THE WATCHERS

T STEDMAN

In memory of Diane Burke, who was first to read all my work from the beginning. I know you would have loved this one. I dedicate it to your wings. May your spirit soar and live on in the Lord's memory.

CHAPTER 1

*R*achel's nan would have turned in her grave. In fact, the whole of her church wouldn't approve. Telling the future was strictly taboo for a good Christian. To Rachel, it was just theatrical and tacky, and Madam Beauregard's laughable tent did nothing to dispel that opinion. It was just part of a school hall psychic fair.

With a "here goes nothing" sigh, she approached the dark doorway.

It was 6.15 p.m. and her allotted time. The evening had been highly entertaining already. She'd thrown herself into buying birthstones, healing crystals, and incense sticks. By the time she'd had her palm read, she was feeling pretty "new age hippie" and totally ready for the cranky old lady in the multicolored tent made of bed sheets.

"You going in?" her friend Lynn called out. "I'll meet you out front. I just want to get the kids some of those cosmic cupcakes before they all go."

Rachel grinned and watched her dart off through the crowd. "See you in a bit," she called after her. She was a blond ball of dynamite all the guys loved. She was also her housemate and one of her closest friends who doted on her niece and nephew. In fact, it was their mum's idea that they were both here. Apparently, Madam Beauregard was red hot in telling your future.

They lived together in a small rented house with another of her close friends, Sebastian, or Seb as he was known. He was tall, dark and sexy and part of their town's answer to The Libertines. He would've simply rolled his eyes and asked if there was hash in the cakes.

She ducked into the dark entrance. "Anyone home?"

"Come in and have a seat, dear," a female voice said, but was nowhere to be seen.

The inside of the tent looked the absolute cliché of every fortune-teller's inner sanctum she'd ever seen in a film. On a dark Persian rug were two plump, patterned cushions in maroon and purple, separated by a low table with a dark red velvet tablecloth and a crystal ball on top. She almost laughed, except the word "sit" made her jump, as the woman appeared from right behind her from nowhere.

After putting her hand to her chest to recover, she smiled weakly and did as she asked, sitting on the cushion indicated. The woman she assumed was Madam Beauregard sat opposite. Rachel watched as she dramatically gathered her robes about her, clearly getting into character. It gave her a chance to assess her. She wasn't as old as she expected, guessing she was around thirty. She was very pretty, quite petite, with dark olive skin and eyes so black you couldn't distinguish the pupil from the iris. A line of gold coins delicately draped her forehead like a Byzantine princess.

"Shall we begin?" she said, in heavily accented English.

Rachel shrugged. "I guess." She already suspected the accent was fake. It took her a full minute for her to realize the woman was waiting for something. "Oh, do I need to pay first?"

Without answering, she beckoned her with her hands already resting on the table. "I need a physical connection to start."

"Oh, I see," Rachel said with a nervous laugh, reaching over her hands and playing along. She'd already been told great fortune and a tall, dark, handsome stranger were coming her way today, *so what the hell*. It perked up her rather dull life, for the next fifteen minutes anyway.

The woman held her hands with a remarkably strong grip for someone so small. "Relax, please. My name is Rose." Then she closed her eyes.

Rachel was about to ask whether she needed to do the same when Rose preempted her with, "Doesn't matter … I just need to summon my spirit guide."

That did strike Rachel as clever, but she shrugged it off. Of course, she would know all the common questions in her line of work.

Rose took a dramatic intake of breath as if she'd been taken by surprise. Then her head began to loll forward and back. It was quite comical at first, but a little alarming.

Rachel began to feel nervous. It was too strange and took her whack-job tolerance way over the scale for one day. She tried to prise her fingers out of Rose's grip, but she held them firmly. "Er … is everything OK?" she said. Now seriously considering making a bolt for the doorway.

Rose's head finally stopped rolling on her shoulders and she settled, now upright and facing front. Her eyes flashed open, but they looked weird—really weird. It was clever as they now looked a cloudy gray, like she had cataracts over them or something. How did she manage to do that? "What is your birth name?" Rose said to the middle distance.

A straightforward question, except her accent had now changed to aristocratic English, like an old-fashioned newsreader.

"Name!" Rose repeated.

"Oh … Rachel … Rachel Fairweather," she said, suddenly realizing she expected some kind of interaction.

"Mmm, yes, I see." Rose's head lolled to the side and righted itself again.

The woman really was a great performer, particularly as this was just a travelling psychic fair Lynn's sister had got out of the local paper. She swore by this stuff and had been here before. Apparently, she was told she'd come into money and had won fifty quid on the lottery the day after. Her enthusiasm had then spread to Lynn, but to Rachel it was just a bit of fun provided by a bunch of enterprising eccentrics who'd found a way to make some extra cash in the evenings. "What do you see?" Rachel asked cautiously.

Rose was staring straight ahead of her vacantly. "Rare, so rare …"

Rachel frowned, guessing the woman just needed time to gather together what direction she wanted to take this. It made her determined to keep quiet and not give anything away. However, when she began to talk it was fast, with such detail and so remarkably clear that her words didn't seem vague at all.

"You are a pure spirit straying from the path … until recently, you were a daughter of Michael—a churchgoer, helper of people … caregiver. Dedicated to Christ since you were a small child. I see the years of devotion shared with a close relative—a grandmother. So close … such love between you. Taken by the reaper only recently … months. You're lonely…"

While the woman gabbled on about her life at double speed, Rachel was transported back to that day four months ago. The day her grandmother never came home. She'd been hit while on a zebra crossing by an impatient driver, travelling too fast and couldn't stop until it was too late. And that was it. In a twinkling of an eye, a good woman who helped people and went to church every week was simply snuffed out. With no reason or justification, here one minute and gone the next, taking Rachel's whole world with her.

She'd sat in the bible group that same evening, numb, in a sense of shock. She didn't listen to the pastor's words or the mundane answers to his questions. All she could think of was: why? How could a god of love take someone as good and kind as her nan—her only source of love and affection, and wreck her whole world? On that day, her security blanket was ripped away, leaving her weak and exposed to everything scary and bad in the world. Despite their calls, she'd got up and walked out, never to return to the church.

"No siblings. Stern father—stepfather. Weak mother," the woman continued. It was then that it dawned on her how accurate she was. With every word, Rachel's eyes widened while she shrank inside. In just a few words, Rose had summed up pretty much her whole twenty years of life. How, along with her nan, she had loved order and goodness and how she couldn't square away in her mind that a god of love could do that to her.

The eerie gray eyes slashed to hers. "But you have lost your way." It was said with narrowed eyes, calculating, as if it threw up a ton of possibilities.

Rachel swallowed as Rose studied her face creepily. It was unsettling. "So ... what brings a good Christian girl like you to Rose Beauregard?"

The question was posed with a satisfied smile and it took her by surprise. As if she knew the answer already. It shook her for a moment because she didn't entirely know what she was doing there herself. "Just bored ... curious ... you know, my friend was coming," she said, plucking things from the air as they came to her.

Rose was already shaking her head before she'd even

finished speaking. "No, make no mistake, there is always an underlying reason. You're searching."

Rachel had heard enough. She wasn't sure if it was the close, airless atmosphere or the uncomfortable line of questioning, but her throat began to feel tight, as if she couldn't breathe, and the tent walls began to close in on her. No one knew her personal business except her small circle of friends and she certainly didn't discuss her feelings about her faith, yet this woman had zeroed straight in on them. Tears began to well in her eyes. This wasn't why she came. The idea was to escape from her problems, not face them. It stirred feelings of hurt and anger buried deep inside and that's where she wanted them to stay. Her grandmother had been all she had when her dad left. Her mother couldn't care less. And now she was gone. *What kind of god allowed that?* She went to stand. All she could think of was getting out of there.

Rose grabbed her arm. "Wait … at least let me consult the crystal before you go. It is the future, not your past, you came here for, no?" Her eyes were now miraculously back to normal and so was her accent.

Relieved, her heart slowed, and she wiped her tears away angrily with the tips of her fingers. "Well, can you be quick, please? My friend is waiting."

Rose ignored her irritable tone and didn't release her hand until she sank back down onto her cushion. Then she began to wave over the crystal ball as if she were clearing smoke. She shook her head and tutted. "It is as I feared."

"What?"

Rose looked her dead in the eye, any sign of theatrics gone. "The birds are circling. Disillusioned and off life's path, you're just ripe for the picking."

Rachel frowned, now totally confused, but strangely feeling a little better. This was familiar territory, where it was all going to get vague and staged. She should have known. She smirked. "I'm sure there's nothing to worry about. I won't be going off to join some cult, or anything. You see, I'm free of all that. I don't believe in anything." *Not anymore,* she finished in her head. "Isn't this the bit where you tell me I'm going to come into money and meet a mysterious guy?"

She could barely keep the smirk off her face, but Rose was too distracted to notice. In fact, she was looking a little alarmed. Rachel put up her hands, feeling bad now. "Sorry, no offence, I just don't believe in any of this stuff either."

Rose took on a vacant look again. "No, you don't understand ... The birds are The Watchers. They scour the Earth in search of souls. Good souls, unblemished ... such as yourself."

She was clearly worried and was making Rachel really uncomfortable now. The act had gone a bit too far. "Look, I'm sure I'll be fine."

Rose picked up one of her hands and held them in both of hers. "Please, if you listen to nothing else today, listen to this. Now you have been here tonight, it is a first step into the dark." She looked up dramatically, as if to an imaginary sky.

Rachel followed her line of vision but, of course, there was nothing to see.

Rose's eyes were wide, as if she was genuinely scared. "You have tested the darkness and they will know, like vibrations on the wind. They will come for you and they will start here with me." Her expression changed to apologetic. "I will have to give you away. There is no denying them. Once they have their sights on their prey, they will stop at nothing, destroying those you love until you submit to them."

The whole tirade was so outlandish that Rachel giggled out of nerves. "Submit to what?" *Time to go.* The woman was clearly mad, but she did really seem to believe what she was saying so, for that, she remained polite. "Well, thanks for the warning." Then she began to stand.

Rose followed her to her feet and pushed a small business card into her hand. "For the next place in your search, you must go there. Please listen to me. You can't escape them now. Face the tests head on and may your God protect you." She took a necklace from her neck, with a fine chain and a polished blue stone pendant. "Take this. From this ancient rune, they will know I have respected their ways and sent you." Then, with surprising strength, Rose literally bundled her out of the tent.

Rachel couldn't believe how she'd been treated and straightened out her manhandled jacket. Outside was brighter, forcing her to blink and take a moment to get used to the light. She looked down at the crumpled card for the first time.

"Angel's Ink", it said. There was an outline of an angel with black open wings printed across it and a phone number underneath. Rose had disappeared back inside. "Wait, what is it?"

"For your tattoo … you must go there," Rose shouted from the blackness of the tent.

"What?" When Rose stopped answering, Rachel was too bewildered to go back in. *How on earth did she know about the tattoo?* It was the very next thing to do on her bucket list of bad things to do before she died. It was a conversation she'd had with Lynn many times and they'd decided to get one together. For Lynn, it was for fashion, to get one before she felt too old, but for her, it was an act of rebellion. Something she could keep hidden and know it was there. Her church would hate it and so would her parents. It occurred to her then that that was what she did—rebel. In her own nerdy way, she'd always been a rebel. Even as a child. She'd turned her back on an indifferent mother and clung to her nan as the last part of her real father, and now she was doing the same, looking for a new life now she'd gone. The idea enthused her and made her feel alive and that was something she hadn't felt in a very long time. *How could Rose Beauregard possibly know any of that?*

"Go!" came from inside the tent. "Ring the number on the card. The rest will be taken care of."

Rachel looked at the card again. It was a mobile number. Then she gazed out at the now-emptying hall. Maybe she'd been longer than she thought. Checking one last time over her shoulder, a closed sign was now in the doorway of the tent. She wandered out into the foyer in a daze, her head still reeling from all the information that Rose shouldn't know and yet did. She'd read her perfectly.

She was still deep in thought when she felt a tug on her arm.

"There you are." It was Lynn, with a brown paper bag full of enough cakes for a netball team. "Ready to go?" Having rushed around, she looked hot but still managed to look gorgeous.

Rachel nodded absently, still distracted by the weird evening. With the business card still in her hand, she walked out of the front doors to the car park at the front of the school.

"What's that?" Lynn said, pointing at her hand.

Rachel let out a deep sigh and shook her head. She held the card up to her friend. "Madam Beauregard said, 'as I'm off the path of righteousness, I need to go and get a tattoo'."

Lynn laughed. "No!" she said, clearly scandalized.

It was pretty funny when she said it out loud like that.

"Spooky!" she said, pulling a face. "Are we going?"

Rachel shrugged. "Seb said we should go to Nicks on the High Street. His friend, Joe, got a good one there of a skeleton on a Harley."

Lynn laughed again. "Er, yeah. Have you *seen* Seb's tattoos?"

Rachel conceded with a bob of her head and a smile. "True. All it's got is a number on it. Not sure where it is, though."

By then, they'd reached the car. Lynn unlocked it with the fob, and they got in and plugged in their seat belts. Lynn's phone immediately vibrated in her bag. Lynn rolled her eyes and pulled it out, first checking the display. "I thought I'd told you not to ring me anymore."

Rachel watched, tuning out the words. It was the same old story with the on–off saga between Lynn and her boss, Colin. He was a rogue, but Lynn gave him a run for his money. It was one of the things Rachel admired about her; she was nobody's pushover. "Yes … I'll see you later," she said, on a weary monotone breath. Then she turned to look back at Rachel, deadpan. "Ring it then and find out," Lynn said, starting the engine as if they'd never been interrupted.

Rachel pulled her own phone out of her bag. It was pretty exciting finally acting on what they'd been talking about for ages.

A female voice answered on the other end. "Angel's Ink, who's calling, please?"

"Oh, hi, my name is Rachel. Me and my friend are interested in getting a tattoo."

"How did you get this number?" the woman said, a little sharply.

Her abruptness completely stunned Rachel for a moment. It wasn't what she expected from a business relying on, *you know, customers.* Irritation was immediately followed by the unease she'd felt with Rose. "Er … my name is Rachel Fairweather and Rose Beauregard from the psychic fair gave me your card and recommended you."

There was a pause at the other end, and for a moment, Rachel thought she'd gone. "Hello?"

"Sorry," the woman said at last. "I was just checking for availability. Come in tomorrow afternoon for your pre-assessment, then Grigori will see you at 9 p.m."

It threw Rachel into a panic for a number of reasons. It was so soon, for starters. She could probably get there for the afternoon one, it was Saturday, but why such a late appointment? The woman should have at least asked if she could make any of those times. And she'd made no mention of Lynn's. "What about my friend?" she said, sure that would at least slow things down a bit. Fitting two people in at a weekend without notice should be nigh on impossible. While the woman went quiet again, Rachel put the phone on mute and said in a stage whisper, "Can you do tomorrow afternoon?"

Lynn nodded enthusiastically. "I don't have to be at work till 5.30."

Shit! She'd really expected her not to be up for it before her weekend shift at the pub. Reeling from the speed of it all, Rachel put the phone back to her ear. "Tomorrow is good for my friend, too. Is there an appointment available for her as well?"

There was another long pause. "Did Madam Beauregard give her a card?"

Rachel frowned. This was all too weird. "Well, no, but we said we'd get tattoos together, you know? We've never had one before."

Another pause. "Tell your friend to come with you tomorrow afternoon. We'll squeeze her in."

Rachel instantly brightened with relief. After her visit to Rose Beauregard, the whole thing was playing havoc with her spidey senses. It was as if they were only interested in her and Rose's golden ticket and there was no way she'd do it alone.

She gave herself a mental shake. It was just a tattoo. People get them all the time. It was what she'd talked about for ages and now that Lynn was coming as well, it was fun again and really nothing to be scared of.

"Right then, remember it's just a chat, you're booked in properly at 9 with Grigori. The postcode will be texted to you thirty minutes before you attend." Then the woman hung up. *OK, that was weird.*

It was up there with one of the strangest phone calls of her life, but she eventually managed to shrug it off as the strange and dark world of tattoo artists. Maybe it was some kind of pop-up parlor.

She looked across at her friend, who turned the radio up and was grinning widely. "Whoop! Whoop! We're actually doing it," Lynn sang. "We're getting tattooed! We're gonna be badass babes!"

Rachel laughed along with her. It was pretty cool, but she couldn't shake off the prickling unease. Instead of excitement, she felt a curious sense of dread. Rose Beauregard had started something and impending doom was now spreading into her life.

"Hey! There you are," Seb said, crossing the hall from the staircase to the living room when they got home. "I thought you'd moved out."

They closed the front door to the semi-detached house they all shared and traipsed down the hall after him.

"We went to the school psychic fair," Lynn said.

It was a typical rental property of magnolia walls, hard-wearing grey carpet and a basic stainproof black leather lounge suite.

Rachel's eyes rested on him as they invariably did, admiring him from a safe distance. She had zero experience with boys, but even she could see he was one of those red-hot but lovable types that you daren't go too near lest you got severely burnt.

He was still a lanky, boyish-looking twenty-three-year-old singer who rarely had cash and had the smallest bedroom so he could pay a bit less towards the rent. The guy was laid-back, majorly cute and used it to his advantage. What he lacked in finances, he made up for in a huge sense of fun and an abundance of hot friends. So she and Lynn often over-looked his late payments and constant borrowing money, when they really should have kicked him out months ago.

"Hey, how did it go? What d'ya get?" he said, already eying the bag Lynn was carrying.

Lynn was far more immune to Seb's charms, treating him like an annoying little brother. She smacked his hand going straight for the cupcakes meant for her sister's kids, then relented and gave him one. "It went great. We're both gonna meet tall, dark, handsome strangers."

Seb stood up straighter and held out both arms in a "come and get me" gesture.

The girls giggled.

"You're not a stranger, doofus. Oh, and we're getting a tattoo," Rachel added. "Both of us!"

Seb's eyes went wide and landed on Rachel with interest. He was assessing her in that speculative way of his, as if she'd definitely surprised him. It instantly made her blush. He did that a lot.

He was the house expert on tattoos, having quite a few of his own. They were often on full view when he walked about the house in just his boxers, although they all seemed a bit random in design. He bobbed his head appreciatively. "Nice! What brought this on? Are you going to Nicks?"

"No, the fortune-teller told her to go to this one and gave her a card," Lynn said, nudging Rachel, who pulled it out of her bag and held it out.

Rachel watched Seb's cute profile as he scrutinized it carefully with a frown. As if it was going to tell him some-thing more than the angel and the number on the front. He passed it back with a shrug. "I suppose it's OK if she recom-mended it. Never heard of it, though. Is it local? Did she have a tat from there?"

It was a good question—one that hadn't occurred to her.

They had absolutely no idea how good the place was. She'd seen all the shows about covering over disastrous drunken tattooing decisions from less-than-reputable places.

Then Lynn butted in with, "We're going to suss it out tomorrow afternoon, before we actually get one."

Seb bobbed his head as if that satisfied him, then he flopped onto the leather sofa and flicked through the channels, his attention waning fast. "What ya gettin'?"

It was said as a flyaway comment, but was staggeringly important. She couldn't believe she'd given it no thought at all. Lynn looked at her with her eyes wide in a question she'd forgotten to ask. "I'm getting a daisy after my niece."

Rachel stared back at her, bewildered. *Honestly.* "I haven't made up my mind yet."

Seb twisted in his seat, put his chin on the back of the sofa and grinned mischievously. "And where are you getting it, Rach? You quiet Bible types are the ones to watch!" he said, waggling his eyebrows.

Rachel scowled to hide a deep, toe-curling blush. "I'm not a Bible type." *Not anymore.* He laughed, and she batted him away with a good-natured hand. Grateful to escape the strong reaction his presence always had on her, she wandered out into the kitchen. She constantly had to tell herself that talking to girls—any girls—was incredibly easy for him. What he'd asked were reasonable questions, though. Ones she hadn't really thought through at all.

THE POSTCODE WAS TEXTED EXACTLY thirty minutes before the afternoon appointment, as promised. Despite all the cloak and dagger, they set off in high spirits.

Colin phoned Lynn again and she promised to talk to him later after ignoring his calls all last night.

"Are you going to put the poor guy out of his misery?"

Rachel said as they crawled through the town's Saturday traffic.

Lynn shrugged. "Meh … I'll make him sweat first. If you'd seen him all over the new girl last week, Rach, you wouldn't be so charitable." Lynn just loved the drama and making Colin chase after her. Plus, judging by the racket that came from her room, they had great sex, which was more than could be said for her.

The doorway to the tattoo shop wasn't immediately obvious; they had to park in the multistory and find it on foot in the end. It was just a narrow door between two shops with a small flyer in the window, identical to the business card Rachel had. They paused outside.

"Do we just go in?" Lynn said.

Rachel shrugged. It looked like the door to a secret club or something. She tried the handle, but it was locked. Looking to either side of the doorframe, she found the small buzzer and pressed the button.

"Hello!" the muffled female voice said.

"Is that Angel's Ink? It's Rachel and Lynn."

The door immediately buzzed. "Follow the corridor out back. Don't go up the stairs."

They looked at each other, both feeling the same thing: how over-the-top it all felt. Nevertheless, it was exciting and the most fun they'd had in ages.

Rachel hefted open the surprisingly heavy door and they both entered and paused just inside. The door closed on a spring and clicked locked again behind them. They walked on as instructed, following the narrow white corridor to the back of the building, past the tiled staircase to their left.

"Whatever you do, don't go up the stairs … wooahh, ha ha ha!" Lynn said, doing her worst Count Dracula impression.

Rachel smacked her in the stomach with the back of her

hand to shut up. Even whispers seemed to echo right up to the rafters. However, it did cut through the tension a bit.

They came to a standstill in front of another locked door, which opened before they could knock. A pretty girl invited them inside; they assumed it was her voice on the intercom. She had several tattoos clearly visible on her bare arms, two purple studs directly into the dimples on her cheeks and a gold nose ring. Her hair was wavy, to her shoulders, and startlingly purple.

The girl couldn't have been more opposite to Rachel. She felt plain in comparison. Today, her mid-brown hair had just been pulled into a ponytail. She wore very little makeup or jewelry; just plain blue jeans, a cream sweater, and boots, with a short navy jacket left open on top. Lynn always said her figure was great and she should show it off more. Her pale skin was clear and her cheekbones high, but she felt bland next to the striking, colorful girl in front of her. "Come on in, ladies. My name is Skye. Can I take your jackets and offer you a tea or coffee?" *Even her name was cool.*

Rachel took off her jacket and shook her head. "No thanks."

Lynn asked for a coffee.

They both sat on a gilt-edged red velvet sofa, like something from the Moulin Rouge, while Skye went off to get the drink. Rachel looked over at Lynn. The seating was kind of gothic, she supposed.

The room itself looked modern and clinical. As if the stuff in it just didn't go. The walls were neutral and white and so were the polished tiles on the floors. There were two dentist-like chairs with little trollies next to them, but they were all brass and leather, straight out of one of the steampunk novels she loved. The few posters with black symbols and sketches seemed the only giveaway that it was a tattoo place at all. The room definitely had a very "just moved in" feel.

Skye came back and handed Lynn a mug. "So, which one of you is Rachel?"

"I am," Rachel said, holding up a finger.

Skye smiled. "Did Rose give you something to show me?"

For a moment, Rachel wasn't sure what she meant. Then she remembered the necklace and pulled out the chain that was tucked under her sweater for her to see. She was grateful she hadn't forgotten to put it on. "Rose said you'd understand what it meant," she said with a frown.

Skye's expression remained non-committal, just the slightest twitch of a smile. "Make sure you wear it when you see Grigori this evening." Then she brightened and altered her stance. "And what can we do for you today?" She aimed the question at Lynn.

She perked up immediately and explained the small daisy idea in honor of her niece, on her shoulder.

Rachel looked on and wasn't sure why she got the distinct impression that Skye wasn't the least bit interested. This didn't seem at all like the TV shows they'd seen. There was usually chatting, back story and plenty of drawing to get a design decided for a tattoo.

"Jet!" Skye called out.

A small Thai girl came through the archway Skye had disappeared through earlier. From what she could see of her arms, her tattoos were intricate, feminine and amazing. Way better than any she'd ever seen. It was a good advert for the place.

"Daisy. Shoulder," Skye said, pointing at her own. She smiled sweetly at Lynn. "Jet can get started on you right away." Then it was as though she was immediately dismissed.

Rachel wasn't impressed with her friend's treatment. Lynn looked a little bewildered and she didn't blame her. She gave her a wink and a smile of encouragement. Lynn stood and shook hands with Jet. She seemed nice enough. Smiling, she led the way to her workstation and indicated for Lynn to get into one of the big chairs.

Rachel continued to keep an eye on her until she seemed confident and happily caught up in conversation. Even Lynn had seemed a little shocked at how fast it had all gone and she was a "jump in with both feet" kind of person.

"Right then," Skye said, sitting down in the black velvet armchair opposite her. "You'll be coming back tonight for your appointment with Grigori."

Rachel smiled, but she was a little unsure. Her eyes tracked nervously to Lynn. Her chair was now flat and she was lying on her front with her off-the-shoulder neckline exposing her skin perfectly, while Jet sketched something onto her right shoulder. She couldn't help wondering why Lynn was getting squeezed in now and she wasn't.

Skye seemed to follow her line of thinking. "Your friend's tattoo won't take long. Yours will take some planning and several sessions."

There it was again—all the weirdness. Her heart was speeding up as if she needed to run and she had no idea why. It was no good; she had to say something now before it went any further. "I'm sorry, but I haven't said what I want yet. And I'm not even sure I know. Isn't that what this appointment is about?"

Skye looked unfazed when she leaned forward and put her hand over hers. "Of course, I know it can feel strange at first. Grigori will be able to help you with any questions." Then she lowered her tone and it sent chills all over her. "He'll guide you through it and you won't regret a thing."

There was nothing ominous in what she said, exactly, but everything felt strange, like it had some higher meaning since she'd met Rose. Plus, she'd have been a whole lot happier meeting this guy and having it done during the day. "Isn't Grigori around now just for a chat?" she said, looking around her as if he could appear any minute.

Skye was already shaking her head. "Grigori never works days. He always says there's less distraction at night for his more intricate pieces."

IT APPEARED that was it for her pre-assessment chat—not that she'd learned all that much. The whole thing seemed more for their benefit than hers—as if they were checking her out and not the other way around.

"Go sit with your friend," Skye said, wandering off to sit behind an old-fashioned desk, with just a brass lamp and oblong green shade on it. "She won't be long."

Still a little uneasy about the circumstances surrounding her own tattoo, Rachel went over and Jet nodded to the rolling stool at the other tattoo station. "Take that one."

Rachel did as indicated, and her mind was quickly distracted by the comical pained faces Lynn was pulling. "Seriously, Lynn?" The thing was tiny, no bigger than a fifty-pence piece.

"Argh!" Lynn said with another grimace. "Just you wait till it's your turn."

In less than thirty minutes, Jet straightened up and said, "Right, lady. You're done!"

The daisy was small, cute and absolutely perfect on Lynn's shoulder. Rachel smiled at her. Lynn sat up and studied it in the mirror Jet passed her. "Thank you," she said, blinking back tears.

It surprised Rachel that such a small thing could have such emotional significance. She wondered if it would be like that for her.

"Let's wrap you up," Jet said, breaking the emotionally

laden moment. She gently rubbed some cream onto the freshly inked skin and taped loose gauze over the top, so her clothes didn't rub against it.

Rachel squeezed her hand. "So pretty, Lynn." It made her wonder for the umpteenth time what she would have. "Love the colors." It really was a miniature work of art.

"Why aren't you getting yours done?" Lynn said, looking puzzled between her and Jet, who was already clearing bottles away.

Rachel shrugged. It was a good question and one she'd like to know herself. "Apparently, I've got to come back for Grigori tonight." She couldn't help noticing the uneasy flash in Jet's eyes at the mention of his name. "Is he good?" she found herself asking.

Jet didn't look her in the eye. Just kept wiping down her workstation. "Sure ... he's the best. You'll end up with a masterpiece."

Rachel frowned at her friend, not sure how big this masterpiece was likely to be. She didn't want to turn into the tattooed lady. Everyone was building it all up so much; it felt like overkill.

"You OK with that?" Lynn said, reading her perfectly as usual.

Nodding, Rachel took in a ragged breath, guessing it was all nerves. It was a much bigger deal for her than for Lynn. It was her two fingers up at the world. She had to get a grip. She was getting a tattoo with someone who appeared to be the best guy in town. "Will you come back with me later?"

Lynn smiled. "Sure. I'll blow off work." Her evil grin said everything. "It will piss Colin off no end." Then she frowned slightly and put her hand to her head. "Might have to have a bit of a lie down first. I think I might be coming down with something."

. . .

With the worst timing ever, Lynn was right. By the time they got home, she had a raging temperature.

Seb was already on the doorstep, saying goodbye to some girl draped around his neck, refusing to let him go. He grinned and extricated himself from her cloying arms as he sensed there was something wrong. The girl trotted past them with a face like thunder.

They walked in past him and he followed them inside. "She's coming down with something," Rachel explained. It didn't deter him, and he still gave Lynn's tattoo the once-over. However, Lynn held her head and had to go straight to bed. It was unlike her not joke around with Seb. Rachel watched her go upstairs. There was no way she'd be able to come with her that night. She felt kind of selfish, only thinking of herself when she was clearly ill, but she was already quite anxious about going.

As usual, Seb saw straight through her. He was often sweet and perceptive, which he brushed off as having four sisters. "I've got a gig, but I can drop you off on my way, though and pick you up after if you like?"

It was the next best thing and she smiled. "Thanks." It cheered her up a little. She couldn't remember the last time she'd had these many butterflies over anything.

It was dark when she kissed Seb on the cheek and got out of his van directly opposite the door. She was grateful for the lift. She could have borrowed Lynn's car, but the multistory could be very spooky at night and she was freaked out enough as it was.

The shops on either side were in darkness. There was just a subtle glow through the glass in the Angel's Ink door to tell her someone was home.

A feeling of foreboding kicked up the butterflies in the pit of her stomach like autumn leaves. She was grateful that Seb hadn't rushed off and appeared to be waiting. Whatever lay behind that door gave her an overwhelming urge to run the other way. It made no sense. All it had to be was a small tattoo, *for god's sake,* just like Lynn had, in exactly the same place. Her tattooist just happened to work nights.

She continued to squash down the strange feeling of dread before she talked herself out of it and that she'd never live down. There was no way she'd go home having chickened out; it was the deciding factor and so she forced her legs to make the few steps towards the door.

This time, no voice came when she pressed the buzzer. The door just clicked for her to push it open. Whoever was at the other end was confident it was her. *Well, it was bang on 9 o'clock.* She was never late.

Rachel turned and put her hand up to Seb, who'd waited patiently with his engine running. Satisfied she was safe, he nodded and pulled away. Facing the door again, her heart beat wildly against her chest. Seb had gone and there was no running away now. She summoned her courage, pushed open the door and went inside.

The corridor was lit for nighttime. Tiny emergency lights emitted a dim light every six feet or so. The staircase they'd joked about earlier seemed creepier and went up into darkness. Skye's words, "don't go up the stairs," echoed. Like she'd actually want to go up there. Cool air settled around her, making her shiver. The place gave her the creeps.

Finally making it to the end, she found the door ajar. She peered inside.

"Close it," a deeply accented voice said.

She did as she was asked without actually spotting who the voice belonged to.

"We don't want any uninvited guests," he said, allowing her to home in on its source.

The room had a warm glow cast only from a light above the workstation; it fell on him like stage lighting. The first time Rachel's eyes fell on Grigori would be stamped on her retinas for ever.

CHAPTER 3

Grigori's sheer presence affected her so deeply, even with his back to her, he had to be about the tallest, hottest, most perfect package of a man she'd ever seen. Not at all what she'd been expecting. In all honesty, she didn't know what she'd been expecting. A cliché of a bearded Hell's Angel, she supposed.

When he turned from what he was doing and smiled, he simply knocked the air out of her lungs. She literally went into a Jane Austen-like swoon and staggered slightly. She wished she had a tissue to dab the perspiration from her top lip, brow and between her breasts. She'd never had a reaction like it.

He, on the other hand, hadn't moved a muscle, but watched her closely. "You want glass of water?"

She shook her head, pinpointing his accent as Russian. Embarrassment at the hash she'd just made of a first impression incinerated her while he chuckled softly as if he knew damn well.

Finally, she was able to dab her hot face with a tissue she

found in her bag. No wonder he worked nights; the man would be a danger to womankind during daylight.

His hair was light brown, overlong in loose tendrils, way past his chin and slashed forward to enhance his rough, stubbled jawline. His eyes were dark and almond-shaped, with a look that was almost cruel in their directness, framed in black lashes any girl would kill for. He was tall and lean, with muscles that looked honed by use rather than by posing in a gym. His tattoos snaked around his arms in Polynesian-like patterns that spoke of tribal ritual rather than the mindless imagery that usually covered boys of her age. They perfectly suited the dangerous aura he radiated.

She tried to drag her eyes away at that point, but his trim washboard waist beckoned her on to imagine what was beneath the shirt tucked effortlessly into narrow black, well-worn jeans. They hugged the length of his long legs and were tucked into iron-gray battered boots with the laces left loose. It took a while. There was a lot to take in.

The effect was total and breathtaking, all at once. When she predicted the questions that would follow from Lynn, she would honestly have trouble describing him because, despite all of the above, she couldn't exactly say he was model beautiful (but heaven knew he would be stunning in a photo), he exuded far too much danger for that. Like he'd plunge a sword right through you as soon as look at you.

Sword? It was a weird association. But that was just it, exactly. It felt like he was from another age.

"You want to come in?" he said, clearly amused. "I won't bite, I promise."

The accent was definitely Russian, or something of Eastern European origin. His tease snapped her out of her paralysis, but did nothing to help the flutter in her heart, which threatened to beat right out of her chest.

She inched forward when he turned to arrange his

bottles. He nodded towards his dentist's chair. "Sit!" She was sure she actually gulped at that point. "Right away? I mean … aren't we going to chat?"

He smiled over his shoulder. "You can hang your coat over there." His eyes went to an old-fashioned hat stand in black wrought iron, next to the door.

Rachel hung her coat and made her way back to him. He adjusted the chair to a more upright position and sat down on his rolling stool. When she hesitated, he held out his hand to indicate for her to sit again and she was forced to get up onto the leather, knowing she would look truly stupid refusing. All she could manage was, "I don't even know what I want yet," in a small voice.

"Isn't that why you're here?"

She paused with those insightful words. Like in that moment, he knew everything about her, and she had to literally shake off his hold. There was something unusual about him. A power. A presence. She wasn't sure what. But whatever it was, it attracted her and yet made her want to run at the same time.

As if to emphasize a point, she flushed red and a film of sweat spread over her again.

He didn't miss that. His eyes went straight to a rivulet of sweat trickling down her temple to her neck and dwelt there. Her hand went to the pendant Rose had given her. She looked away and patted her brow with her already damp tissue, while appearing to study the hundreds of ink bottles lined up on the bench next to her, though she swore she could feel those steely eyes burning a hole in the side of her head.

It was ridiculous, but she thought of the old fairytale of Red Riding Hood. The words, "all the better to eat you with", repeated in her head over and over. She truly thought she was going mad.

She took a fortifying breath and gave herself a mental slap. If she didn't want the bloody tattoo, she should just go.

She flashed him a glance.

His eyes remained calm and knowing, not responding to her uncomfortable silence. "We begin," he said simply, reaching for a sketchpad on his trolley and taking a pencil from behind his ear.

She immediately felt relieved. At least he wasn't going straight to the inking.

"Relax. At this stage, we talk ideas."

She calmed down a little more.

"And where we wanna go with it," he added with a small smile.

Aaaand up her temperature went again. She was now positive he was toying with her. "I'm not sure I can do this." *Why couldn't she have Jet, like Lynn?* Her little daisy flower was cute and homely and safe. She'd been thrilled with it. That was all she wanted. This whole idea had got out of hand.

When she looked back at him, he put his head at an angle as if he was reading her. On closer inspection, his eyes were lighter than she'd first thought. They were black and amber and fiery flecks of red, like a stormy winter sky; the most unusual eyes she'd ever seen.

He put the pencil behind his ear again. "People call me Grigori," he said, with a smile that transformed the harsh lines of his face. It felt like sunlight after a cold night. "Relax, Rachel."

The use of her name in his accent felt like a gentle stroke along her brow. "That's not your name?" She shot the question at him more to gain control and shake herself out of the effect he was having on her.

His eyebrows rose a little in surprise and he shook his head slightly. "No, it is not," he said, but offered no more.

She couldn't take her eyes from him and what that

meant. He was a man that no one knew. In that moment, she knew that absolutely. "I'm Rachel Fairweather." Then she frowned, as he already knew that. She held out her hand anyway. "Pleased to meet you, Mr ... er ... Grigori." She had no idea why she did it; she truly was losing her mind.

Instead of laughing at her, he took her hand somberly in a handshake that affected her utterly. Electricity went the length of her arm in a hot jolt that almost shorted out her brain. His eyes held hers in total confidence.

He knew.

"Let's get down to it," he said, releasing her hand but leaving it tingling.

Her throat was dry and she had to swallow hard. She was even shaking as if she'd taken a nasty tumble.

The pencil was back in his hand and he was sketching in light strokes across the page. It gave her a chance to recover and study him without that affecting gaze. She wasn't sure if she even found him attractive exactly, but there was something powerful in him that was only just contained. She crossed her legs.

After several moments, she decided she did feel safe with him, and that was weird in itself. She barely knew him and yet knew everything she needed to know.

He continued to draw. "I want you to think carefully about what you want from this experience, Rachel."

It was a clever question and not what she was expecting. It went far deeper than the artwork itself. People all wanted tattoos for different reasons.

It made her frown. "I'm not sure exactly. I've never had one." Despite the surface meaning of her words, she knew he understood the deeper undercurrent.

He bobbed his head. "It is why I do this. You need to be sure of what you want. I create a work of art, but it is your life. It affects everything." He finished looking directly into her eyes.

She found herself thinking of Rose Beauregard. She would have liked to think he meant things like public perceptions, or first impressions for jobs, et cetera, but he was driving at so much more. It had echoes of Rose's words and made her feel fanciful, like she was in some weird negotiation for her soul.

She shook her head at the ridiculousness of her thinking. He was simply drumming into her the importance of permanent ink. *Selling her soul.* She almost laughed and shook her head in disbelief.

There was that icy stare again. "No receipts, Rachel. No taking it back."

She swallowed hard. Whatever he meant, he was right, but she couldn't shake the feeling that it went deeper.

He nodded, knowing the exact moment she understood, and sat back and let out a long sigh. "Why do you want this tattoo, Rachel?"

She shifted uncomfortably.

"You must have some ideas?"

At first, she thought he was being curt. Then, after a long look into his eyes with slight creases in the corners, she decided it was his way and relaxed back a little too. However, she wasn't sure where to start and was not sure she wanted to share her reasons with a complete stranger. She'd barely shared them with her closest friends. The fact that he was a powerful, smoldering pile of sin didn't help either.

He cut her thought off as if he knew her dilemma. "The more honest you are, the more I'll be able to satisfy what's in your heart."

The air went from the room again. *Was it getting hotter?* Every time he opened his mouth, whether it was his Russian phrasing, his accent, or his meaning, he unnerved the hell out of her. Looking him dead in the eye, she knew he meant every word with undertones or not. She started to feel sick and the blood seemed to drain out of her face. He was saying something, but sounded far away. "Rachel … Rachel."

The next thing she knew, the chair was flat, and she was lying on her back with him leaning over her.

A tendril of his hair fell forward from behind his ear to touch his chin. He handed her a glass of water. "It's OK. You fainted."

Her hands were shaking when she took the water, but she managed to take a few unladylike gulps. His hand stayed on the glass and she was acutely aware when their fingers touched. Small tingles of electricity spread through her hand, but not as strongly as the last time.

He took the glass and raised the back of the chair a little so she could relax back and not sit up too quickly. The heat of embarrassment pricked her cheeks as the blood flowed back into her head. "I'm sorry. I don't know what happened." She went to sit up straighter, but her energy seemed to have gone, as if she'd had the air knocked right out of her.

"No problem," he said, sitting back on his stool. "The first time can be overwhelming."

Her eyes went straight to his. Another of his weird sayings. She'd barely said more than a hello to him. Surely it would have made more sense to assume she hadn't eaten or ask if perhaps she was coming down with something. *Lynn!* That was it. She was coming down with a bout of what Lynn had. Then she frowned. They'd both jumped to the conclusion that it was to do with this experience.

She swallowed hard; her mouth had gone dry again. "Can I ask you a question?"

He nodded slowly, not taking his eyes off hers. "Go ahead."

She couldn't believe she was actually going to say this out

loud, but she guessed fainting and feeling a little lightheaded somehow gave her the courage. "This place ... what Rose Beauregard told me ... Is it you? I mean ... it can't be true ... can it?"

He didn't answer right away. He put out his long legs in front of him and crossed them at the ankle. His look was intense. "I don't think you are ready for the answer you want, Rachel."

It was a complete evasion of the question, but it was calm and lulling, using her name like a caress across her fears, making the CH in her name into a "sh" sound.

"I can tell you that after today your life will change ... isn't that what you want?"

Despite the obvious deflection, the softness held a hint of something dangerous in those words. *He was right, though, wasn't he?* Wasn't that what she'd wanted ever since she'd turned her back on everything after her grandmother's death?

It felt like he was getting in her head, hypnotizing or worse still, taking something from her.

She sat up sharply. Her head swam again, and she had to grab her forehead. He made no move and it settled in a few seconds. She dropped her hand and flashed her eyes at him. "I don't want to talk about my personal business. I just want a tattoo." It came out more abrupt than she intended. He'd just hit a raw nerve.

His expression didn't change; he just regarded her closely and nodded. "Fair enough. You are happy for me to take care of the design?"

The question was so sane and normal it completely threw her. Like she was acting unreasonable or something. The guy was just talking tattoos and she'd attached all this hidden meaning to it. Heat bloomed in her cheeks with embarrassment yet again. "OK," she said with a gravelly voice. "What did you have in mind?"

The pencil came from behind the ear and he began to work it in elegant strokes across the page. "First of all, I only work in black and grey. I don't do color. Everything is emphatic with me … like life."

She wanted to argue that life wasn't always black and white; that there were very definitely many shades in between, but it died on her lips. Looking at the man drawing in front of her, the idea of pretty daisies coming from his hand was preposterous. The real question was why this place thought she was so suited to him rather than Jet.

His hand worked quickly in feather-like flourishes and she soon forgot the questions forming in her mind to tune into his words, softly spoken as if to himself. "There will be a further six sessions. I will start inking you next time. We will begin with this on your right shoulder."

His eyes went to hers, seeming an even lighter amber than before—almost shimmering in the spotlight angled at his workstation. Then she dropped them to the pad he was holding vertically for her to see.

The bottom of her world fell away. In that moment, all her surmising and questions she'd wanted to ask seemed pointless. They were answered in an A4 sketch and the look in his hooded eyes. There was no placation to what must be a startled expression, because he knew. The exact moment— the culmination of everything since meeting Rose Beauregard—no, scratch that, since her grandmother's dying, had led to this point. This place. To this man, if that was what he was.

Somehow, she managed to follow his words when he began to speak again, but she was in shock.

"We will build from this. Each time it will grow. The

artistry will come from within you and drive the transformation into what you want to become."

She barely had a voice as her mouth had become so dry. "But I didn't tell you anything."

His answer was to tear the page from the pad and hand it to her. "Go home and think it over. The whole point is that you don't do anything you don't want to do. Despite what you believe, everything is your choice." He paused, but his look was intense, boring into hers with meaning. "But remember, Rachel, life is a journey and all journeys need a destination. It is up to you where it will end."

She took the piece of paper and studied the expert lines that perfectly depicted a flower—an iris. Not too dissimilar to a daisy, some might say, although it was larger and more intricate. But it was more—so much more.

"Go home," he said. "We'll meet again the same time next week." He stood and went to get her coat.

She slid down off her chair and robotically put her arms into the coat he held out for her.

"How did you know?" she asked as she turned and looked up at him. "My grandmother ..." she swallowed before she could speak again. "Her name was Iris."

He looked down at her, easily a head and shoulders taller than her. The corners of his mouth curled into the smallest of smiles, but his eyes remained narrowed and cruel. He tilted his head as if she should already know the answer to that. "I am a watcher of people ... it's what I do."

CHAPTER 4

Rachel didn't know where the time went. It was around 10.30 when Grigori told her they were finished for the evening. Seb wasn't ready to pick her up yet, so she told him she'd get a cab. She was grateful, really. There was no way she wanted Seb's joking style of questioning while she was trying to figure everything out. Sleeping on it before she faced her friends seemed a much better idea.

The house was quiet when she got home. Lynn must still be in bed and so, after grabbing a glass of water, she tiptoed up the stairs to her room. However, no matter how exhausted she felt, her dreams were vivid, chaotic and not at all restful.

She dreamed of her grandmother over and over, but somehow Grigori invaded them all. Tall and imposing, he always seemed to be there in the periphery, watching. Even when she couldn't directly see him, her senses prickled, telling her he was in the shadows. Suddenly his arms snaked around her waist, and his breath heated her neck. Her grandmother shrieked, "Beware, The Watcher! ... He's here. Don't let him get his claws into my good, sweet munchkin!"

Rachel sat bolt upright, out of breath and pouring with sweat. The dream was devastatingly real. Her grandmother had called her by the pet name she'd used from when she was a little girl and was so distressed. She'd never seen her like that. She was always so happy and calm. Nevertheless, what disturbed the hell out of her was how the blood heated in her veins at Grigori being close by. It was a fierce desire that seared right through her, making every nerve-ending prickle. She'd never been with a man, but found it hard to believe it was a usual response to someone so quickly.

She was forced to click on her bedside light to absorb the warm glow of relief it gave her. Her room was homely and a little cluttered and she allowed it to comfort her for a moment. The large bookshelf along one wall held her well-loved books. Classic hardbacks were arranged at eye-level and all her trade paperbacks underneath—all alphabetized, of course. A small vinyl record player stood on a table in the corner that used to belong to her grandmother. She'd loved opera and had a small collection of records. Her absolute favorite was Caruso, which she couldn't bring herself to listen to or throw away. Seb noticed and often lent her his vinyl records to play. They were mainly guitar bands she'd only vaguely heard of. Music hadn't ever really been her thing until she came here.

Her eyes rested on the small Italianate painting of Jesus that hung on her wall. That was what had taken up all her time. The face that radiated goodness and hope. It was what had drawn her to the church as a small child. Together her and her nan had had this wonderful thing in common. Then her heart hardened when she remembered how it had all been cruelly snatched away. There was no point in wasting further thought on it.

Except for the small voice at the back of her mind that niggled and pecked away at her. With all this new, bewildering stuff going on around her, if she was going to believe in the dark, then surely she had to admit there was light.

She decided to sleep with the lamp on. The weight on her chest had lifted and her breathing slowed. She reached over to take a glug of water, leaned back against the headboard and let out a long exhale. In the soft orange light, the air tickled her nose from the window and a tiny downy black feather floated on the currents to land gently on her bed.

THE NEXT MORNING was Sunday and she spent it in a daze. Confusion about the meeting and the dreams that followed jumbled around in her head. Strangely, everyone had got up and out by the time she came out of her room. Lynn must have been feeling better and she guessed Seb hadn't come home at all.

Her phone buzzed on the kitchen counter. It was Lynn.

FREE FOR LUNCH?
  Always!
  Wethy's?
  Yes!
  12.30ish?
  See you there!

WETHY'S WAS their nickname for the huge barn-like pub in town that sold affordable lunches and, more importantly, cheap drinks. Everyone in a three-mile radius frequented it at some point during the week. Sunday lunch would be rammed, but it would rouse her from obsessing over everything. So she hurriedly showered and dressed in a comfy grey sweatshirt and jeans and jumped onto a bus with the idea that she didn't have to watch what she drank. The truth was, her grandmother had given her full use of her car while she was alive. Since that tragic day, it had remained in the garage and she hadn't had the heart to drive it. The bus service wasn't too bad. Their house was one of many in a 1960s-built estate of grass-edged roads and treelined pathways. It was perfect, really, with the town center only fifteen minutes away, not counting the traffic.

Typically, she was the first there at 12.40, Lynn arrived shortly after and she should have known that Seb would wander in last, in last night's clothes. He waved from across the room with bedhead hair, gave some blonde babe a peck on the lips after she gave him something out of her purse and sauntered over. He really was incorrigible.

They ordered food and Seb plonked down on the bar what proved to be a ten-pound note that he'd clearly just borrowed from the blonde. They split the bill (which was rare without an IOU) and went in search of a table with their drinks. Spotting a group preparing to leave, they hovered to pounce on it before anyone else. Pleased with their luck, they sat and took off their jackets. Before any of them could open their mouth, Lynn said, "Shit! There's Colin."

Rachel turned her head and saw the good-looking guy making a beeline for their table. Lynn tried to make herself look invisible, but it was too late. She'd been seen. He nodded to Seb, then Rachel and bent down to Lynn's ear.

It was the usual conversation. "Why have you been ignoring my calls?"

"I've been ill—like, really ill. Haven't I, Rach?"

Rachel nodded manically, feeling a bit sorry for him. Despite Lynn telling the truth on this occasion, she enjoyed leading him on a merry little dance. He was really quite a nice guy; tall, suave and stylish. Lynn had batted away being scolded for it with her slightly skewed reasoning that that was exactly why she had to keep him working hard, so he didn't go off with anyone else. Rachel thought it was a dangerous game, but Lynn seemed a master at it. Within two minutes, she'd promised to see him later, and he kissed her on the lips. "Promise?" he said.

"Promise," she repeated.

Then he walked off, satisfied and apparently just leaving.

Seb shook his head with a smirk. "Props," he said with a grin.

"And that's why he pays me the big bucks." They all laughed. It was true, she had made a meteoric rise from barmaid to restaurant manager in no time at all.

It occurred to Rachel then that Lynn and Seb were the same person in different guises.

"Show us then!" Lynn said, taking a swig of her pint of beer.

Rachel almost spat out her vodka and Coke with the hard nudge she gave her.

"Oh yeah," Seb said. "I completely forgot. What d'ya get? Devil on horseback, skull and crossbones, Kermit, a puppy?"

Rachel rolled her eyes but continued to sip her drink.

Lynn frowned. "You didn't get it, did you." It was said flat with disappointment, as if she'd totally let her down.

With the look of exaggerated disbelief on Seb's face, she had to hold up her hand to shut them both up. "Can you let me explain?"

They both sagged and looked at her deadpan, as if it had better be good.

It was hard to know where to start. Anyway she thought about it, she was going to come off as mad. There was no other way but to come straight out with it.

"What's the matter, Rach?" Lynn said, softening her tone.

Rachel nodded once and swallowed, then delved into her bag for the piece of paper. "Do you remember at the psychic fair me saying how weird the fortune-teller was?" she asked, passing the piece of paper into Lynn's waiting hands.

Lynn nodded and looked down at Grigori's sketch.

"And it was her who told us to go to that tattoo place?"

Lynn nodded back at her with a pained expression. "It's beautiful, Rach." She was staring at her with all the hurt she felt for her in her eyes, while Seb snatched the paper out of her hand.

"I don't get it?"

"It's my nan," Rachel said at the same time as Lynn. "There's no doubt what it means."

Seb bobbed his head. "It's a good sketch."

She could tell he wasn't getting it—neither of them was. "The thing is, I didn't choose that," she said, pointing at the paper in Seb's hands. "That guy, Grigori, sketched it out right in front of me with barely a word."

Lynn took the piece of paper back and studied it again, as if it would reveal some coincidence or something.

"It was like he knew everything, Lynn. It really freaked me out."

Lynn shrugged and handed the paper back to her. "Did you get it done?"

"No … that was the other weird thing. He said there would be six more sessions, all at night, starting next week, and I was to go away and think about it, because once I have it, it'll change everything."

"Deep," Seb said, nodding sagely.

Lynn looked at him, exasperated. "That does sound strange. Was he creepy? … You should ask for Jet. She was lovely."

Rachel thought about that. There was no doubt Jet was very good, but she couldn't shake the feeling that a die had been cast and there would be no swapping—not at Angel's Ink, anyway. She shook her head. "Funnily enough, he wasn't creepy at all." *Far from it.* An immediate film of sweat covered her at the memory of the hottest dream she'd had of him.

"What?" Lynn said, half laughing, immediately catching on. "He was hot?"

Deadly serious, Rachel nodded back. "Like you wouldn't believe. He's some brooding Russian or something."

Lynn laughed and Seb's mouth dropped open.

"It's just what you need," Lynn said, clearly delighted.

Seb was shaking his head. "I think we should check him out."

Rachel giggled at Seb's nose obviously being put out of joint, and Lynn nudged him. "You just can't bear another man in Rachel's life."

He shrugged, not arguing with the logic. It made Rachel smile. As hopeless with women as Seb was, he did look out for her in his way.

Lynn picked up her glass of wine and motioned for her to do the same. Then she clinked it with hers. "Go on, live a little. You can always call a halt to it if you're not happy at any time."

Rachel clinked glasses a little less enthusiastically, but it did make her realize that she was probably overthinking it all. She was prone to do that about most things. She went to clink her wine glass with Seb's beer and realized he was checking her out closely, as if he wasn't so sure either.

"Don't worry about him," Lynn said, nudging him again, now playfully. "He's just bummed he's no longer the male center of your world."

He sighed, now resigned, with a "cheers!" and a bump of his glass. "Just let me know if you want me to come with you. I should meet this guy."

It finally made her let go and laugh. Lynn was right. If it got too much, she'd just stop, and maybe Seb could go with her if she felt uncomfortable. Although by the time their food came and their chatter had moved on to other things, she couldn't shake the thought that once she started on this course, she'd have to see it through to the end. And maybe once everything was out of her control, she wouldn't want to.

THE SHORT TIME Rachel had spent with Grigori plagued her all week. Twisting the conversation this way and that in her mind, by Thursday, she wasn't sure if she'd imagined half the double meanings and undertones.

Work had been a welcome distraction because, as well as her faith, she'd always loved books. She guessed it stemmed from her grandmother reading to her and spending a lot of time alone as a child. It had seemed a natural leap to do her work experience in her last year at school with the town library and eventually slide into a job there when one opened up. She'd always intended to go to university, but somehow time passed, and she never went. It seemed like her basic needs were met: church in the evenings and weekends, meeting regular library patrons who felt like friends, and getting paid to surround herself with what she loved most: the route to pure escapism.

Her usual start time was a cool 9.30 and she finished at 6, but they'd done a big stock-take last week and she had some time owing.

She decided to walk home from town instead of taking the bus. She could think better that way. The weekend was getting closer and she was no nearer to a decision about the whole thing. She always seemed to hit a wall. It all boiled down to either cancelling it or just turning up on Saturday and seeing what happened. However, that still brought her back to the inevitable question he would ask: What did she want from it? That's the point that always stumped her.

What did she want from it?

Rachel reached home, turned her key in the door and went in. "Anyone home?" she called, flinging her bag down on the small table in the hallway. The house was silent, so she guessed she was alone. She went into the kitchen to put the kettle on. It was a typical rental kitchen: low-end white-gloss kitchen cupboards, arranged in a square with a small circular table and four chairs in the middle. There were still bowls from breakfast in the sink. She'd even have to wash a cup before she could use it and called Seb a lazy sod under her breath. He literally charmed his way through life with a sexy grin and a wink.

The flower Grigori had so skillfully drawn came back to mind as she rinsed the cup. She imagined what the pain would be like; the ink being pushed into the skin of her shoulder. Pain caused by Grigori's hand. Her insides immediately clenched at the thought, and restlessness followed. This had been the pattern for the whole week.

The only thing she was sure of was that she did want change. Grigori was right about that.

A knock at the front door pulled her out of her daydream. She flicked the switch on the kettle, went back through the hallway and peeped through the small spyhole in the door. She'd never liked opening the door to strangers.

Shit! It was Cynthia Blackburn from her church. *What the hell was she doing here?* The church was way over the other side of town, near her parents' house.

For a moment, she considered hiding and pretending she wasn't in, but after moving from one foot to the other and panicking with indecision, she thought she might as well just answer it. She'd probably seen her shadow through the smoked-glass panel anyway. Then the letterbox opened, and the nosy cow could see her legs.

Rachel snatched open the door and caught the woman

still bent at the waist. Cynthia stood and beamed a smile at her as if she'd done nothing wrong. "Ah, you are in."

She had to hand it to her, it was a real lesson in styling it out when caught red-handed.

Cynthia took a step closer and pulled her into a tight hug. A sickly floral stench of some old lady's perfume and glacier mints wafted around her. She even tasted it in the back of her throat. "Hi, Cynthia," she managed, half coughing and feeling crushed by surprisingly strong arms.

Thankfully, Cynthia soon put her away from her to study her face with an exaggerated expression of concern. "My poor love, how are you? Are you doing OK?" She looked up and around at the house as if she'd come down in the world. It annoyed her a bit. There was nothing wrong with their rented semi.

"We've all been so worried about you since your grand-mother's passing. You've missed so many bible club sessions. Pastor Joseph keeps asking everyone if they've seen you. So I went to your mum's and she told me where you were. "How are you? … Are you sure you're OK?"

It was all said in a whiny voice that made Rachel take a step back, out of range of the awful perfume. She tried hard to appear grateful; the woman had just taken a trip across town, especially to call on her. "I'm fine. As you can see," she said, opening up her arms. "I've got a bit to sort out, since Nan … you know."

The woman pulled a pained face, following her trailing off words with exaggerated nods. "Oh, I know, dear. The whole thing was a terrible business. I want you to remember we're all here for you and you're still in our prayers." Then she tilted her head to the side and really studied her as if something in her face was giving her away. It irritated her, and she shifted her weight to her other foot in impatience.

"You know, even though your nan's gone, and you had

that wonderful bond of worship together, faith goes deeper than that. It was in you from a very small child; I saw it. And you wouldn't have kept it up all those years just to please your nan. It can be a tremendous comfort through your grief, you know, Rachel."

Her words struck her in the center of the chest like a stake. She could barely think of this stuff, let alone discuss it with someone who barely knew her. She guessed the woman did mean well, but she still felt too angry and it was all still too raw. What she really wanted to say was: a lot of good it did her nan, but she remained silent, bit her lip and nodded in the interest of politeness.

The woman assumed that she was choking up and hugged her again. She extricated herself quickly and went to say goodbye, but then she said something really strange. "Please be careful out on your own, Rachel. You're such a good girl and the Devil makes work for idle hands. We need to stay busy in the work of the Lord. Remember 1 Peter 5:8: Your enemy, the Devil, prowls around like a roaring lion looking for someone to devour," she said, nodding with that pained expression again. Then, as if she'd said something as mundane as the weather changing, she said, "Bye then, Rachel." She patted her hand, turned and walked off down the short, Tarmacked drive. With a last look over her shoulder, she called, "All you have to do is resist, and he will flee from you."

For a moment, Rachel watched Cynthia walk away, aghast, with one hand holding onto the doorpost. On the surface, her words were predictable. It was just that with everything else going on in her life, it felt like some prophetic warning. Like she was teetering on the brink of two sides of a war, and the side of good had just sent its agent in the form of Cynthia Blackburn. Strangely, instead of comforting her, the whole conversation had made her angry all over again. It actually made her wish she had her tattoo right then, for her to see.

Thankfully, Seb's old smoky-grey van pulled up like the cavalry, blaring music at just the right moment to pull her out of her nosedive. Both doors flew open and Seb got out of one side and his hot friend, Jules, got out of the other.

It brought her back to normality with a comforting bump. They slammed their doors, and Cynthia gathered her mac around her floral dress and got into her little Ford Fiesta, looking horrified.

Her tension lifted a little. They did look like the antithesis of the people at her church: two hot guys with overlong, messy hair and completely dressed in black. Seb's oversized T-shirt with Badmotorfinger on the front and Jules' Kooks with ripped skinny jeans kind of made Cynthia's point. The clouds cleared from her mind as they made her smile, pulling a huge amp from the back of the van and proceeding to struggle with it towards the house. It was everyday life and it helped her breathe easier again.

"Evenin', all," Seb said, as she stepped out of the way to let the two of them squeeze through the doorway.

Cynthia had remained in her car, watching, and now wound down her window. "You have my number if you need me," she called. Then she started her car and pulled away as if she was fleeing a crime scene.

Rachel frowned and looked down at her hand. She hadn't even realized she was holding a piece of paper. Unfolding it, she read Cynthia's name and phone number in ultra-neat handwriting. Despite how she felt, the word lifeline came to mind. It felt silly the moment she thought it, though.

Male laughter and the twang of guitars behind her broke her out of her musings. Without realizing it, Cynthia had helped make up her mind that she didn't want her old church world anymore. However, it also came with a sense of unease, because not wanting to believe in something didn't necessarily mean it wasn't true.

She took in a deep breath. Cynthia's car disappeared into the distance rather like her old life. In a waft of sickly perfume and mints, Cynthia had gone, taking the last remnants of her safe and stable life with her. An evening chill in the air made her shudder.

Then Lynn's little blue Nissan Micra pulled up where Cynthia's car had been. It warmed her instantly. *This* was her life now. Not the church or any of the weird paranoia going on in her head about the tattoo. It was real and it was hers.

"What you standing there for like a lemon?" Lynn said,

struggling up the path with a bunch of shopping bags in each hand. "Feel free to help."

Rachel rushed to take some of the bags. It was just what she needed. She followed Lynn inside, grinning. *Boy, she could be a weirdo sometimes.*

Rachel helped Lynn unload the bags of shopping in the kitchen and wandered into the living room.

"Who was that?" Seb said, busy arranging an impressive set of effects pedals in a semi-circle around him.

Rachel smiled a hello at Jules, who grinned back. He was lead guitarist in Seb's band, The Shotaways, and was completely heart-throb material. His curly blond hair framed an angelic face, far too beautiful for alternative rock, which was what he played like a man possessed.

"Oh, just someone from the church," she said, feeling heat enter her cheeks with embarrassment in front of Jules. It was the first time she'd used the word "the" instead of "my". It was very telling. She was publicly distancing herself. Shame now added to the pink in her cheeks.

Seb had noticed and flashed her a look, but he kept quiet, thankfully. Both he and Lynn knew her from before and accepted it as an integral part of her—kooky, but part of her all the same.

"And for what do we owe the pleasure of all this?" she said, to change the subject and already turning back in the direction of the kitchen.

"Milk, two sugars!" Seb called from behind her. "We're getting in some extra practice before our gig at the Rising Sun on Saturday."

"Tea is not so rock 'n' roll, Seb," she called back, laughing.

Rachel made the tea and brought the boys a cup. "What

time is it? Don't forget I've got my second appointment at the tattoo place on Saturday night."

Seb's face clouded. "Can't you reschedule?" he said, uncharacteristically snappy. It was so unlike him that it brought her up sharp.

He looked at Jules. "She's getting this tat from a dude that reckons he will need six sessions and will only see her alone … at night." He left his eyebrows up in an unsaid question.

Jules laughed, a single mirthless blast of air, and shook his head.

It irritated the hell out of her. She'd thought Seb understood, but he obviously didn't get it at all. What he said was true, but he'd said it out of context.

She relented a little, guessing that maybe Seb was just disappointed because he wanted all his friends there. "Look, I'll try, OK?" she said, putting up a hand in defense. But somehow she got the impression that Grigori's timescale was pretty rigid. Even that sounded weird. Maybe Seb had a point.

He looked her dead in the eye. "We're doing two sets. 8.30 and 10.00. I'd like for you to be there."

The look he gave her made her swallow hard. Seb was always so easygoing and laidback. This felt like a completely new side she was seeing and it seemed more than brotherly protectiveness. It was a glimpse at something more. Like she was seeing him for the first time as possibly more than a friend. It blew her away. "I'll try," she said, so quietly she wasn't entirely sure she'd spoken aloud.

His eyes held hers for another full moment until Jules twanged his guitar to bring them back to the room. It was her excuse to slip away.

. . .

RACHEL WENT STRAIGHT UPSTAIRS with her heart thumping and her hands shaking. She needed time alone to think. After closing her door, she went and sat on her single bed, hugging her knees to her chest. She slowly scanned the cluttered room. It was a nice enough room. Frilly lemon and white bedspread, freestanding mirror used to hang 'not quite dirty enough to wash' clothes over. It made her realize that everything in her room was serviceable, useful and boring. Nothing was frivolous or bought *just because*. Lynn's room was full and messy; scattered with new clothes, glossy magazines and festival flyers pinned to the wall. It was a stark reminder of how completely out of her depth she felt.

When she thought of Cynthia's visit, it felt like a weight of dread in the pit of her stomach. *Could she honestly go back?* In her heart, she knew that since her nan had gone, she'd changed too much to ever fit in. She turned and knelt up to remove the picture of Jesus. Taking a ragged breath, Rachel took a last lingering look into the sad eyes, then bent down and pushed him underneath the bed. Something stopped her from throwing him away completely. It seemed too disrespectful, or maybe she just wasn't ready.

Sitting back up, she surveyed the room that held so little personality. Now the walls were bare, there was nothing of her left. It felt empty, like a blank canvas.

She'd come to live in the house at Lynn's suggestion, almost immediately after her nan had died. She didn't want to live in her nan's house on her own. And she certainly didn't want to go back to her parents'. Seb shortly followed. They'd all gone to the same secondary school; Lynn was the only friend she'd kept up with all the way through. If she were honest, even members of her church were just acquaintances. She just didn't make close relationships easily. Seb's carefree personality had slipped past her barriers because, frankly, he just didn't see them.

She guessed it stemmed from her real dad leaving her with her mum when she was a little girl. She wasn't too young to remember his love of cars and how she would stand on a chair while his head was under the bonnet, passing him spanners. She supposed that was her first experience of betrayal. One day, he just packed his bags and went. He visited her at first, but as time went by, the visits became wider apart, until they stopped altogether. Her nan had been there to catch her. By the time she was twelve, her mother had remarried and taken on his three younger children. Time spent with her nan gradually increased until she moved in completely. That was how it was pretty much till the day she died. She'd moved in with Lynn the day after the funeral.

Now her nan's house was up for sale and she'd been left most of the proceeds of her will. The solicitor said she would be a modestly solvent woman—whatever that meant. Money had never been important to her—except when she'd had bills to pay and not enough money to pay them after her nan's death. That had been scary, but she guessed that was normal. However, she knew the hole in her chest would take a lot more than money to fill.

Her mind went back to Seb. Crazy, funny, sexy, totally un-boyfriend material, Seb. She'd be lying if she didn't admit she'd had a secret crush on him since school. What wasn't to like? Brought up by four older sisters, he was a cute ladies' man in such a hopelessly adorable way. But never in a million years did she ever imagine being on his radar, let alone in his league.

What just happened? Had something changed without her knowledge? Could she have missed something as groundbreaking as that? It was something only a conversation with Lynn would solve. For now, there were more pressing matters.

She reached down, grabbed her bag from the floor and pulled out her phone. The Angel's Ink number was already programmed in under A. Even that made her pause. It was right at the beginning of her contacts list as if it was top of the agenda. Just seeing the name there in print made her heart thrash in her chest while it rang and rang. Part of her dreaded the voice at the other end.

She quickly got a grip on herself. It had built up so much in her head as something supernatural, it now became a test to see how normal it could be.

Suddenly, the ringing stopped. "Hello?"

There was a weighty pause. Then she let out a breath as the answerphone cut in. She was forced to come up with something to say quickly. "Er … it's Rachel … Rachel Fairweather. Not sure if you remember me, but I've got an appointment this Saturday with Grigori and I need to change it. Can someone call me back?" She left her number and hung up.

She checked the time on her bedside clock. It was 7 p.m. Someone should be there now if it was a regular tattoo shop. Early evenings would be their busiest time. Then doubt crept in again. *What did she know?* Maybe it was only open till six—six-thirty. *Shit!* She had to stop this habit of reading too much into things.

By the time she came out of her room, Lynn had already gone to work. She worked at the same pub that Seb's band was playing in at the weekend. She'd have to catch up with her tomorrow.

Seb took up the living area all evening, so she steered clear after the weirdness of earlier. She nuked a lasagna microwave meal and took it to her room. She ate it while watching the small TV her nan had given her, placed on her chest of drawers at an angle. Then she showered, got in her pajamas and snuggled down into bed. The light soon went, until only the light from the TV flickered around the room. Her eyes became heavy and she drifted slowly into sleep.

She'd been asleep for a while when she became conscious of her phone ringing. It took her a good few rings to realize it wasn't in her dream. Then she remembered the message she'd left. She sat up and snatched up the phone from her nightstand. Her clock read 11.55. "Hello?" she said, even though the phone display told her it was Angel's Ink. *It might not be him,* she told her beating heart.

"Rachel?" the unmistakable, deep voice said, already melting her insides to warm butter.

"Oh!" she said, swallowing hard. "I thought it would be Skye." She was fumbling and awkward and everything came out in a long ramble. "Erm … Saturday … Can't do nine. Can I change it? … I mean, I don't want to cancel or anything. Just change it … you know?" She frowned, wondering if he'd made sense of that at all with the language barrier and everything. He was waiting patiently for her to finish, so it was hard to tell.

Typically, he cut right to the point. "Have you thought carefully about what you want?"

As if their strange conversation hadn't been on her mind since they'd met: the shop, the people there and the fortune-telling from Madame Beauregard. But, in all honesty, she hadn't gotten past her nan's flower.

She had to break it down to simple terms. Did she still want a tattoo? She decided that she did. "I want the flower you drew, Grigori."

There was a pause for a long moment before he spoke. "That is good. It's a beginning."

The silence that followed made her ramble again. She was learning that he kept his speech to a minimum and didn't feel the need to fill silences. "I've just got this thing I need to go to on Saturday and nine is not great for me. I can come before if you like?" It seemed a perfect solution. She could simply go straight to the pub.

"My time is limited, Rachel," he said, making even her dull name seem sexy.

She couldn't think of what to say after that. She didn't feel like she could let Seb down. The tattoo thing felt like it was taking over her life. "Or another day?" she said as a last hope.

"You may come after you finish. It is better with no distraction, and a sitting can take it out of you."

Her mind went to Lynn's illness, but that was obviously a bug or something. And anyway, she'd only sat for a short time. She had to admit coming after the gig was an angle she hadn't thought of and she couldn't really argue with it, except, "It'll probably be more like midnight, though?"

"I am a night owl," he said straight back. "Remember what I said, Rachel. If you start this, it is a big undertaking and you must fully commit to it: six sessions, exactly one week apart."

It sounded like a prescription, but she guessed it was something to do with the healing process.

"Do we have an agreement?"

There it was, the weirdness again. As if what she said next was somehow legally binding. And yet he'd accommodated everything she'd asked for. She could go to Seb's thing, do this and not upset anyone. *So why did it feel like she was signing her life away?*

Maybe it was because it was all said in his deep, sexy accent. His magnetism affected her even over the phone. The alternative was to stop this now. He was giving her every opportunity, but, for some reason, cutting off this new part of her and not seeing Grigori again seemed impossible. Somehow, him and the tattoo were bound up in each other and woven already into the fabric of her life.

"OK!" came out before she could talk herself out of it.

"Please say exactly what you want so I fully understand."

It shocked her into silence for a moment; the weirdness was now way off the scale.

"English is not my first language. The words are a safe-guard for you and for me."

She swallowed, trying to work through what he said. She guessed he was right. With something as permanent as ink, there could be no misunderstanding. "Er, yes ... I'd like your flower design, please."

"And you agree to six sessions?"

"Yes."

In the pause that followed, she sensed relief—no, triumph, she was sure of it, which made no sense at all. "I will see you at midnight on Saturday." Then he was gone.

The conversation left her bereft and tingling all over. As if his presence had been a tangible thing in the room and was now dissipating in the air around her. It made her shiver, so she shimmied down into the bed.

Her mind churned. She'd gone from the most staid exis-tence to one where Cynthia—a woman she barely knew—wanted to save her soul. Seb now looked at her with eyes that could see into her soul, and Grigori? Well, with him, it felt like if she allowed him to get close enough, he would take it.

CHAPTER 6

The next evening, Rachel rushed home from work in the hope of catching Lynn for a chat. "Sorry, babe, I'm really late. Colin's gonna kill me," she said, rushing past her in the hallway. The front door slammed before she had a chance to close her mouth.

Things obviously worked out because Lynn didn't come home that night at all. Nor the next. In fact, Rachel managed to miss Lynn every time she got in from work. She desperately wanted to broach the subject of Seb, but it wasn't something she wanted to say over text or the phone. By Thursday, she messaged Lynn:

When's your next night off?
Saturday. Why?
Miss you. Girl time while we get ready?
Fab! Look forward to it.

THAT SORTED, she'd be able to speak to her then, if the wait didn't kill her.

Saturday finally came at a sloth's pace. She spent the day

cleaning her room, trying to read and browsing tattoos on her laptop. She didn't want to seem like a complete idiot in front of Grigori.

Finally, Lynn came home from a lunchtime shift, showered, and Rachel went to her room to get ready with her.

Rachel was drying her hair at the old-fashioned white kidney-shaped dressing table. Lynn had bought it herself to add to the bright, girly feel of the room that was bigger than her own. She was applying makeup with a small magnifying mirror on the nightstand. "You've been quiet lately," Lynn said. "I've missed this."

Rachel turned to look at her and watched as she dipped her wand into her mascara and leaned into her mirror. She was good at applying makeup. Never too much and a good judge of how much more or less to put on depending on the occasion.

She, on the other hand, always used the same, as little as possible, for fear of messing it up. "You haven't exactly been around. I've just got a lot on my mind," she said, turning back to her reflection and deciding she needed more blusher.

"Yeah, sorry … Like what?" Lynn asked, frowning but not taking her eyes from her mirror.

"Oh, a few things really."

Lynn held her lipstick up and waited for her to go on.

"Cynthia from my church came round this week and asked me when I'm coming back."

"And are you?" She pouted in her mirror and rubbed her lips together.

Lynn was so unperturbed by it that it made her feel a lot better when she said, "I don't think so." She faced back into her own mirror, not sure who she saw anymore. "I feel like I've changed so much since my nan died."

"Give yourself a break, Rach. It hasn't been that long. And

anyway, it doesn't mean you don't believe just because you don't go."

Rachel smiled at Lynn, undoing and teasing out her long blond hair. She could be surprisingly insightful at times. It was an incredibly sweet thing to say, but she didn't fully understand; no one did. She turned back to her mirror and sighed. "I'm not sure if I do anymore, Lynn … I'm not sure I want to."

"Shit!" Lynn said, now shuffling over to sit on the end of the bed nearest her. "You've been into the God stuff ever since I can remember."

Rachel nodded sadly. It was true, she had. "But I did it with nan. It was our thing. Study group, charity fundraisers, cake bakes, everything." It was the barest information. She knew she was skating around the issue. If only life were that simple. She held back that the information Rose Beauregard told her had challenged the very fabric of who she was. That everything in her life now felt like she was being sucked into a heady, dark world of rock music, tattoos, and hot guys. And Grigori.

Grigori. He was in a whole other category. She wasn't sure exactly why he'd popped into her head then, but she had to concede that he was probably at the root of how she felt. It wasn't a simple thing of deciding if her faith had gone—far from it, it was proving that if there was darkness, then there was light too. That meant she had a far bigger decision to make and whether she was prepared to turn her back on it.

It all sounded too ridiculous to say out loud, and so she changed the subject to one Lynn would understand. "Never mind all that. Something else happened this week, even weirder."

Lynn's eyes widened and she frowned comically. "Weirder than that?"

Rachel rolled her eyes and flipped her off. Lynn doubled

over with laughter. "Hey, do you remember when we'd just started secondary school and you were convinced caffeine was a slippery slope to drug abuse?" She fell on her side laughing.

Rachel couldn't help letting a giggle escape her. "Yeah, but I was always first in the queue at lunchtimes in Roasta Coffee!"

"Exactly!" Lynn said, laughing.

Rachel laughed along with her this time. She simply couldn't help herself.

Lynn held her stomach and finally got comfortable, crossing her legs on the bed. "Come on then, tell me!" she said, beckoning her with her hands.

Despite Lynn's cathartic laughter, Rachel was too embarrassed to look straight at her, so she angled her dressing table mirror so she could see her while she brushed her hair. Her cheeks prickled with heat. There was nothing else for it, she just had to blurt it out. "I think Seb might fancy me." It felt ridiculous, like the height of big-headedness to jump to such an assumption, but she couldn't think of another reason for his odd behavior. She looked at her through the mirror.

Lynn's eyes were wide, but she was smiling. "Why, what did he say?"

Rachel frowned. "Well, nothing exactly. It was more how he acted when he thought I couldn't come to his gig. I had to postpone my tattoo appointment and everything."

Lynn leaned back on her arms, shaking her head. "Catch up, girl. He's always had a soft spot for you." Then she bobbed her head. "You, and half the female population."

Rachel laughed. She had a valid point there, but it didn't matter. The fact was she was no longer invisible. She stopped what she was doing and turned to face her squarely. "No he hasn't, Lynn." She was completely sure she'd never got that impression before. "I would have known if he had."

"You've just been too dense to notice. I even teased him about it in the beginning. We thought you didn't like him, which completely battered his ego, but then we realized that you were just hopelessly oblivious. He's really good at covering it up with jokes and being … well, daft Seb. I actually thought you'd never twig … Yay," she said, doing small claps with her hands in front of her.

All she could do was gape at her friend. "Why did you never say anything?"

Lynn pulled a pained face and Rachel sagged. "I can take it, go on."

"Well," she shifted uncomfortably. "I kind of threatened him. He would have eaten you for breakfast, Rach … Not meaning to or anything. Just by being Seb. He just would. And you, you were so … so—"

"Gullible and stupid," Rachel finished for her. She sagged in her seat and looked down at her hands. Lynn scooted over to her on her stool. "No, not at all. You were young, that's all. You know, for your age. You're much more worldly wise now."

Rachel knew Lynn was saying it just to make her feel better, but it did brighten her up. She tried to think back over the last few months for clues, but came up with nothing in particular. "He gave me no idea."

Seb was incredibly cute in a cheeky kind of way. Girls adored him. He had that dark, almost black, ruffled hair and piercings look that a lot of the metal kids had. He was never seen wearing any color other than black and grey and always had a band t-shirt on. He was fun and got on with everyone. So, because of that, she never thought she got any special treatment or was anything more than a friend. It had simply never occurred to her.

Maybe it was to do with her faith and the knowledge that Seb would never wait until marriage, judging by the succession of girls seen leaving his room in the morning. But even she now recognized that as an excuse. More accurately, she'd assumed he'd never look twice at someone like her. She was pretty and curvy in a natural kind of way, but she was into books instead of bands, tea instead of alcohol, and staying in instead of partying in order to do all the above. Her wardrobe had improved, but she was not so stupid as to think she'd ever been cool.

"He's a bloke, Rach. You're complicated and he's used to easier conquests. He was scared you'd give him a knock-back. And then, you know, the living together bit would make it awkward. Tonight's just incredibly important to him. There's a guy coming who might want to be their manager. It would mean bigger gigs and maybe even some studio time."

Rachel was stunned. Of course, this would be huge for him, and she felt bad now for treating it so lightly, whatever he thought of her. "What difference would it make, my being there ... really, though?"

Lynn sagged back on the bed again, defeated. "Think about it, dingus. He wants his close friends there. He wants you there."

She couldn't face Lynn's mocking expression any longer and turned back to finish her makeup. *How could she have missed something like that?* They'd all lived together for months. Surely she would have picked up on some kind of clue.

Then something began to creep over her, something that had niggled at the edges of her consciousness for a long time. That maybe she'd hidden herself away in her church for reasons other than a simple devotion to god. She believed in God, of course she did, but perhaps it was less about religion and more to do with safety and hiding herself away. The answer had been staring her in the face all the time: maybe she'd been too afraid to live.

Her grandmother came to mind as she always did. *Could it be that losing her the way she did had thrown open the shutters and forced her out of hiding?*

Her mind moved onto Grigori—her next most thought-about topic these days. Maybe his effect on her was less about some magical power and more to do with the first potent, grown-up alpha male she'd ever been alone with. It sounded much more feasible. Despite Seb's jokes and bravado, he was still young and not as confident as he made out, so maybe it was easy for her to miss the signals. Unlike Grigori, whose experience and sheer magnetism belted her straight in the gut.

The realization made her feel strangely better. It was all so logical. For the first time in her life, she was waking up. She was setting herself free of her self-inflicted prison of denial. What she was feeling was completely natural.

It was a huge weight lifted off her. Tonight, after years of shunning parties in preference to church meetings, she would dress up for a cute boy for the first time ever. It was exciting. And if she was being totally honest, there was a small part that wanted Grigori to see her like that too. Looking at the new, glowing reflection staring back at her, she decided blusher was no longer needed.

CHAPTER 7

The Rising Sun was halfway between where they lived and the town center. Rachel watched all the lights in the shop windows go by with new eyes. Who knew nighttime could be so exciting? Lampposts shone their orange glow against the night sky, warm and inviting, making her wonder why she'd always avoided the town center on a Saturday night. Everyone seemed cheerful as they chatted animatedly, hurrying with somewhere to go.

They'd left home in good time to get there for 8 o'clock to get a good position and Lynn got a space in the car park easily. The older daytime customers were filtering out and being gradually replaced by the younger evening crowd.

As they walked in, the smell of stale beer hit her immediately. She saw Seb straightaway. He and his band were still setting up in the corner reserved for the live entertainment, so they bagged two rare barstools at the end of the large L-shaped bar. People would kill for them later.

Rachel had been there only a few times. The restaurant part, where Lynn worked, was through a separate door. The pub layout had live entertainment and space to dance at one end, and seating with tables and chairs at the other. The floors were covered in plain grey plastic tiles for easy mopping, but the glow from behind the optics created an olde-pub feel and a nice ambience. It was a great venue for a live gig like this one. Not that Rachel was experienced in these things. Seb's band was the only band she'd ever seen live, but she did know that they were very good.

"Hello … Hello … Hello!" Seb said, testing the mic.

Lynn leaned in close. "Seb looks good tonight." Rachel shot Lynn a warning look, to an amused, unrepentant, embarrassingly knowing expression. She wasn't wrong, though. He looked very cool in his customary black. This time, his band T-shirt was Nirvana—the one with the man with wings.

However, just as seeing him look this hot excited her, it also made her heart sink. She didn't know any of the bands Seb listened to. His music taste was cool and hers was very definitely not. Non-existent, actually, so she wasn't sure if that even counted. Life was confusing enough as it was without Lynn teasing her every five minutes. "So does Jules," Rachel threw back, issuing a dare for her to say one more thing on the subject. Lynn just laughed and held up her hands in surrender. "Just sayin'." Then she got a little more serious. "Are you going to talk to him tonight?"

The thought filled her with horror. "Nooo! And you mustn't either." *God,* she couldn't think of anything worse. "He's far too busy."

Lynn bobbed her head, not able to argue with that. She turned back to the band and watched Jules and Joe do some last-minute tuning to their guitars, and the drummer, Jack, took his place behind the drums, getting ready to begin. They'd joked about everyone in the band having a first name beginning with J, except Seb. Lynn was right about one thing. She had to have a conversation with Seb sometime.

It was at that moment that Seb spotted her. It was close to 8.30 and the place was filling up. He started walking towards them through the crowd on the dance floor. A couple of guys patted him on the back and a girl greeted him and kissed his cheek.

Shit! For a split second, she debated whether to make a dash for the ladies' room, but Lynn put a steadying hand on her leg. "No, you don't." She hated that Lynn knew her so well, but stayed put.

Seb came to a standstill in front of them and called out, "Bottle of Bud, Jim … and whatever these two want," to the barman behind them.

Seb kissed Lynn's cheek and then hers, but his eyes lingered longer on hers. "You came." He looked at her with an intensity that made her self-conscious in front of all these people. There was such heat in them, but she couldn't understand: why now?

"Course we came," Lynn said, saving her from a death by silence. Then she called out her order of beer and a blue alcopop.

Rachel had never managed to drink any drink that tasted of actual alcohol, which was ludicrous, she knew. She did it to fit in, when the truth was, she didn't actually like the taste. "I postponed my appointment till later."

"Thanks," he said, with an earnest look that said he absolutely meant it. *Wow*, he really did have the nicest blue eyes. He had very Celtic coloring. He was clean-shaven and smelled of something lovely. Clean like soap, but quite manly.

Both she and Lynn had opted to wear their black Shotaways t-shirts and skinny jeans. Seb nodded his approval. He'd given them to them for Christmas. Before she was forced to say something and make a real fool of herself, Seb said, "Better go." He grabbed his bottle from the bar and disappeared through the now-packed dance space, back to his band.

Lynn was grinning at her now.

"Stop!" she said, scowling at her friend.

"He couldn't have made it more obvious, Rach."

Rachel sank into her stool. She was right; she had no idea how to handle this. "It's all so awkward, though, Lynn. We live together."

Lynn softened. "Just talk to him. He's not a serious guy. Nothing bad or heavy will happen; he likes you."

The thought of it was already constricting her airways and she shook her head.

"I'm going to say a quick hello to Colin before it starts." Lynn got down from her stool, leaving her coat on top and shot off in the direction of the restaurant.

Rachel was grateful for the headspace. Supposing, for argument's sake, that she and Seb did start a thing: she couldn't jeopardize their whole living arrangement. She loved it. It was the only good and stable thing in her life since she'd lost Nan. She wouldn't mess things up by letting things get weird between them. If they entered into a relationship and it didn't work out, then everything would be ruined.

However, just as she'd talked herself out of it, the band began to play, and she was reminded of how totally adorable Seb was—had always been. She'd just pushed it to the back of her mind as off-limits. Right then, she couldn't help feeling that maybe it was too late.

Lynn returned, lipstick gone and running her fingers through her hair. She got back on her stool and swayed and sang as if she'd never been away. Rachel watched her and wondered how much else in life she'd missed. It was as if the veil had been lifted from her eyes, and she was noticing the details of this relationship stuff for the first time.

Lynn realized she was being watched and grinned. It

made her turn back to Seb. He had such a wonderful, husky rasp to his voice. It wasn't long before the whole crowd joined in with the choruses and she'd gotten the hang of them too.

They did two original upbeat numbers after and a great rendition of Adel's, "Rolling in the Deep". The pub was now jammed and hot and she was grateful for her seat. As she looked around, everyone seemed so trendy and beautiful. It amazed her that Seb, clearly a very talented musician, could actually fancy her. She couldn't really believe it.

They played a couple more original songs and finished their first set with a tribute to Nirvana by playing "Smells Like Teen Spirit", which the crowd went wild for. Seb put his hand up and walked away through the crowd to whoops and pats on the back from the crowd. He was coming towards her again. They really didn't think through their seating position. Seb was always going to gravitate to the bar when he wasn't playing. However, she had to concede that he would have come over to them wherever they stood. He didn't have to, but he always did. *Oh god, Lynn was right.* Seb had been far too attentive for a guy with no interest in either of them. Excitement was quickly eclipsed by terror. This was new territory and she was absolutely out of her depth.

Seb reached them with his band mates forming a group around them, all calling out drinks orders to the overworked bar staff. His eyes fell on hers. "Did you like it?"

She had to smile and nod. His genuine vulnerability after just being nothing short of amazing was adorable. "Of course, you know you were." The rest of the band all said hi and kissed her cheek. It felt good to be one of the coolest girls in the room for a change. Girls looked on enviously, trying to work out which one of the band she was with.

Another girl came over and Jules introduced her. She was

a tall brunette with legs that went on forever. It proved that one of the members of the band did at least date.

Rachel checked her watch: 9.45. The boys were on again in fifteen minutes.

"You have to go?" Seb didn't hide the look of disappointment on his face.

She shook her head. "No, I'll be here a while yet."

His smile of relief tickled the insides of her stomach. It was like she was seeing him for the first time. *How could she have missed this?* He seemed genuinely pleased she was there, and this previously unknown vulnerability was very disarming. With her butterflies now kicking up a storm, she wondered if she'd been too scared to face it before.

In the beginning, Lynn had been his friend at school, and she'd been accepted by default. Living her sheltered life, they'd kept an acceptable distance and crossed paths only on occasion through Lynn. That was until they all moved in together recently. She supposed she'd conditioned herself to never look at him like that. He was the popular guy with girls attracted to him all the time. Now, looking around at the female looks of adoration, she couldn't help feeling plain in comparison—not so much in looks, but definitely in life experience. She was boring.

"Are you still getting it?" Seb said, leaning in because of the noise.

Her butterflies bounced up and down when she breathed close to his neck. She was distracted by the idea of running her tongue along it when she realized it was a question that needed answering.

"Your tattoo," he prompted.

She blasted red and couldn't believe her carnal train of thought. It had never happened with anyone before. "Oh yeah … Later. I've got to be there at twelve," she spluttered.

He frowned. "Twelve?"

She nodded, watching a range of emotions cross his face.

"Doesn't it strike you as a bit late?"

She shrugged. It was. "I know it is, but I think he was just trying his best to fit me in." It did sound like a lame excuse and not half the story, really, but Seb just wouldn't understand.

He didn't argue, although he didn't seem convinced. Her heart slowed a little in relief.

"I'll take you," he said.

She stared at him in shock for what felt like a full minute. Then she dismissed it with a shake of her head. "It's OK, you don't have to. I'll get a cab. I'll have to get one home anyway. I don't want anyone to have to wait around for me."

Seb still looked concerned. Then he leaned into Lynn and said something close to her ear. She nodded and said OK. Then she looked across at her. "I was going to leave my car here and pick it up in the morning. Seb's now gonna drive us back and tell Jules to take the van."

Rachel's eyes fell on Jules. He was laughing and chugging back a pint at the bar. "Are any of you going to be fit to drive by then?"

Seb followed her line of vision. "We will now." He went closer to Jules and said something to him, to which he nodded. Then he came back over and kicked up her butterflies again. "I think I should at least meet this guy. Doesn't hurt for him to know you have people around you."

Lynn must have heard or lip-read because she was grinning and widening her eyes without Seb noticing.

All Rachel could say was, "Thanks." A warm glow had appeared in her chest that she couldn't explain, and it was working its way outwards. No one had ever wanted to look out for her like that before and she liked it. The silence became awkward, so she quickly said, "I'll get some drinks in, shall I?"

Seb smiled and touched her on the arm. "Make mine a Coke." He flicked his eyes to Jules. "And him." Then he went to walk away in the direction of the men's. "Don't go without me!" he called over his shoulder.

She shook her head as her butterflies somersaulted.

"You need a vodka," Lynn said, having watched the whole exchange.

She hadn't intended to drink anymore, but she was right. Despite feeling like some kind of imposter in her own life, she admitted to herself that she liked Seb. A lot.

CHAPTER 8

The rest of the gig went by like some glorious dream. She felt elation, fear and excitement, all rolled into one. It was up there with one of the best times of her life. She'd definitely had more alcopops than ever before, so she was way past merry and feeling a little sick by the time the bell rang for last orders at the bar.

The band had played their last encore and the pub was beginning to empty. A tall, scruffy-looking man was shaking Seb's hand, and the band was dismantling equipment, ready to take out to their van.

Rachel rushed to the ladies', used the loo and splashed some water on her face—though excitement was cutting through her merry haze and sobering her up anyway. She dried her face on a paper towel and stared back at the strange girl in the mirror. What little makeup she'd put on had long gone, but there was a glow to her cheeks and a wideness to her pupils that made her feel sexier. Her heart leapt in her chest. Everything was changing tonight. With a deep, fortifying breath, she went to meet the others.

By the time she reached Lynn's car, Seb's van was already pulling out of the car park. Seb put up a hand of goodbye and Lynn threw him her keys. He caught them easily. Lynn flipped the seat forward and clambered into the back as the car only had two doors and Rachel slid into the front next to Seb. She tried to reason that she was getting out first and not that Lynn was pushing them together.

She glanced at Seb's unimpressed face as he adjusted his seat, flicking switches on the dashboard and swore that he hated these cars. Rachel giggled.

"Hey, stop hating on my little car!" Lynn said from the back.

He scowled at her in the rear-view mirror. "Get a real one then and not a Noddy car!"

Rachel giggled into her hand and looked out of the side window.

They pulled out and passed through the lit streets quickly with very little traffic. "Hey, what about your guy ... what did he say?" Rachel said, remembering there was a whole point to the gig that evening.

"Oh yeah," Lynn said, leaning forward. "I completely forgot. Did he come?"

Rachel looked over at Seb, who was nodding. Then he glanced at her, careful to keep an eye on the road. "Yeah, he came. He wants us to have a chat about some ideas this week."

Lynn touched him on the shoulder. "That's great! You're gonna be a star, Seb. Hey, you're gonna have a rock star boyfriend, Rach."

"Steady on," Seb said, grinning.

Rachel turned around sharply and glared at Lynn. She couldn't say a word to her in front of Seb, and she grinned back, knowing full well. All she could do was smile weakly at

Seb in apology. "I didn't … I mean I wouldn't." She gave up, only making matters worse, and turned red. Although after that, she caught him looking intently at her, gauging her reaction, a couple of times.

Thankfully, the journey was short, and they pulled up directly outside the Angel's Ink doorway. The digital clock on the dash told her she was five minutes late. "Shit! I'd better hurry. Thanks, you two," she said, unclipping her seat belt and opening the door.

"Wait! We'll come too. I want to meet this guy." Seb got out as well.

"And me," Lynn said, already pulling the lever to spring the front seat forward. "I'm not staying out here."

Rachel rolled her eyes. It felt awkward enough as it was. For some reason, she didn't like the idea of mixing the two worlds. Although as the three of them approached the door, she was acutely aware of how deserted this part of town was at night. It probably couldn't hurt to have an escort.

She rang the buzzer and the door clicked open immediately. They all walked in and followed the dim corridor, lit by emergency lighting like last time. They passed the stairway that went off into blackness and reached the door that opened before they got there. Grigori stood, the light behind him, as tall and imposing as ever.

Suddenly, the evening, her friends and the alcohol, even her budding romance, receded into the background. All that was left was him. The darkness of his piercing eyes held hers first, then fell on her friends one by one. The silence crackled around them until she was forced to be the one to break it. "It was late … my friends didn't want me to come on my own."

Despite the harshness of his face, when he spoke, she was always surprised by how softly spoken he was. After a pause, he said, "As it should be. Perhaps their concern would be satisfied if they came inside for a moment?"

Rachel noticed that his words were spoken directly to Seb. To his credit, he didn't shrink under Grigori's intimidating stare. Instead, he said, "Yeah … five minutes and we'll be on our way."

The temperature felt like it had dropped a full degree. Grigori stepped away from the door and the three of them entered the room. The lighting was very low, as before, with only a glow from the lamp at his workstation illuminating the whole room.

Grigori disappeared and came back with three plastic cups of water, carried easily in his big hands, and they all sat silently on the sofa. Seb was in the middle, taking in the room. Seeing it through his eyes, she guessed it was a little weird.

"Are you gonna be alright?" Lynn whispered across to her.

"Do you want us to stay?" Seb said.

Actually, despite how sweet they were being, looking after her, they were making her feel uncomfortable. She shook her head and glanced behind her at Grigori getting his bottles ready on his bench. He might be stern and antisocial, but she didn't think he would hurt her.

Lynn took the hint. "Right. We'll get off then and leave you two to it," she said at a normal conversation level.

"Just give me a call, and I'll come pick you up," Seb said, with a face the most serious she'd ever seen.

Grigori was now folding his arms and leaning back against his bench, waiting.

"No, I can't expect you to do that. I'll call a cab."

Seb was about to protest when Grigori cut in. "Don't worry. I use a specific trusted cab firm. I will personally see to it that she returns home safely." The steely stare directed at Seb moved to her and turned her insides to liquid. Then he moved towards the door, giving no one any room to argue further, and held it open.

After a brief pause and a loaded look at Lynn, Seb kissed her on the cheek. "Call me if you need me?"

She nodded, still feeling the tingle of his kiss.

Lynn squeezed her hand as she passed. In the end, she wanted to scream at them. Grigori clearly wanted them to go, and, despite their concern, they were embarrassing the hell out of her. "Go! I'll be fine," she said, giving Lynn a small nudge towards the door.

"We'll wait up," Lynn said, looking at Grigori as she passed.

He was patiently looking ahead of him, giving nothing away in his expression.

However, Seb paused and spoke directly to him. "How long do you think she will be … so we don't worry?"

Grigori turned his face to him for the first time and she had to admire Seb's guts, because a cold look from Grigori would wither any man. "It is hard to say exactly—two maybe three hours. Have no fear, I will take good care of her." He smiled, but his eyes were as piercing and harsh as ever.

Rachel's insides nearly dropped out of her stomach when Seb didn't move and said, "I'll hold you to that." Her jaw literally fell open. It was more than amazement that Seb was being so protective of her, it was that he had the guts to say it to Grigori at all.

However, instead of bristling, his smile softened as if he understood everything and he inclined his head. "Of course."

Seb took one last look over his shoulder at her and, pulling Lynn along with him by the arm, they left at last.

Grigori closed the door, throwing the catch, and with a last look of amusement, he turned and went back to his bottles.

Rachel was left standing in exactly the same spot. She was

relieved her friends had finally gone, but now she was alone with him and suddenly felt awkward.

"Sit!" Grigori said, still with his back to her, putting together his tattooing machine. When she didn't move right away, he looked at her over his shoulder and bobbed his head towards the big chair next to him. "Your boyfriend has gone. You can relax."

Her heart was thumping as she approached and got up into the huge leather and brass chair. "He's not my boyfriend."

Even though he wasn't looking at her, he smiled a secret smile to himself as if he didn't believe her for a second.

She examined the weird seat and climbed up. It looked like the dentist chair you'd imagine if it had been made for Jules Verne—all tan leather, valves, and brass—but it was soft and comfortable. It allowed her to relax back and watch Grigori. He didn't say any more about Seb.

He sat down on his stool and quickly finished attaching the correct end to his machine, which she guessed was the needle bit. Then he ran a hand through his hair, pushing it back from his face and put on a grey baseball cap back to front.

Rachel openly stared. It was clearly meant to hold back his hair, and on anyone else it would look goofy, but on Grigori, it was purely functional and revealed the starkly handsome face she'd only ever seen partially hidden.

He turned to face her then and moved closer on his rolling stool. He angled his spotlight on them so he could see what he was doing and looked directly into her eyes. All the while, he never said a word. She guessed it was a sign of inner strength that he didn't feel the need to make small talk.

It did, however, give her an opportunity to study him close up. His forehead was clear, with small furrows and his eyes were dark, almond-shaped slashes, with creases at the corners proving that he must laugh sometimes. His cheek-bones were sharp and his jaw stubbled with five o'clock shadow. It seemed like it was always there. She couldn't imagine him clean-shaven or even with a beard. With his hair back, she could see small tattooed stars in his hairline, and on his left side, there was a small tear just below the corner of his right eye.

It made her sad. Not just because a handsome face was marked in such a way, but that it was purely for him. No one else would see it when his hair was in its usual place. It meant he carried a sadness that he wanted to keep private. She found his face utterly fascinating.

He reached to the side for his tattoo machine. His arms were covered in a design that disappeared into the black gauze of his t-shirt. It was left loose over the tight black jeans with rips at the knees, revealing more black ink. It occurred to her then that every inch of him might be covered. Ink addiction was probably an occupational hazard, but there was nothing cliché about him. Far from it.

He was lean without an ounce of excess fat on him. And yet, somehow, she doubted he spent much time at the gym. He looked less like a bodybuilder and more like an athlete or a fighter.

She frowned and wondered how on earth she'd arrived at that decision about him. He smiled at her for the first time, bringing to life those cute wrinkles at the edges of his eyes, and the effect was breathtaking, transforming his tough granite face into something absolutely beautiful.

Rachel smiled back. She couldn't help it; his smile completely disarmed her. Then she hitched a breath, remembering. "Shit! I forgot the picture you drew."

His face transformed to mildly curious. As if he didn't immediately follow what she was saying. Then the smile returned. "Don't worry. It was just a guide. It will evolve as we go anyway."

She sat back in the chair, not sure if she liked that idea at all.

"The placing. You want it on your shoulder."

It immediately brought her back to what he was doing. "Yes. On my shoulder blade." She was leaning with her back against the chair, so she reached behind her with her fingers as far as she could go. It had to be hidden by clothes. Then she realized that he wasn't asking a question.

Grigori proceeded to press a pedal with his foot, and something moved at her lower back with a hiss. She sat forward with a jump, not knowing what was happening.

He immediately steadied her with a hand on her leg and his eyes on hers. "I will turn around, then you will remove the top part of your clothing so I can get to the right place on your shoulder. Then you must face the back of the chair so that your knees go here and your arms can go on there," he said, tapping the leather where he meant her to go.

She could see exactly what he meant, but she wasn't sure about it at all. Lynn didn't have to adopt any weird positions for her shoulder tattoo.

"Try it and see. It is really very comfortable for long sittings."

His look was direct and strong and gave her no reason to doubt what he was saying. She was learning that more and more about him. It was a strange feeling to get from someone she barely knew. He said nothing further and turned around on his stool.

She was left staring at the tight V of his back. Then, with no further argument, she stepped down and pulled her t-shirt over her head, placing it as neatly as she could across her bag. She took a hairband out of her purse and pulled up her hair into a high bun so it wouldn't get in the way.

Without it, she was left feeling very naked and thankful she'd worn a decent bra. It was black and lacy and one she reserved for best.

There was a small pedal-like step that she used to hop back onto the chair and face the way he told her to. It reminded her of getting on the back of a motorbike, except she was facing the high back of the headrest.

"OK?"

She wasn't sure at all, but the lumber part that had moved before had narrowed so her knees could now fit there snugly. With another hiss, the headrest lowered, offering a soft ledge for her to put her chin. The two handlebars she rested her arms on completed the feeling of straddling a bike. Grigori had been right; it was comfortable.

His hand rested lightly on her shoulder, immediately speeding up her heart rate. "Ready?"

Her mouth had suddenly gone dry. She took a breath. "Yes." The warmth from his touch spread over every tense muscle.

"I'm just going to sketch it out freehand, OK?"

Turning her head to face him, she could see the marker pen in his hand. "OK." She swallowed hard, a little relieved that he wasn't going to go straight in with the needle. For a moment, her eyes went to his, and she became lost in them. This close, she could see that they were black and amber and not brown, and they seemed wise and older than their years. As if he'd been alive forever. They were strong and direct, but she could detect sorrow, making his small teardrop tattoo make sense. It made her wonder what had happened for that to come across without a word. Then, as if she'd seen something she shouldn't, the moment passed and he concentrated on what he was doing, wheeling his stool closer.

At first, she panicked at the size of what he was drawing, but she became so absorbed in the man himself that she dismissed it as paranoia. There was something so magnetic about him.

He was left-handed and working this close made her even more aware of him, if that were possible. As his left hand moved across her skin, his right steadied it and pulled the muscles of her back taut. It enabled her to get a good look at the ink on the inside of his bicep. The artwork was intricate and amazing and surprisingly not just meaningless lines. They were miniature works of art. "Your tattoos … who did those? They're the best I've ever seen."

He stopped what he was doing and sat up for a moment as if the question had thrown him. "A friend … no longer here," he said softly, more to himself. He leaned back in and didn't elaborate. It was obvious that it was someone he cared for deeply and she ached to ask him more, but she could tell it was too personal a question.

"Do they mean anything?"

He turned his head to her then and the look on his face was a mixture of horror and disbelief. The reaction was so strong that it made her want to shrink away from him. "Sorry, you don't need to answer … The pictures, they're so small and detailed …" she said. "They're beautiful."

His face relaxed and he turned back to what he was doing. His hand moved quickly across her skin. "It was done a very long time ago … just a story of how I got where I am." He left a pause long enough that she thought that was all he was going to say. Then he looked at her through the corner of his eyes. "You know … rather like I'm doing here." It made her swallow.

As quick as the dark cloud came, it lifted, and he appeared to shake off his broodiness. "Anyway, I'm here for you, not the other way around." He turned to her slightly and winked.

She smiled in relief. It was a rare moment of playfulness

on his part, but she could tell she'd touched upon something deeply personal.

"You will choose him," he said, crouching over her again.

The sudden subject change completely threw her for a second. "Who?" She wasn't sure what he meant at all. He was shifting the spotlight back onto her.

"The one that came in here … The friend," he said, raising an eyebrow.

She was shocked. Her mind scattered. She wasn't even entirely sure he was asking her a question. She was beginning to realize he spoke in statements. It was amazing that he would think there was a line of men battering down her door. It almost made her laugh. "I'm not sure yet," was all she could say without bursting red. He must feel her blush through her skin. "He's a bit of a Casanova."

Again, the secretive smile. "Isn't it a better prize to win what others want?"

"Everybody wins where Seb is concerned. That's the trouble."

His grin widened, but he didn't say anything further, which frustrated her. She found herself wanting to know what he thought about her and Seb, but she let it go. They barely knew each other.

He continued to work, and she became increasingly aware of his wonderful smell. She was sure it was no kind of cologne that she knew, and it had become stronger the longer he worked—a mixture of clean skin and pure masculine odor d'Grigori. The room was hot. Maybe the heat was bringing it out. "Well, we have six sessions. I've got time if you want to swap guy troubles?" she said.

The look he cast her then was nothing short of flabbergasted. Well that and a hint of irritation and maybe a little amusement. As if she had the cheek of the Devil. It *was* rather forward of her. She had no idea where it came from, but she'd found the courage and just said it. However, instead of commenting, his jaw clenched, and he returned to his work, his beautiful whiskered jawline in full view. She noticed it clenched every so often with concentration. The line of it was mirrored perfectly by the starkness of his cheekbone. It made her think he might not have been eating enough carbs. Keto was her latest reading at the library.

Although she couldn't take anything away from him, the guy was just beautiful—lethally beautiful. She instinctively knew he didn't play at anything. She guessed that put her in pretty good hands for a tattoo.

At last, he sat back, having finished the sketch, and reached for his machine sitting in a cradle next to him.

"Is it going to hurt?" she asked, with a flutter of fear.

"It will a little, but the place you have chosen is one of the better ones." He smiled his heart-rending smile then. "But nothing is worth anything unless you pay a price."

It was an odd choice of words, but she didn't have long to consider it before she tensed and braced as he neared her skin with the machine.

He paused just before he touched her. "Relax." He turned to her, his eyes clear and direct, but there was a rare kindness in them. "It will hurt you less if you relax your muscles." There was something so knowing and believable in them that she took some breaths and gradually released some of the tension in her back. She felt herself loosen into the leather seat.

The machine began to whirr, and she realized she'd become completely unaware that she was sitting in just her bra and jeans.

"Better," he said, with the gun whirring next to her skin.

At first, it felt like a hot scratch, then an ache she quickly got used to.

"Good," he said. "You're doing well."

She felt herself flush under his praise. It wasn't nearly as bad as she was expecting, and she found she could relax completely.

He felt so close. She guessed he had to be, but his proximity was doing all kinds of things to her. It felt so incredibly personal. Maybe that was what he'd been driving at all along. That they were embarking on an incredible journey together, one that couldn't be shared with anyone else in the world.

CHAPTER 9

Rachel concentrated on Grigori's profile again to get her mind off the heat in her blood now radiating beneath her skin. She was soon absorbed by the total look of concentration on his face. The daft backwards baseball cap did its job perfectly and didn't detract at all from the hard lines of his face. In fact, she had to admit he looked hot in it. Something she thought impossible for anyone. "Why do you really work nights?" The question just came out with absolutely no forethought.

He finished a tricky line he was doing, sat up a little and grinned. "Because I turn to dust during the day."

She stared at him, not knowing what to say, until he chuckled, and she frowned. Was he batting away a question that he deemed way too personal to answer, or had she been that obvious in her thinking about all the Rose Beauregard stuff? Had he caught on to how wary of it all she'd been? Then she remembered he would have seen Rose's necklace.

She suddenly felt foolish and embarrassment prickled her cheeks. It turned to anger, which made her a little reckless. "Why did Rose Beauregard send me here—why you particularly?" It left her a little shocked at her courage. Perhaps it was just the weird vibe in the place or the alcohol she'd consumed earlier. She did, however, know one thing: to continue, she needed to understand his connection with Rose, as she was in no doubt there was one.

Grigori didn't so much as blink at the weird question. His hand remained steady while he either ignored it or thought about what to say. "There is no connection to me and your psychic, other than she knows who I am. She gets a little—how do you say? kickback, for sending people here."

Her heart stalled. *Was he saying that she worked on commission? Was that all it was?* But it didn't make sense—all the cloak and dagger, weird phone calls, texting the location and everything. Then her heart began to sink with irrational disappointment. The necklace simply told him who sent her so she could get paid. "So, you know she's a psychic," she said flatly. It was the only sane thing she could salvage from her tumbling train of thought.

"Only a soothsayer would see the humor in sending you wearing a rune of the damned." He adjusted his position on his stool and grinned at her. "In your books, have you ever looked into the history of body ink and from where it came?"

Her mind struggled to process his last sentence and her eyes darted to him, startled. The chain Rose gave her felt tight against the skin of her neck and the abrupt change of subject was bewildering. *Love of books?* She knew she'd never told him.

He tipped his head to her bag, dumped against the wall on the floor. A hardback was just poking out through the zipper. "In this age, a physical book, and a hardback, would suggest someone who cares a great deal about them."

She felt foolish again. He'd read her perfectly. Why was she determined to see all this as something otherworldly? She gave him a wan smile.

The machine whirred away. Grigori straightened up and changed something on the gun. "I notice things others do not." Then his face transformed with that disarming smile again. "You had books in your bag the last time you came."

She let out a blast of air she hadn't realized she'd been holding. *God, she was losing it.* She was reading far too much into everything. Although he hadn't answered a single question properly. "So, I think we've established you're not a creature of the night."

His mouth twitched with amusement and he glanced sideways at her. "No, I'm something much worse. I am real and vampires are not." He grinned widely, but it didn't reach his eyes.

Rachel found herself swallowing hard. He seemed to find a way of disarming her with his sexy magnetism one minute and then scaring her the next. He still hadn't revealed why he didn't work days. There was nothing to do but let it slide.

He continued in rapt concentration and she remained silent, letting her eyes wander languidly over the sexy lines of his face. She wasn't ever going to get a straight answer from him. He had given her a clue, though. The history of tattoos was a place to start. She wasn't sure her library went back that far. 'The beginnings of body ink' were the words he'd used. She wondered if there was a difference.

The machine buzzed and her back ached where he was working over a bony part. She closed her eyes to breathe through it.

"You're doing well," he assured her.

Praise again. Her heart fluttered a little. Her mind meandered again with the soft whirr and the pain subsided with a fleshier part of her back.

Had he read her easily because of the way she looked? Did she come across as being plain and boring because she was a librarian? Her heart sped up at the thought of all the beautiful babes he must see in his line of work. That kind of jealousy was ridiculous with a man like him. She doubted whether any single woman could hold him. *Or man?* The thought of him being gay was becoming a voice in the back of her mind; she couldn't ignore it. Maybe the guy who'd tattooed him had been more than a friend. He certainly mourned him.

The machine vibrated on her skin and the heat in the room sent her drifting off to sleep. Her troubled mind produced weird and realistic dreams.

Her eyelids flickered and she found herself lying on her side on a cold slab of stone. It was covered in soft moss and under a canopy of trees. She felt instantly chilly, and goose-bumps sprang up on her arms. For a moment she was disoriented, trying to rack her brains to remember if she'd fallen asleep outside. Her eyes gradually adjusted to the speckled light and she realized she was deep in a forest, where the sun only just broke through the trees in javelin-like bars.

It felt so real, but the light was strange and disorientating. Birds called, foxes yapped and she could even smell the decay of leaves on the soft earth.

There were men's voices. A woman, too. Close by. All seemed to have accents like Grigori. His was among them. It sounded like there were three or four. She lay still, pretending to sleep.

"Is she the one?" a deep voice said.

"Yes." *Grigori?*

"And the flower?"

"The first thing she needed." Definitely Grigori.

"It will be your downfall. You know this."

"Remember Abaddon, he will know what you're trying to do."

"You think I could ever forget that?" Grigori sounded furious and Rachel's eyes widened in fright.

"Pass this one to me, brother."

There was an agonizing pause where she was dying to turn to see what was happening.

"No. I am on a path with this girl now. I must see it through to the end."

"Sentiment."

There were grumbles as if there was some sort of posturing or scuffle—slam and an oomph, as if the air had been knocked out of something. "Pragmatism. There is a difference," Grigori said.

Rachel took the risk of revealing she was awake to see and turned towards the noise. Grigori had a man by the throat against the wide trunk of a tree. The man he held had black, much longer hair and eyes as black as a crow. Facing her, he noticed her immediately. "She wakes."

As Grigori released the man and began to turn, a light blinded her. She could hear only the beating of large wings and feel cool air on her face. "Angels," died on her lips as the sounds receded into nothing.

"Angels," she said again.

The next thing she knew, Grigori was rubbing ointment into her back.

"You slept. It is done. You sat very well."

She was blinking, still trying to get her bearings. She was in Angel's Ink and a fan was on, explaining the breeze she'd felt. *Shit!* "I was having the weirdest dream." It felt so real. Then his words finally registered. "I'm done?"

Grigori stood from his stool, stretched out his long arms and rotated his shoulders to loosen his muscles. Then he began to dismantle his tattoo machine. "Dress." His back was already to her. "Careful. You may feel a bit dizzy."

Rachel felt more stunned that her first session was over already. "Can I see it?"

"Over there." Grigori nodded towards a full-length, free-standing mirror by the coat stand.

She stood slowly. He was right and she wobbled a little. Strong arms immediately caught her and held her against a hard, surprisingly warm body. Shocked into remaining perfectly still, his smell wrapped around her while she absorbed the feel of his sheer size encasing her. The heady mix made her heart hammer in her ribs.

It felt like a long moment before his warm breath was next to her ear. "OK now?" With her heart threatening to drive right out of her chest, she nodded. Only then did she realize she was still in her bra and jeans.

His arms released her slowly and his presence moved away, but the impression of him stayed like a warm tingle next to her skin. She had to literally push him out of her head; he affected her that much.

She walked towards the mirror.

Whether it was the low lighting or the fact that she'd fallen asleep, she wasn't sure, but she didn't recognize the woman walking towards her in the mirror. She looked tall, seductive, and dare she think it: *sexual?*

For a moment, she put it down to an overtired brain becoming fanciful, because the awkward, average librarian was nowhere to be seen.

The tall, imposing frame of Grigori came closer until he loomed behind her. He was holding a large oval mirror, which he angled so she could see.

And there it was. The days of worry, soul-searching and anguish were over and made manifest in a work of art like nothing she'd ever seen. It wasn't just that a simple, perfectly formed flower could convey all the hurt and love she felt, but that it seemed to glow in its center as if it had a power source of its own.

Still looking into the mirror, her eyes tracked up to Grigori's, hooded and knowing, behind her. All feelings of bashfulness were gone. "It's so beautiful," she said, at a complete loss. "I don't know how to thank you." The weight of it was suddenly overwhelming and tears welled in her eyes.

For a moment, he seemed troubled, but recovered quickly. "The iris is perfect for you. It can symbolize many things—eloquence, wisdom, faith, hope … passion." The pause before the last word brought his eyes directly back to hers in the mirror in front of them. "And purity when it is perfectly white."

His look held something dark and made her swallow. She had no idea the flower signified all that. It added so much more to the piece. She turned to face him and was instantly aware of how close he was.

This close his eyes looked ravaged and desolate. So much so that she had to ask, "What's the matter? It's stunning. I love it."

The clouds in his eyes immediately dispersed and he smiled a little. "Nothing. For others, it holds a different meaning, that's all." His eyes dropped and took a leisurely gaze over her body. There was no misinterpreting it. It was the way a lion looked at its prey before it ate it. It was surprising because, up to that point, he hadn't appeared to notice her in that way at all. It was her own reaction that surprised her. Instead of wanting to hide herself, she bloomed and opened everywhere his eyes touched, like a flower seeking the morning sun. It was liberating rather than demeaning, as if he were releasing something long kept inside.

By the time his eyes meandered back to hers, her blood was on fire. No one had ever looked at her like that. Then, while her breathing was still labored and her chest rising and falling as if she'd been running, he said, "Go home to your friend, Rachel," and the master switch to it all got thrown off. It was said softly, like a warning, but it still felt like rejection.

It brought her back to her senses like a cold shower. She

wasn't sure what had come over her, and she looked down at herself, feeling foolish at her nakedness. "Sorry," she whispered, completely mortified. Cheeks searing with embarrassment, she scurried over to her bag and, with clumsy hands, pulled on her shirt. Her eyes closed as another wave of humiliation washed over her and she said, "I'd better call a cab."

"Your car is outside."

Rachel opened her eyes, stooped and picked up her bag. She had no idea when he'd managed to arrange that. He already had his back to her, at his bench, putting away his bottles of ink into a wooden box with a handle. The dismissal seemed so quick. "Bye then," she said.

He turned and leaned against his bench-top, with his arms folded. "I called them while you slept."

She nodded. She'd forgotten about that.

"How do you feel?" Grigori asked, smiling. He seemed completely unaffected by the embarrassment of a few minutes ago.

Maybe she'd made too much of it as usual. "I feel fine," she said with a small, awkward shrug.

"You feel different?" He was smiling widely now as if he saw something she didn't.

"I don't know," she said, thrown by the way he could switch from deadly serious to laid-back and amused, as he was right then. Her mind went back to the strong, confident woman she'd seen in the mirror.

"You're an inked woman now." His grin widened.

She half-smiled and half-frowned as she walked hesitantly to the door. She didn't know how to take him at all. Every time she thought she was getting to know him, he flipped her onto her back.

With her hand on the handle of the door, she turned and looked back at him. Her tattoo burned on her back, just like his eyes. "What comes next?" The thought surprised her. Despite everything on this, the weirdest night of her life, she wanted it again. Even when she knew it was a dangerous feeling. Like she'd just sampled the most addictive drug in the world and loved the way it felt.

Grigori's eyes were hooded. Of course he would have seen this reaction before. It was probably nothing out of the ordinary for him. "Go!" he said, with a flick of his hand, and pushed off his bench. "Think. It will come to you."

Rachel was beginning to think that he only ever spoke half of the sentences he wanted to say. "Bye then," she said again, snatching open the door when there was no reply.

Embarrassment went through her like molten lead. By the time she got in the surprisingly posh taxi and rode the short distance home, she was burning up with fever.

CHAPTER 10

Rachel was shivering violently as she tried to get her front door key into the door. Finally, she managed to get in, and she went to tiptoe past the living room in darkness except for the flickering light from the TV.

Seb had fallen asleep in front of it. She paused and watched him stir and turn over, the noise of her coming in not enough to completely wake him. Seb prided himself on being able to sleep anywhere. It was really late and she wondered if he'd waited up especially for her. She should really tell him she was home so he could go to bed, but a wave of nausea threatened to do that for her. So she left him and staggered to the kitchen to grab a glass of water, then shakily climbed the stairs. The strength felt sapped out of her, and the climb was like a mountain. Having to lean against the wall two or three times, she finally reached the landing. She used the loo, grabbed some paracetamol from the bathroom cabinet on her way and wet a cooling washcloth for her head. She felt strangely proud of herself for thinking of it all. Once she got in that bed, there was no way she was getting out of it.

Every bone in her body ached. She hurriedly shed her clothes and grabbed an oversized t-shirt, teeth nearly chattering out of her mouth. It was a job to get the two paracetamol to stay long enough to glug them down with water. The sheets were painful, they were so cold as she slid down in between them. She lay a full minute trying to get control of her shudders. Then she reached for the cold flannel, folded it into a rectangle and put it across eyes that were now killing her.

This was one hell of a virus—whatever it was. It had to be the one Lynn had after she came back from Angel's Ink last week. That had come on suddenly too. The parallel struck her for a moment, but sleep was dragging her down. It had to be easily 4 a.m., if not later. She was soon sucked into a world of shivers, where heat and cold entered the most vivid of dreams.

She was back in the forest she remembered from earlier. Except this time, she was walking and heading for a clearing of brilliant sunlight. When she blinked and got used to it, she could see her grandmother standing there. She wore exactly the same glasses and floral pinnie she always wore. Her hair was grey and neatly tucked away in a bun. At some level, she knew it was a dream. Surely she would be a young woman if she'd come from Heaven, but she looked well, really well. "Come here, munchkin," she said, and held her arms open.

Rachel ran over immediately and sobbed into her. "I've missed you so much," she whispered into her shoulder, already wet with tears. She felt exactly the same, small-boned but tough, soothing her as she'd always done. The smell of her lavender perfume wrapped itself around her. "Why did you leave me, Nan?" She hugged her even more tightly, afraid she might disappear.

But she didn't. The wonderful embrace went on long

enough for her to lean back and look into her face. It was her. "Nan!" came out on a sob.

Her nan got out her handkerchief from her pinnie pocket, where she always kept it, and dabbed her eyes. "There, there." Then, she moved stray pieces of hair from her eyes. "Blow!" she said, holding the handkerchief over her nose like she'd done when she was little.

Rachel laughed as she did as she was told. She couldn't take her eyes from her, afraid she'd disappear any moment.

"Shh," she soothed, running a warm thumb over her cheek.

Where are we, Nan? You seem so real." Her face began to crumple as she began to cry again.

Her nan smiled weakly as if what she was going to say was very sad. "We're at the top of the stairs in the Angel's Ink shop."

Rachel frowned in confusion as doubts started to form, but she didn't have time to say anything as her nan added, "We're at a crossroads, that's all." She looked over Rachel's shoulder. "That's where you came from and must go back." Then she bobbed her head backwards, "And that's for me."

Rachel understood then. Her nan would go back to Heaven and she would go back to her life. It was a dream she'd conjured to see her nan, but she was OK with it and resigned to enjoy it while it lasted. "I know Nan," she said, picking up the small, bony hand.

"I don't think you do, my lovely girl. The crossroad is for you, not me. You have a choice of two directions when you go back." She pointed with her free arm into the distance behind her, first towards the right and then to the left.

Rachel tried to look beyond her nan to see where she came from, but the sunlight was so bright it blinded her. "Where does that lead?"

Her nan smiled kindly. "To one possible end of your journey."

"When I ... ?"

Her nan nodded slowly. "When you pass over."

A lump came to her throat. Suddenly, everything became so overwhelming. "I don't know, Nan. I feel so ill. What way do I go?"

Her nan pulled her into her arms for a few moments to soothe her and put her away again. Her grip felt so firm and real on the tops of her arms. "The Watcher has you. You already bear his mark."

Before her nan finished speaking, she felt a tug on her ankle, then another. She pulled her leg up sharply. It happened again, then at her back. She squealed, turning and putting her nan safely behind her.

Little spindly grey men were everywhere—except they weren't people. They had long, straggly arms and were moving and morphing into different shapes, moaning and crying as they went. All the while, they were trying to grab her clothes.

She screamed. "What are they, Nan?" Her feet were sinking. "Run, Nan!" They were pulling her this way and that.

Then everything went dark as if a huge cloak came around her. She felt it cross her face like soft velvet. It felt wonderfully warm and the smell familiar. The silence was restful and even though she couldn't see a thing, she relaxed into it. Safe and warm in the knowledge that nothing could hurt her.

There was warmth behind her. A body that was simply too big for her nan. The heady, familiar smell wrapped itself around her like another layer of protection. She turned into it, burying her nose in the smell. "Be at ease," the deep, familiar voice said. "You are protected. Now and forever."

The words sounded echoey and far away, but still swept

away her fear. In the darkness, she looked up and could still make out the strong stubbled jaw. His smell was overwhelming, even sinking into her pores. "Grigori?" Her own voice sounded weird, too, as she wrapped her arms around his waist. She held him tightly and felt his muscles move beneath her hands like iron under silk. The last thing she knew, her feet left the ground.

The next moment, she woke and turned into a soft, wet pillow. Her washcloth had fallen off, or she'd sweated and made her pillow soggy. Her sheets were a damp mess. *Shit!* That was the most insane dream she'd ever had in her life. Her fever had broken, and she must have been delirious.

She reached over to grab her water and nearly dropped it, her grip was so weak. Sliding back down in the sheets, she knew there was no getting up yet, however badly her bed needed changing. Instead, the weird dream bounced around her head, making her heart palpitate.

Then she heard something—whispers, from right outside her window. Male. "Seb?"

"Shh! She'll wake."

"Grigori?" She tried to sit up, but the world spun. Instead, she leaned up on an elbow and craned to listen.

"What are you doing?"

"They came for her and you stopped them. Let her go, Xenon."

"She was identified, consented and marked. She's ready."

"She is not ready. She remains on the brink. The contract is for the full six marks. Trust me, she'll be worth a hundred times more."

Then followed indiscernible muttering.

"He is right."

"She wears Layke's mark. Are you claiming her or calling him? Which is it?" A woman's voice said, "Have you taken leave of your senses? You'll call Abaddon's wrath upon us all."

There followed a hiss and raised whispers as if holding someone back. "Hold your tongue, Oleander. I did nothing. The Iris is her own, it's a sign." It sounded like Grigori, but angrier than she'd ever heard him. "Never utter his name in my presence."

"Maybe you've become too close to the subject, Brother."

"Or seek to cut a deal to squeeze us out."

A gust of wind blew her curtains and she pulled her sheet up under her chin. Her heart smashed against her rib cage and her eyes were wide in terror. A golden figure stood in the center of her room. He looked like a Greek god with wings—yes, stunning white wings, tipped in silver. Her eyes nearly popped as he came closer and put a finger to his lips.

The voices outside her window receded to nothing. The last words echoed. "Enough! ... The sun rises. You have until the Atonement Moon, Brother, otherwise she will be out of your hands."

The light in the room didn't feel real, like the flickering projection of a film. Everything felt strange. Wind billowed her curtains and the golden angel had gone.

Rachel flopped back onto her pillows with her heart pumping and exhausted as if she'd run a sprint. Her head was pounding. Her bedside clock read 4.36 a.m. Barely any time had elapsed at all.

She closed her eyes and took some deep breaths. She was dreaming; she had to be. Her sick brain was exaggerating her fears and throwing them up to scare her. Seeing her nan, Grigori, the tattoo, Seb, and even the golden angel were signs of anxiety. It had been an emotional day; it was just her brain's way of processing it.

Sleep must have taken her under at that point because the next time she looked at her clock it was midday. She remembered it was Sunday and was grateful. Her limbs were painful lead weights and she wouldn't have been able to go to work anyway. Bouts of fever came and went until a gentle tapping on her door brought her out of a light doze.

"Rach … you OK?" It was Lynn's voice. "Did you get home OK? Is it done?"

"Come in," Rachel said with a barely audible voice.

Lynn peered in. "Oh yuck! What's the matter with you?"

"Don't come too close, I'm really ill."

Lynn's face immediately crumpled in concern as she sat on the end of the bed. Then she drew in a sharp breath. "It's probably what I had. Nasty."

Rachel nodded. It had knocked Lynn over just as viciously and quickly.

"At least it only lasts about twenty-four hours."

"She awake? Can I come in?" Seb's voice came from outside of the door.

Lynn looked into her face. "You can, but she's ill."

Seb came in regardless and walked straight over to the bed. His face contorted. "Ouch!"

Rachel was too ill to even get embarrassed. "I know, I look like shit," was all she could manage.

"You gonna show us then?"

Lynn clapped double time. "Yes, show us!"

Rachel rolled over onto her front. It was just a dull ache on her right shoulder blade. "You'll have to pull down my top to look."

She felt the oversized neckline of her t-shirt being pulled down as far as it would go and then there was silence—a long silence—and whispering.

The neck of the t-shirt got pulled the other way to the wrong shoulder. The whole thing went on for so long that curiosity even overrode how crap she felt. She rolled back over to glare at them. "What's the matter, don't you like it?"

Seb and Lynn both looked at each other. "There's nothing

there," Lynn said, her eyes worried and sympathetic. "Maybe you got ill there or something?"

Rachel sifted through all the weird dreams she'd had and back through her memories of the night before and shook her head. "That's ridiculous. Bloody hell, Lynn, I'm too ill for jokes." She struggled to get up and Seb immediately sprang into action to help her sit up.

"I'm not joking," Lynn said.

Rachel's eyes tracked to Seb's. "She's not," he said, quietly.

Her head was banging now she'd sat up, but the earnest look in Seb's eyes when they locked with hers made her pause. "Really?"

He nodded; his expression worried.

"Come on, help me get up and look." She was so weak that her knees buckled when she went to stand. Lynn and Seb took her weight under each arm. "Take me to the bathroom."

The three moved slowly towards the small bathroom adjacent to her room. They led her to the mirror over the sink, where she shuffled to put her back to it. The tattoo hurt like hell. It felt sore and bruised, aching with every arm movement.

Rachel held an arm across her chest as Lynn pulled the hem of her nightshirt right up to her neck. Bunching it at the nape so both shoulders were clearly visible.

She looked over her right shoulder and there it was, as breathtaking as she remembered.

It was red and slightly raised, giving it an almost 3D effect, but it was there, and it was beautiful. An intricate mandala-style iris the size of a small melon. It nestled among leaves with droplets of dew and everything. She'd never seen anything so beautiful. "Thank god," she said, relaxing. "You had me going for a minute." The skin felt tight across it as she moved to try to get a better view, but it was totally worth it.

"So, what happened, Rach, did you chicken out?"

Rachel whirled around and scowled at her oldest friend. "Cut it out. It's the best tattoo that I've ever seen." When all she got was an incredulous look and silence, she was forced to turn to Seb. "You like it, right?"

His eyes flashed to Lynn's and then he looked into hers, the most serious she'd ever seen him. "Maybe we ought to call a doctor."

Rachel pulled down the back of her shirt, out of their grip. "That's it! Get out, I'm going back to bed."

The two just stared at each other.

With a cry of frustration, she pushed past Seb, went across the hall and slammed her door loudly.

"I'll bring you a cup of tea in an hour or so," Lynn said, softly through the door. Another voice joined her in hushed tones. *Colin.* He must have stayed the night. *Great.*

Rachel crawled back under her covers and turned onto her left side, smacking her pillow to make it more comfortable. Even that hurt her shoulder. She couldn't understand why they were being so awful—especially when she was so ill. Maybe Lynn was jealous. It was obvious that it was a far superior tattoo to the one she had.

Whatever the reason, they'd just taken a joke to a whole other level. They were both acting like she was losing her mind.

She sat up and punched her pillow again, quickly regretting the fast movement. How ridiculous they both were. Enough was enough now. They'd better drop it by the time she got up.

CHAPTER 11

It was a strained week. Lynn was either at Colin's or still in bed most mornings when Rachel got up for work, and, if she timed it right, she would have already left for her shift at the pub by the time she got home. On the rare occasion they bumped into each other on the landing, Lynn gave her a sympathetic look as if she wanted to say something. It drove her mad. It was beyond a joke. She couldn't understand why she insisted on keeping it up. It was plain mean.

And Seb. Well, he wasn't so subtle. The very first day she got up from her sickness, he came up to her in the kitchen and asked how she was.

"OK, thanks. Just a little shaky, so I'm going into work today. I need to get out."

"You know we weren't winding you up, right?"

Rachel turned around to face him squarely with her hands on her hips. "Stop it, Seb. That's enough."

His cute crooked grin wasn't there today. He was deadly serious. In fact, he looked the most concerned she'd ever seen him. "So, you're completely happy with your tattoo?" he said, finishing with his eyebrows raised and no smile.

"Yes!" she hissed out through tight lips. "It's the most beautiful one I've ever seen. Stop it, Seb, stop it." Her face started to crumple, but she didn't want to cry in front of him.

Instead of allowing it, Seb quickly pulled her into the heat of his body. His arms hugged her tightly and with his few inches of extra height, she fitted snuggly against his chest. He was still a little lean and willowy like a youth, but he had a frame that would bulk up into gorgeous shape one day. He smelled soapy and clean from a recent shower.

Grigori flashed into her mind and the brief contact they'd shared. This was nothing like that. That was amplified like a dream and this was real. Her anger and upset slowly ebbed away and she found herself remaining still, softening into his arms and letting him hold her. It was the sweetest embrace of her life. There were no more tears, but she couldn't bring herself to pull away. She wanted to prolong the moment as long as possible.

She felt him bow his head, so his mouth was next to her temple. "Can we look at it again together, just in case, you know, one of us got it wrong?"

It irritated her that he was persisting, but only for a moment. He was being so sweet that maybe it was a good idea to finish it once and for all. She nodded into his shoulder. "OK."

He picked up her hand and led her out into the hallway, up the staircase and back to her room. She didn't protest. She was more amazed that he hadn't let go of her hand. Her heart fluttered and the seed of attraction she'd always tamped down for this boy threatened to break out into full bloom. She was beginning to develop feelings for him.

Once they were there, she made sure the curtains were

pulled back so daylight spilled into the room. She wanted no misunderstandings. Then she threw all the hanging clothes, obscuring her full-length mirror over a chair. She was instantly reminded of the new confidence she'd felt at Angel's Ink when Grigori first showed her the tattoo. She felt a little like that now—like nothing could derail this new course she was on.

Seb stood in the middle, watching her every move. As she neared him, she dropped the back of her robe right down to her waist, so her back was on full display in the mirror. Then she turned and looked over her right shoulder.

There it was, in full majestic glory. The dots and the fine lines depicting a flower so delicate and so complete in its honesty and detail that it made her want to cry all over again. The swelling had receded, leaving a little redness at the edges, which only served as further emphasis. "You see?" she said, her voice threatening to break.

She looked across at Seb with unshed tears in her eyes. He looked from the mirror to her and back again. Then he seemed to take a large swallow, not from emotion but discomfort.

She couldn't believe him. "What, you don't see it? Look, it's there: petals, raindrops, bugs and everything."

He shook his head wearily and looked down as if she'd defeated him. "I'm sorry, Rachel. I won't lie to you. There's nothing there, not even a bruise."

For a single moment, anger seared through her, like a hot furnace, and she wanted to throw him out, but he looked so upset that it died as soon as she looked into his face. His dark hair was particularly unruly this morning and it tumbled into his eyes. They were very blue, perhaps the bluest she'd ever seen. His lips were a little apart and he was clean-shaven. She suspected he never grew a beard because he didn't grow enough to have one; he had a boyishly irresistible look. She remembered how he felt when he held her downstairs—how he smelled, clean and fresh.

Her own thoughts startled her. Here he was, basically calling her mad and she was thinking he was hot. *Why had she not admitted this about him to herself before?* She'd lived with him for three months with him clearly throwing hints that he liked her. If Lynn was right, and she'd missed them all until now, what had changed? It all boiled down to this weekend.

Grigori was right. Everything did feel different. *She* was different. It felt like she was that confident young woman walking up to the mirror in Angel's Ink. She'd sensed it immediately. Gone was the plain, awkward girl of before. The one who hid away from people, emotions and all the wonderful new experiences in life. She liked the idea of the new girl. She *was* that new girl.

The misery reflected in Seb's eyes was changing to one of curiosity, as if he'd just noticed it in her too. She took a step closer, then another, until she stood right inside his personal space. A thing she'd never had the courage to do with anyone in her whole life before.

He didn't step back. Instead, a little startled at first, he looked down into her eyes speculatively, as if he didn't have a clue what was coming next.

Her eyes went from his to his lips and she thought how beautifully soft and pink they were. "Thanks for looking out for me on Saturday night." Her voice sounded husky and quite unlike her. She sounded sexy. She hadn't forgotten how good it felt to be protected by him.

He coughed as if it took him a while to find his voice. "No worries. I couldn't let you go alone that late."

His eyes mirrored hers and dropped to her mouth, and she knew then it would happen. She'd never been more certain of anything in her life. She was going to kiss Seb.

Right there, in a situation she herself had engineered. It was as terrifying as it was empowering. And hot—*so hot*. It was a position she'd never been in before and she wasn't running away. She didn't want to.

His mouth was almost there when she closed the distance, brushing her closed lips against his. He did the same thing back and she felt his arms come softly around her. His lips brushed hers again, feeling soft and tentative, as if he was afraid he'd scare her off. She knew then that she must be in the driving seat and it answered everything. This was why it had taken them so long and her heart soared.

She lightly ran her tongue over the seam of his lips. He answered by parting them slightly. He softly touched his tongue with hers and they stroked and swirled together. It was enough to set her whole body alight and she closed the gap between them. Her body followed, feeling every inch of him as he tightened his grip around her, and she moved against him. The kiss ran deep for both of them as if they'd been starved of each other.

Then it was over. The whole kiss lasted no more than about five seconds and they were left staring at each other in wonder. For both of them, it was the shock of discovering something for the first time. "Sorry," he said, taking a hard swallow. "It's just you looked so hot, I couldn't ..."

Then, not able to bear to see the first flicker of regret, the shutters came down and she stepped back out of his grip. "Don't be silly. Er ... better get ready for work." She looked down and weakly pointed at the door as a hint for him to go. She was beyond embarrassed.

He paused awkwardly as if he had no idea what just happened. "Er ... OK then. I'll leave you to it." Then, after taking a couple of hesitant steps as if he was going to say something, he hurriedly left her alone.

Rachel stared at herself in the mirror after she heard the

door close. Her cheeks were red, and her lips were rosebud swollen. Even her hair was messed up in a come-to-bed kind of way. *What just happened?*

One minute she'd been angry, and the next, she'd turned into this ballsy, don't-mess-with-me vixen. She'd kissed Seb. *She had actually kissed him.* It was her first real kiss and she had initiated it. She touched her mouth, looking in the mirror. He was still a tingle on her lips.

He'd responded. *Boy, had he responded.* She'd seen Seb kiss a hundred girls and never dreamed of being one of them. He was still a heat in her lower abdomen and between her legs. She remembered how sensitive and soft he'd been and also how fierce and sensual he'd become when she'd given him the green light. He was completely sexy.

There was no doubt in her mind then. She wanted to do that again. She wanted more of Seb. She wanted him to be her first.

Memories of Grigori and Saturday night threatened to squash this new notion of her and Seb, but she knew without it, she'd never have had the confidence to do what she just did.

It galvanized her into action. Something Grigori said popped into her mind: 'The history of body ink.' As soon as she got a minute at work, she would find out.

Everything felt out of kilter; she was both confused and excited. Life was changing and she felt more and more out of control. She had to get a hold on things to take it back.

However, she was still staring at herself in her bathrobe. She wore no makeup and had the worst case of bedhead she'd ever seen. She'd just vowed to sleep with a guy. She *was* changing, and for the first time, she liked the person she saw.

· · ·

RACHEL SET her mind to looking up anything connected with tattoos. After leaving Seb, she rode the bus in a daze. Getting herself a car was going to be the very next thing on her to-do list and not a sensible old banger either. The tattoo was for her nan, but the car was for her real father—a salute to him, wherever he was. It had to be one he would whistle his appreciation at if he ever got to see it, just like she remembered him doing with a cool car parked in the street. He'd run his hand across the paint like the flank of a horse and whisper, 'What a beauty. And no one would notice the real passion in his eyes but her. That was the type of car she would get.

The journey passed lightning fast, she was so lost in her plans. Her friend and manager, Mabel, smiled through the glass door as she unlocked it to let her into the library. "I've put the kettle on," she said as Rachel put her bag down behind the big, curved librarian's reception desk.

Mabel was a lovely, kind maternal figure with a red corkscrew perm and a warm smile. With her apple-shaped figure and floral dresses, Rachel put her at around sixty, but she'd never asked. She brought them their tea from the small kitchen behind the desk and they swapped stories from the weekend. Mabel had enjoyed a weekend of grandkids staying over and Rachel glossed over the weirdest weekend of her life, saying she had been really poorly, and it was touch-and-go whether she came into work today.

"Well, I'm glad you did, but go home anytime if you need to," Mabel said with a genuine smile. She was lovely like that.

Regular patrons started to arrive soon after. Some were elderly and loved to get a new book, meet with their friends in the adjoining cafe and pass a few hours in conversation. Then, later on, came the harassed mums with a toddler and baby in the pram who used the library to distract their kids for an hour or to just get them out of the house. Rachel had always loved her job as it felt like the very hub of the town.

Not today, though. The morning passed achingly slowly. She couldn't muster up the enthusiasm to chat much with the customers. She stamped books in and out and must have made her preoccupation so obvious that Mabel sent her out with the trolley to put the returned books back on the shelves. "You're putting people off," she laughed, pointing to the rows of books.

After a visiting primary school finally left, it was quiet enough for her to scour the library computer catalogue for books that might help her find out what she wanted to know. It was disappointing.

The ones the library held contained only the basic facts about tattoos. Things like, they'd been around since about 3370 BC and evidence of them had been found in places like Alaska, Mongolia, Greenland, Egypt, China, Sudan, Russia and the Philippines—basically the whole world. It was all very interesting, but she was sure Grigori had been hinting at something far deeper than that.

She sat back in her chair and rubbed her forehead. Or maybe she was reading too much into things again.

Her break passed quickly, and a lunchtime rush of people meant she had to leave it for the time being. Mabel would soon lose patience and tell her to pull her socks up if she didn't hurry up and do some work.

Her afternoon break didn't bear much fruit either. The book supply on the subject was minimal and she started to search for tattoo uses to see if that got her any further.

She discovered that until the twentieth century, tattoos were used only by the stigmatized or outcasts of society. Usually, criminals or slaves, but some had them for medical treatment. The most interesting fact she found was that the young chiefs of ancient Samoa had tattoos to dedicate them-selves to their culture upon ascending to the throne.

Dedication. Maybe there was something in that.

Webpage after webpage only rehashed what she already knew. Nothing was really hitting on what her gut was telling her that Grigori wanted her to find out. It sounded stupid, even to her, given that she didn't have a clue what that was. It was more to do with the way he spoke of it; like it was some-thing of which to be proud or revered, and until she under-stood whatever it was, she wouldn't fully understand what she was embarking on—this journey, or whatever he called it. It all sounded daft when she thought about it in the cold light of day.

They had a steady stream of customers for the rest of the day. After being ill, she was exhausted by the time it came for her and Mabel to close up. "Go home and get an early night," Mabel said, reading her perfectly.

Rachel smiled weakly. "Yeah. I need it. See you tomorrow. Thanks." She waved and walked off towards the town center, unsure whether to walk or take the bus. She was in no rush to bump into Lynn.

She opted to walk via the shops in the end. It was 6.30 p.m. Lynn would definitely have left for work, but she wasn't sure what day she had off this week. And Seb? She closed her eyes and her heart twisted in her chest. She'd managed to put him out of her head all day with her preoccupation with tattoos. He made her feel a whole lot of stuff she wasn't used to and wasn't sure she liked yet. There'd been no time to process it, so she wasn't ready to bump into him yet.

Instead, she took the long way home, window-shopping through the town. It wasn't big. It had as many good and bad points as any, she guessed: all the main high street shops, restaurants and cafes, but not big enough to have its own cinema. Old people pulled trolleys and chatted on corners, teenagers hung around the burger bar or drank cider in the park. Just average, she supposed.

By this time, most of the smaller shops were already closed—except the hairdresser's, 'Shebangs'. It was trendy, modern and loud. The kind of place she would never normally be drawn to, but today the music seemed so cool and the atmosphere alive with people. The pictures in the window were exciting and edgy, with young girls showcasing varying lengths of hair. Some were black and white. Others had vibrant colors and eyes that said, 'I dare you'. The whole thing was captivating.

A thought struck her. What was to stop her from getting a new look? *Wasn't she all about new starts?* One of the things that had stopped her getting out there dating had always been how invisible she felt. Whether that had been deliberate or not, this was a great chance to change all that. With a mental picture of Seb looking deliciously ruffled this morning, she went inside.

The place was a cacophony of hairdryers, music and chatter. A pretty young blonde girl in a ponytail smiled brightly. "Hi! What can we do for you today?"

Now she was inside among all these brightly colored, fashionable people, her newfound confidence fell on the floor. "Erm … not sure." She went to turn to run straight back out again. "Was it a cut you were after, or a cut and color? We've got some great new shades this year."

It made her stop in her tracks and turn back. Perhaps the girl hadn't noticed she was an imposter here.

A young, wiry man with bleached-white, spiky hair sashayed over to the desk, rang something up on the till, and took money from a glamorous redhead. "That's all booked in for you, darling. Friday the fourth, cut with Bernice and color with me."

The woman pushed what looked like a ten-pound note

into his hand and blew him a kiss. "See you next month," and then smiled at Rachel as she breezed out of the door in a cloud of expensive perfume.

The male hairdresser's heavily charcoaled eyes then fell on her and drew in a sharp, dramatic breath. "And who do we have here?"

The blonde girl quickly said, "This lady isn't quite sure what she's after, Gavin."

Rachel stared at him, wide-eyed like a startled deer, not sure whether to speak or run. He didn't seem perturbed, but pursed his lips and squinted while he assessed her hair. Then he waved an arm extravagantly, widely encompassing her whole body and shook his head. "I dunno, Sade. She says rock-chick to me. What do you think?"

Sade went and stood shoulder to shoulder with him, looking at her as well. Nodding, she said, "Yeah, deffo."

The mental picture of her on Seb's arm as a confident, no-messing, fashionable, tattooed rock-chick really kick-started her imagination. It was exactly the type of girl Seb would date, and maybe she could be that girl with a makeover. "You can make me look like that?" she said, hating that she sounded more like a lost waif than a sassy go-getter.

"Abso-bloody-lutely." Gavin came around from his side of the desk, pulled the hairband from her ponytail and fluffed it out. "You're lucky I have a cancellation on Thursday." He clicked his fingers and pointed at Sade.

She immediately tapped away on her computer keyboard and nodded. "Yeah, your 5 o'clock."

He clapped his hands as if extremely pleased. "Book her in, Sade." Then he looked at her questioningly.

She gawped at him for a moment and then realized. "Oh, er, my name's Rachel—Rachel Fairweather."

"That's it. Book Rachel in for the works. I do so love a beautiful blank canvas." He air-kissed each cheek. We're gonna have such fun, darling. You'll have a new life and a new man after Thursday," he said with a wink.

Rachel was left stunned while Sade clapped double-time. "It's gonna be great."

She hadn't had a single bit of input as to what she was going to have, but they both seemed to know everything, so she went along with it.

Gavin patted the back of her hand as if he knew. "Don't you worry about a thing, babe. I've got just the thing for you. I reckon darker. Don't you, Sade?" he said, looking over his shoulder at her behind the desk.

"Deffo," she said, shaking her head slowly as if she was sure of nothing more.

"Some neon-blue slices," he said, holding up strands of hair.

"Oooh, yeah," Sade said, eyes lighting up as if he'd just said the cleverest thing ever.

"Cut here, here, maybe number one here," he said, sweeping a hand through her hair from her temple. "What do you think?"

She had no idea what he was talking about; he was speaking another language.

Sade was clapping. "Oh yeah. You should deffo go with that," she said straight to Rachel, which was about the only thing she understood.

It sounded as if he was going to make her a new woman and that was exactly what she wanted, so she nodded. Bewildered.

Gavin kissed her on both cheeks theatrically, Sade put her name in the diary and she was walking down the street again as if she'd been swept up and dropped by a tornado.

CHAPTER 12

After leaving the hair salon, it was inevitable that Rachel would pass the Angel's Ink doorway. She stopped and stared at it, then at either side of it where the shops were empty and the staff gone home. A strange impulse pulled her towards the door. The small Angel's Ink poster had gone from behind the crisscrossed, reinforced glass.

Her heart thumped. *Had he gone?* It struck her as strange, even to her, that she only associated the tattoo shop with Grigori. As if the sole purpose of it being there was for him. The thought of not going through with their journey was devastating now she felt she'd come so far. Surely he wouldn't have run out on her after making such a big deal over the six sessions.

No, she refused to accept that and pressed the buzzer.

Nothing happened. She put her fingertips on the door and it clicked open as if it had been left on the latch. Looking up and down the street, and seeing no one she recognized, she went inside.

The corridor was as dingy as always, so she hurried through to the back and the Angel's Ink parlor door. It was ajar. "Hello," she called, sticking just her head inside. Despite no answer, she felt a certain amount of relief. It was as she remembered it. Artist's stations, boudoir chairs and everything, but no one was there.

Rachel checked her watch. 7.25. *Maybe it closed at 7?*

She turned and pulled the door closed behind her. Then she went towards the street door. A bump and a scrape on the ceiling made her look up. Then her eyes went to the forbidden staircase she and Lynn had joked about. Drawing nearer, she could see a small emergency light at the top illuminating a regular door. It was a pretty inoffensive door, and someone was definitely up there. It could be a storeroom, but perhaps it was where someone lived—more precisely, where Grigori lived. What would it matter to just give it a knock? Suddenly, it seemed imperative that she speak to him. She slowly climbed the stairs, ears straining for every sound, until she stopped directly in front of it.

There it was again: a bump and a scrape. Her hand went to her mouth, as if someone would hear her breaths. She shouldn't be there. She raised a shaky fist to knock the door.

"Can I help you, Rachel?" the soft, deep voice said from directly behind her. She jumped and swung around with a yelp.

Grigori was still climbing the stairs until he came to a standstill and loomed over her. She had to crane her neck to look into those dark, intense eyes, trained on her like a hawk. It struck her that he reminded her of a bird of prey at that moment.

She gathered herself with a small cough. "Erm, sorry to come unannounced, but I was passing, and I thought ... I wondered ..."

Grigori smiled, but there was no warmth in it today. He half turned and held out his arm towards the staircase behind him. "Come down to the studio, I'll make some tea and we can talk."

Despite him obviously steering her away from the door, it surprised her that he sounded resigned. As if it was inevitable that she'd turned up there. She nodded, took a last look at the door, knowing that someone must still be in there and walked past him and down the stairs. His presence was a tangible force behind her.

He seemed irritated. Perhaps her visit was inconvenient. Maybe it was because she'd been just about to knock the mysterious door. Or perhaps he was just a moody sod, and this was his personality when he wasn't tattooing.

They walked back into the tattoo parlor and Grigori went past her to what she assumed was the kitchen out back. "Sit!" he said.

She perched on the black sofa and surveyed the room. Nothing appeared to have changed since her last visit. After no more than a couple of minutes, Grigori came back with two cups of steaming tea for both of them. He hadn't asked her how she took it and handed her what was weak and black.

Maybe that's how they took it where he was from and she sipped it without comment. It was comforting to hold it in hands that suddenly felt superfluous and awkward.

Grigori sat across from her in the high-backed armchair, sipping his tea with his eyes riveted to hers. The silence went on for ages until he said, "Do you have a problem, Rachel?" It was said with that wonderful lulling tone he had.

She wasn't actually sure why she was there when it came down to it. Her emotions had been bouncing all over the place and she was confused. If she were really honest, something just called her to come in. Suddenly, everything going on in her life felt like a huge weight.

He seemed to sense it and relaxed back into his chair, stretching out his long jean-covered legs in front of him.

"I was ill all weekend—you know, after I left here." She wasn't sure exactly why she'd told him that.

Grigori just bobbed his head and took another sip of the hot tea. "And you're recovered?"

She nodded, sipped her tea and put it down on the low table between them.

"Speak, Rachel. We are on a journey, you and I. You can tell me anything." He smiled a little and his eyes held a twinkle but were as cold and calculating as ever.

"Like a friend," she said, thinking aloud.

Grigori narrowed his eyes. "Never get me confused with that, Rachel."

Her eyes widened in shock.

His softened for the first time. "Think of me more as a mentor." His smile widened. "Your life is changing. Isn't that what you wanted?"

Her head hurt with the strain of figuring all this stuff out and it felt way beyond weird. She had a sudden need to get the hell out of there. "Do you live upstairs?" she blurted, to get some of the heat off her.

He bobbed his head. "I stay there sometimes." He wasn't going to help her out; it was as if he was enjoying her discomfort. "Spit out what you want to say, Rachel. I won't be hurt. I'm a big boy." His grin widened at the look of horror on her face and he actually winked at her.

He was mocking her while it felt like her life was in pieces. She wanted to scream at him. Instead, she said as calmly and as controlled as possible, "I think there might be something wrong with my tattoo."

"You don't like it?" he said, raising an eyebrow and not seeming fazed at all.

"Yes, but ..."

"It makes you feel good about yourself?"

She thought of how she looked in the mirror and the kiss she and Seb had shared only that morning. "Yes, I know, but ..."

"It is early yet."

"Look, they can't see it!" There. She'd said it out loud.

He didn't react at all. He nodded slowly as if it was incredibly interesting. He sighed deeply, still holding his cup with elbows resting on each arm of the chair. "Rachel, people see only what they want to see. And you ..." His eyebrows rose in question, then lowered as if he were deadly serious. "You show people only what you want them to know."

Rachel frowned. What was he talking about? Was he referring to her life now or before? He always appeared to know more than he let on. She shifted in her seat with irritation.

He cut across her thoughts. "Did you look into the history of ink, Rachel?"

She didn't know what that had to do with anything. "Yes. But it only told me it was for outcasts of society, like criminals, and has been around for thousands of years."

Grigori leaned forward, put down his cup, then stood and put out his hand to her. The movement was so sudden it startled her for a second. The meeting was clearly over and there was no arguing with him. Dazed, she put down her cup and followed him meekly to the door, still wondering what she'd said exactly to end their chat so abruptly.

He stopped and faced her before he opened the door. Then he pushed a stray strand of her hair out of her face and tucked it behind her ear. She froze. The gesture surprised her in how gentle and intimate it was and sent tingles all over her. A mere moment ago, he'd said they weren't even friends. She felt the burn of his intense gaze because she couldn't look up at him.

"Perhaps you have the wrong question, Rachel," he said, softly.

That brought her eyes immediately up to his, as if he'd posed a riddle. "What are you talking about?"

He smiled a little and let his hand drop to her shoulder, where he gave it a squeeze. It instantly ignited. "I can make the pictures on your skin that can take you anywhere you want to go, but the real secret is in the ink itself."

She stared at him then, taking in every nuance and micro movement in his face. He was communicating something without outright telling her, and rewarding her, by rhythmically rubbing his thumb along the inside of her shoulder until he knew she got it. "So," she coughed as her throat had suddenly gone hoarse. "I should be looking at the history of the ink itself?"

He smiled and nodded almost imperceptibly. "You are a bright student, Rachel. Learn this small thing and the world will be revealed to you, and maybe even to your friends."

The last comment left her cold and she pulled the door open and left. She never knew where she was with him. He pulled her in and then pushed her away. Made her feel beautiful and then clumsy and foolish. Everything went around in her head on the way home. Nothing he said ever made any sense.

The history of the ink itself. The power to show her what she wanted. She repeated it over and over, like something she hadn't seen might reveal itself. Everything he said always made it sound like the choice was up to her—even Seb and Lynn seeing her tattoo. *What choice? How does that work?*

Walking up her garden path, she made a plan to grab

something quick to eat, shower and then lock herself in her room and find out.

THE HOUSE WAS empty when she got inside. It was 7.30 p.m. She showered and sat cross-legged on her bed with a huge pile of nachos, melted cheese and salsa. As she opened her laptop and tapped in her password, she remembered her nan joking that she should win awards for a healthy diet—always eating salads and stuff like that. It made her smile sadly. There was no one to tell her that now. She cracked open a sugar-filled Coke. She *was* changing.

Rachel quickly put her nan out of her mind. She had a job to do before she went to sleep tonight. Her fingers ran quickly over the keys, searching combinations of words: history of ink, then the history of tattoo ink, tribal tattoo ink, et cetera.

It was all very interesting. She found that early Christians tattooed children to ward off plague and that they were once worn by them as badges of persecution under the heavy yoke of the Romans but then evolved into symbols of belonging and devotion to their faith.

Rachel stopped typing to think more about that. Maybe that was the type of thing Grigori was getting at: belonging, devotion, *ownership?*

She continued on and searched the components of the ink itself: Iron oxides, metal salts, plastics—even glow in the dark, but there was nothing remarkable there. It was when she looked at the more traditional components that it got a little more interesting.

They started unremarkably with pen ink, soot, and dirt. Mineral and geological ingredients seemed to be the main sources, with the carrier always some kind of alcohol, which increased skin permeability. Then she came to a rare medium for metals and her fingers stopped working. Why that struck a chord with her, she wasn't sure. It couldn't be the case today. It would be illegal for starters. However, Grigori seemed to want her to find and understand something very specific and that's what made her uneasy when finding the rare carrier for heavy metals had been blood.

CHAPTER 13

*R*achel's head was aching with information overload. She couldn't absorb another paragraph. She checked her digital clock by the bed. *Shit!* 11.50 p.m. The evening had gone so quickly. It was no good; she needed sleep.

She was about to close down her laptop and give up for the day when one last thing to search came to mind. Her fingers rapidly clicked over the keys: *ANGEL'S INK.* Then she hit Search. The list loaded and her eyes skimmed the page. Various titles came up, some to do with a New Wave band ending in C instead of a K, a few obscure songs, and a similarly titled film, but nothing really of note. Then she clicked onto the second page, which was something she seldom did. Results were often too old.

Halfway down, she found what she was looking for in the heading: Angel's Ink by Dr Nicola Harding.

It was a book.

She read the quick description before she got too excited, making sure it wasn't a fiction novel. She breathed in relief.

It was a non-fiction book on the author's life's work and seemed exactly what she was looking for.

Rachel clicked through to the author's website. It seemed pretty uniform. Her bio said she was at Oxford and had completed her doctorate in Theology and Anthropology; her main interest being the human struggle for good over evil, both in the Bible and its correlation with ancient legend and folklore.

She went next to the book page itself to read the blurb. She was hooked by the first line:

ANGEL'S INK is Harding's lifetime study of the Grigori—The Fallen Angels.

Cast down and banished from Heaven for their fascination with human women and carnal knowledge, they were rumored to have fathered the Nephilim—the "giants" and "men of fame", recorded in the bible. God destroyed their evil offspring through the flood, but the Grigori and their hordes merely returned to their spirit form and escaped. However, they could never return to Heaven and were forced to roam the Earth looking for souls.

Dr Harding is convinced that not only are they still here, but also active and among us to this day. And we are just as in danger as we ever were ...

RACHEL WAS BARELY BREATHING, heart pounding by the time she finished the short paragraph.

It was more than the words on the page; it was the forcing her to face what she already knew inside. It hit her so hard because she knew, without a doubt, it was true. Years of Bible study proved it. She'd seen it with her own eyes and buried it deeply in her subconscious. The final band-aid was ripped off in Harding's final tagline:

. . .

THE WATCHERS ARE VERY MUCH alive today.

GRIGORI HIMSELF HAD ALLUDED to the fact that it wasn't his actual name and called himself "a watcher of people". She'd just put his choice of words down to a language thing. She shuddered, suddenly feeling cold. She was overtired and needed to rest.

She clicked all over the website to see if there was an excerpt, but there wasn't. There was, however, a "buy" button, which she clicked without hesitation. £12.99 for a paperback. Weirdly, there was no eBook option. She tried all her usual stores to get it quicker, but it didn't appear anywhere. The confirmation of her order pinged into her emails and she would be forced to wait the two to three days it said it would take to arrive. The wait would kill her.

Then, just as she was about to close the lid on her laptop, right at the bottom of the email was a link: *Join our closed Facebook group.*

Rachel hovered over it for a moment. This could mean there were others feeling exactly like her. It was mind-blowing. Surely such an obscure, unknown book could have only warranted a group if it was of interest to a lot of people.

She tapped and was taken through to Facebook, where she clicked the "join group" button.

"Your request is being reviewed", came up. *Of course it was,* she thought, rubbing her tired eyes. Perhaps it was for the best. It would have kept her up all night if she'd been accepted straight away and she was dog-tired already.

After a final double-check of the book's delivery date and realizing it would probably arrive over the weekend and possibly even after her next appointment with Grigori, she closed down and shut the lid on her laptop.

It was a relief to leave it, really. When she got up and went to the bathroom across the hall, her head lightened straight away. She used the loo and quickly brushed her teeth. Then she padded back over to her room, slid into the bed and clicked off the lamp.

Her ceiling had speckles from the streetlight piercing through the loops at the top of her curtains. Despite her extreme fatigue, her mind tumbled with what she had found out. It felt like a dark and scary world. Her thoughts flicked from one thing to another.

She shouldn't get ahead of herself and become paranoid. Grigori, even though he was like no one she knew, had really been nothing but kind to her. She should try to be objective about all this stuff. It could be some huge coincidence.

Then she remembered Rose Beauregard's obvious fear and it mixed her emotions all over again. *Didn't Grigori himself admit that it was just what people called him and wasn't his name?* She made a vow to ask him what it was at the weekend. *Why leave it till then?*

She sat bolt upright, clicked on her lamp and snatched her phone off the nightstand. Working quickly, she spelled out the words, *what's your real name?* and hit Send to the Angel's Ink number.

Even though there was a risk someone else would pick it up, she knew he'd get the message. She leaned over and put the phone back, then turned off the lamp and lay back down, trying to slow her rapidly beating heart.

Say he was one of these—she wasn't sure what to call him, exactly—*Fallen Angels, why did he insist she find out more about it and risk getting found out?* If he was trying to warn her then surely that meant he wasn't all bad.

On and on her mind went, turning this way and that,

until finally she must have slept as her alarm, that came all too quickly, woke her up. Every part of her body felt heavy and half asleep as she threw her legs over and tried to get out of bed. Her eyelids felt like sandpaper and her mouth like an empty drain. She took some hefty glugs of water from a glass by the bed and seriously debated phoning in sick, but then she risked embarrassing encounters with Seb or Lynn. Admitting she would want to pursue all that she'd learned last night, she guessed there was little to be gained by staying at home.

The day passed agonizingly slowly. She barely got a break; the library was so busy. When she did get a chance to check her phone, she was disappointed to see that her request still showed 'under review'.

At last 6.30 came and she hurried home. She couldn't be bothered with staying out of everyone's way tonight. All she wanted was to grab a baguette to save time with cooking, get home and lock herself in her room.

The bus came, and she was there in under half an hour. She put her key in the door, rushed through the hallway, and almost bumped right into Seb, who was just coming out of the kitchen with a plate and holding toast up to his mouth. For a moment, he looked as shocked as she was to see her. "Hey," she said, immediately slowing to a stop.

"You seem like you're in a hurry," Seb said, looking the most taken off guard she'd ever seen him.

"Erm … got homework," she said, holding her large sub up in her hand.

He cracked a smile and she turned and bolted up the stairs, incinerating with embarrassment and cursing the ridiculous comment the moment it had left her mouth. He continued to crunch his toast, watching her all the way up.

Thankful for the sanctuary of her room, she flipped the lock and dumped her bag. She lived the embarrassment of downstairs one more time before she cursed and kicked off her shoes, perched on the bed and started her laptop. While it whirred and loaded, she got out of her work clothes and put on the oversized t-shirt and sweatpants she reserved for lounging around.

She took a huge bite out of her baguette and sat back on the bed. Crossing her legs, she went straight to her Facebook notifications and there it was: *Your request to join the Soul Rebels closed Facebook group has been accepted.*

Cool name. Then she spotted a direct message. Not being able to resist a quick scan of the page first, she was amazed at the many posts with questions and topics that could have easily come from her.

It was frustrating as many questioned quotes from the book she was yet to read. The newbies spoke of initial fear, the more experienced of excitement, but many talked about tattoos. Her heart-rate was double time when it hit her what a mine of information this group was.

Before she got too into reading some of them, she clicked on Messenger. Her breath caught when she realized it was from Dr Nicola Harding herself.

Dear Rachel, welcome to the Soul Rebels' Facebook Group. If you're here, then I guess you think you've come into contact with Grigori. You're in the right place. It is a place for support and help and to be among friends with similar experiences. I'll take this opportunity to give you the group rules. Please read them carefully and respect the other members. I normally dip in and out of the group and answer any questions not answered by other members. Good luck and kindest regards, Nicola.

Luck? Would she need it?

She went over the rules listed in bullet points: *Don't give out personal details. Be polite and courteous at all times. Do not judge others for the decisions they make.*

Decisions?

She tried to cast her mind back to any decisions she'd had to make for Grigori. There was the tattoo itself, which she'd definitely decided to have before she'd even met him, and there were the six sessions. He'd been adamant that she was clear on her agreement to that. Apart from that, there didn't appear to be any so far. She was intrigued to learn more about the other users.

The last point was to introduce herself by posting in the group. That seemed pretty standard.

She took another large bite of her baguette and thought about what to say. *Where to start?* Scrolling down the News Feed, there hadn't been any new members over the last few days to see what they wrote. In the end, she opted for short and sweet, to test the waters. This wasn't about baring her soul; it was about giving enough information to compare with other people's experiences to see if there were any similarities.

She began: *Hi everyone, my name is Rachel. Thanks for having me here in your group. I'm yet to understand whether it is somewhere I'm supposed to be. So please excuse me if I'm in the wrong place.*

I was an active member of my church until I lost my nan just over three months ago. To say I was kind of lost is putting it mildly. She was my world. Don't ask how I ended up there, but I went to a fortune-teller and she sent me to Angel's Ink. I thought it was strange. It was there that I met my artist, Grigori. He works by invitation, alone, and only at night. After the initial consultation, he said I needed six sessions. So far, I have completed just one. I guess the reason I'm here is that it was all so strange. But in his defense, it has been him all along, encouraging me to find out more about tattooing and, most of all, the history of ink. That's how I found Dr Harding's book and this group. Apologies if I'm rambling. My point is, he promised me change, and I do want to change, more than anything. Anyway, that's me.

Rachel hit Post before she could think better of it. Now that she'd done it, she felt disloyal and kind of a fraud. Grigori hadn't exactly done anything wrong. Perhaps it was because opening up to strangers made her raw and exposed. Nevertheless, she felt guilty, like she was betraying him in some way. Writing it all down did feel kind of cathartic, though, like a cleansing of the soul. She had to remember she didn't know any of these people. They'd never meet, so she shouldn't feel ashamed.

There was, of course, the not-so-small detail of her housemates not being able to see the tattoo she'd suffered all night to get, but if she was honest, that sounded just too mad to air right then. And she still wasn't entirely convinced they weren't winding her up.

Rachel began to read some of the earlier posts. Many were talking about the great tattoos that all their friends envied. *At least their friends could see them.* What struck her most of all was how they seemed to be boasting about the turnaround in their lives since having them. They spoke of a new confidence and unbelievably good luck. Boys were posting that girls who had been previously aloof were jumping into their beds as easily as clicking their fingers. It sounded bizarre, but the girls were saying it too. They recounted over and over that boys just couldn't resist them. It also revealed the obvious age group of many of the members.

However, some spoke of getting a promotion that had eluded them for years, or suddenly being noticed at work when they'd previously been invisible. Everything was landing in their laps and they were generally winning in life when they were losers before. It seemed to be the theme of them all.

None were moaning of anything weird. None seemed frightened or even questioned anything that was happening to them. They seemed to be rejoicing in their good luck as if they'd been completely brainwashed or bought.

Her mind stopped churning at that last word. *Bought.* Wasn't that what the book blurb had alluded to—that the Fallen Angels were scouring the Earth for souls? For some reason, she had expected this to be some sort of support or action group. Instead, it seemed to be a place for the ones who'd fallen prey to connect. *Had they, though?* They all seemed so happy.

A notification popped up on her Messenger, then another and another. It was like her phone had suddenly lit up. She opened it and began reading them, her heart pounding with each one.

Welcome, I'm Chris. I'm the group's administrator. Please don't be put off by the posts on the main page. THIS is the real group for those of you considering saying No to your Grigori. If you want real answers to your questions, then you can get them here. Good luck and stay strong.

Rachel swallowed, her heart in her mouth, and read the next one.

Has the Grigori told you his name yet?

And the next: *How did you feel after your first session? Did you get really ill?*

Another: *It's not too late. Whatever you do, don't sleep with him—whatever he promises.*

Her eyes went wide at that one. Like she knew he was off-the-chart sexy, but he was way older and out of her league and the idea hadn't really entered her head. *Or had it?* Not consciously, but he had left her feeling something breath-taking whenever he got near her.

Another message came through and her heart stopped when she realized it was from Dr Harding herself.

Hello, Rachel. It's Nicola. Don't be afraid. After you have received and read your book, call me. And she left a mobile phone number.

She read it and re-read it. It sparked excitement, but her alarm bells were ringing all over the place. Wasn't it the first rule of the Internet, not to contact strangers? She was about to write something back to that effect when there was a light tap on her door. *Bloody hell!*

Rachel glared at her door. "What?"

"It's me. Can you let me in for a minute?"

Seb. She sat frozen for a few seconds while her mind raced at what to do, but there was such a plea in his voice that she couldn't ignore him or tell him to go away. She put aside her laptop, slid off the bed and went to the door. Flipping the latch, she opened it a bit.

"Hey!" he said, looking relieved.

"Hey." Her eyes felt bleary and her mind struggled to catch up and leave what she was doing. "I'm kind of in the middle of something?" It came out more abrupt than she'd intended.

His eyes narrowed and his face went red. "That's it? That's all you've got after yesterday?"

Rachel was shocked at how angry and hurt he looked. She wasn't used to dealing with romantic stuff and had been so caught up with everything that she hadn't really given him the headspace he deserved. "I'm sorry," she said, sagging with exhaustion. "Come in." She pushed open the door for him to come inside. "I've got a lot on my mind at the moment."

He was standing a couple of feet away, studying her face as if he was mapping it and absorbing every word. "So, it's not the brush off?"

She frowned in horror. "No ... oh god, no," She instinctively went to him, slammed straight into his chest. His arms immediately came around her protectively.

It felt alien but so good. She reveled in the warmth and

the smell of him. He said nothing and held her for a full minute before she broke away. His eyes were beautiful this close, ice blue and surrounded by thick dark lashes. He pushed away stray locks of hair from her face with the back of his fingers and studied her as if he was as amazed as she was at this sudden closeness. "I like you, Rachel." He swallowed and bobbed his head, adorably unsure of himself. "Like, really like you," he said, meeting her gaze again.

With her heart missing beats, it felt like a dream. She had always thought he was hot, but she'd never allowed herself to ever even daydream about this happening.

Her mind was suddenly clouded with the group posts she'd just read. They were all getting their hearts' desires, too. *Was this real? Or had she already sold her soul?* And the most alarming thought of all: *would she stop it even if she could?*

Seb was moving closer and her thoughts scattered, leaving only one. Her eyes closed and his wonderfully soft lips touched hers. She melted into it and became fluid in his arms. When his tongue stroked along them to gain entry to her mouth, all the other stuff didn't matter. She wanted him.

Rachel opened her mouth and devoured him. He went rigid for a second and then matched her ferocity. There was nothing tentative in this kiss, only hunger, like they'd been starved for a lifetime. All she knew was that she needed him; his taste, his smell, the feel of every inch of him. She plundered his mouth. Even taking his gasp as she took over everything.

His arms crushed her to him and her hands went up into his hair, pushing through it with her fingers and pulling him tighter by the roots. He accepted and responded to her roughness, slamming her roughly up against the door. Releasing her mouth, he bit and sucked down her neck, making her gasp next to his ear as his hand found flesh under her slouchy top.

There was no time to think about how she looked as her body came alive under his touch and ran molten between her legs. She'd never felt like this. There were no nerves, no fear or even hesitation, only need.

Her breaths became measured and shallow as he bit her shoulder and moved his hands up her ribcage as she writhed under them. His thumb passed over her nipple and sent shock waves through her. She bowed backwards, exposing her neck, which he bit in tiny nips, whispering, "You're so fucking hot."

As her hips ground into his, an image of Grigori's intense gaze flashed into her mind. She wasn't sure why it had happened. It was just for a moment, but enough to bring her to her senses. She became aware of her surroundings and realized she was out of control. In precisely two minutes, she and Seb would be having sex against the door. Her heart was still hammering and her cheeks were burning red while his hips pinned her and he took her mouth again.

She pulled out of it and patted his back. "Stop!" she said, patting harder while her eyes rolled and he bit her neck again. "Please!" She managed to get her hands between them and gave him a hefty shove. "Please stop!"

He released her instantly, looking completely bewildered. His face was flushed and his lips wonderfully red and swollen from use.

She couldn't look him in the eye. "Sorry," she said again, closing her eyes.

After a moment, she felt the rush of air as he passed her, pulled open the door and slipped out without even nudging her.

She pushed it shut and leaned back against it. Her body was thrumming so badly, it was painful in her lower abdomen and thighs. There was no real reason for stopping things other than she'd panicked. She'd become more aware and attracted to him since the kiss they'd shared, but she never imagined the strength of her physical response. And why did she think of Grigori at a time like that? She could only think that it totally overwhelmed her. She wished he hadn't gone so quickly, so she could have explained—even though she had no idea what she would have said. He probably wouldn't have believed her anyway.

She brought up a shaking hand and rubbed her forehead. The sound of a bedroom door closing echoed behind her, meaning it was safe to go out. She wasted no more time and went as quietly as she could to the bathroom across the hall.

She locked the door and went to the mirror over the sink. The person staring back was wild and unrecognizable, but she liked what she saw. Her pupils were dilated, her cheeks pink and her lips plump and red. She *was* sexy.

Her blood pressure gradually slowed. She turned on the cold tap and ran her wrists underneath to cool down. She made a promise to her reflection there and then. If she hadn't totally messed things up, it would be Seb. There would be no running away, bucket list or not, she wanted to lose her virginity. Grigori had definitely woken something up in her, but she wanted it to be Seb.

She brushed her teeth and changed into her nightshirt. Then, padding back across the hall, she closed her door and slid into bed. Her phone dinged loudly, reminding her to put it on night mode.

Her breath caught. It was a message from the Angel's Ink number with one word: *Xenon.* A name she'd heard once before.

CHAPTER 14

*R*achel had heard that name in one of the weird dreams she'd been having lately. She'd never heard anything like it before, so not even her subconscious could have conjured it up. That threw up the disturbing angle that maybe they weren't dreams at all, but that was unthinkable; the thought too frightening to even contemplate. For that reason, she pushed it out of her mind. The sheer emotional exhaustion from the day finally dragged her under to sleep.

The next morning, she woke up feeling like she'd had no sleep at all. She sat up and the weight of everything tumbling back to mind was a tangible weight on her shoulders. The first thing she did was check her phone. *Shit!* Her notifications had maxed out, showing twenty-plus messages, and her stomach fluttered when she saw there was another text from Angel's Ink.

Rachel read that first.

"I'm going away for a few days. C U Saturday. DON'T go to the shop X.

It looked like he'd signed off with a kiss, but she noted the first use of his real name—the name she shouldn't know.

She checked and it was sent half an hour after the last one. It made her look at the current time and swear. The other messages would have to wait, or she'd be late for work. Quickly showering, dressing and grabbing a handful of cereal and her coat on the way out, she left, pulling the door closed behind her.

She only just made the shuttle bus, found a seat and scrolled through as many messages as she could. There wouldn't be another chance till lunch to look properly.

Most carried on in the same vein as the night before: Direct Messages saying stuff like: *Don't be sucked in by him; Resist, it's like a drug.*

What is? she almost messaged back, but she wasn't entirely sure if the page wasn't a meeting point for conspiracy theorists and crackpots yet.

Watch out for the woman—she's a bitch. That was a new one. The only females connected with the shop had been Skye and Jet, and neither would she class as a bitch. Then she thought of the dream she'd had while in Grigori's chair. There had been two men and a woman there.

Has he put his stamp on you yet? There were a number of messages saying something like that. Others called it a brand or his mark, but all were getting at some sort of ownership. How she wished she had the book to refer to.

Then another seemed to imply that it was a good thing: *If he offers his mark, take it. It's safer if he's claimed you.*

Another said: *Accept the mark, you can fall prey to the others if you don't.*

Some were more supportive, but others seemed to alarm her even more: *Don't be scared. Nicola is great. She's helping us all. Read the book. Memorize it if you have to. It saved my life.*

By the time her bus pulled in near the library, she was

terrified of what she'd got herself into. It made her think that maybe she was better off not knowing a lot of this stuff. However, she knew, as soon as that damn book came, there would be nothing that would stop her from reading it.

Before she got off the bus, she did manage to message back to Grigori—*Xenon?* It felt too weird to call him that just yet. *Don't worry. I'll be there.* She hated text-speak and never abbreviated. She doubted he cared. As she hit Send, a wry thought struck her; the group was right about one thing: he had her in the palm of his hand.

Work dragged. Customers came in steadily, peppered with stolen moments checking the endless Direct Messages that kept coming to her Facebook profile. No one said anything new or remarkable, just a rehash of what had already been said before.

The group page had a lot of people posting a welcome under her intro post too. She found she had a knot in her stomach reading those. None of them were horrible—far from it. They all wished her well, basically saying enjoy her good fortune and to share the love and encourage others. It felt too weird and automatically repelled her.

That feeling did strike her as strange, having come from the church. All the years she'd attended with her nan were filled with a similar tone of encouragement from the parishioners, but this felt like something different. More like the stranger you were warned about at school, enticing you with sweets.

The disturbing realization was that, whatever any of them were saying, just how many people all this affected. It was astonishing. It made her wonder where all these people lived. They couldn't all be from her hometown, surely.

That led her to wonder just how many Grigori there were, if they had hordes of followers—presumably other Fallen Angels, and whether they had the same purpose on the

Earth as the Grigori. The mind boggled at just how huge all this could be. Surely governments must know about them. *Maybe they were there because of this.* Her mind skated on like that all day. Thankfully, the day passed. She finished work, locked up with Mabel and went home.

No one answered when she walked in the door and called out. Her conscience pricked her when she was glad. Lynn, she knew well and could deal with, but Seb, she had to face sometime—even if it was just to apologize. How did she explain she was just too plain chicken when things got physical? Guys like Seb simply never dated virgins. She cringed inwardly at how he would take that. Luckily, she had a reprieve; he was noticeably absent.

Not so for Lynn. She bounded down the stairs just as she was about to go up. *Damn.* They both stopped and said an awkward "Hi." Then "sorry," and a nervous laugh, at exactly the same time.

"You go," Lynn said.

Rachel touched her forehead. This was harder than she thought. "Look, I'm sorry. I never wanted to fall out. I'm just working through a lot of stuff, OK?"

Lynn sagged in relief and instantly hugged her. "No need to apologize. Really. I'm like a herd of elephants sometimes."

Colin came down the stairs behind her, putting the collar down on his shirt and tightening the knot on his tie with perfect timing.

They both laughed, the tension disappearing. She wasn't at all like an elephant. She was honest and direct with people and it was one of the things Rachel loved about her. It just wasn't always easy to hear.

Colin gave her a small smile of hello and a hint at what they'd obviously just finished doing. She must ask how that was going when they got a minute alone.

"But seriously though, Rachel, you need to talk to Seb. He's really upset."

Rachel immediately flushed and her eyes darted to Colin. "You know?" Dying seemed a great option to cope with her embarrassment right then.

Lynn shrugged and looked a little pained. "Not everything, but enough," she said, indicating something tiny with her thumb and forefinger. "He really does like you, Rach, but he won't hang around for long. He was already in the pub when I left."

Rachel took in the jeans, boots, sweatshirt and loose hair. Her uniform for work was always hair up, black slacks and a white shirt. That meant she must have done a lunchtime shift today. "Got it. You off now then?" she said, already moving past her. Colin turned sideways so she could pass. She couldn't deal with where the conversation was going—especially not in front of Colin. She barely understood men at the best of times and certainly didn't understand what it was between her and Seb. Lynn touched her on the shoulder, making her pause. "Whatever happens, we're here for you, Rach, OK? Don't shut everyone out."

Rachel managed a small nod at the extremely accurate appraisal of her and darted up the remainder of the stairs. She only breathed again when she reached the safety of her room and locked the door behind her.

Embarrassment stung her cheeks all over again when she imagined the conversation between Lynn and Seb. How Lynn would have pulled him aside, all concerned and explained how she was just inexperienced with men and probably freaked out. The fact that it was the truth made it all the more humiliating. She closed her eyes and leaned heavily against the door behind her. Then she went and flopped onto the bed. She supposed she should really be grateful to Lynn. She'd only really ripped the plaster off something that she would've skirted around for ages. It needed tackling. She would talk to him; she just had to think of what to say. She liked him. She'd always liked him, she just never imagined he would feel the same way. Maybe it was because, deep down, she couldn't fully believe that he did and it was easier keeping him at arm's length, so she didn't get hurt. He would come to his senses sooner or later and reject her anyway.

She knew she was just scared, but she also knew it was the old her. The whole point of the bucket list was to force her out of her comfort zone to achieve all the stuff she never otherwise would. She guessed she really did owe Lynn. Thanks to her, he probably wouldn't hate her now. No, now he would just feel sorry for her. She groaned with humiliation and hefted herself up off the bed.

Lynn had left with Colin and Seb still wasn't home. A shower made her feel marginally better, but she stayed in her room after that. She spent her evening taking her mind off Seb by scouring the Internet for fresh leads on the Grigori, but found very little. Dr Harding's book seemed to be the only real source of information. More of the same types of comments referring to it filtered into her Facebook profile. All the while, she couldn't help keeping half an ear open for Seb coming home, but he didn't. She dismissed her feelings of disappointment as just tiredness and fell asleep fully clothed.

The next day, she woke early, remarkably refreshed. She decided that the sensible thing would be to go into work early to make up to Mabel for how preoccupied she'd been lately.

The book still hadn't come and that frustrated the hell out of her. Everything felt at a standstill until then.

She couldn't believe the day had come for her hair appointment. It felt like a pivotal point in her life. To some, it would seem like nothing, a surface adornment like a new dress. But for her, it was the most daring thing she could do —even more so than her tattoo. She would be stepping out of the shadows into the spotlight. It was a major deal.

It wasn't that she didn't want it, but, just like with Seb, it had crept up on her. She wasn't ready.

There was a niggling voice that said she'd never be ready and would need to jump in with both cases. They were so connected. The letting go of the old and embracing the new. It was a quandary that stayed with her all day.

So much for being more use to Mabel. She had to re-check in several books and re-file those she put away on the shelves. She looked blankly back at Mabel when she tried to make conversation, until in the end, the only safe thing to do was to give her a feather duster to dust the top shelves.

It was all still on her mind when she approached the Shebangs doorway and while her feet carried her all the way past. She paused in a doorway, just out of sight, and dialed the receptionist. "Hi there, sorry, this is Rachel. I know it's last-minute, but I've been kept late at work. Can I postpone till next week?"

The girl put her on hold to check the diary and Gavin's voice came on the phone. "You have kind of left me in a bind, love ... erm, let me see. The best I can do is in a fortnight, unless someone cancels. There will be a cancellation fee. Is that OK?"

The reprieve flooded through her in a wave of relief. It was the breathing space she needed. "Thanks, Gavin, that's great," although it was tinged with disappointment at not moving on with her life.

When she clicked off the phone, she decided there was absolutely no way she would let him down next time. She couldn't expect change if she kept on chickening out all the time. If a cancellation came up, she would take it no matter what—even if it meant taking time off work.

Her phone beeped with a message from Lynn: *Happy hour is quiet if you want to join?*

With the feeling of disappointment in herself still weighing heavily in her stomach, she messaged back: *OK, just for one.* Then a thought panicked her. *Who else is there?*

Don't worry. Just me waiting for the evening rush.

She messaged back, *OK,* then jumped onto the shuttle bus that went the two stops to Lynn's pub.

When she walked in, the bar had a few regulars in after work. Lynn wasn't in the pub bit, so she followed the L-shaped bar round to the part that disappeared into the restaurant. Lynn was sitting on a stool, joking with a couple of customers, leaning into Colin with his arm loosely draped around her. A pain stabbed in her chest at how easily they interacted with each other. How lovely that would be.

Lynn spotted her. "Hey! You came!"

She tried to hide her annoyance at her surprise. Although she did deserve it, as she'd been more antisocial than usual lately. Colin smiled hello and walked away to do some work. The two men sitting at the bar moved so she could have a stool next to Lynn. She climbed up.

"What's up with you?" Lynn said, immediately putting a glass under the optic of vodka. Rachel knew it was useless to protest and rolled her eyes. "Medicinal," Lynn said, adding a tonic, ice and a slice of lemon.

She sighed. "I just feel worn out, that's all." She took a huge swig of her drink and it went down surprisingly well. *So that's why people went straight to the pub after work.* She got it now.

"Stop obsessing," Lynn said. "You're always like this. Just relax. You're a beautiful girl, you've just got to learn to let go and get out there. Just learn to accept opportunities instead of immediately shutting them down."

Rachel looked at her for a long moment while she digested her words. "I do, don't I?" She downed her drink while Lynn grinned and immediately poured her another.

"I could have … you know." She looked quickly around her. "Done it with Seb, the other night. Then I had this hair appointment booked today and I cancelled." She picked up the new drink and drank that down too.

Lynn fixed her another. Colin noticed and Lynn frowned at him and shook her head for him not to say anything. Rachel saw and guessed it was because she hadn't paid a thing yet. "Make me a tab," she said, pushing her empty glass towards her. She was starting to feel warm and fuzzy and the dark cloud was shifting from her heart. "Do you know what I'm starting to think, Lynn? I'm not capable of deep feelings for anyone." When she looked up from her glass at Lynn, she felt a bit woozy, but it passed.

Lynn fixed a drink for each of them this time and pulled her chair closer to the bar. "You wanna know what I think?

Rachel shrugged and nodded.

"I think you have the deepest feelings of all."

Rachel frowned with surprise and waited for her to go on. It wasn't what she was expecting.

"I'm going to go all Dr Lynn on you now and totally shrink you. I think you loved your dad and your nan very much, but they all left you and I think you're frightened to get close to anyone in case that happens."

Rachel took a sip of her drink and digested what she said. It was very insightful. "What about the church?"

Lynn bobbed her head. "Lots of people go to church. It doesn't mean there's anything wrong with you. You believed it. You just took a knock like lots of people do. You like order and knowing where you are with things. It suits your personality, like working in the library."

Rachel scowled for a moment. "Boring, you mean."

Rachel half-laughed and rolled her eyes. "No, I wasn't saying that. You alphabetize the bloody kitchen cupboards, Rach." Lynn was laughing by the end and so was she.

"I do, don't I." They laughed harder at that.

When they held their stomachs and got their breath, Lynn said a little more quietly. "Maybe you've just got to accept who you are, but try to go with the flow a bit more." She sat up straighter and her face brightened. "And here is the perfect person."

Rachel, now completely slouched on her stool, turned to see who she was looking at, just as Seb and Jules came to a stop next to her. The surprise robbed her of speech for a moment.

"Usual, please, Lynn, and whatever this one is having."

Jules took his beer back into the bar and Lynn annoyingly winked at her and went to get on with some work.

Seb pulled up a stool next to her.

"Hey," he said, warily. As if he wasn't sure of his reception. "Don't usually see you in here?"

She shrugged. "Been a hard day." It came out a bit more snarky than intended.

"You OK?" Then he looked for Lynn and she smiled from the end of the bar. "Are you pissed?"

"Pissed angry or pissed drunk?"

He shrugged, amused, looking mildly surprised.

"Bit of both, I think," she said, frowning. "Maybe."

He laughed and nodded. "I like this new you."

She looked up at him sharply then, to see if he was making fun of her, but he didn't appear to be. She poked him in the chest. "Don't just think that because you're Seb Newly and looking all cute and sexy that I'm going to go all gooey over you, because I'm not. I'm a smart, independent woman." All the while she spoke, she poked him in the chest until he caught her hand, grinning and trying not to laugh.

"I won't, I promise."

Then he was saying something about how she'd had a bit too much to drink, but all she could do was watch his luscious lips move.

"Are you listening …?" he asked, laughing.

"Do you think I'm boring?" she said a little too loudly, cutting straight over him.

"What? No, of course not. You're beautiful and smart."

"But not cool or hot," she said, resigned, knowing it for a certainty.

He called over to Lynn, "I'll take her home." He threw down a twenty onto the bar and she went to push him off when he tried to help her down off the stool. But when she eventually slipped and ended up flush against his gorgeous-smelling body, all she could do was look up into his amused eyes. "Are we going to have sex?"

He burst out laughing at that. "Not today. You're smashed. And it might surprise you to learn that I like my women conscious when I do that."

She frowned while he steered her through the bar and put his hand up to Jules, who read the situation in a single look and returned it. She was angry and wanted to argue with him, but couldn't think of how to start.

He helped her into the van, went around to the driver's side and started the engine.

Then she thought of something that had been really bugging her all day. "What happened to you last night?"

He took his eyes off the road to look at her and grinned. She just couldn't seem to rile him. "I stay out a lot, Rach."

"I know!" she said, irritably. She knew she was being an irrational pain, but she just couldn't help herself.

"We've got a gig in Bootsies not this Friday but next, if you wanna come?"

She glared back at him. He hadn't answered her question, but he was right; he did stay out all the time. That was him. It had always been him and she knew that before any kissing had started.

All of a sudden, she felt unbelievably tired. "Yeah, sure." She looked out of the passenger window at the familiar houses in their road. She knew exactly the place he meant. Kinky Boots was a bikers' bar just out of town. It wasn't the sort of place she would ever normally go, but she wasn't boring, and she should do daring things.

Seb's expression of uncertainty showed he half expected her to say no.

"I'll try," she said, honestly. The place should definitely be on her bucket list of bad things to do.

"Cool," he said, pulling up to a stop in their small drive-way. "Let's get you in bed." He grinned at the shock on her face.

She got out and he opened the door to let them in with his key. "Do you want anything to eat?" he said, as they passed the kitchen.

She shook her head, already feeling a little sick.

He followed her into her room and stopped right in front of her. She felt herself sway and he held the top of her arm to steady her. "Do you need some help?"

She shook her head again and began to step out of her skirt. He pulled back the quilt and she got in with the remainder of her clothes still on. He smoothed back her hair. "Sleep, party girl!"

She was already drifting off when she heard him close her door. The evening was a blur, but it had felt a bit of a rest from the constant churning in her mind. Sleep felt like her last hiding place from it all. Seb, the book, tattoos. If they did hold some kind of power, then they'd better get the hell on with it; she was sick of waiting.

FRIDAY CAME and went with a hangover. After grabbing something quickly to eat on the way home, she got into bed for a much-needed early night.

Her heart was heavy, and she couldn't explain why. Maybe it was boozers' gloom or maybe it was because she was a lonely failure. *That was it.* She was still that sad, lonely girl who spent all her time with her nan when everyone else was out partying with their friends. And now her nan had gone, she was just sad.

A solitary tear trickled down her cheek. It put her in mind of Grigori, sad enough to have his permanently inked there. She wiped her tears away with angry fingers and texted Angel's Ink: *Do you have a private number?*

She wasn't surprised when nothing came back. A single sob escaped her. She hunkered down in the bed, pulling the covers right up under her chin. *What a sorry mess she was.*

Sometime later, a message pinged her subconscious awake. Remembering instantly, she snatched the phone off her nightstand. *It was him.* All that appeared was an eleven-digit number. Typical of him to give nothing else away. It also made her feel curiously elated. He was a private person and had given her his own number. It made her wonder if she was more than a customer to him.

Then, as usual, doubts crowded in with the warnings on messenger. *Was this him just cleverly luring her in?* She instantly shook the thoughts away. She'd messaged him, *remember?* He'd done absolutely nothing wrong or inappropriate, ever.

She kept it simple and messaged back, *thanks.*

Is everything OK? Came right back, causing her heart to pump.

Every nerve prickled in anticipation, but now that she had his attention, she had no idea what to say. She opted for as honest as possible. *Just a bit low.* Her finger hovered. *Not sure I'm worthy of the tattoo.* It was cryptic, but she'd learned already that he was extremely perceptive, and it was interesting to see how he would answer.

There was a gap so long she didn't think he would. Then came eventually, *are you having second thoughts?*

Second? Try a million thoughts. Could I if I wanted to? She was holding her breath through a pause that must have lasted a full minute.

Of course. There is always freedom to choose in life, but we are enslaved to consequences.

Her stomach rolled. It was a deep statement that could be taken in a number of ways. If she went with her paranoid side, it could sound like a threat, but if she went with her gut, that he was like some sort of savant to her, then he was right. Deep down, she knew she could never be happy unless she saw this through. She would forever be dissatisfied. *I'll see you tomorrow,* she answered, simply.

He commented no further, just sent an *X,* and this time she was sure it was a kiss.

CHAPTER 15

*R*achel was pinned against the door and she could feel his hardness against her as he whispered, "You're so fucking hot." Then, as she turned into his cheek to find his mouth, he was pulled away. A bright light was behind him, pulling him further, while his hand reached out for her. "Don't get sucked in," he called out. "It's me you really want."

Then she felt something and turned to look at her right shoulder. It was Lynn. "Chill out, it's only Seb. Just go with the flow," she was saying with a shrug.

She looked back at Seb's hurt and angry eyes. The same ones as the other night when she'd pushed him away. She whirled around to escape the guilt, straight into the hard, unforgiving chest of Grigori, resplendent with the huge raven-black wings of The Fallen. They fanned out and encased her, soft and downy, shielding her from the outside world. His tattooed arms came around her and held either side of her face. His soulless eyes were black like endless pools and she was mesmerized by them. *If you stand with me, I can protect you now your grandmother has gone. I would never hurt you.*

She sobbed into the inky softness of his wing. When she blinked, she was crying face down into her pillow. It was a vivid dream, but so real. Even Grigori's distinct smell was still around her, in her mouth, nose, hair, everywhere. She needed him and willed him to return.

She closed her eyes and was amazed to be transported straight back there. *Can a person know they are dreaming while they're in it?*

He was still holding her, his eyes trained on her like an eagle.

Always? She found herself saying.

His face softened and he nodded.

Where are we? she asked, still unable to see anything but the shelter of his wings.

Tartarus, he said, but before she had time to process it, she was lying on her side facing him in her small bed. His wings relaxed and trailed behind him on the floor. He was stroking and studying her face closely. There was nothing human about his features. His eyes were completely black and his skin pale and taut over his bones. She reached out to touch the curve of his wing behind him and he jolted, then relaxed into her touch. They were huge, even folded back, and reached down to well past his bare feet. *Magnificent,* she whispered, wondering how they must look in flight.

Grigori, I'm so lost. I don't know where to go next. Even in her dream, she knew she wasn't making sense. She didn't know if she meant lost in life or the next session with the tattoo that she knew he'd insist she guided. How could she guide where he went when she had no idea herself? The iris had been easy, but she had no idea what on earth he expected her to say next.

Her eyes went back to his, still studying her intently. *Isn't it obvious, little dove? After the iris, there is pain.* His eyes held pity as if the answer was inevitable.

A childhood memory of putting her hand into one of her grandmother's rose bushes came to mind. Her hand had bled from the vicious thorns. She held her fingers up in front of her face as if she was back then and remembered it like yesterday. She'd wondered even then how something as beautiful and fragrant could have been that cruel.

Life and death, Grigori said, even though she was sure she hadn't uttered a word. *Light and darkness always exist together. It is what reminds us we are alive, in a world that increasingly makes us feel dead inside.*

When she looked into his eyes, they'd lightened into tawny sparks, and she saw anger and devastation there. He was thinking of his own pain and she ran a thumb across his cheek to bring him back from that terrible place. *Hold onto the pain, Rachel,* he said vehemently. *Hold it and cherish it and they never truly leave us.*

A single tear escaped the corner of his eye and she caught it on her thumb. She understood his tear tattoo then. It was how he held onto the one he loved. *Little dove?* She remembered and looked at him quizzically.

The peacemaker, he said. *You bring me peace.*

Her heart soared.

It SEEMED like she blinked for a moment and it was morning. For some reason, her heart felt as heavy as a medicine ball. She normally woke up low when she remembered her nan as her first thought, but today felt worse than usual.

She remembered it was Saturday and thanked God, as she just couldn't face getting up today.

She checked her phone for any other messages and flopped back down into the bed when there were none.

Tonight was her next appointment. After all the exhausting dreams she'd had last night, she was quite glad of it. Despite all the warnings from the group, it felt like the only thing keeping her going at the moment. It was becoming really important to her, like a lifeline.

When she did eventually get up, it was about three o'clock in the afternoon. Starvation had forced her in the end. Her nan would have frowned at the chicken nuggets and chips she bunged in the oven for quickness sake.

Seb came in through the front door just as she was getting them out. He looked at her cautiously and put the beers he was carrying in the fridge. "You're up. How you doing?" he said, pinching a chip off her baking tray just like his old self. She knew he was referring to her embarrassing display of not handling her alcohol.

"I'm fine," she said, not meeting his gaze. "You want some of my cordon bleu cuisine?" she said, holding out her hands like a TV presenter.

He smiled, giving away a little of his relief that there was no weirdness. "No, you're alright. I wouldn't want to deprive you." But he did steal a chicken nugget. He sat heavily in a chair at the table opposite her. "You want a lift tonight?"

It surprised her that he'd remembered. She hoped it didn't mean that he was worried about her going. He didn't seem to trust Grigori and she wondered if it meant he was just a tiny bit jealous. "Yes, thanks. Don't you have a gig tonight?"

"No, we're rehearsing in Jack's garage."

She nodded. It was the place they did most of their rehearsing as Jack's dad had soundproofed it for them. It didn't leave her with much else to say. "I'm sorry … you know … for the other night." She couldn't meet his eyes.

Seb, however, took it as his cue to go. "Don't worry about it, I do it all the time," he said, getting up from his chair with a forced laugh. He left the kitchen, then loud footsteps sounded on the stairs.

She was left feeling a little flummoxed. He was undoubtedly referring to her getting drunk and ignoring completely the fact that she'd cruelly turned him down. It proved, despite what he'd said, that they weren't OK with each other. It had gone weird, which was exactly why dating a housemate was a bad idea.

After that, Rachel spent the rest of the day taking her mind off Seb with a long bath and getting ready for her appointment with Grigori. The time and effort she put in was as if she were going out on the town. Seb passed her a couple of times, either plucking her eyebrows in the bathroom mirror or painting toenails on the sofa. His eyes were knowing and easy to read. *What are you getting all tarted up for?* he may as well have said. Even Lynn came in and actually said the same. But her wink after completely said she knew why. "There's not … it's not," she blustered, not able to mention Grigori's name aloud. She *was* dressing for a hot guy, she just wasn't entirely sure at that stage which one.

"It doesn't hurt to keep Seb on his toes, Rach." Lynn smiled knowingly and went to get ready for work

It was 8.40 p.m. when Seb tapped on her door. "Be ready in five."

She studied herself in her full-length mirror. Her hair was up in a high bun so it wouldn't get in the way. It was hard to gauge where Grigori would go next with the tattoo. She had on a cute short-sleeved white blouse, with a white lacy bra she saved for best underneath. She convinced herself it was everyday enough because she paired it with black skinny jeans. Black lace-up pumps added to the illusion of casualness. They also looked great with the jeans if she went down to just her bra again.

Lynn, of course, would have insisted on black. That, she was sure, would have totally given off the wrong message.

Who was she dressing for, really? Heat entered her cheeks with guilt. She was an independent woman who could dress how she wanted.

Seb's visual sweep of her as they left told her what she wanted to know: she looked great—that, and the fact they travelled in his van in silence. Eventually, after ten minutes of awkwardness, they pulled up at the curb with the engine ticking over.

Tonight felt like a turning point—for what she didn't know, but they both sensed it. "You don't have to go in, you know. No one's gonna judge you for it," Seb said, staring out the front window at the fairly empty street. Hardly anyone was walking and only the odd car went past now and then.

"Well clearly I do, as none of you could see the first one." Rachel studied his profile, illuminated by a streetlight overhead. Despite her words, she wasn't angry. It felt like one of Grigori's warnings, making sure she was completely sure of what she was doing and was OK with it. He turned and looked intensely into her eyes. He was always the joking, light-hearted one. She relented. "I know … but I'd hate me if I didn't do this."

After a moment of studying her face, he nodded and looked out the front windshield again. A muscle ticced in his jaw as if he was holding in something that he was using every ounce of willpower not to say. She wanted to tell him not to worry, as he wasn't going to lose her to the much older, experienced man inside. She'd already made up her mind about Seb, but something far stronger was driving her and now wasn't the time to go into it. "Right, then," she said, opening the door and turning to get out.

"Take care," he said softly behind her.

She nodded and stepped out onto the pavement.

"You want a lift home?" Seb called out as she went to walk away.

"No thanks. I'll get a cab," she called back and held up a hand of goodbye. She rang the buzzer and prayed it opened quickly before her resolve crumbled. The door clicked and she hurried inside while Seb's van revved and pulled away.

GRIGORI WAS where he always was when she reached the shop at the back, arranging his bottles as if they followed a particular order. "Sit!" he said straightaway, barely giving her enough time to take off her jacket. Strangely, after the journey there, his off-hand no-nonsense way about him was kind of comforting. It was much easier to deal with than complicated feelings and guilt.

She hung up her jacket on the coat stand next to the door and wandered over to his workstation.

"Top off," he said, with a flick of his hand. He hadn't turned to even look at her.

Feeling a little foolish at the effort she'd put into putting her outfit together, she began to undo the buttons on her shirt. "Where am I having it? We haven't discussed that yet."

Grigori turned, still not looking at her, and pumped the chair's lever with his foot to raise it to a more upright position. "Sit for now," he said, pointing with his finger to get in. "Discussion will be quick. It's gonna be a long night."

Rachel was unclear why that statement made her heart flutter, but it did. She went towards the chair, watching his face. He was grumpy most of the time, but he seemed extra stern tonight. It made her wonder what went on in his life to make him like that.

She climbed up into the chair as ladylike as she could, and it hissed immediately as he raised it and tilted it back slightly.

"Is everything OK, Grigori—Zen—? Sorry, I don't know how to pronounce your name."

His eyes flashed to hers; the first time he'd looked at her. "Xenon—like Zen-on. It is an old name."

She nodded, slightly relieved that he seemed to be relaxing into conversation a bit. "Yeah, I've never heard anyone called it before."

He still hadn't answered her question when he sat down on his stool and wheeled it closer.

It emboldened her to say, "You prefer Grigori, don't you? It means you don't have to reveal anything then. Someone knowing and using your name is getting a bit too close."

His eyes flashed to hers while he readied his machine in its cradle. Anger and annoyance surged through them—and just a little bit of curiosity to check that she wasn't mocking him.

"Of course I can call you that, but if you are bad, then it'll be 'Xenon'—Surname?"

"Of Kryta."

"'Xenon of Kryta, get yourself back here, or else,'" as my nan would say."

He remained absolutely still and openly stared at her. Like he couldn't tell if she'd slapped or tickled him. Then he raised his eyebrows and shook his head slowly. "How did your grandmother say it to you?" Then the corners of his mouth twitched for the first time in the whole time she'd been there. "You're always so damn good."

Rachel let out a blast of shocked laughter, delighted that he actually had a sense of humor. She'd managed to cheer him up! She didn't miss a beat and, in her poshest version of her nan's voice, said, "Oh, she'd say something like: 'Rachel Leticia Fairweather, do not willfully disobey me. Get yourself here before I spank your bottom and send you to bed with no supper.'"

Grigori laughed. Big old scary Grigori actually laughed; a deep, rich sound that came right from his diaphragm. It really was beautiful and rare, and when he looked at her again, his look had completely softened. He tipped his head in kind of an unsaid thank-you and her heart swelled in the heat it created. It was pride in the fact that she was able to do that, and she hadn't felt anything like that since her nan was alive.

"Turn for me." It was said less like an order and more like a request that sent heat to her cheeks.

She turned in the chair to face the same direction as last time. Then he gestured for her to sit forward more. His warm, rough hand ran lightly over his work from the previous week. "It has healed well."

She'd intended to mention again that she'd been ill, but he seemed so wrapped up in what he was doing that she really didn't want to risk upsetting him again. She just nodded and leaned into the chair, hugging it like a racing bike.

Grigori picked up a marker pen from the bench and rested a steadying hand in the center of her back.

"What are you doing? It's perfect as it is," she said in panic.

His pen hand gently landed on her knee as if to calm her, but it just sent her heart surging to a hundred and fifty beats a minute and her face exploding with heat. He was very close when he spoke. "We want it to flow into the next piece, as if it was one piece created in one sitting."

It sounded reasonable, but she wasn't sure. "We haven't discussed anything yet and I only wanted one tattoo originally," she said while his expression remained impassive and relaxed.

He didn't argue. Instead, he put his head at a slight angle as if she'd surprised him. "But we have discussed this, Rachel. You gave yourself into my hands because you wanted change.

It is your journey from the security of your grandmother to where you are now."

Rachel openly stared at him. What he said was insightful and absolutely true. He had managed to convey into words that which had swirled and confused the hell out of her all week.

He bobbed his head. "Your grandmother's passing caused you great pain, did it not?"

She frowned, not sure where he was going with it. "Well, yes, but ..."

"Then this part must show that—from the cotton wool of your grandmother's care to the harsh realities of life ... and to finally living it." He sat back on his stool and she was stunned by his shocking but accurate appraisal of her.

She stared at him while he assessed her body. It wasn't in a male ogling a woman kind of way, but in the way an artist stands back and reviews his canvas. He moved his hand in a sweeping but whisper-light arc from her shoulder with the iris down to her side, to beneath her breast in a downward swoop. "You trust me?" he said, leaning back, engrossed in her form, marker pen in mouth.

"Yes, but—"

"I'll sketch you, then you can see what I mean." He was already taking the lid off his pen and moving in to draw.

She guessed it wouldn't hurt to see.

His pen worked quickly over her skin, taking the same route he'd made previously with his hand. Then he got up, went to his bench and came back with a big rectangular mirror.

She could see instantly what he meant. It was a beautiful climbing rose, but it wasn't stylized in any way. It was raw and lethal—almost predatory. The parallels to her earlier childhood memory took her breath away. *Did he know?* She wasn't sure.

"It has the thorns of hardship. And here, the budding roses show promise of new life to come." The seeking frond under the swell of her breast pointed gracefully downwards in the direction of her groin. "With a promise," he said with the smallest hint of a smile, but again, there was nothing sexual in it. Like he was lost fervently in the image he had already created in his mind.

It didn't stop the rush of blood to her cheeks though. There was no mistaking what it meant. However, he was the consummate artist and she was beginning to feel like the muse that the great painter painted over and over.

It was completely confusing and frustrating, because he was always so incredibly perceptive and seemed to get her completely. The budding roses could so easily signify her budding relationship with Seb. And where they were pointing—well, that was inspired.

She liked it and nodded. She really did. His talent for not only the artwork itself but also its placement, making it work with the contours and muscles of her body, was incredible. It was subtle and not at all over the top and yet held all the meaning in the world to her. Then a thought struck her: "I get the thorns, but it doesn't really signify the lonely despair —the physically debilitating pain I've been in … are still in," she finished almost spitefully, not able to meet his eyes. If he was truly mapping her journey, then these last months had been a living hell. Thorny roses weren't exactly going to cut it.

Grigori didn't say a word. Instead, he got up and walked to his bench, where she noticed an old-fashioned audio system that stood stacked at the end. He pressed a button and turned a large knob all the way around. "You haven't felt where it is yet." He took a six-inch piece of doweling out of a drawer.

Rachel looked at it with alarm, then up at his face.

"To bite on," he said, handing it to her. "The ribs are probably the most painful part of the body to be inked."

The music kicked in, atmospheric, then building to hard rock that filled the room completely. "Don't worry, Rachel, you will live your hell tonight." Then he pulled his baseball cap from the back of his waistband, turned it and scraped back his hair while he put it on. He sat, snapped on his Latex gloves and smiled at her wickedly. His machine whirred and he wheeled in closer on his stool.

All she could do was stare at him like a frozen deer, thinking him the most sexually scary man she'd ever encountered in her life.

"Lose yourself in the music; it will carry you through."

His words were perfectly timed. The lead guitar wailed, the singer screamed, and the bass guitars thrashed. The last thing she heard before she descended into misery was the singer wailing, "Together we're doomed."

Grigori didn't lie. The next three and a half hours were agony. It didn't start off too badly as it went downwards from her shoulder blade to under her arm, but the minute he hit rib cage, they felt bruised and tender and he hadn't even done anything yet. In ten minutes, she was counting so she didn't seem like a wuss and ask for the doweling too quickly.

He checked her eyes a few times and asked if she needed a break, but she was determined to see it through and shook her head. She knew if she stopped, she'd never want to get going again. It was strange, as it was those sideways looks that spurred her on. They were deep and intense, and it was rare to get the opportunity to look at him—really look at him. He was startlingly handsome. His eyes seemed to take on the dim light around them, almost becoming iridescent. His teardrop was a strategically placed jewel on the highest point of his cheekbone.

Then she was sure she lost consciousness because he nudged her shoulder, making her blink with bleary eyes. He was holding out a shot glass filled with clear liquid. "Vodka," he said simply.

Without questioning him, she took it and knocked it back like a seasoned drinker. "Get on with it," she said, not trusting herself to stop for longer.

Grigori bobbed his head in appreciation and resumed his position on his stool. "You sit well," he said, while his instrument of torture worked right over bone.

"Yeah," she hissed. "Well get on with it, comrade, my life's ticking away."

He laughed loudly. She'd never get tired of hearing that; it was a beautiful, resonant sound. Although the pain was now such that she wanted to scream, and she snatched up the doweling and bit down.

The music pounded loudly in her ears and joined her heartbeat, thrashing with the stress of her pain. Perspiration trickled into her eyes. Grigori continued to work as if he was used to killing people this way. He began to talk, and she became riveted to every word like a lifeline. Later, she would wonder whether it was a tactic to distract her from what he was doing. "That's it, Rachel. Control the pain. Think of it as a purging. Absorb it for your loved one—like a penance for them." She followed every single thing he said and lost herself in the agony. Until even she saw fatigue mixed with the sweat on his brow.

He sat back and stretched out his back. "Time to turn," he said, closing his eyes and frowning as he stretched out his taut, aching limbs. Then he stood and held onto her arm as she shakily maneuvered herself in the chair until she faced the other direction. He draped some soft muslin down her back and his gloved hand guided her shoulder back into the chair. Every movement was firm but caring.

The backrest hissed and rose up, so she was in a more upright position. "This last bit follows the breast line. You will need to pull your bra wire up," he said, watching her reaction carefully.

She'd come too far for what felt like hours to get coy now and pulled it up so it barely covered her right side. The pain had already worn her down to the point of exhaustion.

Without saying a word, she watched him pour each of them another shot of vodka. He knocked his straight back in a single swallow and passed her the other. She did the same. "Go," she said, with a flick of her hand and winced at the strength of the burning liquid warming all the way down to her stomach.

He tipped his head, straddled his stool, and moved in one adept move. "Ready for the last part of the ride, daredevil?"

She laughed and hissed at the same time when his machine cut through her warm, fuzzy thought; she liked that he called her that. She'd been called a lot of things in her lifetime, but daredevil had never been one of them. Maybe that meant she *was* changing.

When she cried out and lost her grip on her doweling with her teeth, he distracted her with questions. "What is the first thing you want to do with your new life?"

She had to blink to clear the pain fog from her head to absorb the question. It was a good one. It made her focus on how close his face was to her body. For the angle he needed, he was almost between her knees, hunched over her. Close enough to touch his hair if she had the courage to. He had other small tattoos around his hairline; tiny symbols amongst the stars she'd never noticed before. "I'm going to treat myself to a car. Not just any car; a little red soft-top, like a sports car or something." She kept quiet about the connection of cars and her dad; she rarely talked about him. Plus, the acquisitions of the shallow people on the Facebook page came to mind, so she left it at that.

He straightened and smiled as if she'd surprised him. "And then what?"

"And I'm going to get my hair done—a completely different look, you know? Colors and everything."

He paused and tipped his head. "Nice."

Then her heart raced when he said, "I look forward to seeing that." His eyes held hers for a millisecond too long and then the moment was gone. He was concentrating on inflicting pain again.

Needing the distraction, she said in clipped, tight words, "What would you do then?"

He sat up and frowned a little as if the question had knocked him a little off balance.

"You know … if you had a new start. What's the first thing you would do?"

He looked out into the distance for a long moment as if he was giving her question real thought.

"Would you get a Harley?" she prompted, convinced it would suit him. Then she could have kicked herself, because he just laughed and went back to what he was doing. "I already have a motorcycle … and not a Harley," he finished dryly.

It made her feel a little foolish. Trust her to say something silly just when he was opening up. He would feel caged in a car. There was absolutely nothing conventional about him at all. "Oh, must be one of those racing-type bikes you have to crawl across then," she said as a statement.

He laughed again. She'd clearly redeemed herself as he nodded. "Something like that."

She was just thinking he'd evaded her question when he asked, "What, a new start from today, or if I could go back in time and start again?"

She looked at him, completely astonished that he was

seriously considering her question. "Both," she said, hedging, intrigued by what he would say.

"If I could go back in time and know what I know now," he said, looking above her thoughtfully. "I would understand how transient human life is, and that when you love and it's returned, it's the greatest of all gifts. That it's spiritual and not physical, and I would hold it like the precious thing that it is and do anything to keep from frittering it away."

When his eyes flashed to hers, they were full of anger and desolation. His passionate statement made her swallow down a lump in her throat. There was such unbelievable pain in them that the words slipped out before she could stop them. "Then you're living your pain with me too tonight."

He stopped inking and stared at her for a full moment as if she'd slapped him. Then he clenched his jaw, bowed his head and resumed filling in a delicate line. "As I do every night," he said eventually.

"And what about now? What if you could start again from tonight?" She winced again and counted. Tears were forming in her eyes—a mixture of the pain and the subject area she had steered him into.

He didn't look up or even pause in what he was doing. The inked teardrop was clear for her to see—a perfect example of miniature realism. "I would choose to die, Rachel. My journey ended a long time ago."

She couldn't believe her ears. *Suicide? A strong man like him?* It threw up so many questions, none of which she had any right to ask. The main one being, what stopped him? Why did it only come up as a 'what if' scenario?

Despite all her own pains—emotional and physical, she felt desperately sorry for him. It was obvious he'd lost someone he'd loved deeply and had lived a very long time without them. "What was her name?" she said, not able to help herself. It was tactless and rude of her, but she had to know about the person who had caused such grief and devotion in a man so strong.

"Him," he corrected, looking her dead in the eye. "His name is Layke."

She stared at him, stunned—more to do with his choice of words than his gender. "He's alive?"

Grigori pushed his stool back. "That's it, you're done." Question time was over, the spell broken.

Rachel was still watching him, slightly open-mouthed, as he stood and rolled the stiffness out of his shoulders.

He frowned now, slightly amused as if he knew exactly what she was thinking. "I don't like labels, Rachel." He reached for the tube of cream on the bench and held out a hand to help her out of the chair.

She was a little wobbly on her feet; it had been a long sitting. She walked slowly over to the full-length mirror and lifted her right arm to look at his handiwork—the cause of her suffering for hours.

It was breathtaking. Swirls and arcs swooped and curled around the iris with several branches down her side, under her breast, curving perfectly to accentuate her shape. It was stunningly beautiful. She pulled her bra back down into place and winced as it rested on sore skin. She couldn't wait to take it off and see the full effect.

Grigori stood directly behind her, looking in the mirror over her head. Their eyes met and he gave her a single nod of appreciation. "You sat better than most men." He didn't smile, like he meant every word.

She felt too emotional to acknowledge the compliment and looked back at the artwork. The rose and its thorns wrapped themselves around the iris as if it were captured and dragged down. She wondered if it was more than a coincidence that the fortune-teller that had got her into all this had also been a Rose. "What comes next?" Two fronds pointed to the center of her chest and down into her groin. She had no clue where he was going with this.

"You came to me," he said, eyelids low and making him impossible to read.

Came to him. Her cheeks flushed red. The inference in the artwork was obvious: heart or sex. It made swallowing almost impossible. It automatically made her think of Seb and her vow that he would be her first. *Was that what it boiled down to with him: love or sex?* She had no clue where Grigori fitted into any of it. She blushed when only pure animal sex came to mind. However, after the way he opened up tonight, she wasn't so sure. It was confusing.

She stood up straighter. She had to remember Seb was real and this whole situation, as captivating as it may be, was not.

No sooner had she had the thought than Grigori rested a gentle hand to steady her shoulder and began to rub some of the medicated cream into her back. Her heart rate soared and felt painful in the center of her chest. Every touch tingled like electricity and she found herself holding her breath, anticipating his hand working its way round her front.

Instead, his arm came around her with the tube of cream for her to do the more intimate parts herself. While she did that, feeling a little foolish, he taped some gauze over her shoulder, so her clothes didn't rub.

She dressed in silence. For some reason, everything felt really awkward after that. Grigori handed her bag to her. The music had finished; maybe that explained the gaping silence. It really did feel like they'd travelled on a grueling journey that night, and now they'd arrived, there was nothing left to say. However, she felt it had drawn them closer because they'd suffered trials together. It was a fanciful idea, but she did have a deeper understanding of him and she hoped she was right and that he had a deeper respect for her.

Grigori's voice sounded a little cracked when he broke the silence. "Your car is outside."

She turned and looked up at him. He looked drained too. "Thank you … for everything, I mean." He looked a little quizzical, as if he was surprised at that. After a brief pause, he tipped his head. "You gave to me too tonight, Rachel."

She looked into eyes that were now soulless and dark, for a long moment. Then she turned to open the door. Her chest hurt with real physical pain at the thought of leaving him. All she could do was go as fast as she could, out to the street and all the way to the waiting car.

WHEN RACHEL'S car left Angel's Ink, she was overcome by an overwhelming fatigue. The late night, the vodka and, undoubtedly, the pain all played a part. The skin around the freshly tattooed area felt like it was burning. However, by the time she tiptoed in quietly through the front door and passed the living room lit only by the flickering TV, she came to the conclusion that the tiredness was emotional and not physical. It really felt like she'd purged something toxic from her body that had left her weak and feeble.

"You OK?" Seb's groggy voice came from the living room.

She turned from the staircase, walked over and stared down at him stretched out on the sofa. She found herself wondering if he'd waited up for her or just fallen asleep watching something. "Yeah, just really tired."

His eyes looked silver in the reflected light from the TV. His overlong black hair framed his face against the cushions. He looked relaxed, half asleep and his smile was inviting. She noticed the way his mouth was slightly parted as she said, absently, "Sorry I woke you."

"I'm glad you did. I was waiting for you."

Strangely, with her earlier thought answered, it felt perfectly logical that he should wait up to make sure she got home safe, and she wasn't plagued at all by the nerves and lack of confidence that saying something like that would normally bring. He simply shifted his body into the back of the sofa to make room for her without saying a word.

Rachel slipped off her shoes and coat and stretched out next to him, carefully nestling her sore back right up against him. His arm came around her like a warm blanket and his breaths gently stroked her ear and neck. Everything felt like the most natural thing in the world. So much so that she had to keep asking herself why she wasn't freaking out.

Her mind wandered back to the strange conversation she'd had with Grigori and his huge revelation about his lost love. A small part of her was a little disappointed that he was gay, but he had given her a great deal tonight and more than just the artwork. It felt as if he'd swapped with her a little of himself. *Prid pro quo*, she thought.

It was weird that she thought of Latin at a time like this, *but wasn't that Grigori all over?* For all his gorgeousness, he seemed like he was ancient. And he was right about the journey. They were definitely travelling together, and she felt strangely good about that.

Seb stirred and she became conscious of the feel of him. His wonderfully masculine smell was now all around her like a warm cocoon. Sleep was softly beckoning her down into a warm bed of feathers. However, when she turned into the welcoming body heat of Seb, it was to the damp coldness of earth and the smell of wet leaves.

CHAPTER 17

The earthy smell and the cold slab of stone against her cheekbone woke her up. Turning onto her back, it took her a full minute of blinking up at the green canopy high above her to remember she was back in her dream of the woods. Grigori was always in this dream.

Voices were raised again. This time she couldn't help but turn her head in their direction. She was laid out on a horizontal plinth and four people were arguing in loud whispers in the circular clearing in front of her. One of them was Grigori. With him were two others and a woman dressed for the wrong era. Her hair was piled on her head under a bonnet, and her lace-edged scarlet dress was heavily corseted, with a full bustle skirt right to the floor. She was a little smaller than the men, but she appeared to be the aggressor. Her hand was against Grigori's chest and she was right up in his personal space. The two men were on either side of her, as if they were all united against him and sideways on so they couldn't see she was watching. The sun poured down on them through the circular gap in the trees above in a single beam, lighting them up like a stage, along with bugs and butterflies, spectacularly. Their skin appeared to be glowing and pale; a stark contrast to the ring of moving blackness the thick trees made around them.

Rachel blinked. *Moving?* She squinted to see if she could see past the beam of light illuminating the others. In the end, she had to sit up to get a focus on what she was seeing.

A dream, Rachel. Wake yourself up. It's a dream. No matter how hard she tried to justify the sight before her eyes, it didn't stop the terror creeping up her body.

Wings. The four people in front of her had huge black wings tucked behind them. They arced easily a foot above their heads and reached all the way down to the floor. Grigori's splayed out slightly in his anger, giving her a perfect view in the light. Layer upon layer of ink-black feathers, magnificent in design and as luxurious as velvet.

The woman must be tall, as she was almost nose-to-nose with him. The forest went deathly quiet; not a bird nor a cricket made a sound. She moved closer to his ear, but she heard her say clearly, "I think he intends to let the little sparrow escape."

"Have a care," one of the others said, resting a cautioning hand on her arm.

Wise words when she saw the black look on Grigori's face, like he would plunge a knife into her as soon as look at her. Instead his hand raised lightning fast to grab her around the neck. She jumped as if shocked and grimaced. Then her leering smile returned. "I think he wants a new pet ... poor gentle Layke would never be enough."

Rachel had never seen anything as scary or as magnificent as what was to happen next. Grigori rose by around three feet in the air, dragging her with him by the neck. His glorious wings outstretched and circled to give him his vertical hover. Hers flapped awkwardly like a caught bird. The two on either side of her shouted and rose too, not knowing whether to intervene or stay back. It was a wonder he hadn't snapped her in half already.

Rachel was sitting up now with her legs hanging over the plinth.

Grigori, his eyes now huge black disks lit by specs of silver, began to speak through gritted teeth. "You will not speak of Layke and you will speak no more of her. The claiming has begun. The brand will come on the last waxing moon." Blood was pooling in the woman's mouth and running down her chin. Without showing any pity, he threw her away, so she barely had time to spread out her wings to soften her fall.

"You can't hide her. Mephistopheles himself is interested in her," the woman said, shaken but gathering herself together remarkably quickly. "Abaddon will come and there is nothing you can do."

Grigori landed softly and the others followed. He narrowed his eyes at her.

"Have you sent word to Wode?"

"You must, Brother, what's stopping you?" the other said, sounding as anxious as the woman.

"You'll get us all killed."

Rachel looked on, making a mental note of all the strange words to find out about later.

Grigori gave him an equally withering look, which he tracked to each of them in turn. "She will meet Abaddon at the appointed time, have no doubts on that score. In the meantime, no one touches her but me. My blood works through her already."

The men visibly relaxed. The woman brushed down her skirts. "I think we've exposed a nerve, brothers." She didn't appear to be scared of Grigori at all, because she went right up in his face again and prodded his temple with a sharp fingernail. "Think, Brother. You will bring the whole of Wode down upon us all."

The other two males were quickly on either side, ready to jump in. Grigori stared at her for a long moment, then turned and strode off into the forest.

She called after him. "There's no escaping it ... you can never escape. If you don't claim her for the darkness, one of us will. Don't fight it, Xenon. It's too late for you—too late for any of us."

When the woman trailed off, she wasn't jeering at him any longer but looked desolate, as if the reality of all their situations hit her. Then her eyes rested on Rachel and the smile slowly turned up the corners of her mouth. The other two caught on and followed her line of vision. Rachel shrank back, realizing there was nowhere to hide.

Suddenly the air was wrenched out of her with huge, powerful arms. Grabbed around the middle and under her knees, she was pulled up into the darkness against a warm chest. The dark spice smell was familiar, and she breathed it in like she couldn't get enough. "Don't let me go," she whispered, feeling dizzy and disoriented.

Deep, rhythmical beats like a muffled drum sounded around her and she was lifted away from the smells of the forest until the air felt colder and smelled fresh like the ozone of the ocean.

Her head gradually cleared. "Grigori?" She had no idea where she was. Everything blurred into dark and light, whizzing past her. "It's OK, it's me," his deep voice rumbled through his chest against her cheek.

Strangely, she wasn't scared at all. Somehow, whenever she was near him, he instilled confidence in her, more than she'd ever had before.

Her stomach churned as she felt herself go higher, until the arms were suddenly gone, and she fell heavily. A shrill noise deafened her, louder and louder, but she realized it was coming from her own mouth.

"Rachel! ... Rachel!"

She couldn't see or breathe because of the strength of the wind. All she could do was flail her arms and legs in a vain attempt to slow down her fall.

"Hey! Hey, it's OK. It's me, Seb. You were dreaming."

When she dared open her eyes, she looked blearily around her. She was sitting on her sofa in the living room with Seb standing in front of her. The lamp cast a warm glow on the coffee table next to her and Seb was wearing his coat as if he was about to go out. She glanced at the clock next to the TV. It said 5 a.m.

"You're up early," she said, rubbing her eyes.

He laughed. "I just got home. You were shouting away in your sleep in here." He couldn't keep the laughter out of his voice.

Rachel looked around her, completely disoriented. "But ..." she wanted to say she was only just in the forest and cut herself off before she sounded really stupid. Then she remembered the last time she'd seen Seb. "But I fell asleep with you on here," she said, resting her hand on the sofa.

Seb's eyes widened in surprise. "Well, I'm totally down with that," he said, grinning. He pointed his thumb over his shoulder and bobbed his head towards the doorway. "It's more comfortable up there though." He raised his eyebrows in a teasing invitation.

She was beginning to feel foolish and embarrassed. He seemed to relent and stooped to help her to her feet. "Come on, party girl."

Rachel winced when he took her weight on her right side.

"Sorry," he said, immediately, and loosened his grip.

"Ribs," she said, not explaining any more.

He nodded, but weirdly didn't ask to see what she'd had

done. Instead, he walked with her up the stairs to her room like a little old lady who needed an escort in case she fell.

Seb seemed to sense her preoccupation and left her to it at her bedroom door after asking again if she was OK. She nodded and went inside, feeling dazed and a little sorry he'd gone so quickly. *Wow,* those dreams. She was convinced she fell asleep with Seb, but he'd been out all night again. However, she had to admit that it was much more likely than him waiting up for her.

At least she wasn't unwell. The tattoo burned on her skin, but she was more concerned with what had happened between getting in the taxi at Angel's Ink and waking up on the sofa. She couldn't stop thinking about it until sleep inevitably took her.

THAT DAY SHE SLEPT LATE—REALLY late. It was 1.30 p.m. when she ventured downstairs. Seb hadn't got up yet, which wasn't unusual. Lynn was drinking something fast at the sink when she walked into the kitchen.

Rachel went to walk straight out again, but Lynn turned the moment she sensed she was there. "Oh. You're up. I'm just going out. A package came for you yesterday." Lynn looked around the kitchen and spotted it on the bread bin. "Looks like a book. I didn't think it was urgent." She went to grab her keys off the side. "Oh, and how are things with Seb?" she said as she went to walk out.

"Better," she said, her cheeks automatically coloring at the mention of him.

Lynn stopped and looked at her enquiringly, amusement clearly on her face. "Has something happened between you?"

"No!" Rachel said, a bit too forcefully. "You know me," she said, a little more softly.

Lynn laughed and looked at her sideways as if she wasn't convinced. "Mmm, and I know Seb too. Be careful."

As she disappeared, Rachel almost called out for her to see her new tattoo, but closed her mouth as soon as she thought it. She didn't want to start any of that old fiasco again. It was better to stay silent for the time being until she could fathom it all out.

After checking that the tattoo was definitely there herself, she pulled the cardboard open to reveal the book she'd waited five whole days for. It was a plain black hardback.

Discarding the cardboard into the recycling bin, and grabbing a whole carton of juice, a glass and a pack of bagels off the side, she hurried up the stairs with the book under her arm.

It wasn't so much that all it said was 'Angel's Ink by Dr Nicola Harding', on the front, nor the sub-heading: 'A user's guide to The Fallen'. It was the embossed design of an open-winged angel with his bald head bowed that brought her heart up into her throat.

It was exactly the same design as the card given to her by Rose Beauregard and the small poster on the tattoo parlor door. It held meaning.

She got back into bed. She had no plans of going anywhere anytime soon. She poured a full glass of orange juice, took a huge glug and an equally unladylike bite of bagel and settled back to do her favorite thing in the world.

The spine gave a comforting crack as she opened the book and she sniffed the pages for that blissful mixture of new paper and musty ink smell.

There was barely anything on the copyright page, suggesting it was self-published. It pretty much just said the copyright belonged to Dr Nicola Harding and it was published in 2005. She wondered if the image might be from something famous, not this weird coincidence she was seeing.

The first few pages were the same as the blurb she'd read on the website. Normally, she would skate over the dedication page, but even that drew her in and made the small hairs stand up on the back of her neck.

I couldn't write this book without a special thank-you to everyone who risked everything to contribute his or her experiences to it. For those of you reading it for the first time, you have many to thank who went before you. Some are no longer with us. They sacrificed their life to the darkness so you might understand the peril you are in. For the first time in history, you are being given an informed choice when dealing with The Watchers.

Because, make no mistake, that's where you are. You have come to the notice of a special type of fallen angel, with the power of the universe behind them and interested in nothing but your soul.

Rachel's heart was almost beating up into her mouth. Her gut twisted, and she put down her bagel. There was no way she could eat. If this book were the beginning of a thriller, it would be a bestseller. The hook was so strong. However, the coincidences to her own life were simply too many to ever assume it was that.

She turned the page to the introduction.

Choice is a wonderful thing, you would have thought. And that's true in most cases, but it can also be a double-edged sword.

Imagine two drinks. One where if you drank it, you could put on blinkers, go back to your life and have your every heart's desire, or the other, to truly see, and have your eyes fully opened to the terrible responsibility and danger that it brings. Only you can make that awful choice. And I'm afraid once everything has been revealed to you, you cannot un-see it. You are at a pivotal crossroads. Whatever way you go, it will affect and change your outlook on life forever. Because once you accept that angels are real, then everything else must be too—that means God, demons, everything. Some people are simply not strong enough to handle knowledge like that.

So, think carefully before you read on. Do you have the courage and strength of mind to know?

RACHEL'S MOUTH had gone dry. She reached over and took a huge glug of orange juice. Next was the contents page and she skimmed down the list. *Who are the Grigori? What's in a soul? How to survive The Watcher's tests.* And the one that stopped her breathing; *The secret of the ink.*

Every heading made her want to go straight to that chapter. Instead, she calmed herself and methodically worked her way through. The first heading was "About the author."

I'M NOT GOING to go on about all my qualifications and educational degrees. I'm simply going to tell you what you want to know: I, too, am a survivor. It's what got me into all this. I needed to know whether I was the only one. I guess that's why you're here too. It happened when I was barely out of childhood—a young woman at university, alone, with no one to look out for me.

RACHEL WAS STARTLED by the similarities to her.

. . .

YOU SEE, angels are real, and they mix with us invisibly every day. They mix with us in the flesh at night (more of that later). However, the ones that are the subject of this book are the ones you don't want to meet. They are The Fallen and they've got no place left to go (Except Tartarus, and we'll cover that too).

HER MIND SHOT straight to the dream she'd had only the night before. She could barely breathe, and her hands were now shaking the page she tried to read.

I'VE LIVED through all of the trials you now face, and my sole purpose is to pass on all the knowledge I've accumulated in order for you to make an informed choice during the tests. I'm going to tell you exactly who you're dealing with and what your fate will be, depending on the choices you make.

Read on to find out ...

RACHEL TURNED TO CHAPTER ONE: *The Biblical explanation of The Fallen.* She knew pretty much all this. How Jesus had battled in the heavens and cast down forever all the bad angels so they could no longer go between Heaven and Earth, causing trouble, as they'd always been able to do.

What she hadn't seen was the relevance of the history that had got them to that point. How it had all started with them being preoccupied with human women and wanting sexual relations with them, manifesting human bodies to do it. It was so fascinating that it made all the years of Bible study that she'd looked on as wasted, suddenly worthwhile. She knew exactly what the author was driving at. That is, until the very end, when it touched on something she'd never heard of before. *The Grigori were a special breed of fallen, and the most dangerous angels of all.*

FLIPPING THE PAGE STRAIGHT OVER, she began the next chapter: *Who are the Grigori?* It went straight into the explanation. However, she was still wary of being taken in too quickly. She couldn't really believe this could be talking about her Grigori.

THE GRIGORI AREN'T JUST any group of angels. They were the elite group who fell right at the very beginning. Around for eons, they've seen every sin and inclination of mankind. In short, they know you better than you know yourself. They are cunning and they're clever. They can conjure your dead relatives, turn friends and family against you, and make that elusive boyfriend or girlfriend think you're irresistible. They can offer you the world because it belongs to their master: the first of all The Fallen, the Devil himself.

There are really only four that should concern you. They are The Watchers. The Watcher of the North, The Watcher of the South, East, West—you get the picture. They are the very top tier of Grigori. They are the ones who deal directly with the demons. They broker deals for themselves with your souls.

CHAPTER 18

Time literally had no meaning. All there was was Rachel and the book. She was sweating and shaky from stress, achy and stiff from concentrating in the same position for so long. But she couldn't stop. She shifted and lay on her side with the book propped in front of her. She read on. *What's in a soul?*

To understand their motivation, we must go back to the time before the Biblical flood. Some of the angels had become curious and accompanied the lead instigator, Lucifer, in his roamings on earth. They began to pay special attention to the human women and grew restless in the heavens, which they saw as a sexless place. And so they materialized human bodies for themselves and had sexual relations with all the women that they chose. From those unnatural joinings, the Nephilim were born. They became huge, fierce men who spread fear and evil through the Earth. God could not allow them to continue to taint mankind and so he sent the flood—of which you probably know.

It destroyed the Nephilim, but the angels simply discarded their physical bodies and escaped to the spirit world. However, in the scheme of things, that wasn't for long. The heavens were eventually cleansed in a great war between the good angels and the wrongdoers, and the Fallen were cast down to Earth forever. (Hence the name.)

Well that's the party line, anyway. There is more to know that is extremely important to you, to me, and to the rest of the human race. This is where your soul comes into it:

Some angels became the demons and managed to escape with Satan (Lucifer) to a realm they call Wode, but the high-ranking Grigori and their followers, who you could say were the scapegoats in all this, were imprisoned in a no-man's land called Tartarus. It is neither in this world nor the heavens. It's another dimension, parallel to ours, that's set completely apart. There are links to our world with doorways and only The Fallen know where they are.

God himself is said to have imprisoned them until he sees fit to judge them along with the whole of mankind.

Lucifer rarely appears, preferring the sanctuary of the kingdom of Wode, but his reaper Abaddon and his closest followers, the demons, merrily roam the Earth. They know the clock is ticking for them and seek to take as many souls down with them before God exerts his final judgment. It is their final mockery of God that even the pure and the good among the human race have a price. And so they struck their deal with the Grigori.

Abaddon, who is the most powerful of all the Fallen, often referred to as the Angel of Death, offered them a get-out clause. They could walk the Earth only if they forwent their wings and lived in human form, only ever seeing the night. To earn that, they had to gather the right kind of humans—because the evil were theirs already. They had to be the ones who would fall from a great height. Only they would satisfy the demons to while away what time they have left until God judges them all. For humans, the temptation is an old one: they must sacrifice everlasting life for a few good years on Earth.

That's it. That's all it's about. Sorry to disappoint you, that it's not for some more high and lofty reason. It's as basic as living out your natural life with all your wishes granted and at the end of it there'll be nothing. Of course, they'll never know when they'll be called upon to do some atrocious act. In short, the real price for them is that there will be no Heaven and no resurrection. Not even a fiery torment of Hell—which, incidentally, is just a metaphor for non-existence. The demons know this, the Fallen know this, everyone knows this, except most of us. The ones who stand to lose the most. When you think about it, it's the biggest punishment of all. To be forgotten, like you never existed.

But here is the thing you must remember, having already been singled out: The better and cleaner the subject is, the higher the price and the more it is worth. It is simply a bigger sacrifice. In Grigori terms: when they offer you over to Abaddon, the longer they get to walk the Earth.

To recap: your soul gives them their "get out of jail free card".

IT WAS ASTONISHING INFORMATION. A lot of it she knew from her years of Bible study. The scary thing to someone like her was the undeniable ring of truth to it. That was if you believed in God, Demons and Angels, which in the three months since her grandmother's passing, she had proclaimed to not. The whole thing kind of shook her to her foundations. Maybe that's what made her valuable; that she knew all this stuff. Or, more disturbingly, that she *did* believe, and had consciously chosen to turn her back on it because of grief. It was a lightning bolt moment.

It made sense that the Devil ruled the world with all the evil in it. However, when she thought of Grigori—coincidence of his name aside, she couldn't believe there was no good in him at all.

She shelved her doubt and turned the page to the next

chapter: *The secret of the ink.* This was what Grigori had wanted her to know, so it held special interest.

So why the tattoos? Something so modern and frivolous and I agree. It does seem a little superfluous.

What if I told you that every single person I interviewed for this book is heavily inked and is branded by one of the four top Grigori? That's right. I can safely bet that if you're reading this, then you're already somewhere along the six sessions or the six tests.

Somewhere in the middle is the marking or branding.

THE AIR SEEMED to leave Rachel's lungs. It took her a full moment to gather herself and slow down her heart rate.

It doesn't make any difference how you got there; the important thing is that's what The Watchers do. They look for the vulnerable, hook them in, brand and serve them up to the Devil, again and again. That leaves them free to roam the earth like princes. That's the secret of the ink, plain and simple.

The ink comes into it because it is how you are identified and controlled, because it is highly addictive. The common belief that once you have a tattoo, you can't stop has never been truer, except that with these, it's not the pictures and coverage of the body that's the objective, it's the ink itself.

You've probably had vivid dreams, maybe even become unwell after a session—particularly the first one. That's your body's natural defense mechanism, trying to fight it. Once you begin the sessions, it indicates to the other demons and angels that you are already on the six-step program to damnation.

So how does it work?

Amongst several mineral compounds, it contains your partic-

ular angel's blood. Yes, you heard me. You are contaminated and owned by the blood of your Grigori, and once branded, with some sign or another of his name, you are well on the path to destruction.

But it's not all lost yet. That's just his signature in the contract. Yours comes later. I managed to get beyond this point, although I will never be completely safe, and neither will you. All you can do is survive the tests.

Remember the two drinks? Read on if that's your choice.

RACHEL ALMOST RIPPED THE PAGE; she turned it so fast, but there was nothing there. It was completely blank and so was the next. Ten whole pages had absolutely nothing written on them. She stared at them, horrified.

She felt cheated and upset, like she'd been the victim of some sick joke. She kept flipping pages until she got to the back matter.

SORRY I COULDN'T GIVE *you more. My life is in constant danger. I have to move around all the time. Hopefully, you have my latest number through the Facebook group. Please contact me quickly before I have to change it to discuss your options.*

Some members have reported not receiving their book, or, worse still, that it had been tampered with in some way. I pray that it's not you.

So, in case you're uncertain, here is a recap:

1. *You are a good person who has hit hard times—you're vulnerable.*
2. *Someone or something has guided you to a pop-up parlor whose advert matches the symbol on the front cover of this book.*

3. *You've been ill and suffered scary psychedelic dreams since you started your sessions.*
4. *Your life is changing, and you are getting everything you could have ever wanted.*

If all the *above is happening, then this is you. Stop! Think! You are being groomed by the most cunning, seductive creature that has ever walked the Earth.*

You must fight. You are in mortal danger. Your everlasting soul is at stake.

Call me for the answer
Nicola

It was powerful; she'd give her that. But why leave out the most crucial chapter of all if it wasn't some clever marketing hoax to get her to call a number? No book she'd ever read ended with an invitation to ring the author directly. Anger and curiosity nearly made her do it, but it scared her. What if this Dr Harding was the head of some mind-controlling cult? You heard of all kinds of nutcases on the Internet these days; her pastor was always warning his flock of the dangers of false prophets.

Rachel glanced at her clock and couldn't believe the time. She'd been reading most of the day. It had been gripping, to say the least.

What was strange was that she was more terrified of being sucked into something because of the book and less about her Grigori.

There were an awful lot of unexplainable coincidences she had to admit, ones the doctor couldn't know about her. But so far, Grigori hadn't done anything except what she'd asked for. She wasn't suddenly being showered in money and clothes, so it all seemed a little far-fetched.

She needed time to think about all this—certainly before she contemplated phoning the doctor's number.

Rachel dozed for the rest of the day. Strangely, now she'd actually received and read the book, she could relax. She lazed about and re-read certain parts, but, in the end, she just put it on her bookshelf figuratively and in reality. There didn't seem to be enough to make her do something about it yet.

Later, she took a bath and stood naked in front of her full-length mirror. The redness surrounding the tattoo was disappearing remarkably fast.

Grigori was right about one thing: she liked that she'd suffered for it. It was satisfying, like a last gift to her nan. Tracing the sharp lines with her finger, she couldn't help being aware that he had made them. The idea that they contained his blood because he wanted to lay claim to her didn't repulse her nearly as much as it should.

THE BOOK WAS on her mind the whole day at work the following day. Because of it, she purposely stayed off Facebook, resisting the urge to check it for messages. She didn't want anything to sway or affect her. The thing she chose to take her mind off it was the idea of popping into the car dealership on the Princes Road on the way home.

At last, 6.30 came, and she said goodbye to Mabel and began walking in that direction. A text dinged in her bag. She was almost too scared to look. In the end, curiosity won out. It was from Shebangs, the hair salon. She hurriedly clicked it open.

It's your lucky day! A cancellation has meant a slot is available for you at 3 p.m. on Thursday. Confirm or cancel. Gavin.

It was so what she needed. She replied to confirm, hoping to square it with Mabel tomorrow. That done, she continued on her slow walk while her mind went straight back to her dilemma. *Could she actually stop going to Grigori?* The knot that immediately twisted up her gut told her that was doubtful. She liked going. She liked him.

CHAPTER 19

The Mazda MX-5 convertible caught her eye immediately through the window from the road. It was a pile of red, shiny, shallowness that called to her on many levels.

She went in and ran her hand over its smooth lines. *Wow!* This was exactly what she had in mind when she thought of owning a cute little sports car. The low long bonnet and cute little soft top that just asked you to pull it down. Her dad would have loved it. He would sit her on his lap and read his car magazine with her and the ones he always whistled at were just like this. In her daydreams, she would always pull up to the curb, and a man would happen to walk along and admire it. She'd look up the long legs and body, straight into the eyes of her father.

An over-groomed, smooth-looking salesman in his late twenties came straight over to her, having lost interest in an older couple deliberating over a sensible hatchback. "Nice, isn't she?" he said.

Rachel gave him a brief glance and nodded. He wore far too much hair gel and his suit looked more appropriate for a night out than the workplace. He ran his hand over the car like you would a thoroughbred horse, as a thing of beauty. He wasn't wrong.

She didn't want to listen to any of his patter and immediately cut across him, "Can I take it for a test drive, please?"

The guy spun on his heel and narrowed his eyes on her like he was working out whether she was a time-waster. She stared back at him defiantly. "Well, can I?"

His eyes widened as if he was surprised by her assertiveness and said, "I'll get the key." He walked back over to a glass cube set up as the office and said something to a guy sitting at a desk. He came back over and asked, "What do you currently drive?" He nodded for her to get in the passenger side.

"I don't have a car. I used to drive my nan's." She looked out of the front windscreen and felt his eyes burning into her as he started the car. It roared into life and settled down to a soft purr. They eased out the huge double doors and onto the street.

The car drove like a dream while Car Salesman of the Year Simon went through all the mod-cons the car had to offer. Most of it went over her head. All she cared about was that it was beautiful, fast, and not in the least bit sensible. This was about recklessness and getting exactly what she wanted for a change, not making do. If she wanted to change, she had to make bold decisions.

Looking sideways at her, doubtfully, he said, "It's quite a lot of car, you know?" And when she continued to stare out of the window, appearing to ignore him, he added, "More under the bonnet than you think."

She turned to face him squarely and didn't miss a beat, "Well then, it's perfect. Just like me."

He stared at her for so long that he had to swerve a car at the last minute. How sick she was of everyone underestimating and compartmentalizing her into a boring, safe cubbyhole. "I'll take it," she said.

His foot jarred the pedal and the car shuddered. "But you haven't even driven it?"

"I don't care. I'll take it."

He narrowed his eyes a little. "I'll need to do a credit check."

"No need. I'll pay cash."

His eyes went wide, and he actually went red with embarrassment at getting her so completely wrong and missing an up-sell.

"I've been waiting my whole life for this," she said, more to herself. She'd saved since she was a little girl for that thing that would come along one day and change everything. She wanted to be ready and have the money in the bank for whatever it was. Somehow she always knew she was a caterpillar who'd one day turn into a butterfly.

The change in Simon was miraculous. Suddenly he couldn't do enough for her. Without having to arrange finance, the paperwork was very quick. He went through the rudimentary controls—how to flip the bonnet and put the top up and down, stuff like that. Then she finally got behind the wheel.

It was terrifying. It felt like she was almost sitting on the ground with the bonnet the length of a bus. She stalled three times, much to her embarrassment, in front of the salesmen standing shoulder to shoulder, watching her pull away.

By the time she was nearly home, she had relaxed and was really enjoying herself. She felt *alive*. The top was down, radio blasting and, for the first time in a very long while, she was happy; just high on life.

Then, as always, the thoughts of Grigori came crashing in. Her life *was* changing. *Was she turning into one of those braggers on Facebook who got everything they ever wanted?*

She immediately got ahold on her tailspin. Even if she *was* being lured a little into temptation, the car was bought with her own money, saved over years. She hadn't allowed herself to buy anything selfish since she was a kid. Hardly going out and no holidays away, she hadn't even touched the money she'd got from her nan. And even if she had dipped into her inheritance, her nan would want her to have it. She was now a relatively well-off woman who could make purchases like this if she wanted.

She pulled into the drive with a huge grin on her face, right behind Seb's van, just as he got out of the driver's side and Jack the other. He wolf-whistled as she pushed the button and the roof smoothly closed.

He came over, then stood back to admire the car as Jack did the same on the other side. "Serious wheels," Jack said to Seb across the top.

Rachel got out and stood and looked at it next to Seb. "It's beautiful. Whose is it?"

"Mine!" she said, grinning at him. "I literally just bought it on my way home from work." She could scarcely believe it herself.

She headed for the house, smiling to herself, leaving him staring after her. He could stay out all night if he wanted. She was an independent woman with a cool shiny new car.

He came in five minutes later and stood, watching her get things out of the fridge to start making some dinner. "Want some?" she said.

"What's going on, Rach?"

"Dinner," she said, continuing to pull out a saucepan from the drawer below the cooker. "Pasta OK?"

He nodded, looking a little exasperated with her. "Where did you get the car, Rach?"

"The dealership on Prince's Road."

"Rachel!" he shouted, almost making her drop the bag of

dried pasta. "Will you stop what you're doing and talk to me?"

It was her turn and she slammed down the saucepan onto the kitchen side. "What, Seb? What do you want me to say? I'm telling you the truth, but you're not listening. You're just the same as everyone else. You want to look down on me, being invisible. Maybe I should get a nice little Noddy car like Lynn's?" She hated herself for saying that. There was nothing wrong with Lynn's car, but he'd riled her and her pressure valve had gone. What with him, the book, and the tattoos they refused to see. Wanting to change and no one accepting it. She wanted to scream. Instead, she breathed like she'd been running and gripped the handle of the saucepan so her knuckles went white.

He was already shaking his head and putting his hands up in defeat. "You know what, Lynn's right. There's something wrong with you, Rach. You're all over the place." He tutted, walked out of the room and up the stairs. She marched after him, furious, and stood at the bottom of the stairs. "No, you both just don't like it that I'm not staying in my neat little box, Seb. Safe and boring, where you know where I am. Well, I've got news for you, sunbeam, that's not me, and you had better both get used to it!"

By the end of her tirade, she was almost crying, and her face was burning red. She couldn't remember the last time she'd lost her temper like that. Dinner was forgotten as she snatched up her keys and her bag and stomped up the stairs to her room. Angry tears welled up and she threw herself face down on the bed. The whole episode had come from nowhere ferociously quickly. She could only put it down to yet another thing that was a big deal to her that no one appreciated. The last straw had finally snapped because she was sick of everyone trying to keep her down.

At least that's what she thought it was. She was so confused.

A couple of weeks ago, she had her job at the library and her books. She'd come home to Seb and Lynn, have a laugh and a joke and that was enough. She'd confidently turned her back on her church, convinced it was all lies and had nothing to do with her life anymore.

Now, everything was different. She'd seen it in Seb and Lynn's eyes when they couldn't see the tattoo and she saw it again just then when Seb couldn't make the connection between her and the car. And now Grigori and the book had come along, and instead of freeing her, she was forced to face the fact that all the church had taught her was true, not the lies she was determined to leave behind. Seb was right. Her life was in tatters. Everything had changed. Everything was gone.

The sobs wracked her body until they gradually subsided along with her anger. She sat up and pulled her phone out of her bag. She clicked Contacts and her finger hovered, not able to make up her mind whether to tap Dr Nicola Harding *or ...?*

Her heart flipped and she knew exactly who she needed to speak to.

He picked up straight away. "Is everything OK, Rachel?"

For a moment, it threw her. It had been such an impulse and she didn't really expect him to pick up. It was so flattering, her heart fluttered.

"Rachel?"

"Er, yes. It's me ... sorry. Just been a hell of a day." She cringed at her choice of words. Then she frowned; she was really losing it.

As always, he was the consummate professional. "Is the tattoo healing OK?"

"No—yes ... I mean, that's not the reason I'm calling. It's fine ... great." Then she knew exactly what she had to ask. "What will the tattoo design be this Saturday, Grigori? I mean, I know you said it will signify that I found you, but how will you show that in a tattoo exactly?"

There was a short pause before he spoke. Then he let out a long breath as if it was the end of a long day. "I never know exactly, Rachel. All artwork has a signature, like a tag somewhere, so it can be attributed to a particular artist. As for the illustration itself, it will flow on the night."

He was answering her question and yet he wasn't. "Like a brand kind of thing?" She pushed down her heart, starting to rise up into her mouth.

His voice remained soft and lulling when he said, "More like a sign-off of an artist on a painting. Is everything all right, Rachel? You sound upset?"

She felt ridiculous and silly and she had to take a minute to control the wobble in her voice. There was no way she wanted to make any more of a fool of herself with him than she already had. "It's nothing, honestly. It's just my friends. Ever since I started all this, they seemed to have changed and not been very supportive of me. They don't seem to like that I want to be different. They seem to want to keep me as I've always been. A person I don't want to be anymore."

A sob escaped her before she had time to stop it, so she had to put the phone away from her so she could get a hold of her emotions.

She could just about hear Grigori saying, "Rachel … Rachel," over and over. "Please, Rachel, don't cry."

Seeing the soft side of such a strong, mature man, who never seemed to show emotion himself, made her put the phone back to her ear. It amazed her that he seemed to know she was now listening.

"Don't be hard on them, Rachel. They couldn't possibly understand loss as we do." His words softened her towards him even more. He was assuming they were both the same and that felt like the biggest compliment he could have given her.

"It hurts though, Grigori. They refuse to even acknowledge my tattoos."

"It's because they refuse to see you as you really are. Soon they will have to because you won't be going back to the Rachel they think they know."

His words were so true and insightful; she was scared and excited by what the future held. She couldn't stop now. Even if what Dr Harding said had some truth in it, she needed Grigori because he knew her so well. He totally got her.

In fact, it was a revelation just how much she needed him. He'd become a lifeline. *What on earth would she do when the six sessions were over?* The thought terrified her and sent her heart into panic. "What will I do without your advice?" Her voice was cracked with emotion.

There was a pause at the other end, so she thought she'd embarrassed him or come over too needy.

"You will be stronger by then," he said, eventually.

Even that was the professional answer. Nothing he said could be construed as overly personal or creepy. Maybe Dr Harding could steer people toward her way of thinking, but to her, then, although a little rough and closed off emotionally, Grigori was a great teacher of life skills, and maybe she could even call him a friend. "OK then. Thank you, Grigori. Sorry I bothered you. You must think I'm daft at times."

Again, a pause. "Not at all, Rachel. You're strong. Deep down, you always know what you need to do. You must have confidence." Then he was gone, and she was left staring at the "Call ended" on her phone.

THE NEXT DAY was beautiful and sunny and Rachel was

thrilled to be able to drive her new car to work with the top down.

Seb and Lynn weren't up, so she had the breathing space she needed to get ready without any more questions and scrutiny about the car. It was becoming hard work defending the choices she was making. Although she was acutely aware that Lynn had to be faced at some point.

Work passed quickly and uneventfully. In fact, it was the most relaxed she'd felt for ages. Even Mabel commented on it. She was still ignoring the Facebook page, so she turned off her notifications. She would call Dr Harding when she was ready. Right then, she didn't feel she needed to. Now that she had her car, she was starting to look forward to her hair appointment on Thursday—the third thing on the 'new Rachel' bucket list: Tattoo, car, and then hair. It felt like she was on a roll and really getting things done. She didn't want to wimp out now. Mabel gave her the OK to go early, so she was all set. She drove home with the top down and the radio on, happier than she'd been in a very long time.

It dissolved the minute she pulled up outside the house and Lynn was just going out. *Talk about a buzz kill.* Her sensible side, the one that always said, 'maybe she has a point,' was quickly squashed flat. Lynn was already taking in the new car with a frown, making her hackles rise. It was going to come down to her defending her choices. The roof came up and Rachel got out, clicking it locked with the key fob. Then she hardened in readiness.

"Must have cost a bomb," Lynn said, coming to a standstill next to her.

Rachel shrugged. "I needed a car, I've always fancied one, so I thought, why not?"

"You never said."

"I always pointed out little red sports cars whenever we saw one." She was sure she did.

Lynn tipped her head. "Well, yeah? But people don't usually actually go and get one. I point out dishy Hollywood stars all the time, but you don't see me pulling up with Brad Pitt!"

Rachel sagged a little and rolled her eyes. *When did Lynn turn into her mother?* It felt like she had to justify her actions yet again, so she turned with a huff and said, "Why, aren't I good enough, Lynn? Is it out of my league? Like red lipstick, high heels, or maybe Seb?"

Lynn's face looked so shocked that she may as well have slapped her. "No, that's ..."

But Rachel was already walking away and dismissing whatever she had to say with a hand. When she reached the doorway, she stopped and turned. "You know what would have been really nice, Lynn? My friends being pleased for me for a change."

Lynn hitched a breath in shock and marched back up the path towards the house, angrily, behind her. "That's not fair, Rachel. I've been there for you through everything." She came to a standstill at the doorstep and glared up at her.

Rachel looked down on her, sadly, and softened her tone. "Yes, you have ... through all the bad times and the tears. Can you not be there when something good happens for a change?"

Lynn was struck dumb by that and Rachel fought back tears. Then she shook her head, turned around and left Lynn standing aghast.

It was several minutes before Lynn came and found her in the kitchen. "You're right, OK, and I'm sorry. It's just that you're changing so fast, I can't keep up."

"And what about Seb?" Rachel said, now feeling awful that she'd been so spiteful to her dearest friend. It had flared up in her so fast, she'd had no control over it.

"Seb is a hopeless dope, but he adores you. You know

that. I think he thought he knew you and you keep on surprising him—surprising both of us." She smiled. "Don't worry, your major concern should be when he asks to borrow it."

Lynn was so right; Rachel couldn't help smiling back.

"And I never said you weren't good enough for him, red lipstick or high heels … ever!"

Rachel tried not to laugh along with her and went over to hug her friend, who hugged her back tightly. "I'm still here, OK, I'm just trying to find out who I am after hiding away my whole life."

Rachel felt Lynn nod into her shoulder, then pull apart to look at her. She gave her shoulders a squeeze. "Listen, I've got to rush. I'm late." She turned and walked back towards the open front door, then stopped and looked over her shoulder. "This Thursday, me and Colin have got a rare night off together, we're all going to Cinderella's. Come."

By all, Rachel understood that she meant Seb, his bandmates and any dates they wanted to bring. It would be a big group. Something she didn't usually do. An image of the bustling club in town hit her: the cracked grey paint outside with a single pink neon sign and a queue around the block. It had never been her thing. However, after the fuss she'd just made about changing, how could she say no? "OK, I'll try."

Lynn's eyes went wide, but she was smiling. "OMG, Rachel." She shook her head, laughing, and went out the front door.

Nothing much happened over the next couple of days other than a growing feeling of unrest. It was as if she was waiting for something and she didn't know what. Her heart seemed to palpitate for no reason and that made her more and more irritable. Sometimes it really felt like she was losing her mind.

She bumped into Seb a couple of times, awkwardly. He looked like he wanted to say something, but nothing except "Alright?" came out. She always cut him off, wondering where he spent his nights and who with. She didn't want to open a conversation she'd quickly regret, so she kept it surface too. She had to admit he did look good, though. She was noticing him more and more. The clothes he chose, the way they fitted him, the way he moved, everything. It made her wonder if he'd always looked this good or if he was making a special effort these days. Either way, she was thinking about it a lot lately. Not in a macho, scary, Grigori kind of way, but more chilled, sexy, casual, like he'd not made too much of an effort. Her eyes followed him all the time.

In bed, she wondered how it would feel to be skin to skin with him—his soft, full lips travelling over her body. She didn't know what had jump-started her libido in the last few weeks, but he was the subject of many an erotic dream.

However, daydreaming about Seb did give her respite from Dr Harding and her book. She'd purposely not picked it up since Sunday. However, she couldn't help occasionally checking the Facebook page.

The Soul Rebels page continued on with a constant stream of posts of people's acquisitions, new jobs, or partners. The common message being, 'you only live once, so grab it with both hands.' She guessed it was easy to slip into that kind of thinking if you ignored the other side: the price paid with your immortal soul.

Thankfully, Messenger was quiet. All the warnings seemed to have stopped, except for one from Nicola Harding herself:

Rachel, how did you get on with the book? I haven't heard from you. I wanted to check you were OK.

Despite the obvious answer to a ridiculous question that annoyed the hell out of her, she ignored it. She wasn't ready yet. Instead, she flipped back to the main Facebook page. *I wonder?*

Her finger tapped away, and she uploaded a picture she'd taken earlier of her car looking gorgeous. Then she added a simple caption, *'Just call me Shirley Muldowney!'* and hit Post. Her dad had pointed out the famous drag racing driver in magazines and it had always stuck with her that it was a woman. It felt braggy and shallow, but it was also a test just to see what reaction she got.

Hits to the page were immediate.

Way to go, girl!

Looking good!

Every girl's perfect accessory

You can pick me up any time ;)

Every single comment was upbeat, lighthearted and supportive. More than one hinted at a date. It was remarkable. It made her compare it with the reaction she'd had from the friends she lived with.

Messenger remained deathly quiet. *Guess the naysayers didn't have much to say about the red sex magnet parked in her drive.* Much like the reaction she'd probably get from members of her old church. The slight polite nods and smiles, but no one actually saying how great it was. She didn't need them or the church.

CHAPTER 20

Rachel tapped out of Facebook, having come to a decision. She wasn't going to be put off by people who put her down because they were too sad or too chicken to get off their backside and do something for themselves.

It was Thursday at last. Mabel's expression was intrigued when she saw her get into her car the following day. "Don't go getting into mischief in that, will you." she said, laughing and waving her off.

Rachel grinned. "I'll try not to," but she couldn't resist putting the roof down even for the short distance to Shebangs.

There was a small car park behind the shop. She parked and walked in through the tradesman's entrance, which was really a fire escape propped open with a chair. It was quicker than walking all the way around the front. Following a small hallway, she quickly found herself in the main room of the salon. It was a mix of grey, pink and chrome, thumping dance music and chatter. Hairdryers blew and the air was filled with the pungent smell of peroxide. It was a blast to her senses.

"Ah, there she is," Gavin said, spotting her from his station where he was blow-drying a girl with extremely long, poker-straight hair. "Have a seat. Be two ticks."

A little nervous, Rachel nodded and made a beeline for the sofas in the corner, arranged around a low table, covered in magazines.

"Coffee?" the receptionist said.

"Please … black, no sugar." She wondered if that was a good idea. She didn't want to be running off to the loo every five minutes, but it was something to do with her hands and she sipped gladly when it came.

At long last, Gavin led his client over to pay at the reception desk. Rachel watched as he took her money and gave her a few hair tips. He really was very good; the girl looked great. After an air kiss on each cheek, he said goodbye to her and walked over to where she was sitting. "Now, my lovely, all set?"

She was nodding, but she wasn't sure at all.

"Still up for the full Gavin Savioni makeover?"

He was so outrageously camp that she couldn't help smiling. "No," she said, honestly. "But I put myself in your capable hands."

Gavin clapped animatedly, double time, and called over a pretty girl with pastel-pink hair. "Sophie will settle you in while I go and mix up your colors and then we'll be away."

GAVIN RETURNED with two pots with brushes in and got to work. She watched in the mirror as he painted strips of hair and wrapped them in tin foil. When he'd dotted them all over her head, he lathered the rest of her hair in a blue goo that went into a foam.

She was plied with more coffee and left to relax with a magazine. It seemed like ages until Sophie came back, peeked under a piece of foil and asked her to come over to the sinks. That was the best bit; her hair was washed with slow, head-massage movements, rinsed, and a wonderful-smelling conditioner applied. "It's gonna look great. You're so lucky," the girl said. "Your hair's so thick, like Asian hair."

Rachel smiled. "Thanks," she said, but didn't really know what that meant in terms of hairstyles and followed Sophie back to her chair.

Gavin stood behind her, completely engrossed. He picked up slices of hair, appearing to decide how best go about his masterpiece. "You're gonna look magnificent. Do you trust me?"

Rachel looked into his eyes in the mirror. They looked honest and direct back at her. "It's gonna be different, but I promise you it will be rock chick gorgeous."

His choice of words was an amazing coincidence because that was exactly the look she was going for. Probably to catch Seb's eye. "Go on then. Yeah, I trust you."

Gavin grinned like he always knew the answer would be yes. He clapped his hands gleefully. "Yeah, baby. Here we go. Turn up the music, Christina," he shouted across the salon. Lenny Kravitz's "I'm gonna go my way" came on and suddenly held new meaning.

The music bounced around the salon and everyone sang along and chatted while Gavin's scissors worked their magic. It was such a happy, vibrant place; she wondered why she hadn't done this years ago, but she knew why. She'd been hiding.

In no time at all, Gavin said, "Voila, beautiful lady." He brought a mirror up behind her so she could see the back.

The finished hair was amazing. She stared at herself, frozen in the mirror, not believing it was her. Several other hairdressers came and stood on either side of Gavin to look.

"Bloody hell, Gav. It's fabulous!" one said.

"Beautiful," Sophie said, too.

Rachel was lost for words. She was astonished by what was hiding under all that librarian. Jet-black, silky soft hair to just past her shoulder, cut asymmetrically very short above her ear on the left side and left to sweep over her eye on the other. Through it all were thick slices of neon blue, catching the light and emphasizing the feather-like cut. It was choppy and angled just like a Japanese Manga character she'd once seen in a comic book. It was a far cry from the mid-length mid-brown hair, with no particular shape, she'd had before. She loved it. *She abso-bloody-lutely loved it.*

Everyone around her had gone quiet. Eventually: "Say something?" Gavin said.

"I love it, but you do realize that I'm gonna need a whole new wardrobe now."

Several people around her laughed.

"Yes, you certainly will and I know just the place. Come on over to the till and I'll sort you out."

She followed Gavin over to the desk, where she gave over her card, careful to give him a generous tip. This style would need upkeep.

After a few moments of preening her sweeping fringe, Gavin gave her a card with "Suki's Vintage Boutique" on it. "It's just inside the precinct," he said. "Tell her Gavin sent you and she'll give you a ten per cent discount off your first shop."

She turned and looked at him adoringly. She simply couldn't thank him enough. It was like a dream.

"Stop it," he said with a wave of his hand. "You'll have me gushing … Go!" he said, shushing her away. "It's open till six. Go get an outfit to knock 'em dead. You out tonight?"

Rachel remembered Cinderella's and guessed she actually was. She nodded.

"Well, you'll never get a better opportunity to make a first impression," Gavin said kindly.

He was right and, weirdly, it brought a lump to her throat. She thanked him two more times, they kissed cheeks and she left quickly, vowing to be back.

Gavin was true to his word. The assistant at Suki's helped her pick out the perfect outfit, including a leather jacket and high-heeled pixie boots, which she would have never picked for herself and gave her ten percent off. Then she took her time going home, not wanting anyone to see her before she made her grand entrance at the club later on. New hair, new clothes, and, after checking out a few YouTube tutorials, fabulous femme fatale makeup.

Luckily, Seb was out and Lynn was in the bath when she got home a little after 7.30. Lynn called through her door an hour later, "Are you coming with us, Rach?"

"I'll meet you there," she called back, praying she didn't come in and ruin the surprise. But Lynn had no reason to think anything was different and said, "OK," as if she'd heard it all before and didn't expect her to come. She'd be wrapped up in meeting Colin first for early drinks somewhere, anyway.

Rachel couldn't help feeling a little sad that their lifelong friendship seemed to be growing apart. Lynn had Colin, and she had, well … confusion. Rachel sniffed, refusing to allow herself to get maudlin. Tonight, she'd decided, was going to be the first day of the rest of her life.

FINALLY, Rachel eased herself into her killer dress. It was the little black dress that everyone was meant to have in their wardrobe; figure-hugging, backless and perfectly showcasing her tattoo.

With her new hair, which she fell in love with more every time she caught sight of it in a mirror, her new dress and arriving in her new car, she felt she could chew up the world and spit it out.

Whenever the terror of turning up at the club alone took over, she remembered that she was living a new persona tonight—the newly vamped her. It didn't matter that she was quaking inside. The real point was that she was actually going and that was huge. Tonight, she was being the person she'd always wanted to be.

Everything fell into place like the script to a movie, right down to being able to pull up and park right outside the club. The whole queue turned their heads to watch as she put her silky-smooth leg out of the car, stood and smoothed down her dress. Excitement was keeping her warm. The street felt alive with lights and cars and a buzz of anticipation filled the air.

Careful not to make eye contact with anyone except the two bouncers, she crossed the wide pavement as confidently as she could.

One of the bouncers stepped forward immediately and unclipped one side of the dark red rope. "Evenin', Miss."

"Rachel," she said, dropping her eyes to the name badge on his lapel. "Good evening, Charles."

The other bouncer put out an arm, urging her through the doorway into the orange light. "Go straight through, Rachel."

She almost faltered at being allowed in for free, but she recovered immediately with a small nod and a smile, as if she was used to this treatment every night of the week. Inside was wall-to-wall red paint and she could already hear the thump of the music. A girl whispered, "Who's that?" behind her. She couldn't believe all the attention she was getting.

She was glad she hadn't bothered with the jacket. She breezed through the corridor and didn't want to ruin her flow by putting anything in the cloakroom. It was now a little after eleven, and she wanted to hit the main room before this "new her" evaporated and everyone realized she was a fraud.

But it never happened.

The loud music and tropical heat hit her as soon as she walked in, and the crowd appeared to part, checking her out while they allowed her through. She'd never felt like this: absolutely confident that she looked great.

Lynn was the first to spot her while standing with her back to Colin and his arms around her. She elbowed Seb and he scowled and rubbed his ribs. They were standing next to a pillar with a ledge laden with drinks. As she approached, Seb followed Lynn's line of vision and his jaw dropped.

"Hi, guys," Rachel said, leaning in to kiss them both as if she met them out all the time.

Seb's bandmate, Jack, turned at just the right time and his eyes went wide. "Want a drink?"

Just as she was about to reply and possibly ruin her new image by saying "Coke", a girl came over from the bar carrying a huge bucket with a magnum of champagne that must have cost a fortune. Rachel looked around at the faces of her friends, shocked at whoever had spent out on it, but the girl answered her question with. "Compliments of Mr Kryta." Rachel's heart missed a beat and she looked around. "Is he here?"

"No, I think he arranged everything over the phone."

She swallowed hard, a mix of relief and a little disappointment, and looked at the others as each was passed a glass.

She took hers gratefully and tried to regain her composure. Her eyes went back to Seb's.

"Oh my God, Rachel! You look amazing!" said Lynn.

Seb's face had taken on an expression she'd never seen before. His eyes were soft and dewy and hadn't moved from hers.

She dragged them away to look at Lynn. "Do you see them now?"

For a short moment, Lynn looked confused, then she held her arm, partially turning her to look at her back and side revealed by the dress. "Yes … Oh my God, Rachel. They're amazing … Oh, stunningly beautiful." Then she looked back up into her face. "That's it, though, right?"

It irked that she'd gone straight in with a negative comment, but she was just relieved that she'd finally admitted to seeing them. Perhaps Grigori had been right. The time had finally come when no one could ignore the new her. So, whether it was something magical or not, Lynn had finally admitted to seeing them. So, she would take it and, ignoring the question, smiled sweetly. "Thanks."

She turned her attention to Seb, who was still looking at her in a state of wonderment. After Jack topped up her drink, she took Seb's hand and led him away to the far side of the packed dance floor. She sensed their friends' eyes burning holes in her back.

She didn't care. She was on a mission tonight, and nothing was going to knock her off course.

As soon as they got to a quieter corner, far enough away not to be watched, Rachel turned and put her arms around Seb's neck. He rested his hands gently on her hips, studying her face like he was expecting to see the real her hiding behind the makeup. "What happened, Rachel?" he said, eventually.

It wasn't the opening she was expecting. For a split second, she wavered, but refused to be taken down. "This *is* me, Seb. I just never had the courage to let it out before."

Looking into his eyes, she pulled him closer to her lips. He brushed hers with his warily, as if he was still trying to work everything out. "Do you like it?" she whispered next to his mouth.

He took in a deep breath and shook his head. "What's not to like? … It's just a lot to take in." Then he took her hands from his neck and put her away from him. Holding her by the shoulders, he took her in from the feet up.

"Can you see my tattoos?" she said, willing him to say yes. It had come to signify his acceptance of the person she was becoming.

He turned her body slightly so he could see her back and nodded. "Yeah … it's pretty badass." He grinned his crooked grin at her. "Who knew you were this cool, Rach."

Her heart swelled with the praise, which meant everything coming from him.

"But you know I liked you before, right?"

Her delight quickly drained away. He must have read it on her face as he crushed her to him and said in her ear, "You're beautiful, you always have been."

She allowed him to hold her while she thought about what he said. It was the right thing, she knew. It was good that he liked her, however she looked. She'd just wanted a bigger reaction to her new look. She gradually relaxed and snaked her arms around his neck and they moved a bit to the music. It was upbeat but not too fast that they couldn't move to it.

It was a milestone, really—the first dance with a boy in her whole life. She'd never stayed out long enough anywhere to have one—not even at school. She'd always avoided large social situations outside of the church.

They were interrupted by a nudge to the arm. Jack grinned and winked, then offloaded their drinks. "Enjoy," he said, waggling his eyebrows. She couldn't help laughing. Seb grinned.

They didn't really say too much after that. She guessed they were both a little stunned at their new status and slowly drank their drinks and danced. She had to be careful. She was driving and wanted a clear head to savor the evening, not sure if it would happen again. They remained glued to each other through several songs.

Eventually, the inevitable happened and their lips finally came together. They shared the most intimate and softest of kisses. It was over too quickly and ended with Seb's forehead against hers. "Ready?" Seb said. They instinctively knew it was time to leave.

They went via the bar to leave Jules with the keys to Seb's van. She didn't ask who was in a fit state to drive it. Lynn watched them approach and clocked their joined hands.

"We're going," Rachel said.

Lynn looked a little stunned. Then she had to go and ruin it by saying, "What have you done with the real Rachel," and laughing.

It stung a little that she felt the need to say this kind of stuff, but Rachel shrugged it off, determined not to let it get to her. "I'm out to play now, Lynn. You'd better get used to it."

Lynn frowned and hugged into Colin's side, who put his arms around her protectively.

The guys from the band had all heard and cheered. Lynn, who still seemed unsure what to do, kissed her goodbye. "Please be careful," she said in her ear as she pulled apart. Lynn was clearly scared she'd get her feelings hurt by Seb, but she was treating her like a child and needed to let her go.

"Be good!" Lynn said a little more loudly to Seb, who frowned.

"Always," he said with a grin.

Rachel couldn't wait to get them out of there, and she pulled Seb away in the end. They hadn't let go of each other's hands. Both bouncers said goodbye to her by name and nodded at Seb. He looked at her, amazed—like he'd entered some parallel universe. She kind of liked it. It gave her the advantage.

He recovered when he caught sight of the car parked right outside. Like he'd forgotten or didn't expect her to bring it. He walked around to the passenger side. "You've turned into a rock star overnight, Rach."

She got in. He was right. She had, and her mind went straight to Nicola's book and the Facebook page. "Now that makes two of us."

He laughed, still shaking his head and waved her on. "You'd better get us home quick."

"Yes, sir,' she said, laughing. Revving the engine and pulling away fast.

The drive took no time at all. "I never knew you could drive like that," Seb said. Then he frowned. She smiled a little, knowing he knew as well as she did then, how guilty everyone was of underestimating her.

They walked shoulder to shoulder up to the front door. She locked the car with the key fob over her shoulder and got out another set for the door from her bag. "My dad liked nice cars. He always had his head under a car bonnet. I think he would have preferred a boy." She didn't bore him with the details of the real dad who left while she was still young.

Seb nodded, looking at her quizzically, taking in all the new information as if he were seeing her for the first time.

Rachel headed straight for the kitchen and filled a pint glass with water from the tap. "I get thirsty in the night."

He grinned like he had a wise-crack come-back but didn't say it. Instead, he pulled her into a hug. Then he kissed her gently, taking his time, exploring and seeking with his tongue. "Where have you been?" he whispered.

"Here, Seb. I've been right here."

They searched each other's eyes in awe at what appeared to be happening between them. Then he picked up her hand and led her up to bed.

CHAPTER 21

*R*achel had the strangest feeling while walking up the stairs with Seb. Never in her wildest dreams —and there'd been a few, had she ever imagined it would happen like this. Not just to have the opportunity with Seb, but to do it without being a quivering mess. She did have butterflies, but it felt right. Like it was the most natural thing in the world with the perfect person. They'd known each other for a long time, and she trusted him. She just never thought he would notice her in that way.

He shook his head as they got to his door. "I'm not sure a tramp isn't living under my pile of laundry." She giggled as his room always looked like a bomb had hit it.

By the time they reached her door, she became totally convinced that all this had happened since she'd met Grigori and got her tattoo. There had to be something in that.

The thoughts flitted away along with her bag onto the floor. There were more pressing matters. She clicked on her small lamp next to the bed and Seb killed the overhead light.

Seb studied her for a long time, taking another visual

sweep of her. "Wow," he said, making a fierce glow in her lower abdomen.

Her mind flicked back to the Facebook page where everyone got their heart's desire. *Was this hers?*

"Second thoughts?" he said, putting his head at an angle. There was no animosity in it, just a question. His hair was ruffled and his lips full and sensual in the warm glow of the lamp.

Whatever the reason, she wasn't going back now and shook her head. "I'm throwing caution to the wind tonight, Seb." She went to him and he crushed her to him. His mouth nestled in her hair by her ear. "I won't hurt you," he whispered.

She felt a slight burn at being exposed as a virgin, but she guessed Lynn had done her a favor in telling him in the end, however embarrassing. This was Seb and he would look after her, and if she did this, then she wouldn't shrink away.

He shed his leather jacket and threw it on the floor. Her heart cranked up a gear and she began to unbutton the buttons of his black shirt—quickly revealing his silver cross and a couple of leather surfer-type necklaces. They were totally him, but the cross made her pause. "My mum gave it to me as a boy," he said, looking down at her, still smiling. "She died of cancer when I was very young."

He'd barely known her. It made him feel even closer to her then. They'd both suffered such terrible loss. She'd already known he'd been brought up by four older sisters, but it answered so many questions about him; why he was easy in the company of women, but didn't invest in anything emotionally. It was in case he got hurt. Guess they had more in common than she thought.

Rachel ran her hands over his smooth cream skin. He had a geometric pattern over his left pectoral that ran over his shoulder and down his arm. "Do you like it?" he asked, smiling more widely.

She nodded. She'd just never seen it this close up. He was very slim, like he had a lot of filling out to do as he aged, but it was perfect for his young rock-singer persona. When the shirt went the way of his jacket, she realized he had quite a few small tattoos, mainly on his arms and over his back. They weren't Angel's Ink standard, but there were no horrors.

He bent down to take something from the breast pocket of his leather jacket on the floor and put it on the nightstand. *A condom.* His eyes locked with hers as if to say that if they were doing this, then they were doing it right.

Seb went up a notch in her estimation, if that were possible. Her heart was beating a military tattoo when he came to her and pulled her against him again. He peeled her dress slowly from her shoulders, planting soft kisses where it went until it fell to the floor and she stepped out. She was left standing in her new lacy black panties and resisted the urge to cover her chest.

His eyes took her in feverishly and she was gratified. There was no disguising a look like that and it made her feel powerful for the first time in her life. It felt amazing. He wanted her and it felt like she held all the cards.

She walked up into his space again and kissed him, making sure she loosened his belt and popped the button on his skinny black jeans.

He gasped next to her mouth and then helped her push them down so he could step out of them easily. He never once broke their kiss and she deepened it, realizing the only things between them were the lace of her panties and the soft cotton of his skin-hugging shorts.

Her hands ran down his back, over the material and the sides of his long legs. His skin was silky smooth over surprisingly hard muscle. It was the first time she'd touched him, and he felt wonderful.

Now they were skin to skin, the temperature appeared to get hotter. Hands travelled but more urgently, demanding and seeking. When his fingers ventured beneath the waistband of her panties, she pulled him down with her onto the bed. She wasn't ready to lose them yet.

Seb seemed to sense it in her and slid off to the side, slowing things down. He leaned up on an elbow and pushed the stray strands of blue and black hair from her face.

"Do you like it?"

He nodded, smiling. "I love it both ways."

The warm light reflected in his eyes, making them look misty. She closed the gap and kissed him. "But you like it more like this." Then she kissed him hard.

Seb groaned and rolled on top of her, crushing her into the bed. The weight was welcome—his hardness pushing into her pelvic bone and stomach. Her hips were already undulating beneath him. She was hyper-aware of the tight gauze of her panties pushing into her folds, soaking wet already.

After nipping hungrily at her mouth, he left a trail of kisses down the side of her neck, down to her breasts. Gently passing a thumb over the hard pebble of her nipple, he lavished them with kisses and suckled them gently. She was mesmerized, watching the whole thing, only closing her eyes when the sensation overwhelmed her completely.

He paused and hovered when he came to her ribs. The rose fronds split and curved underneath her breast towards her heart and pointed downwards in a graceful arc to her groin. She wondered if he contemplated the choice like she did. It was beyond deep and she absolutely knew it was how Grigori meant it—love or sex.

There was no time for further thought as his lips closed,

kissing reverently the center of her heart and his hand smoothed over the flat of her stomach and gently pushed her legs apart. His fingers slipped easily between lace and slick wet skin.

She gasped and his eyes flashed to hers, checking she was OK, while his fingers glided over her. "You're so ready," he whispered.

There was no answer except to circle her hips into his hand. With the silent permission, he eased the panties down from her hips, all the way, where she kicked them off her feet.

Somewhere along the line, his went too. His mouth went to her stomach while her heart hammered and her cheeks went red. "Seb!" she gasped, as he neared the small mound and his fingers still worked through her wetness.

He met her gaze just before he dipped his head. His eyes looked bleary and lost to lust. "If you want me to stop, just say, Rach." Then his head went down, nipping with his lips until he teased her small bud.

She cried out; the sensation was so strong.

He paused, allowing her to catch up.

"Don't stop … don't stop! … Oh god!"

He smiled and kept his eyes on hers while his tongue lapped and swirled until something reared up within her so quickly that she lost all sane thought. Her body bucked and arched, but he held onto her thighs hard and remained glued to that place, holding his mouth and circling his tongue over it.

A single beat of time and a whiplash of fire shot through her whole body. Rushing through her veins, right to her fingers and toes. Ecstasy pulsated through her for several seconds.

Her hips circled as it subsided and Seb left her to crawl up her body. The crackle of paper made her open her eyes and watch enraptured as he slid the condom over himself, hard and erect. It was the first time she'd ever seen someone do it. *Who was she kidding?* It was the first time she'd seen a real one at all.

He smiled when he realized she was watching and hovered over her, looking into her eyes. His knees went between hers and he eased his weight down.

Her heart raced when she realized this was it. She was actually going to do it. He placed himself at her core and, taking most of his weight on his arms, began to rock his hips gently. She held her breath with the sensation of him inching into her little by little.

Excitement was unfurling in her stomach again as she began to get used to it. Her hips involuntarily began to move to meet his. Then he slowed, barely moving, and closed his eyes. He looked utterly beautiful in that moment and she couldn't help but reach up and touch his cheek. His eyes opened at her touch and he smiled angelically, then pushed into her completely on one final thrust.

Scalding pain blinded her. "Seb!" she cried out.

He instantly dropped his weight down to hug her tightly. He didn't move but remained tightly inside her. The pain was intense, searing and all-consuming. With her eyes shut, she felt him find her mouth and kiss her ardently. As the pain slowly subsided, he whispered, "Sorry," next to her lips.

She'd heard the first time was painful, but she'd never imagined it like that. She guessed unused muscles were ripped apart. However, as she felt them loosen their vice-like grip on him, he began to move again. The pain was beginning to give way to indescribable pleasure. She found she was able to move with him and the feeling grew.

He held her to him, and they moved together like one person. It began firm and slowly at first. A wonderful feeling of togetherness built with every roll of his hips. *Wow,* she had no idea anything could feel like this. Both of them lived every moment in the moment, getting equal pleasure directly from each other. They became one body as they grew in confidence that he wouldn't hurt her. She began to lose herself to it.

Each thrust built in strength and he pushed her on and on, pulling her knee over his hip. She found she was panting with every thrust. Any thought that he might be young and inexperienced disappeared with every deliberate push he made into her. He totally knew what he was doing. He sat up on his knees, holding her buttocks firmly, and she felt herself begin to float again. It must have been reflected on her face because he whispered, "Yeah, that's it."

In that perfect moment, he dropped down next to her ear again. His thrusts became deeper and more measured and his whole body appeared to tense around her. It was when she realized they were both going to finish together.

Everything felt so perfect. Moving as one, sweat making their skin slick between them, he threw back his head and let out a long, audible breath. With the sight of him like that, her mind shattered as the sensation she now recognized flashed through her body, longer and much more intense than the last time. Her sheath pulsated around him and she heard him groan her name as he burrowed as deep as he could inside her. Biting the soft part of her shoulder, he lost her to sensation at the wonderful feeling of primal ownership.

Eventually, their movements slowed, and they stilled to a tangled heap. The bed linen had disappeared onto the floor, and they simply lay where they found themselves and caught their breath. The wonderful crispness in the cool night air caressed their bodies. She was grateful for the gentle breeze that blew the curtains from the window she never opened.

. . .

SEB. The person she'd fantasized about, but never expected to notice her all the way out there in the friend zone. But he did, and she couldn't imagine anyone so perfect.

When they recovered, he helped her remake the bed. "Four sisters," he said with a grin, when she looked at him, amazed. He also came with her to shower as her legs were still wobbly. He was so caring and attentive, she was surprised over and over. No wonder all the girls loved him. He was laid-back and playful, but that night she saw him as a caring man—a real heart-breaker.

For the first time in her life, she slept the whole night wrapped in another person. They were tangled in each other, wanting to touch as much as possible, and all without any conversation. There was no need; touch was the only medium needed.

"You OK?" was all he said, and it was perfect. Any more and the moment would be marred.

She nodded and he was satisfied. She guessed they were both still a little stunned. Sleep was pulling her into a warm, soft cocoon, and she remembered what Grigori said about acceptance for what she was. "I'm glad you could see my tattoos," she mumbled just before she dropped off.

She felt his lips smile against the back of her neck. "Oh yeah, I saw them alright."

She fell asleep grinning.

IT SEEMED like five minutes until her alarm went off. Even though she'd set it for as late as possible, it still felt like no time at all. Reluctantly, she extricated herself from Seb's arms at 8 a.m. to get ready for work.

She could have thrown a sickie, but the sun was shining and she was so happy to be making the short drive to work with the top down. It gave her valuable time alone to process and relive the most amazing night of her life.

That day, everyone remarked on and loved her new hair. She didn't look at Facebook, not wanting to ruin her buzz. Instead, she spent the morning with a huge grin that she simply couldn't shift from her face. Mabel smiled at her knowingly a few times. "Someone had a good time last night."

Rachel blushed, but didn't deny it and the morning passed on a pleasant cloud. At lunchtime, she checked her phone. There were two messages, one from Seb: *Thanks for last night! XXX.*

It made her heart flip. They were really doing this. It was a thing—a real thing. She wanted to shout from the rooftops, *I have a thing going with Seb Newly.*

The other was from Lynn, which she was definitely expecting. *How'd it go? You little ...* She ended it with a red devil emoji. The irony wasn't lost on her. It made her giggle. She had been bad—very.

Rachel messaged straight back: *Best night of my life!*

Seriously—Seb—! Then the emoji of being sick.

He has hidden talents!

Yuk. Spare me. Seriously. Happy for you. About time. X

Then she wasn't sure why she did it, but she texted Grigori while riding her high: *You were right. Had the best night of my life last night. New car, new hair, new man.* Then she hit Send before she had time to think about it.

Rachel finished work and locked up with Mabel, exhausted. She hadn't done a lot of sleeping the night before. She waved and got into her car, still smiling every time she thought about it—along with a stab of delicious pain in the pit of her stomach.

She made the short drive home and found a cute note with a hand-drawn heart and the words: *Band practice at Jack's. B naked when I get back*

It was way too presumptuous of him, but it made her laugh. It was typical Seb. However, it did mean it couldn't have been too bad for him if he wanted her again.

It felt good to have the house to herself. She was still reveling in the memory of what had actually taken place between them. She made herself a microwave dinner, took a long soak and went to bed at around 9.30.

Somewhere between 10 and 1 a.m. Seb must have eased himself between the sheets with her. Thankfully, it was Friday, so no work the next day. So, when they turned into each other instinctively and had the gentlest, sweetest sex, she didn't mind at all. It felt perfect. There was nothing forced, just two lovers whose bodies simply found each other in the darkness. She felt safe with Seb, like he'd protect her and be there till the end of the earth.

They lay replete in each other's arms as dawn came stealing into the room. "I have my tattoo appointment tonight," she said, tentatively, not wanting to ruin the moment.

Seb didn't answer right away, but she could tell his mind was working.

"What's the matter?" she asked, leaning up on an elbow. The blue-grey light gave his skin an angelic glow against the black of his ruffled hair.

He looked from the ceiling to her and touched her cheek. "Nothing ... it's just ... do you really need any more? ... I mean, you look great—more than great."

Rachel recoiled, a little stunned. She thought he understood the journey she was on. "But I have four more booked sessions, Seb. You know that."

He sensed her hurt and turned on his side to face her, resting his hand on her shoulder. His thumb gently massaged just under her collarbone. "Please don't get upset ... it's OK. All I'm saying is that you're perfect as you are."

She studied him for a long moment and then relaxed back into her pillow. What he was saying wasn't wrong, really. The feeling of panic came from deep within her. She just recognized it for the first time. "I can't explain it, but I need this, Seb."

He lay down too to face her on his pillow. Then he leaned over and planted the gentlest of kisses on her lips. "Don't worry. Forget I said anything. Maybe I'll even get another one myself."

. . .

THEY DIDN'T SAY any more after that. Seb fell asleep and she pretended. She found she kept analyzing the scenario of never seeing Grigori again and the thought terrified her. Whichever way she tried to talk herself down and rationalize it, she was filled with absolute panic. Despite knowing that Seb was completely right, she had to go, and it wasn't simply because of her so-called journey. She needed it. She needed Grigori.

She sat up and remembered she'd had no reply to her text, which was unusual. Grigori had not answered one of her texts before. In fact, since he'd given her his private number, they'd usually been straight away.

Fear gripped her heart for a second until she took some breaths to calm herself. Seb slept soundly next to her and she tried to relax back down next to him, but her thoughts went to Dr Harding's book.

It had spoken of the addictive lifestyle the Grigori could offer—the good fortune, the possessions and, particularly, the ink. *The blood is in the ink,* she repeated in her own mind. It seemed too far-fetched for words. *Could that be it?* Was that the reason she had to go back and risk something good and real with Seb? Come to think of it, her moods had been erratic for a while.

Rachel tried to take some deep breaths to control her racing heart. It was nothing really to worry about. She'd simply broach the subject of the book and its warnings with Grigori tonight. She'd gauge his reaction and all this silliness would go away.

It was a plan at least and that helped her relax enough to fall into sleep.

SEB WAS SUBDUED and already drinking a beer when she got ready the following evening. She felt for him, but she couldn't set a precedent and let him control her in this way. It made getting ready difficult, as she wanted to make an impact with Grigori with her new look, but she was conscious that Seb would think she was dressing up for another man—which she kind of was.

In the end, she opted for a plain black shirt and skinny jeans combo with the new pixie boots she'd worn with Seb the previous night. It looked good but still kind of casual.

When she was ready, Seb stood from the bed and swept his eyes over her like a physical touch. "God, you're too sexy, Rach." He pulled her to him, bit her neck playfully and gave her butt a squeeze through her jeans.

She giggled. "I can't help that. What would you have me wear?"

He pulled back to look into her eyes and nodded. "No, you can't." He pushed back a stray lock of neon-blue hair. "But you could make an effort, like wear glasses, a big hat and a floral dress or something."

She laughed and he cracked a smile, not able to stay serious. It was what she loved about him.

"Come on, I'll take you," he said.

Rachel shook her head and grabbed her keys from her nightstand. "No need," she said, shaking her keys in the air. "Have babe machine now."

He smirked, but it was obvious it was covering his unease. With a prickle of guilt, she pretended not to notice, kissed him quickly on the lips and left him standing in the middle of her room.

When she pulled away, she didn't look back at the house. She felt Seb watching her go and it felt weird. Like she was abandoning or betraying him or something and that was just ridiculous. She wasn't doing anything wrong. All she was doing was keeping a pre-booked appointment.

The whole thing ruined the drive to Angel's Ink. She parked right outside and walked across the wide pavement to the front door. It was unlocked and clicked open without her even buzzing. *Weird.*

She walked quickly, straight through the corridor to the parlor at the back, but the door was locked. She was so excited to show him how much she'd achieved in just a week. She knocked loudly three times. "Come and look at my car, Grigori." She knocked again, but still didn't hear a sound.

She frowned, then got her phone out of her bag. She was bang on time and not late. Grigori had never been late and there was no message.

She tapped quickly. *Where are you?*

There was no reply.

A thump and a scrape brought her head up fast to look at the ceiling. Then she considered the staircase that went up into darkness. She slowly walked back, stood at the foot of it and looked up. The door stood in the gloom at the top.

Slowly, one at a time, she climbed the staircase. The closer she got, the more she heard voices; it sounded like a heated discussion. She stopped right outside the door and strained to hear whether one of the voices was Grigori. He'd made it quite clear that she shouldn't come up here, but surely these were extenuating circumstances and she didn't know what else to do. She had to get to Grigori. Her hands were shaking—like really shaking and there was a huge knot in the pit of her stomach. Like hunger but not hunger, she couldn't explain it. She knocked, figuring she had no other choice and took a step back from the door.

The voices went quiet for a full minute, then the door opened. A woman stood in the doorway. Rachel was speechless as she had to be the most beautiful woman she'd ever seen. She was very tall and looked like she was dressed for a ball. Her red dress was long with shimmering silver edging, contrasting perfectly with her warm, honey skin. Her long black hair swept down over one shoulder and her eyes were large, dark-lashed and the most vivid shade of violet she'd ever seen. "Hello, Rachel," she said in a warm, accented voice. "We've been expecting you. Why don't you come in?" She pushed the door wide open, so Rachel got the full impact. She was Jessica Rabbit sexy, showing off far too much cleavage. Like, even a straight girl could get lost in those curves.

Rachel hesitated, still speechless. Two men came and stood behind the girl, taller by at least six inches; a formidable wall looking down on her. One had dark-brown hair and eyes the color of a glacier, ringed in black like a wolf. The other was very dark, with jet-black hair and the most unnaturally beautiful eyes; obsidian, like a crow. Lethally handsome, they both smiled at her with full sensual lips.

"I'm looking for Grigori—I mean Xenon. I have an appointment. Er … Are you his family?" she eventually got out, like a star-struck idiot.

The three of them nodded. "Come in. He said you'd be coming by," the one on the left said. "I'm Bohdan. Oleander and Raephe," the one with wolf's eyes said, nodding at the other two. "Come in and wait. Xen shouldn't be long."

Despite the outward friendliness, she wasn't picking up a friendly vibe. There was a weird excitement in the air, like electricity. It made her think of a den of wolves and she had to fight the urge to run and appear rude. Somehow, she remained rooted to the spot.

Oleander stood aside. "Come in and be with us for a while."

Her words sounded inviting—seductive, even, and Rachel found her feet moving despite her better judgment. Alarm bells were screaming, but she still moved forward hesitantly into the apartment.

With the slam of the door, her head began to swim, and the words "Come, be with us" echoed like a whisper through her mind.

The two men appeared at her shoulder as she walked. They were huge—Grigori huge. She wanted to move away from them as they were too close. They began fawning over her, running their hands over her arms and through her hair. One even kissed her on the cheek—and not in the way of a hello.

Terrified, she looked up to see Oleander walking backwards in front of her, beckoning her forward with a finger. Her feet kept moving, *damn them*.

The small hallway suddenly became impossibly long. It became a tunnel with a white light at the end.

A hand ran up her spine. She looked left and the one called Raephe smiled with sloe-black eyes that appeared to glow like diamonds.

Something was happening and coming over her and she didn't seem able to do anything about it. Her heart beat hard in her chest and her whole body was shaking uncontrollably. Then she was positive she stopped breathing and, for a moment, she couldn't see. There was absolutely no sound— weirdly reminding her of freshly fallen snow and when she could see again, she was in the forest of her dream.

Her breathing came with a rush and a splutter as if she'd come up out of water. *This was good, right?* It meant she'd probably fallen asleep. Maybe she'd gone back to her car and waited for Grigori there. This was simply that weird dream she'd had while she was waiting.

"Come," Bohdan said, and she went with him a little easier now that she thought she was dreaming.

She squinted. The light was weird, artificial-looking, and everything seemed a little out of focus. The dream gave her an uneasy sensation she wasn't enjoying. She tried to will herself awake. It wasn't good to be there. Danger was so close that her fight or flight mechanism was kicking in, but she couldn't make herself move.

Rachel managed to turn a slow circle. She was in the same clearing of trees that she'd seen before—the one where Grigori had argued with the strangers. *These strangers,* she realized when she turned and all three stood in front of her with the most spectacular black wings. "You're ... you're Grigori," she whispered.

They all grinned. "You're well informed for an Earth child," Bohdan said.

Oleander beckoned her with a finger. "Come, let's play a while. Abaddon will be here soon. We can give you exquisite pleasure, such as you've never known."

Rachel watched, helpless, as Oleander struck out at her with talons for nails and shredded every one of the buttons on her shirt, leaving her black lace bra on full view.

Raephe smiled at Oleander. "She has no mark."

Bohdan appeared next to her in the blink of an eye and cupped her face. "I'll mark her myself. Taste the ambrosia, child, that Xenon has so cruelly denied you." He slowly bent his head and began to cover her mouth with his own.

At first, she recoiled, wanting to push him away, but the moment his tongue touched hers, her body ignited. A feeling of warmth and absolute joy spread through her. It was so intense that it made her gasp.

He broke his kiss, and she was bewitched by his wolf's eyes, seeming to see right into her. Something nudged her other shoulder and she turned towards it dreamily. Raephe was there and bent and kissed her too. A similar feeling returned, but different, like a different flavor or signature. It went on for longer and drove her heart so fast, it felt like a drug.

It was as though her feet left the ground and she floated in a cloud. The next thing she knew, she was lying on cold, hard rock.

"It is a shame Abaddon is almost here; it would have been gratifying to take such a pure, untouched spirit."

Rachel opened her eyes to see the three of them looking down at her, nodding.

"Still, we can leave her with a lasting memory."

The euphoria was subsiding, to be replaced with a horrible, creeping fear. Instinct was gradually breaking through, telling her this situation wasn't good. The sky was darkening behind them. A slow beating was coming closer—wings, she realized. The sound was getting louder, and the wind whipped the hair around their faces.

The sound echoed as if she were delirious. It sounded like a wailing or a shouting. *Nooo*.

Then the three standing over her appeared to be swept aside as if hit by a wrecking ball.

A great wind came with it and took her breath away. She struggled to sit up and found she was on the same plinth as in her dreams.

Grigori—her Grigori—stood like a barrier between her and the strangers. Her heart was still erratic from the strange kisses they'd given her. "Dare you touch what you know is mine?" Grigori said. "My blood runs with hers and you dare taint her?"

"Abaddon comes, Xenon," Raephe said, like it was all some joke that had got out of hand. "Your job is done."

"He knows she is here with you," Oleander said, winding a lock of her hair around her finger. "You risk yourself and us for a mortal."

Grigori became suddenly terrifying, as he seemed to

double in size and loom over them. "Rest assured, I will not forget this betrayal. You are premature in calling Abaddon. *You* risk us all as she is no longer pure."

Rachel watched the horror and indecision spread over their faces, but the words echoed. She tried to concentrate on what he was saying, but her focus drifted in and out, so she couldn't be sure exactly what she heard. Dreams were like that, *weren't they*? The weird rhythm in her heart was making her woozy.

Then Grigori was right there, easing her back into his tattoo parlor chair. He passed her a glass of cold water. She expected him to say she'd slept, but it was as though all pretense had gone and she was seeing the unguarded version of him for the first time. "Why did you go there, Rachel, when I explicitly forbade you?"

Her head was still swimming, and she felt dreadfully sick. Sipping the water helped slightly. "What's happening? I don't get it. What is that place?" She turned to him. "Wake me … wake me up, Grigori." She said it over and over, grabbing onto his arm. He didn't react at all but watched her dispassionately until she calmed down and remained quiet. It felt remarkably like waking from an anesthetic, where disorientation subsided, and your doctor waited for you to come around properly.

Now she could see the coldness in Grigori's face was fury. He was pissed like she'd never seen him before. His amber eyes looked almost red in the light. "Stop this nonsense now and give it up. You know what is happening and refuse to see it."

The shock of being told off by him, of all people, unclouded her mind. It was enough for her to focus on her surroundings and realize she was in the tattoo parlor, with Grigori standing over her, rage barely contained beneath the surface.

"I … I don't understand," she said, looking around her. "I came and you weren't here."

"I was bartering for you, Rachel. Trying to save you from the fate of your poor decisions. It took a little longer than expected."

She stared at him, trying to compute what he was saying to her. *No, she was trying to lie to herself.* Trying to come up with a cozy, plausible explanation or another meaning. However, try as she might, there was none.

With a final glare, he took his baseball cap from the back of his waistband and straddled his stool. Her eyes never left him while he ran his fingers back through his hair and put it on. Despite his anger, he never looked more handsome or more severe.

She sat stunned, as if she'd been knocked silly. She supposed she never expected him to voice all the stuff she'd pushed out of her head and into the background. And on top of all that, he was continuing on with the tattoo.

He snapped his blue Latex gloves into place. "The shirt and bra must come off for this one," he said with a wave of his hand.

Rachel looked down. She'd forgotten that Oleander's talons had ripped open the front of her shirt already. She looked up in shock, drawing the buttonless shirt together protectively.

"My mark must be over your heart."

She continued to stare at him, speechless.

He leaned towards her with his hands on his knees. "Do you want to be claimed by another? Because that was exactly what would have happened if I hadn't arrived when I did."

"I don't under—"

He came even closer so she could feel his hot breath. "Yes you do, Rachel. You just don't want to see it. It is the story of your life. You hide yourself from the world, refusing to see it for the cesspit that it is. Always it must be butterflies and flowers. You of all people should know it is full of lies and loss. That is the reality that no amount of sports cars and flashy clothes can gloss over. When your time is up, nothing can buy you a single minute longer on this planet." His tone softened as he relaxed back onto his stool. "I know this, and so do you."

She continued to stare at him while he put the ink into his machine. The ink she knew would contain his own blood. Everything was true; she knew that now. "All this has been a contract for my soul," she said, more to herself.

He looked at her then, with his eyelids low, and didn't correct her. She swallowed hard.

"Tonight, I sign with my mark. Without it, you are carrion for the birds. Do you understand?"

Her eyes were filling with tears, but she nodded. The day had started so happy and full of promise. "Seb," she whispered. Everything she imagined for their future had gone in an instant.

Grigori pointed, indicating that she remove the shirt, with no further argument.

With her mind still reeling, she did as he asked—too numb to feel embarrassed.

He adjusted his machine and moved in closer. "The boy was a complication just hours before the deal was struck. Instead, it became your saving grace." His eyes flicked to hers. "Bra!"

She moved slowly, doing what he asked without argument. She was living the book she'd read only a few days ago. Everything was a nightmare. A tear ran down her cheek. "I trusted you," she said, reaching behind her back. The bra went loose, and she let it fall, dropping it on the floor next to her. Exposure was the furthest thing from her mind, and his, evidently.

His gun whirred and he leaned into her chest as if it was any other part of her body—always the consummate professional. A stray lock escaped his cap and covered the tear on his cheek. "In the words of Cobain, 'No one dies a virgin, life fucks us all,'" he said with a mirthless blast of breath. Then he got to work.

CHAPTER 23

Grigori worked silently, fixated on what he was doing. Soon, Rachel was oblivious to sitting there, topless. Tears tracked down her cheeks in wordless misery until she had to ask: "You know about the book?"

His eyes flicked to hers for the first time in ages. "Of course. There have always been prophets. Scrolls, parchments, books, they are always there, and many subjects find them. It is part of the process. Sacrifice only has worth when it comes freely given."

What he was saying simply blew her mind; how old all this was, how far-reaching, and what it meant. As a Christian, she was well aware of the prophets. "Dr Nicola Harding?" she said, finding that hard to believe.

"Of sorts. Why not? A modern-day prophet, sent by …" And he didn't bother to finish. Instead, his eyes flashed to hers as if he couldn't bring himself to say it. "The scales must be even. You must have free will."

It felt so incredible and yet it all made sense. What she didn't understand was how she could have seen something so vulnerable in him and yet he was this—this soulless creature—she didn't know what else to call him. "How is it free will when you tricked me? I thought I could trust you. I confided in you." She was openly crying now, not able to help herself.

His jaw clenched and she could see the anger building in him, but she didn't care. "Free choice would have been telling me you're a demon."

That was it. He slammed the gun he was holding into its cradle and came frighteningly close. The light from the lamp played in his eyes like flames. "Demon," he repeated, making her shrink back into the chair. "You would know it if you came face to face with a demon. It is a demon from which I have saved you. I am from the highest tier of angels ever created."

"And yet you chucked that all away, didn't you?" she shouted in his face. She was beyond angry now. Misery made her reckless. "You're no better than me. Can you honestly say if you knew you'd be living like this, you would have done what you did? And where is this lover you gave everything up for, eh? Best buds with Satan?" she ended up screaming into his face.

He looked at her as if she'd just backhanded him across the face and he was dealing with the shock of being struck.

It went on for a long moment, until she remembered to breathe and swallow at last. His eyes searched hers as if he would find his retort there. Instead, he slowly blinked and said very quietly, "No, he went back." Then he picked up his gun and roughly pushed her back by the shoulder to continue what he was doing.

Rachel allowed it, staring at him now, bewildered and confused. "What? He didn't come down to Earth with you?"

Grigori went on tattooing so long she thought she was never going to get her answer, until he said, eventually, "He did initially. We were among the earliest assignments among humans. We made plans. We wanted to be physical to have—"

"What humans have—a physical relationship," Rachel finished for him.

He nodded and then sighed. "When it came to it, he tried to talk me out of it, but I was stubborn. We argued. We had just twenty-four hours together and he left me to my fate." He held out his arms and tipped his head down, indicating his own tattoos. Just a blink of an eye in time for an angel, but long enough to leave his mark all over his body. A cruel, lifelong reminder.

Rachel watched him for some time after, seeing the sadness hanging over him like a wet cloak. It all made dreadful, weird sense. They had just been two lovers who'd seen a chance to be together and that person had let him down in the most tragic way possible. "Why didn't you go back too?"

The look he gave her then pierced through her like a knife. "My heart was black. There was no returning for me ... I knew this. Layke had never truly committed." He averted his eyes before she could see the hurt.

"So, you found a way to survive in the only way you knew how," Rachel said, more to herself.

He didn't look at her, but his jaw clenched again. "Save your pity," he said. "When you've existed eons, empathy has long left you."

She didn't believe him. He had been an angel once. The golden, glowing angel of her dream came to mind and she tried to imagine him like that. Surely he wouldn't have saved her from the others if he had no feeling at all? She decided to change tack and get some more information while he was this talkative. "If the scales have to be even and I'm supposed to be able to make an informed decision, what happened to the pages of the final chapter of the book on how to survive the tests?"

Grigori sat back on his stool to ease his back. "It is not blank, it's veiled. Those who want gratification in this world will not put in the effort to see it. If that is your path, then it will be revealed to you."

He smiled at her, but it held no real warmth. It was weird because, despite everything, she still felt like he was acting a part; that all this wasn't really him. Bitterness had simply made him this way.

Her eyes never left him. He worked purposely and professionally after that, as if she were any other regular client. A full hour and a half went by.

She was still living in a haze of disbelief, but her feelings of hurt and anger were very real. She was devastated, but strangely, it seemed he wasn't faring any better.

When she finally looked down at her chest, his mark wasn't that big; just the size of the back of her hand.

"It is done," he said, wheeling back a little on his stool. He appraised his handiwork and she could tell he saw only artwork, not a semi-naked woman in front of him. She guessed a gay angel wouldn't.

"What is it?" It was hard to tell upside down.

He reached over, grabbed a large hand-mirror and held it up in front of her. "It is my mark."

She looked at it in horror. It was a badass piece—Seb would approve, maybe on a bloke—a Hells Angel, or something. It was a Roman numeral X with a dry skull of a horned steer over the top of it and the whole thing was bang smack in the center of her chest over her heart.

Tears spilled down onto her cheeks and she closed her eyes for a moment. "Oh my god, what have I done?"

Rough hands yanked her around in her chair, so she was forced to look at Grigori in all his flaming anger. "This is what you agreed to from the beginning, Rachel. This is where your journey has brought you: to me!" he said, jabbing his thumb into his own chest. "This is what I am!" He covered the new tattoo with his palm and spoke a little more softly. "The contract is binding, and those who matter will know my mark instantly without even seeing it. You belong to me till death, but it is also a protection. Please see it as that. No angel—not even demons—will dare touch you now."

Tears were streaming down her face as she tried to hold in her sobs.

"You got what you wanted. Your life *has* changed, Rachel. You have many of your desires already."

They seemed only empty, shallow possessions now. How stupid could she have been? She was now sobbing, never taking her eyes from his. He was shouting at her and shaking her by the tops of her arms, but there was pain there. She knew it and he knew it and it made him angrier. He hated her for making him feel. He was fierce, but he was concealing something that ran deeply within himself. Rachel continued to sob into her hands. It felt like she was emptying every feeling and hurt she'd ever had, until she felt a nudge on her shoulder and he passed her clothes.

"Stand," he said, a lot more softly.

She did it mechanically and he rubbed some cream into the reddened skin. She'd stopped crying and felt the numb calm that always followed crying. However, even in this wrung-out state, she felt the moment was laden, like something had changed between them.

He was no longer reluctant to touch her. She must have stiffened because he said immediately, "Have no fear, Rachel. You're not my type." However, the sardonic look held no animosity. At another time, it may have even been funny. "One kiss and I would ruin you for other men."

Her cheeks blushed with embarrassment, but it did pique her interest as to what he meant. He chose that point to move away. At first, she thought he was arrogant, but then she remembered the feeling she'd had from the two angels that had kissed her earlier. It had been a heady, all-consuming experience and she didn't even know them.

"An angel's saliva holds drug-like properties. And because of our bond, mine would be the most addictive of all," he said, smiling ruefully. "A human partner would pale into insignificance after that." He narrowed his eyes and put his head at an angle as if studying her for her reaction. "And, besides, we have our boy to think about now."

It made her uneasy speaking about Seb—especially when he referred to them as together in taking him into account. She didn't like that. She didn't like that at all. Something told her to keep quiet about it though. She didn't want to give away how much Seb meant to her. She averted her eyes instead and busied herself putting on her bra and tying her shirt in the front to cover up that there were no buttons. Seb would go mad if he noticed. "What happens now?"

Grigori was now screwing bottle tops on and tidying up his workstation, just like any other day at a tattoo parlor. "Nothing. Life goes on exactly like before. Except now you have me behind you." He leaned back against the worktop and folded his arms. "Some kind of like it."

Rachel scowled that he was able to be so flippant, but he narrowed his eyes, changing the subject quickly. "You have three more sessions to bind the contract and then you will never see me unless you call."

"That's never going to happen." She didn't wait for a reply, slung her bag over her shoulder and walked towards the door. Then she turned and, with a final thought, said, "And that's it? Don't I get handed over to the devil or something?"

Grigori laughed and shook his head. "You pulled off a very clever maneuver last night, Rachel." He pointed a finger as if he was pretending to scold her. "But you offered up something more valuable—and interesting for me." He tipped his head. "So, thank you for that."

She frowned, confused, not following at all. "So, I'm off the hook, then?"

"In a manner of speaking, until your dying breath … yes."

Rachel studied him for a long moment after he finished speaking, hoping she would read honesty or compassion in those hardened eyes, but she could see nothing apart from an amused, cunning mind.

Sifting through what he'd said, she got the gist that the game had changed, he'd renegotiated the terms of the contract, and she was now free to do what she wanted, all the while she was alive.

His smile widened and so did her eyes. "You know what I'm thinking?"

He laughed again and waved her off with a hand. "Go! Enjoy your life, but be here next week." The smile fell from his face. "Don't make me have to come and get you."

Any anger she felt quickly gave way to real fear as his eyes swept over her in an anything-but-gay appraisal.

She snatched open the door and glared back at him. "In the book … who the hell are you?"

Grigori straightened up from leaning on the bench. "You know who I am, Rachel." And he went to move away.

"No I don't. At least have the decency to let me know who I'm dealing with?"

He looked sideways at her and was terrifying then—his height, perfect lean frame and muscled, sinewy arms. She could just imagine the huge wings, inky and black, from her dreams. "I am Xenon, Watcher of the North."

His eyes seemed dark and sorrowful, drawing any light from the room into them. It was then she realized he had no pride in what he did. She nodded once and left him.

· · ·

RACHEL HALTED IMMEDIATELY when she got outside. The chauffeur-driven car was waiting as usual at the pavement. Her car had gone.

The driver got out and held the rear door open for her to get in. She got a look at him for the first time. It was always the same guy, she realized, and he was insanely good-looking. Tall, around six feet, perfect physique in his uniform of black slacks and shirt. Then there was the perfectly groomed dark hair, tawny owl's eyes and winning smile. *"Fallen"* came out on a breath. "Where's my car?" she said, cautiously getting into the back seat.

The driver got in and looked at her in the rear-view mirror. "It will be at home in the morning."

He returned his attention to driving and pulled away, but she studied him when he'd finished speaking. He was far too good-looking and in shape to be any kind of cab driver, executive or otherwise. Come to think of it, now she looked more closely, the car looked more like a limousine than a cab. She was surprised she hadn't noticed before. She'd been too distracted or exhausted. "Are you one too?" she said, a little annoyed that someone had taken it upon themselves to move her car. This was starting to feel less like freedom and more like ownership.

He didn't speak, but looked at her in the rear-view mirror and nodded. The air left her in a rush and she swallowed, looking out of her window. She was shaking now and wanted to cry. There was no escape.

They were everywhere, just like Dr Harding said. It was all so crazy and unbelievable, but she knew it was true—all of it. The pain stung the center of her chest as a reminder. She needed to speak to her urgently. She needed to know where she stood now that she wore his stamp. She had no idea whether Grigori's explanation of the blank pages was true.

Maybe she'd never be able to read them now. With just three sessions left, she was running out of time.

She got out her phone and double-checked her number was in her contacts. She sent off a quick text just as the driver pulled up outside her house.

Nicola, it's Rachel. You have my number now, so you know it's me. Will ring you later. R

The driver opened her door and she got out just as her car pulled up. Another gorgeous man or whatever got out. He nodded at her once and got into the front passenger side of the car she'd just got out of. He was one of them, and now she was in the know, they were treating her like she was one of them, too. Her throat constricted a little more.

Just as she went to walk off, the driver called, "Wait!"

She turned and he gave her a business card through the window. "Whenever you need a car."

She took it slowly and met his gaze properly for the first time. They were the oddest shade of hazel she'd ever seen— more like a mustard yellow, just like an owl's.

She nodded and he pulled away. Her mind went over and over the weird evening's events as she walked up the path to the house. A huge weight of dread was sitting on her chest, one she couldn't shift. It felt like she'd sold her soul to the Devil. Yet Grigori had said he'd got her some sort of reprieve. She didn't get it and that worried her most of all. All she could do was wait for the catch.

CHAPTER 24

Seb was a wonderful surprise in her bed when she got there. It was late and he was fast asleep in rumpled sheets with the duvet pushed down to his waist. His kissable, boyish face was to the side, and his recently showered hair looked more messed up than usual.

Rachel stood over him for a full minute, smiling, drinking him in. Without doubt, he was the best thing to have happened to her since her nan died.

Before he stirred and was weirded out by her watching him sleep, she seized the chance to get out of the ripped shirt before he saw it. A little frantic, she stuffed it behind her bedside cabinet temporarily. She'd whisk it away on bin day.

After a quick shower, she slid between the sheets next to him and was gratified when he instinctively folded himself around her. Her chest ached and not just because of the wound the tattoo made there, but because of the unforgivable trouble she'd brought onto the people she loved. It hurt with a fresh weight of loss, like she was mourning all over again. Except this time, it was for everything light and good in her life. She was Eve, having eaten from the Tree of

Knowledge tonight, damning Adam and everyone else to the consequences. If only she'd remained innocent of all this. Dr Harding sure had spoken the truth about the two drinks.

The nightmares came as soon as she closed her eyes—thick, fast, and in vivid color. They were full of the fear, screams and terrified faces of other lost souls floating around in the black. She was with them, crying and not able to control which way she went. They were all buffeted and pushed this way and that, terrifyingly out of control. She woke a couple of times to Seb's worried face looking down on her, dabbing her face with a cold flannel. "Sorry, Seb. Sorry … I'm so sorry," she said, over and over.

"Hey! Don't worry. You're sick … Just sleep. I've got you," he said, smiling and soothing her. "You're fine and I'm fine."

In the morning, she awoke with a start. A strange man was feeling her head and tapping her chest.

"It's OK, Rach. He's a doctor."

It took her a moment to take in Seb's disheveled appearance and see the stethoscope around the man's neck to catch up with what he'd just said. "I'm ill," she said. It came out a barely audible whisper.

"You certainly are," the young, well-spoken doctor said, barely older than her. "A nasty bug by the sounds of it."

He stood, tore off what looked like a prescription and gave it to Seb. "See that she has plenty of fluids." He gave her one last smile and left with, "I'll see myself out."

Seb perched on the edge of the bed and pushed the hair out of her eyes.

She tried to swallow but had very little spit and her mouth tasted of metal. "I must look awful," she croaked.

He passed her a glass of water. "Drink! You still look beautiful. Doc said you'll feel better in about twenty-four hours, once I get some of these down you," he said, waving the prescription.

Her hand went instinctively to her chest.

Seb raised a brow. "Total badass, Rach. Had you down for hearts and flowers. Impressed." He nodded in appreciation.

She couldn't help the scowl that appeared on her face. She hated the tattoo and didn't want him to like it either. Grigori's ownership of her would now be a wedge between them because there was no way she wanted Seb involved in any of this.

She remembered the text she'd sent just before she got home last night. She must speak to Dr Nicola Harding.

Then she noticed the worry on Seb's face and didn't want to hurt him. She gave him her brightest smile. "I'll be fine … you must have loads more important things to do than nursing me."

He pulled her up into a hug to his chest. "You were delirious, shouting some crazy things in your sleep. Scared the shit out of me."

Rachel put her hand under his t-shirt and felt the smooth skin underneath. He was probably right about the delirium, but not because of some virus. It was the high concentration of Grigori's blood pumped into her with the ink. Her body reacted to it until it gave up the fight and accepted the invasion. That scared the shit out of her too. She'd been invaded, conquered and was now just owned. Misery washed over her with a wave of exhaustion. "You must have things to do," she mumbled into his chest.

He pulled apart to look down at her. "Are you trying to get rid of me?" he said, half smiling, half serious.

"No … I mean, I just want to sleep … you know, with some space," she said, patting the bed next to her and pulling a pained face.

He laughed in that beautiful, easygoing way of his and leaned down and kissed her. "I'm only winding you up. Of course, you want to sleep. I'll pick up your pills and head over to Jack's for practice. Text me if you need me," he said, standing and already wandering over towards the door. "Seriously, though … badass!" He grinned, pointing like he was still amazed and left her in a mixture of emotions. He was so kind, looking after her and giving her space when she needed it. Everything felt like such a betrayal. He was lovely and caring and she had all this stuff going on he knew nothing about, putting him and Lynn in real danger.

She waited to hear the slam of the front door and leaned down and grabbed her phone from her bag that Seb had left thoughtfully next to the bed.

Her head swam and she had to swallow a few times so as not to be sick. Her hands shook violently as she tapped her contact list for Nicola's number. After finding it under H, she hit call. It rang four times, then a female voice said, "Hello?" It sounded silky and warm and not at all old, which was what she was expecting. "Hello," the woman repeated. "It's OK, it's safe to talk."

"Hi," Rachel said eventually, but her voice sounded cracked and raspy. "You might remember me. My name is Rachel. You messaged me on Facebook."

"Yes, Rachel. Of course, … Hi, please call me Nicola. I've been praying you'd call."

The reference to prayer and the kindness and warmth of Nicola Harding's voice made her burst into tears. She just couldn't hold them back and sobbed brokenheartedly into the phone.

"Oh, Rachel, please. Just tell me what's happened?"

The more she cared, the more it seemed to turn up the outpouring of emotion. "It's too late … everything is too late," she wailed. "I'm marked and the people I love aren't safe."

"Shh," Nicola said. "It's never too late. Do you hear me, Rachel? It's never too late. Please stop crying. You did the right thing in calling me. Listen, can we meet? It can be somewhere neutral of your choosing—a coffee shop, maybe? I'm in London, so I can travel to you."

Suddenly, even getting out of bed seemed an insurmountable problem. "Sorry, Nicola, I've been very ill in the night. I don't think I'm able to get out of bed today."

Nicola said a very un-Christian-like, "Shit!" at the other end of the phone. "I'm sorry, Rachel. I'm not angry at you. It's the bloody ink they use. It will pass within twenty-four hours when your body adjusts to it. Can you do tomorrow, do you think?"

Even though the next day was Monday, Rachel agreed. She doubted she'd be a hundred per cent fit to work and this seemed far more important. Although she had doubts, she'd be well enough even by then. She felt as weak as tissue paper. Whatever it was he used this time had really knocked her sideways. She couldn't remember ever feeling this ill or having to ring in sick, for that matter.

Nicola knew the town she lived in from her Facebook profile—something she needed to rectify. Turns out, it wasn't too far for her to travel to and from London by train. "Text me a coffee shop in town and I'll meet you there at 1 p.m. tomorrow. And please don't worry, Rachel. I won't lie and say that you are not in trouble, but it's not something we can't get you through, OK?"

Rachel nodded and sniffed as if Nicola could see her down the phone. She seemed so strong and convincing that she did feel a little better.

"Are you OK with all that, Rachel?"

"Yes," she said. "See you tomorrow." Then she ended the call. The feelings of fear and anxiety it invoked gave her an overwhelming urge to be sick. She leaped out of bed and just made it to the bathroom in time. She spewed every last bit of liquid from her stomach and had to hold onto the doorposts on the way back.

Easing herself back under the quilt, she lay violently shivering. She was wretched. Her body and her whole world felt out of control. So far, the new life that was supposed to give her independence and courage felt very hollow. All she'd ended up with were a few trinkets. The only truly good thing that had happened was Seb, and she might have thrown him under the bus. Now she was just pulled and pushed by a wind, determined to send her over a sheer drop—into a chasm that would take her straight down to Hell.

Lynn popped in later to see how she was. She sat on the bed and caught her up with chitchat and gossip from the pub. She checked out her new tattoo and saw it fine this time, if not a little quizzically.

Saying, "The artwork is great," didn't exactly impart that she liked it. *Who was she kidding?* Even she didn't like it.

Rachel was relieved when Lynn patted her hand and said she was going off for a bath.

Seb came home some time later and, after checking whether she needed anything, offered to sleep in his own bed. She didn't want to come across as needy, but her emotions were so close to the surface lately and tears brimmed in her eyes.

Seb noticed immediately and came and sat on her bed. "Hey, are you OK? Do you want me to call the doctor again?" he said, picking up her hand.

She shook her head. "Can you sleep here tonight?" It was out before she could check herself.

For a moment, he looked away as if he wasn't sure, and she could have bitten off her own tongue. It was too much too soon, of course it was. Then he searched her eyes for the briefest moment until his whole demeanor softened. "Course I can. Let me change those sheets first, you've been in them all day."

Rachel had never known Seb change his own sheets, let alone hers. He disappeared to the airing cupboard in the hall and she got out of bed a little light-headedly.

After much struggling and laughter, they managed to do it together. When they both got back into cool, sweet-smelling bedding, she relaxed. "I never knew you knew how," she said, when he pulled her to lie on his chest.

He kissed the top of her head. "I'm full of surprises."

She remembered he'd been raised by four sisters. No wonder he was easy around women. "Can you cook a mean casserole too?" She looked up and he mock scowled at her, making her giggle. She snuggled into him and her heart swelled. She liked him in her bed; it felt like he was the good guy protecting her from all the demons. She shivered at how close to the truth that actually was. Except he stood no chance and that terrified her. Somehow, she needed to find a way of protecting them all. Right then, the only person capable was Grigori, and he was the one who'd gotten them into this in the first place.

RACHEL FELT a lot better the next day, but she still had the shakes and tremors in her hands and her head felt light at times. More precisely, she felt worse every time she thought of her tattoo, Angel's Ink, or Grigori; it was really strange.

Seb had managed to get a really dossy job at a music shop that didn't open till 10. It was probably the only job he was ever likely to keep. She assured him she was OK, and he left for work at around 9.55. It meant he would be late, but Seb hadn't been on time for anything in his life. Then she phoned work and a very sympathetic Mabel made her feel guilty even though she was genuinely unwell. She guessed it was because she was meeting Nicola and there was always a risk she'd be seen.

It couldn't be helped. This was way bigger than her job. Lives were at stake.

Lynn was in bed, so she didn't want to risk waking her and getting the inquisition. So, she made sure she got ready slowly and quietly. She was still wobbly anyway.

At 12.30, wearing just a light jacket, loose top and jeans, she got into the car to make the short journey to Carol's bakery in town that had a seated area for coffee. It was also the furthest one she could think of from work, and was nestled down a cobbled street, in the older part of town, between a trinket shop and a dry cleaner. She would have preferred to walk. Not just because her car might be spotted by anyone going to the library, but because Nicola might judge it as a symbol of her sellout to the Devil, which, of course, it was. Carol's had a small parking area at the back in which, after waiting for one person to vacate, she pulled into a rare parking space.

Rachel was a bag of nerves when she clicked the key fob to lock her car. Her hands were shaking so badly she could barely close the zip to her bag to put her keys away.

She straightened her jacket, ran a hand through her hair to look presentable, and walked in.

Nicola was easy to spot. She was a very pretty, slim woman in her thirties, with auburn mid-length hair, worn loose and wavy to just past the shoulders of her tan leather jacket. She was the only person seated on her own under the age of sixty.

She immediately smiled when she saw Rachel and stood up to greet her.

"Dr Harding?" Rachel said.

"Nicola, please. I got you a coffee. I hope a flat white is OK?"

"That's great, thanks," Rachel said, genuinely grateful for not having to risk carrying a hot drink and spilling it everywhere with her shaky hands.

They both sat. "It's so nice to finally meet you," Nicola said, smiling at her with real warmth. She was a real redhead with pale skin and a rich spattering of freckles. Her strawberry brows were perfectly arched and her mouth the color of an antique rose. In fact, she looked perfect in her rust rollneck, checked skirt and long brown boots, which Rachel took in quickly as she hung her jacket on the back of the chair.

Rachel wasn't sure what she was expecting; maybe someone older, oozing goodness like she'd expect from an emissary of God. It was a silly assumption, she knew. She just seemed calm and friendly, which was exactly what she needed when she felt like she was going out of her mind. "I'm sorry I didn't contact you sooner, it's just … I couldn't—"

"Bring yourself to believe it?" Nicola finished for her. "It's perfectly natural. The important thing is that you're here now." She stirred her coffee and said, "Why don't you just start from the beginning."

Rachel hadn't touched her drink for fear of giving away her shakes, so she took a deep breath and recounted the whole thing, from losing her nan to the lover in her bed she was terrified of hurting.

Nicola listened without interrupting, nodding and smiling encouragement throughout.

"And isn't it too late to do anything, anyway?" Rachel said. "The last chapter in your book was blank."

Nicola let out a long sigh and played with her spoon in the froth left in her cup. "A few I've helped have said that. It's some sort of clause the Grigori put in when allowing the book. It's to do with free will. They will only allow those directly opposed to them to see it. When you become sure in your heart that you want to fight this, then I think it will become visible to you. So, I guess the question you need to ask yourself is, how much do you want out of all this? My power to help you is limited to that."

Rachel listened closely. It made a weird kind of sense. She could just imagine it being said by Grigori in his strong accent: *The scales have to be equal, Rachel.* The enormity of it all was overwhelming. She sipped her coffee, holding it with both hands. They still shook, but her throat was so dry she had to drink.

Nicola watched her silently until she finally said, "It happened to me too, you know."

Rachel's eyes shot to hers. "Really? But you ... you're free."

Nicola angled her body away from onlookers and pulled down the neck of her top. There, Rachel could clearly see a partial solar eclipse held in vines like a crystal ball. It was a stunning piece—one to even rival Grigori. "Whose mark is that?" she asked, immediately thinking of the heady kisses she'd shared with the two angels.

"His name is Raephe," Nicola said quietly, letting the neck of her top go and picking at small pieces off her paper napkin and discarding them.

It wasn't the angry or defiant reply she was expecting, more like when someone spoke of a relationship that hadn't worked out, where feelings still ran very deep.

"But you got away. So that's good for me, right?" Rachel felt uneasy about Nicola's demeanor when she talked about her Watcher. "I think I met him recently," she said, remembering exactly the eyes and body any woman could get lost with. "I know it sounds weird, but Grigori isn't like him. He's ... I dunno ... he doesn't seem bad." And he didn't. When she'd had time to think about it, even after their last meeting, it felt like he was coming down hard on her for her own good.

Nicola straightened in her chair as if her words were the slap she needed. "First of all, Grigori is a collective term for the top tier of angels. Second, don't waste your sympathy on him. He's been alive for thousands of years—maybe millions. He knows exactly how to gain the trust of a young, impressionable girl like you. He'll make you his slave so you can't live without him."

"Like you!" Nicola had started to pique her anger. She didn't need to be patronized, she needed advice. Dr Nicola Harding wasn't coming across that professionally at the moment. Far from it; she was making her feel uncomfortable, like she wanted to leave.

Rachel went to stand, but Nicola grabbed her wrist fast. "Whatever you think of me, know this: you can never run, you can't hide. Look at you." Her eyes dropped to Rachel's shaking hands. "You can't control it, can you?"

"It's nothing. I was ill after the last session."

"You're becoming addicted, Rachel … Soon you'll be begging him for more tattoos. And when he can no longer give you that, you'll be in his bed for what little of him you can get, like some crack whore. All you'll be is a minion—an empty shell—who can think of nothing else but getting her next fix of Angel. Because, believe me, once you've been there, no one else will do, Rachel. Nothing even comes close."

Rachel stared at her for a full minute in a tempest of hurt and pity and, mostly, anger, until she snatched her wrist out of her grip. "I need to leave." This wasn't at all what she was expecting. Probably more of a female Indiana Jones-type who'd lead her through a series of clues to help her escape. Not some psycho who was no better off than she was. "You're as hooked as me," she said, not hiding the accusation in her voice.

Nicola slowly stood, looking as awful as she felt. "Look, I'm sorry, I've handled this badly. I don't mean to scare you. Please listen before you get too involved with your Grigori … which one is it?"

Her first instinct was to go, but she'd made her curious. "Xenon."

Nicola repeated it while she thought hard. "He's the Watcher of the North." Then she looked at her with even more concern than she did before. "I know of him. He's notoriously ruthless, Rachel. You are in a very dangerous position right now."

Something in Rachel snapped at that point, probably due to information overload. "Well, you seem far from OK. I'm not being funny, but I came here to get answers and have learned absolutely nothing about how to get out of all this."

Instead of getting angry, Nicola's face softened. She put out a hand and squeezed her shoulder. "That's because it's different for everyone. You need to decide to leave Xenon by any means necessary and read the chapter that will, hopefully, become visible for you."

Rachel rolled her eyes. She'd heard enough and put her bag over her shoulder to leave. "Really? That's it? You haven't even told me how you did it?" She huffed, turned and walked away.

"That's because I didn't," she called after her.

Rachel froze and turned back, horrified. "You're still? …"

"Trapped."

$\mathcal{R}$achel frowned and walked slowly back to Nicola. It made no sense. "But you wrote the book. You've helped loads of people."

Nicola nodded along with everything she said. "And I do."

Rachel recoiled in horror. The woman's life must be miserable. She lived those warnings of addiction every day in order to help people.

"The only way I can do what I do is by being so close to it. Call it atonement," she said with a weak smile. "It's my price for balancing the scales. Raephe gives me distance but not freedom. Then maybe ... you know, one day, when my time comes—"

"He might free you from your contract," Rachel finished for her. She was horror-struck at her predicament, but mostly because this was supposedly the one person who had it all figured out, and her life must be a living hell. It made her heart plummet in despair, because if this woman hadn't figured anything out better for herself, what hope was there for her? "And Raephe ... he allows what you do?"

A tear escaped down Nicola's cheek. "They're all for

scales and fairness—plus he finds it mildly amusing. He has such a low opinion of human nature that he assumes he can win everyone around in the end."

"Even you?"

Nicola nodded. "You see, they've lived so long, it's just a game to them." Her eyes were dewy with unshed tears. "I'm merely an interesting distraction."

Rachel remembered Grigori saying something very similar to her. It forced her to sit back down heavily into her chair, the last of her energy knocked right out of her.

Nicola slowly sat back down opposite her. "I'm sorry. Are you OK?" There was genuine concern in her eyes. "Your redemption and chance of escape will be different to mine. Everyone's is."

"Has anyone managed to ... you know, escape?"

Nicola looked less sure. "I think so."

"You think so?" Rachel repeated, raising her voice. *This just got better and better.*

Nicola put out her hands to calm her down. "That's because those who succeed just seem to disappear."

Rachel just stared at her. "Doesn't that mean that they died, or something. Or that one—Abad-something ... has taken them?"

"Abaddon. Yes, and that could have happened. What I have started to believe is that they may have had their memories wiped after, Rachel. Because no one can be allowed to remember all this, it must be veiled to you. It doesn't mean once saved, always saved. You're simply a fish thrown back into the pond. In fact, you've probably just doubled your value if you managed something like that."

Rachel stared at her a moment, taking it all in. "So, if it can be done, why haven't you?"

Nicola nodded with a deep sigh. "That's a good question." Then she shrugged. "It's hard to explain ... I've come to think of it as my purpose in the world. Like I've been left here with Raephe for a reason. You see, Abaddon has never come for me."

She wasn't making much sense. As if she didn't fully understand it herself—*how could she?* It was bigger than them all.

Grigori had spoken of modern-day prophets. It seemed almost cruel that Nicola didn't even recognize it in herself and nobody had ever told her. The information only seemed to set Grigori apart again. "Grigori—I mean Xenon—is different, though, Nicola. I don't know how to explain it, but he has tried to put me off the whole way. Got me to find out every piece of information as if he didn't want to trap me."

Nicola was already shaking her head. "It seems like that, I know. All it does is up your price. He knows that the more informed and purer-spirited you are, the greater the sacrifice and therefore the more expensive you become. Think about it, Rachel, if you were already a witch, who knows all about this stuff, doing terribly wicked things, the Devil already has you for nothing. If you're a clean-living, kind-hearted girl and you sacrifice everything you love in this world and all that's good, even when you know all the facts, then you turn yourself into something the Devil would want very badly. Abaddon, the broker, knows this, and—rest assured—Xenon knows it too. It makes you more attractive when he takes your soul—and your body too."

Rachel was now shaking her head. "It can't be true, though, because I'm not pure." Nicola couldn't be right. "I abandoned my faith and slept with my boyfriend a few nights ago. And, anyway, I'm almost positive that Xenon is gay."

Nicola simply smiled at her sadly, which just made her want to scream. "All you've done is upped the ante. Angels aren't anything, Rachel. They take on any form they choose when they're on Earth, mainly so they don't scare the shit out of us. They had no physical form before that. That's why their coming here causing so much trouble is such an abomination to Him," she said, looking upwards.

"No sex in heaven," Rachel said, repeating the words Grigori had once said to her.

Nicola heard and nodded along with her. "Sex is a major reason they all fell in the first place. And if you're right, and Xenon truly isn't interested in you in that way, I'm damned sure I'd be thinking along the lines of what the hell he does want, because if he's struck a deal with Abaddon already, you don't have long."

Rachel was left staring at Nicola, terrified. Everything she was saying fitted perfectly with what she already knew, but she still had no answers. Surely there was nothing left in her miserable life that he could want. "So, tell me about Abaddon then. Who is he?"

Nicola slouched back into her chair as if the mere thought of him exhausted her. "He's the most dangerous of all The Fallen. He's the go-between for all the imprisoned in Tartarus. He brokers for their time out with the souls they bring him, with the demons and Satan himself. They give him prospects they've already marked, and Abaddon decides their worth. The best are taken to Satan. Some go right away, others he keeps around till death. But you don't want that at any cost."

"Why? ... You seem OK."

"Raephe has bartered to keep me with him for my purpose here, but for most, they might have a life full of material things, they might even be huge stars and insanely rich, but it also means working for Abaddon, only to be Satan's toy at the end of it. And, rest assured, Rachel, there is no empathy in Abaddon. His heart is granite."

By the time Nicola had finished speaking, she felt hopeless. On top of how ill she felt, all she wanted to do was sleep. She had no more idea of what to do now than when she came. Her eyes brimmed with tears when she looked back at Nicola. "You haven't helped me at all. I have no idea what I'm doing, what he wants, or what's going to happen. I have my fourth appointment on Saturday. What happens then?"

"You'll know who owns you from the deal Xenon has struck."

To her credit, Nicola didn't look any happier than she did when she left her. She was in her own world of misery. Even though she tried to reason that it was all too fantastic on her drive home, with her heart in the pit of her stomach, she knew it to be true.

SUFFERING from information overload and with her sickness coming back with vengeance, Rachel went straight to bed when she got home. It was a dead, dreamless sleep that lasted hours. When she finally awoke, she felt quite a bit better. Her headache had gone, her temperature seemed fine and she only had slight tremors in her hands.

Seb came and checked on her and looked relieved that she was awake. He even made her a cup of tea, which made her giggle. "Don't tell anyone," he said. "I have a 'bad boy' reputation to keep up."

She felt so lucky to have him. He was gorgeous, sexy and thoughtful. Who knew that he had all that going for him all along? He even kissed her when she knew she looked like hell. He perched on the bed and updated her on all the gossip on who was getting off with who and their antics in the band. She could watch him talk all day. Every moment of closeness was precious and savored with the weird detachment of knowing she could be cruelly taken away at any time. *How did she manage to land him?*

The thought that just being with him was putting him in danger brought a lump to her throat.

"Hey, you OK?" he asked, stroking the side of her face.

She nodded, trying to give him her best smile.

"I'm not boring you, am I?" he said, with an adorably insecure expression.

She laughed and cupped his cheek in her hand. "Never."

Seb instantly brightened. "Listen, do you think you'll be well enough by tomorrow night to come out? We've been asked to support 'Black and White Town' at the Roxy."

Rachel had never heard of the band, but there weren't that many she had, so she shrugged. "OK. Are they any good?"

It was Seb's turn to laugh. "Yes, they're good, but they're a little heavier than us. They're kind of in the next league, so it'll be great exposure."

She bobbed her head. "OK then."

Seb eventually ended up in bed without fully undressing until hunger forced them up and he dialed for a pizza. Lynn came home just as it arrived, and it was like old times; all three of them sitting cross-legged on her bed, making a mess, telling old stories and laughing.

Every now and then, she would go quiet and just watch their happy faces. It reminded her of a time when everything felt warm and safe. Whatever happened, these people were her family and she'd sacrifice anything to protect them.

By the time they'd guzzled their Coke and finished off the chocolate bars that were ordered with their pizza, it was late. Lynn kissed her cheek. "Night, babe," she said, waggling her eyebrows and giggling at the two of them as she closed the door.

It made Rachel laugh. She guessed it did take some getting used to, them being together after all this time—although neither of them had mentioned whether they were actually dating. Seb piled all the packaging and empty glasses near the door to take down later and then just stood and looked at her.

"What?" she said, seeing the weird expression on his face.

He frowned and scratched his head, but he didn't look unhappy. Just a little baffled. "I'm kind of in new territory here."

"How?" she said, turning in bed to face him squarely.

He walked over and pulled her closer, threading his fingers through her hair. She looked up at him from his abdomen.

"I've never seen anyone I've been living with before."

It did sound the wrong way around.

He laughed and shook his head. "It's weird. I get to this point in the day and I don't know whether to go back to my room or stay here. I don't know if it would hurt your feelings if I left or be presumptuous if I stayed." He laughed as if he was genuinely analyzing his feelings.

Rachel gazed up at him, understanding perfectly. "Well, I can't speak for any other evening, but I have no intention of going to work tomorrow, so I think it would be beneficial to my recovery if you stayed."

He laughed and his eyes softened as he ran a thumb over her cheek. "Move over then, bed hog."

She laughed and scooted over, pushing her legs under the covers. It was strange territory with them already sharing a house together, but surely it meant something that they'd barely been apart since they first slept together.

Seb turned off the overhead light, whipped off his clothes, and joined her. "Too many clothes, Rachel," he said, laughing into a kiss, already pulling the hem up on her nightshirt.

They shared a deep, probing kiss, as if they'd been starved of it all day. It built quickly and became all-consuming, and before she knew it, he was inside her again.

She accepted him gladly, gripping his back and biting his neck. He smelled of pure Seb. She sighed and moved with him until the feeling of togetherness culminated in a euphoria that permeated her whole body, and the two of them were left slick with sweat, breathing heavily, in a tangle of limbs.

That night, she allowed herself to just be with him and fell asleep with her head on his chest. The warmth of his skin, his smell on every part of her and his gentle breaths in her hair sent her into the deepest, most contented sleep in living memory. Her dreams were a bubble that protected them both. Beyond that, there was always darkness where she knew that danger lurked, waiting.

The time for work came and went the next day. Now, it felt of little importance, as if her whole life were on borrowed time. Like someone with a terminal illness, she wanted to cram as much of the good stuff in as possible, before it was too late. Work was very definitely at the back of the queue.

That day, she felt almost back to her old self, just a few tremors in her hands that were easy to hide. She spent the day with Seb, bathing together and making a dreadful mess of the bathroom, cooking and doing the same in the kitchen, until Lynn had to scold them for acting like a pair of kids. "I'm not being funny, you two, but this shithole better be cleared up before any of you go out, or I'm going to blow my top!"

They both found it funny coming from Lynn, but promised they would.

Soon, it was time to get ready. Seb looked unbelievably hot. Dressed in his trademark black ripped jeans and band t-shirt, his hair was loose and barely dry around his face and he looked infinitely kissable. He was going earlier for sound checks. "Don't look too hot," he said, squeezing her butt before he went to go. "I can't fight all the men off from the stage."

She giggled and waved him off at the door. Lynn came flying in soon after in a whirlwind of activity so they could leave together at 7.30 p.m.

They totally looked the part when they left ten minutes late. Both had gone for skinny jeans, a long t-shirt, and boots. Lynn's were over the knee and Rachel wore her new pixie boots. With her black leather jacket slung over her shoulder, they both hopped into her little red sports car and sped off towards the next town, twenty-five minutes away, where Seb's band was playing.

"You and Seb look good together," Lynn said, turning her head to her from the passenger seat.

"Why, you surprised?" Rachel answered, already beginning to prickle.

"No, Rachel, god, you're so touchy lately. I was just saying it's nice to see, that's all."

She felt instantly guilty. She guessed she was just dealing with a lot. They were quiet for a few moments. The radio was on in the background, barely loud enough to cover the purr of the engine. The indicator blinked at the next set of lights.

"So, has he mentioned being exclusive yet?" Lynn said.

Rachel frowned slightly, not knowing how to answer that. She hadn't thought about it before.

"You're all over each other, I don't think he's slept in his own bed since Cinderella's," Lynn said, staring straight out of the windscreen.

Rachel turned to look at her to see if she was trying to wind her up and looked out front again when she appeared to be serious. "No, not exactly … I just kind of assumed … well, haven't thought, really." It was such early days yet. She'd had a lot going on in her own life, but even if she hadn't, she doubted whether she would have brought it up yet. She hadn't felt the need. Seb had been so attentive. She hated to admit it, but Lynn did have a valid point.

Lynn looked at her, then out the passenger window. She felt guilty again. Lynn wasn't saying what she really thought for fear of offending her, and it was her fault. "Please say what you want to say, Lynn." Her heart was beating fast, dreading what it was.

Lynn must have read the fear in her expression because she shook her head and smiled. "Relax, Rach. Just be careful, that's all. This is Seb, remember? The babe magnet we know and love, that has girls calling him to do his ironing."

Rachel tried to keep a straight face but couldn't at the goofy look on Lynn's face. Plus, she was so right. "So, you think I should have the 'exclusive' conversation with him?"

Lynn sighed and then shrugged. "Or, you could just go with it for as long as it lasts." Her expression was apologetic. "He *is* a wonderful, warm, attentive guy … with *everyone*," she emphasized. "He can't help himself."

Rachel understood. She was effectively saying that the conversation could make him run for the hills and make everything between them weird. There was also all the Grigori crap going on, which would probably make any such conversation obsolete anyway. "Point taken."

Lynn smiled in relief and pinched her leg. "Welcome to the world of dating, sweetheart."

Rachel smiled weakly, beginning to realize what a minefield it was. "Where's Colin?" she said.

"Where I want him."

They both laughed. "No, he's working tonight," she said, more seriously. "I'll see him tomorrow."

Rachel envied her friend's confidence in everything. It was why men loved her—why Colin doted on her. They all instinctively knew she didn't need anyone; that they were privileged to spend time with her. She was amazing like that.

She turned the music up and they drove in companionable silence after that.

It was such moments of inactivity that the enormity of what was happening to her sank in. Otherwise, she loved her newfound confidence and life. She even toyed with seeing how it went and taking this new life for everything she could get, but deep down, she knew she would be a good girl who would fight for all that was right. That meant she had to let something go from this life. And soon.

They reached the town center and the crowded streets and lights from the shops and office blocks moved slowly past her steamed-up window. A feeling of absolute terror constricted her throat. It must have been painted onto her face because Lynn asked if she'd forgotten something. She swallowed, shook her head and turned up the radio. "No, it's OK." Then she put it all to the back of her mind. Tonight, she'd give herself a night off. Tonight, she was going to be the new her. *What could happen in one night?*

THE CONCERT WAS BRILLIANT. It was big and in an old theatre that doubled as a dance venue when live bands weren't playing. It was dark and sweaty, with a bar up one end and a sloping floor all the way down to the stage, all the seating taken out.

Lynn phoned Colin from the foyer before they went in and a bouncer whizzed them down to the wing on the right of the stage. There were definite advantages to knowing the band.

Rachel got to see that Seb and his band were very good—like, wider appeal good. Her heart fluttered when he winked at her a few times. She jumped up and down with Lynn and the rest of the crowd and sang along to the choruses she knew. From her vantage point, she could see that the main act's fans were a bit more Metal than theirs, so Seb's band played their heavier stuff—along with a few covers the crowd would know.

The headliner came on at nine, and they listened to a couple of songs. Seb came and found them and asked what they wanted to do. "Where is everyone?" Lynn shouted over the noise.

"They're over the road. You can stay or come with us. Jack knows this bar over there," he said, pointing.

Rachel looked at Lynn, who shrugged. "I don't really know this band," Rachel said, already preferring to go but not wanting to ruin it for Lynn.

Lynn made up her mind and nodded. "Come on, then." The three of them wended their way through the crowd and outside into the crisp night air.

Rachel could see the place he meant. It was not even a five-minute walk, which had the added bonus that they didn't need to move their cars.

In the after-gig high, the rest of their party let loose in the bar, all chatting shop about riffs, chord changes and missed notes. A shedload of drinks were consumed. There was no way they'd leave the van filled with equipment overnight, so Jules and Rachel were the only ones who didn't drink.

Rachel quite enjoyed watching Seb and Lynn verbally spar while drunk. It was an education and very comical.

"Do you remember when I walked in on you at Samantha King's sixteenth birthday party with those two six formers on everyone's coats?" Lynn said, doubling over with laughter.

Half laughing and without missing a beat, Seb shot back. "Do you remember the threesome you had two months ago with the two male dancers from Vader's?" His eyebrows were up, trying not to laugh, and Lynn hit him hard in the chest.

"Where was I?"

They both turned their heads and said, "Asleep," at the same time.

God, she really had been totally clueless.

They continued on with their banter, which gave Rachel the opportunity to observe their rowdy, happy group. The reality of her situation threatened to crash the party a couple of times, but she forced it out. *One night,* she reminded herself.

Jules had had enough by eleven. He leaned into Seb, but she heard what he said. "I'm driving back so I can drink."

Seb nodded. "Where?"

"We'll meet you at the Rising Sun."

Seb explained to everyone what was happening and she agreed to drive back too. They settled the bill and the three of them were left to dawdle their way back to the car park behind the Roxy, with Seb and Lynn continuing on with their drunken arguing.

Rachel couldn't help noticing how quiet the street had got. It seemed like no one was around, particularly the closer they got to the Roxy. It was bustling and alive earlier, but now it felt lonely and isolated. The car park that was previously packed only had a handful of cars left in it. The band's van had gone, leaving her little red car all on its own. A group of hoodies on bikes huddled at the base of one of the few working streetlights, haggling over something between them.

Rachel felt immediately nervous. Seb seemed to straighten up and took her hand. Lynn went quieter, too. It was amazing how a happy evening could nosedive so quickly into serious territory.

A youth noticed them and elbowed one of the others. They all turned around to look. One got off his bike and leaned it against a wall. Rachel could have kicked herself for not parking somewhere else. Even the multistory would have been busier at this time. It just didn't occur to her as she'd parked right next to the band. Now, of course, its protection was gone, and her little red car looked exposed and conspicuous.

"Nice car!" one of the boys shouted.

She went to turn towards the voice, but Seb gave her a hard nudge. "Get in!"

Feeling his nerves made her heart pound and she went to the other side of the car.

"Who you looking at, goth boy?"

Despite being in black, there was no way Seb could be described as goth. It was ridiculous. Rachel hovered too long, watching from the driver's side, finally making Seb shout, "Get in!"

He threw the passenger seat forward so Lynn could clamber into the back, but it left him standing outside the longest.

"Oh no," Rachel said, watching the tallest of the boys stride over. "What d'you say?"

Seb could do nothing else but stand his ground. It was Rachel's turn to shout, "Get in!" But it was too late.

The boy bumped aggressively into Seb's chest while the others caught up and swarmed around them.

Bile came up into Rachel's mouth at the turn of events. "What shall we do?" she said to Lynn, glued to the scene too. She couldn't stand it a moment longer, and with a "Sod this," she opened the car door and got back out.

It was, of course, the totally wrong thing to do. Seb took his eye off them to say, "Get back in!" and one of them shoved him.

"Hey, look who's coming out to play."

"Goth boy and wonder girl," another said, making them all laugh.

"Look, we just want to go. We don't want any trouble," Rachel said.

The tall one grinned. "Whose car? Bit posh for you, innit?"

Rachel ignored the question and called to Seb across the roof, "Come on, Seb," in the calmest voice she could manage.

Seb went to turn, and she thought they might just escape by the tips of their fingernails when one of them shoved Seb in the back, so he stepped into the tall, aggressive one. He didn't wait for explanations and promptly pushed Seb back hard in the chest, drew back and punched him with all his weight in the jaw.

Seb went down on the floor. Hard. They descended on him like a pack of hungry wolves and Rachel screamed, running around to try to stop them. They kicked him in the back and chest, again and again. One even got him in the head. Rachel's shrieked appeals to stop were lost in the jeers. Seb had closed himself off in a ball, so all she could do was throw herself on top of him to protect him from the blows.

For a moment, the sound went off and time stood still. The kicks and punches that were now landing on her felt like rough nudges and sounded as though she was underwater. All she could hear properly was her own breathing. Then, just as abruptly, the sound came on again. Lynn was screaming at the top of her lungs and there seemed to be a loud beating and strong wind.

The boys who had been laughing had stopped. One said, "What the fuck?"

Rachel didn't look. Her eyes were welded shut throughout the whole thing and she continued to lie over Seb.

Despite her mind being a scrambled mess, she sensed someone else was there. There were no more blows landing on her, but she could hear grunts of effort and footfalls and stamps around her. Lynn had stopped screaming and a fight was going on around her.

Grigori. The thought came to her on a gust of wind that brought the scent of him to her nostrils. She hadn't even needed to open her eyes to know he was there. Perhaps it was his blood tingling under her skin, she couldn't be sure. He was protecting her, as he said he would—correction: protecting his investment. She wasn't going to haggle over semantics now. When his heavily accented voice said, "Get in the car and go, Rachel," she finally woke from her daze and opened her eyes.

CHAPTER 26

When she was sure no more blows were coming to harm Seb, she slowly sat up. What greeted her was carnage. It seemed impossible for Grigori to speak so calmly to her mind and be issuing such a beating. There were six of them and one of him. His wings were not there, and his movements were fluid and beautiful like a choreographed dance. Twisting, blocking, kicking, it was mesmerizing to watch. Even knives glinted in the boys' hands and were snapped off like an old twig—their screams earsplitting.

It occurred to her then that Grigori could have killed them very easily but chose not to. It was just a little workout for him—someone who had killed many people over thousands of years.

"Come on, Rachel," Lynn said, pulling her by the arm to get up. It snapped her out of her trance just as a couple of boys ran off. She scrambled to her feet and, together with Lynn, bundled Seb into the passenger seat of the car.

She checked Grigori one last time across the roof of her

car before she got in and saw him swipe the last boy effort-lessly with the back of his hand. He had things under control.

Lynn hurriedly got in the back, behind her seat, and she finally got in and turned on the engine. Lynn was crying and saying, "Oh my god, what *was* that?" over and over.

Rachel reversed, careful not to hit anyone, and pulled away. Shock was now making her shake all over. "We have to get Seb to hospital."

Grigori's tall frame stepped in front of her bonnet and made her slam on the brakes. He made a circular motion with his hand for her to wind down her window and walked calmly around to her side of the car. He stooped down to speak.

"Drive … drive," Lynn was saying hysterically.

Grigori flashed Lynn a single look and she sank back against the seat. To Rachel's look of horror, he said, "She sleeps," without any further explanation or anything. Then he looked across her to Seb, huddled, with his knees still up to his chest in the seat next to her.

Rachel could see him very close up now. Apart from a sheen of sweat and his slightly disheveled hair falling into his face, he looked completely unharmed. "Thank you," she said. He turned that unblinking gaze to hers, no more than six inches away from her face and there was a moment, just a single moment, when she thought he would kiss her. It was stupid, but it was there, nonetheless. Then his eyes went back to Seb.

"We need to get him to a hospital," she said.

He shook his head. "No need. There is no lasting damage. Some cracked ribs, nothing more. Take him home and I'll meet you there."

Groans sounded behind him as the last three of the boys got to their feet and limped off. "You wait," one of the boys shouted. "My dad'll 'ave you!"

Grigori stood and turned, and the boys quickened their pace until they disappeared around the corner. Then he leaned down. "I won't be long, just need to clear up first."

Rachel could see that a couple of knives were on the floor. "OK then. Be careful," she said, but felt odd about it as soon as she said it. She pulled away and saw Grigori stare after her in the rear-view mirror until she turned onto the road.

Her mind scrambled over all the events. There was probably CCTV in that car park, and what about her address? She'd forgotten to give it to Grigori. Then she frowned. He probably already knew it. If he owned her soul, he'd sure as hell know something as basic as that. He'd know everything. He was probably invisible on CCTV, or he would frazzle it. Either way, no one would ever know of his lethally graceful dance with the thugs. And the thing that had amazed her most of all was that he could have annihilated them easily in a second and had just let them go. Despite what they'd done to Seb, it was strangely comforting that he showed that sort of humanity.

At that time of night, they were home in less than twenty minutes. "Lynn! … Lynn!" she shouted, who roused as if she'd fallen asleep on the way home after a drinking session, which was entirely feasible.

Lynn got out, still half asleep and helped her pull out Seb, who hissed and moaned with the pain as they helped him into the house. Every movement seemed like agony and he looked awful.

"Let's get him straight up to bed, Rach. I don't think we'll be able to get him up again if we put him down."

It was a struggle to get him up the stairs as three of them couldn't fit side by side on a step. They tried a few times, rearranging themselves to get further than the third step, but it was impossible.

"Let me," a deep voice said, making them turn around sharply.

Grigori.

He reached out a heavily tattooed arm and took Seb's weight from both of them. As Seb went to slump, he scooped him up as if he weighed nothing.

Rachel looked at Lynn to gauge her reaction to all this and she actually blushed. Despite the whole evening's events, Lynn was clearly totally affected by him. She guessed he had saved all their lives like some sort of superhero.

Grigori carried Seb easily across his arms, all the way up the stairs. She overtook him at the top to open the door to Seb's room. After throwing all kinds of mess off his bed, she pulled back the duvet, ready for Grigori to place him down.

She couldn't see properly, but his face looked awful. One of his eyes was like an egg welded shut. The eyebrow above it was split, and so was his lip, and he had a bruise on his cheek, going purple already. She dreaded to think what he looked like under his clothes.

Strangely, it was then she began to feel the most uncomfortable of the whole evening. Grigori was looking down intently into Seb's face, while holding him in his arms, talking in hushed tones so she could barely hear him. Seb was nodding in response.

Rachel and Lynn stepped back while he placed him down with incredible gentleness. Arranging his pillows, he helped him out of his boots and jeans. It was done so slowly and reverently that she wanted to push him off and say that she would do it, but it seemed irrational.

Then Grigori turned to the girls and herded them towards the door. "Give us a minute."

This felt wrong. She was grateful that he'd saved them, but this—him being here in her house, around her friends—

she didn't like it at all. She went to protest, but he held her eyes meaningfully. "Trust me."

Then he looked over at Lynn, who was watching the whole thing and more than a little confused. "Make us all a drink, sweetheart."

Instead of balking at the patronizing tone, which was normally Lynn's M.O., she gushed, "Sure. Coming right up." Then she turned and skipped down the stairs.

Rachel scowled at the odd behavior, not sure how much Grigori controlled.

He turned his attention back to her. A cacophony of emotions went through her so fast that all she could do was stutter. She couldn't seem to articulate a question fast enough because there were so many. "How did you ... why? ..."

Grigori seemed to know and just gave her shoulder a squeeze. "There are advantages to being mine, Rachel. One of them being: I don't allow my subject to be manhandled."

Her mind immediately went to Seb. She could just see past Grigori at him lying still on the bed.

"Go down. I'll be there in a minute."

His eyes were calm, but she was scared of what he intended to do. "Trust me, Rachel. You are mine." Then he looked at Seb over his shoulder. "And he is yours—which also makes him mine."

She frowned at the logic.

"I'm going to heal him, and I don't want to risk Lynn coming back up. It won't be enough to create suspicion, just knit a few fractures and stop some internal bleeding. I'll simply leave the show of bruising."

She looked up into his eyes and swallowed hard. To think he could actually do that was astounding.

"I promise," he said, with a genuine smile that lit his battle-hardened face into something unbelievably handsome.

For a moment, she stood and marveled at what a contradiction he was, until Seb moaned and prompted her to move.

Grigori stepped back into the room and the door closed without him touching it.

Lynn had the kettle on and was talking animatedly into her phone by the time Rachel got down to the Kitchen. *Colin.* She was filling him in with all the juicy details on how heroic Grigori had been while arranging a row of cups and putting a teabag in each. "Bye, babe … yes, I'm fine, I promise. Speak tomorrow … love you." Then she clicked off the phone and put it on the kitchen side.

"Make one for Seb, Lynn. I don't think Grigori will be up for tea." She wanted him gone as soon as possible. It pricked her conscience, but she couldn't help it.

Lynn raised an eyebrow as if she was mad and continued as if she hadn't said anything.

"Grigori's looking him over," Rachel said, trying to keep the worry out of her voice. "He seems to think it looks worse than it is."

Lynn was putting three sugars in Seb's cup, just as he liked it. "That guy was amazing tonight, Rachel. Did you see what he did? Six of them, Rach, six!"

"Yeah … he's a guardian angel alright."

They were just sitting down at the circular table when Grigori's footfalls sounded on the stairs and he came in to find them. He took the cup Lynn held out to him; it looked tiny in his hands.

He smiled and she blushed with her most ridiculously flirty smile. "Sit down," she said, pointing to the chair next to hers. It was sickening to watch. He was deliberately turning on the charm and she was falling for it, lapping up every last bit. *Putty.*

"Could I speak to Rachel privately for a moment, Lynn? Then I will leave you all in peace. I'm sure you can't wait to go to bed," he said, with a disarming smile.

Rachel rolled her eyes as Lynn batted him away with a hand. "No problem." Her chair scraped on the tiled floor as she stood up. "You must let me buy you a drink sometime… to say thank you." She flashed red again.

He bowed his head slightly. "No need, but thank you."

"Seriously, though. Thanks for what you did." She leaned in and he stooped a little so she could reach to kiss his cheek. He smiled and played along to the point Rachel thought he was enjoying himself.

It felt like she took forever to go. Then Grigori stood menacingly opposite her, drinking his tea. "How is he?" she said.

"Sleeping. He'll be fine."

The relief pulled her down into her chair, where she picked up her cup. Her hands were shaking badly again, probably the shock coming out, although it was always worse around him.

His eyes went straight to it, not missing a thing. "It will pass in time. I'll put something in the mix on Saturday to help."

"What was that tonight? What if you were seen?" she said.

He leaned back against the counter, like she'd seen him do so many times at the shop. "Your blood called, I answered … you are around The Fallen all the time, you just don't notice."

It was a surprise to her. "Even in the day?"

He bobbed his head. "Maybe not in physical form … but, yes."

It was useful information. She'd assumed they were chained to Tartarus during the day, but it just meant they couldn't materialize. "What happens on Saturday?" she said.

"It's the fourth session—the sealing of the deal."

Grigori tipped his head in deference as if he was impressed that she'd found out that much. "That depends."

"On what?"

"On whether or not you're going to fight me?"

The air seemed to go out of the room. He was looking her directly in the eye, making her swallow hard. "I know you went to the prophet, Rachel." He drained the rest of his cup and put it down on the counter. "It's as it should be."

His look was so piercing she found it hard to meet his eyes. "I haven't made up my mind yet," she said, looking at the remnants in her cup, as if the answer might be there.

He shifted his weight to his other leg. "It will not be as bad as you think. I am not a demanding master."

A derisive blast of laughter left her, and she shook her head. "Let's cut the crap, OK, Grigori. Who will own me come Saturday night? I need to know." She finally met him in the eye.

He continued to look at her steadily, not missing a beat. "Nothing has been finalized … and you're taking the boy …" He bobbed his head and flicked his eyes towards the door. "Inspired," he finished, nodding with respect.

Her mind raced and she frowned at what he was driving at. He'd rescued and healed Seb and for that she had to be grateful to him.

He seemed to assume their time together was at an end and straightened up.

"So, all this … it's really happening?" Despite everything, she knew if he'd said something completely feasible at that point, she'd have latched onto it like a life raft. Instead, there was a loud snap like the shaking out of a wet sheet and Grigori stood in all his full-winged glory, exactly like in her dreams.

Now she doubted they were dreams at all. The layers of velvet feathers overlapped in exquisite patterns. The light catching their downy sheen made her want to skim her hand over them. They were huge and magnificent. Their tallest arch reached the ceiling and the splaying feathers at the bottom skimmed the floor. Outstretched, their span would be at least thirty feet, so she wasn't seeing the half of them. The sight rendered her utterly speechless.

He curled one around, so it was inches from her face and she brushed a hand against its softness.

It jerked, surprising her that the feathers had feeling right to their ends. "You truly are …" She didn't know whether to say, an angel, beautiful, amazing, but he cut across her with, "Fallen."

His look was deadly serious. "Never forget that. I'm not some puppy-dog you wanna pet."

She swallowed hard. Every time she thought she'd gained any common ground with him, he pushed her away. She barely got out the words, her throat was so dry. "Thank you … for proving it to me."

Then, in a single step, he was right in front of her, looming down, cupping her cheek in his large hand. "I will not hurt you and I will not take from you that which you are not willing to give."

The weight of his eyes boring into hers nearly buckled her knees. All she could do was nod. Any words would have given away how totally weak she was in front of him. Maybe he knew that anyway, as he continued to search her eyes.

"In all my years on the earth, you surprise me, Rachel. I will seek to preserve you as long as I can." With that, he snapped his wings shut and left by the back door. By the time she got there, he was nowhere to be seen.

CHAPTER 27

For the next couple of days, Rachel gave herself over to nursing Seb, although she had produced some pretty impressive bruising herself on her arms and legs, but nothing life-threatening. It would have been a different story for Seb had Grigori not done his job so well and healed his more serious injuries.

The thought of losing Seb lay heavily on her heart. She brought him hot water bottles, cold compresses and comforting soups and he appeared to be enjoying the attention. By Thursday afternoon, he had to confess that he wasn't nearly as unwell as she was determined to treat him. "You are so lucky, Seb. You could have been killed. Don't you remember anything about that night?" she said, as they lounged on his bed watching daytime TV.

"I know," he said, putting his arm behind his head to stare up at the ceiling. "Bits and pieces." He narrowed his eyes as if he had to think really hard. "I remember the guy from the tattoo shop."

She shifted nervously and he turned to face her. "He said you saved my life."

He was looking deeply into her eyes and she found it hard to hold his gaze. They hadn't discussed her leaping on top of him at all yet. She'd assumed he hadn't remembered. "It was a stupid, reckless thing to do, Rachel, but the most amazing thing anyone has ever done for me. I don't think any of my male friends would have had the guts to do anything like that." He leaned in and kissed her, and her thoughts scattered. His lips were sore and cracked, but it was the sweetest, most sensual of kisses. "You're the absolute real deal, Rachel." Then, in one fluid move, he rolled on top of her and, taking his weight on his elbows, stared down into her eyes.

"Careful, you're still healing." She tried not to show her own aches and pains on her face.

He smiled at her as if she was some kind of living miracle, which was probably the furthest thing from the truth. "That's just it, Rach. I should be in hospital and I'm not, thanks to you. I'm fine—more than fine. I'm going to get up tomorrow."

Before she could protest, he kissed her again and she had to give in, despite her increasing worry that she'd brought something bad into all their lives. All she wanted to do was wrap Seb in cotton wool forever.

After their kiss, Seb relaxed down next her, still covering her with half of his weight. "Are you OK, really?" She couldn't get out of her head the time Grigori had insisted on spending alone with him. Seb had said nothing and she couldn't press him without it all sounding too weird. "Do you remember anything after?"

He thought about it for a moment and shook his head. "Not really. Flashes. Falling down. Curling into a ball. Feeling you hugging me. That's about it." He smiled at her and ran the pad of his thumb across her cheek. "You could have got yourself killed."

He was right. Then Grigori had arrived like the cavalry,

just in the nick of time, and stopped anything happening to her. "And nothing after that?"

He shook his head. "Been having really weird, vivid dreams since, though. The tattoo bloke's in them all. Post-traumatic stress, I guess."

She didn't give him an inkling of the churning horror she felt inside at the mention of dreams. She wasn't sure exactly how they worked, whether it was the mind's way of processing the supernatural things going on around them, or Grigori literally taking them to another place. Whatever they were, they were more than just simple dreams.

He distracted her by kissing her again. "Don't worry, OK? I'm well enough to get up, and I have a surprise for you tomorrow night."

She was shaking her head, ready to tell him there was no need, but he stole the thought with the mother of all kisses. "Let me do this for you, Rach. Please." He rested his forehead against hers. "Whatever happens, you mean a lot to me."

Her heart beat and broke at the same time. There was no telling what the future held. She couldn't think beyond the weekend. Then he struck the killer blow. "Don't you get it? I think I'm falling for you, Rach."

A tear escaped as the words registered and a dream came true. Seb, the coolest boy she'd ever known, had admitted he was falling for her. She should have been whooping for joy, but instead, she wanted to cry. It was too late. She didn't know what Grigori had in store for her, or if she'd even be alive by the end of the weekend. And if by some stroke of luck she was, she wanted the people she cared about the most as far away from her as possible.

His eyes were beginning to fill with hurt at her lack of response. He was, naturally, assuming she didn't feel the same way. So she wiped her tears away and gently touched the side of his face. "I'm feeling it too, Seb. How could I not?

I've got nothing to compare it with, but it's always been you."

The relief in him was palpable. It was the knife that twisted in her gut even more. He kissed her solemnly, as if it meant everything, like a sealing of a pact. It was so moving; for those few moments, she gave herself over to it and kissed him back for all she was worth. Their clothes were soon gone and they were moving together, lost in each other. He, demonstrating what she meant to him, and she, offering a farewell to the only thing left that was good in her life.

THE NEXT DAY Seb was as good as his word and after more early morning lovemaking, showered, dressed and left to run some errands.

Rachel couldn't help but worry. It was his first time out of bed in three days, his eyes were still purple and his back and ribs were still pretty shades of the rainbow. He did seem well in himself though.

After he'd gone, she sat at the kitchen table with Lynn, stirring her coffee and turning things over in her head. "I can't believe he's up and about so soon ... Guess Grigori was right."

"Mmm," she said, trying to keep the sarcasm out of her tone. "I should really go to work," Rachel said, thinking aloud. It was hard to concentrate with her life in limbo like this.

Lynn grinned. "You really have changed. Where's lover boy gone today, then?"

Rachel smiled. Lynn had insisted on ribbing Seb all week about his heroics, but she knew it was only to plaster over the terror of knowing he could have died. "I dunno. He had some stuff to do. And he said he's got a surprise for me tonight."

Lynn didn't look nearly as intrigued as she should have and was trying to hide a small smile.

"You know what it is, don't you?"

Lynn laughed and put up her hands in defense. "OK, you're right. But I don't know everything. He swore me to secrecy. All I can say is it's incredibly sweet and it's to show you how much you mean to him." She grinned. "I don't know how you managed it, but he's crazy about you."

Rachel laughed at the backhanded compliment. It was lovely to hear though, and terrifying at the same time. This was Seb they were talking about, not some geek at school from book club.

Even though she was waiting for the fall of the axe to learn the fate of her everlasting soul, having another person love you like that was the most amazing feeling in the world.

Lynn kicked her under the table. "Don't get carried away. This is Seb. It's not going to be an engagement ring or anything like that."

It broke the tension. She was so right, and they dissolved into giggles. Lynn was the tonic she needed right now.

The afternoon came and went, and a feeling of unease began to give way to real worry. "Have you heard from Seb at all today, Lynn?" she called, as she was just about to leave for work.

Lynn stopped and backtracked to put her head around the living room door. "No, but don't worry. He's been cooped up all week. He's probably doing the rounds. I'll see you later." She left her with a smile. "I'm staying at Colin's," she called, closing the front door.

Nevertheless, she did worry. She tried his number a couple of times, under the pretext of checking in for a chat, but got no answer. Six, seven, eight o'clock came and went and there was still no sign. There was no reply to a text either. By 8.30 she was scared to death something had happened to him.

At nine o'clock her phone went. She snatched it up only to sag in disappointment. It was Nicola. "Hi, Rachel. Hope you didn't mind my calling you so late. I just had to see if you were doing OK before your appointment tomorrow. Have you decided what you want to do?"

Honestly, with all that had happened, she hadn't given it much thought. She relayed the events of Tuesday night, along with Grigori's part in saving them all.

The line went quiet.

"Hello. Are you still there?" Rachel said, her heart speeding up in fear.

"Yes ... sorry. So, he's safely home with you?"

"Yes ... well, no. He has been until today. He's gone out to organize some surprise for me and he hasn't come home all day. I'm starting to worry, actually."

"Oh ... I see." Then the line went quiet again.

"What, Nicola? Please. Start talking. I'm going out of my mind here."

"And you say Xenon was alone with him—after the incident, I mean?"

"Well, yes, he healed him and wanted me to make sure Lynn didn't walk in on him."

Nicola sighed. "So, let me get this straight. There was a fight. Your Fallen arrives just in time and, during that fight, you throw yourself between your loved one and his attackers?"

"Well, yes, on top of him, really. It was all I could think of doing—well, I didn't think, I just did it. They were killing him. Six against one."

"So, you sacrificed yourself—risking your life for this boy?"

The constant line of questioning about the same thing

over and over really began to irritate her. Then the tentacles of fear began to wind themselves around her heart. "You think he could use this?"

"Rachel, it was probably orchestrated." Fear turned her blood to acid in her veins as she started to get what she was driving at. "I have to go." Then, without waiting for an answer, she ended the call.

Jules was in her contacts and she hit call straight away.

"Hello, Rachel?" he said after a couple of rings. "How's my man?"

"He's not with you?"

"He was earlier. We smoked and jammed for a bit. I think he left around seven.

"Do you know where he went?"

He laughed in his easy, laid-back way. "Yeah, well, not exactly. I don't want to ruin the surprise."

She thanked him and ended the call with her mind racing. She could be worrying foolishly, but maybe not. The kitchen clock said 9.30 and still no sign. She hit Lynn's number next, praying she'd pick up as she was at work, but it went straight to voicemail. She left a message: *Lynn, please call me back urgently. I need to know where Seb is. It's important, before he does something stupid.*

That was it. She couldn't wait any longer. She grabbed her keys, slammed the door shut and got in her car. She backed out of the driveway too fast, scraping the bottom and went in the direction of the only place she could think of going.

CHAPTER 28

*D*riving way too fast, Rachel called Grigori on her hands-free. *Come on, come on, pick up.* There was no answer, which stoked her anxiety, threatening to engulf her thinking ability completely.

The clock on her dashboard said 9.41. She tried Seb's phone again and it rang and rang. *Come on, Seb, where are you?"*

It took precisely six minutes to get to the Angel's Ink shop and she sat looking at it with the engine idling at the curb. Despite no evidence to support it, her gut had sent her there. She had to at least check it out, even though it would piss Grigori off.

She switched off the engine, got out and jogged up to the door where she held her finger on the buzzer until the door clicked in the jamb. The corridor was lit for nighttime as she briskly walked through to the room at the back.

The door opened as she got there, with no one on the other side to open it. Her eyes swept the room until they rested on Grigori's familiar physique, hunched over someone in his chair with reversed baseball cap and everything. It was a back piece and they were cuddling the chair like a motor-cycle, the way she had on her first visit.

"Come in, Rachel," Grigori said, without looking up. "For what do we owe this unexpected visit?"

"I'm looking for Seb," she said, walking further into the room towards him.

Grigori straightened, put his machine in its cradle and removed his cap. As he slowly stood, running his fingers back through his hair, Rachel had a clear view of the young, masculine back already inked. The closer she got, the more familiar the other tattoos on his back became. One was a 1950s pinup girl, and the other a Union Jack flag with the script "Rock n Roll Forever" underneath. "Oh, Seb."

Her heart stopped when he didn't look up. She quickened her steps until she stood right over him. His eyes were closed, and he didn't move. "What's the matter with him?" she asked, shooting a look at Grigori and shaking his shoulder. "Seb! ... Seb!" she said, then tapping him. There was still no response. "Is he asleep?" But in her heart, she knew that it couldn't be as simple as that. He would have at least stirred.

She turned angrily on Grigori, who was resting against his counter, watching her. His attitude incensed her and she flew at him to smack her hands against his chest. His hands moved so quickly to catch her wrists; she didn't even see them move. She was forced to collapse into him, sobbing. "No ... no, not Seb. Not Seb."

Before she knew what was happening, he had her shoved against the wall behind his station, pinned by his weight. The more his body pushed against hers, the harder her heart beat and her body shook. There was no controlling it—particu-larly when he bent his head and whispered next to her ear; "Listen to me very carefully."

Her shaking got worse, and perspiration covered her face in a light sheen. She was acutely aware that it was his hips pinning her into place. "Wake up Seb then. Seb!" she called, trying to peer around his big frame.

Grigori grabbed her chin and shut her up by covering her mouth with his. The moment his tongue touched hers and their saliva mixed, her body lit up. It was over in a second, but it left her gasping, unable to think of anything else. "You are for Abaddon. Do you understand me? ... The reaper himself."

She wasn't listening and dissolved into sobs. "Seb ... not Seb," she wailed. Everything was out of control. Her heart was out of rhythm, her knees shook and she couldn't string more than a few words together, but he wouldn't allow her to crumple. He held her chin painfully while he glared down at her and pointed a finger at Seb. "From the moment you gave your virtue to him, you put him in danger. Then, when you sacrificed yourself for him during the fight, you sealed his fate. He became the perfect offering: something you love more than life itself. The scales became balanced. You did this," he said, tightening his lips and speaking viciously between his teeth. "You gave your answer."

Her mind was reeling, and she didn't fully understand what he was saying. Only that she had somehow dragged Seb into this.

He pushed away from her and walked over to Seb's sleeping body. He looked down as if appraising his work. "It is done ... my best work." He picked up a tube of cream and gently rubbed it into the tattooed area.

Rachel was flat against the wall, breaths still heaving in her chest. She finally forced herself to move and come closer to look at the piece he'd just finished.

It was magnificently complex and the artwork exquisite. Grigori was indeed a master artist. A naked girl was embracing a skeleton with a thorn-covered vine wrapping itself around them and binding them together. As it left the neck, it became straight like a thorn-covered spear and into the dry head skull and X that she knew to be Grigori's mark, and behind it all was the hooded shadow of the reaper with his scythe. The girl was clearly meant to be her. He'd even picked up the blue in her hair in a lighter grey. On her back was the iris, so small and so detailed that it was a miniature work of art in itself.

It was brilliant, as on the surface it was Seb's gift. Him, locked in an embrace with the woman he loved until death. It was incredibly sweet, but only she knew what it meant. That she'd bound him to her to be owned by The Watcher of the North, to offer to the Reaper at death. It was very clever. Even the script beneath was a play on the scripture: "The wages of sin is death." It said: "The freely giving of life is a sacrifice paid in full." A contract, if ever she saw one. The air left her, and she would have collapsed if Grigori hadn't caught her.

"He knows?" she whispered.

Grigori nodded. "On the night of the healing, I took him to Tartarus and we struck our deal."

The news was unbearable. She went to struggle, but he held her fast, only putting her down onto her feet when she ceased. "I don't understand, Grigori. What does it mean? I thought you said I was for Abaddon?"

"And you are. Tomorrow you will be in this chair to have the Reaper's scythe and mask on your left hip. It will be masked because your guarantor, Seb, has put up collateral for your freedom."

Her eyes dropped to Seb, who appeared to be sleeping so peacefully. "And that's where he is now—Tartarus?" The thought of him there alone, being tormented by the other Angels, killed her. "Take me there now, Grigori."

There was no haggling over it. He pulled her to his chest, and the next thing she knew, there was a loud beating of wings and the smell of leaves and earth of the forest. As they swooped in, feelings of disorientation and nausea made her head swirl and the refracted light through the trees glinted and made her eyes narrow. It was then she understood why. They were between worlds—the spiritual and the physical. No human could survive any length of time there.

They came into the clearing fast, but Grigori landed them expertly like an eagle with its prey. Her eyes went straight to the plinth where Seb stood with his back to it, with Oleander running a sharp talon down his bare chest. Raephe and Bohdan lounged nearby, against trees, looking bored.

"Oleander!" Grigori called sharply. "Leave the pup. He is marked as mine."

Oleander turned, smirking, eyeing Rachel ravenously. "You've become greedy, Xenon. The girl has given him. Why not share your spoils with us? Abaddon comes for him soon anyway."

Grigori swept her away with a mere look and she was left picking herself up from the dirt. Seb fell against the plinth as Oleander let him go of whatever spell she was holding him with and Rachel ran to him. He seemed bewildered and dazed, as if he had no clue what was happening to him.

He looked at her and smiled lazily as if he were drunk. "What are you doing here, babe?"

She sighed, exasperated with him. "Bloody hell, what have you done, Seb?"

Oleander moved closer again and the other two joined her. Grigori was forced to stand between them. "Why have you brought two humans to Tartarus, Grigori? You play with fire. Abaddon will sense his prize and come straight here. The ink is barely dry on the contract and she has none at all." Her eyes moved to Rachel lasciviously, the pupils closing like a serpent.

It was then Rachel began to realize the concession

Grigori had made. He was genuinely offering her a way out and Seb had offered to stand in her place. It broke her heart that Seb would do that. Although she doubted he fully understood what he was doing.

It did, however, make up her mind on the thing she'd been deliberating on since she'd met Nicola. It was no longer just her eternal soul at stake. She had to fight this with everything she had. She needed to get back to Nicola and let her know she would be contesting the contract. She had to win Grigori's tests and for that she needed to read the last chapter.

She put a hand on Grigori's arm as he still stood sentry in front of them. His eyes went to hers. They were that unnatural amber color that they always were here. Then she phrased her words as quietly and as assertively as she could. "I know you want Seb because he is acceptable to you, but this is my contract and it's not acceptable to me. I don't accept this sacrifice as payment." For a moment, he looked confused, as if her words simply didn't compute with him. She didn't know where they came from or if they'd work. His look was one of amazement when her meaning seeped through to him. "If you refuse this arrangement, then everything will fall to you as it was before."

She nodded. "I know." She looked quickly around her at the other three Angels' growing smiles. Oleander's eyes appeared to glisten, as if she'd just been served up as dinner.

Rachel reached up and touched Grigori's cheek. "Take us back."

For some reason, they returned to Seb separately. Grigori said he must travel back to his body still in the chair. She, on the other hand, had travelled there in reality because she was with him. It made no sense to her already scattered brain.

Nevertheless, it felt strange to be travelling back in Grigori's arms while his strong wings beat in a reliable rhythm back to earth and the shop where they'd started.

The night air was black and cold, and his t-shirt-covered chest felt smooth and warm against her cheek. She was conscious that under the soft material was muscle as hard as granite. It was impossible to get her head around: the dream and the reality, Earth and Tartarus, the physical and the spiritual—even with all her Bible training. It was easy to suspend belief, turning pages, sitting in a Bible study circle. Grigori spanned both worlds and so, it seemed, did she. Now she knew everything, he no longer needed to drug her or put her out. It was obviously the early stages for Seb. His sacrifice brought fresh tears to her eyes as she never wanted him to have to know about any of this.

They didn't go straight back to the shop. Instead, Grigori brought them down on a grassy hill where they could see the lights of the whole town in the distance. Rolling countryside lay between them. The moon, swathed in clouds, was just enough to illuminate dark clusters and lines of trees. Her feet touched wet grass and the air smelled of fresh rain.

Grigori's eyes were midnight black when she looked up into them. "Why will you not take the sacrifice?" he said. "It weighs equal on the scales. Do you realize how hard that is to achieve?"

Rachel continued to stare into those fathomless eyes that she could no longer kid herself were human.

"You saved his life and he saved yours ... You gave him your fleshly body which, by rights, already belonged to me, and he offered his own as recompense."

Rachel narrowed her eyes. "I find it very hard to believe that Seb fully grasped the situation. So, I don't think it is a fair exchange if it's not given with a full understanding of all the facts." Frankly, she was flabbergasted that Grigori actually thought she would go through with such an arrangement.

He looked initially impressed, but then his expression changed to pity, then sardonic. "You don't think Seb has his own desires to fulfill?" His eyes looked crafty then. "Maybe not all to do with you?"

Anger seared through her at what he was implying. "Seb doesn't deserve to be a slave, Grigori. No one does."

"And you will fight me for your own price?" He didn't seem the least bit angry—far from it. He was acting like it was the most entertainment he'd had all day.

Rachel nodded slowly, communicating all the hatred she could through her eyes. "I don't know how. I don't even know what the test is, but I'll fight you … for Seb."

"But not for yourself," he said, sounding truly mystified. He put his head at an angle, trying to gauge her. "You would forgo everything you desired. A full life span, all the riches you wanted, I myself would see to it?"

She still nodded. She could understand why many would fall for an offer like that. Life is so hard for people—especially if they think this life is all there is. Maybe, for a moment, she may have even been tempted, herself, but now Seb was involved. "I want you to nullify Seb's arrangement."

His lips twitched at the corners. "Only he can ask for that, and you see …" He shifted his stance and tried to school his features. "I like him."

Rachel's heart dropped. "He's mine, Grigori, not yours."

He laughed loudly, and despite how she hated him then, she was still in total awe of how handsome he was. Devilishly so. *Wasn't that what Nicola warned her?*

He stopped laughing and seemed to relent. "Please understand, Rachel, that both your contracts are with me. A deal was struck, and Abaddon was set on you. Then I renegotiated for the boy. You can refuse to let the boy go in your place, but both your contracts are still binding to me."

She knew he was being cunning and narrowed her eyes. "I think you somehow caused the fight and you tricked Seb. I don't see how that can be legal with your ridiculous scales."

He looked mildly amused as if what she said hadn't fazed him in the slightest. "Come, I'll take you back. You have bigger things to worry about now."

Rachel and Grigori arrived back on the flat roof of the shop. They walked down the fire escape, past the ominous doorway, which she now strongly suspected was a portal to Tartarus.

Seb stirred as soon as Grigori entered the shop, she assumed by his design. He smiled a heart-wrenching smile as soon as his eyes focused on her. "Hey, babe. You guessed. What do you think?"

She swallowed a lump as big as an apple and brushed away a stray tear. "I can't believe you did that for me."

Grigori busied himself clearing up his bench, but she knew he was alert and listening.

Seb grinned, which turned into a grimace as he tried to sit up. She knew that feeling. The skin would be pulled tight like sunburn. He put his hand to his forehead.

"Careful!" she said, quickly holding his arm in case the dizziness pulled him over. "Will he remember?" she said to Grigori, over her shoulder.

"It can only be a sacrifice if he knows what he's doing." He passed her the large hand mirror.

She felt miserable as she angled it so Seb could see, careful not to catch his eye.

When he saw it for himself, he nodded. "Bad-ass, isn't it, Rach?"

She was only just about holding it together. "Can we go?" She needed to get out of there. The atmosphere was stifling. Part of her desperately needed to speak with him about it, and another was scared half to death of what she'd find out.

"The car is waiting."

Grigori answered her next question without her even asking."It will be delivered to your home."

Sure it will, she thought bitterly. No favor is too large or too small. She felt like she'd cry if she stayed another minute —or hit him, so she didn't argue.

Instead, she passed Seb's shirt to him calmly and helped him down off the chair, along the corridor and into the cool night air.

The usual driver was leaning against his executive car when he spotted them and immediately opened the rear door. They slid into the leather seats and Seb picked up her hand.

Seb looked deeply into her eyes as they pulled away. His were bloodshot and heavy. They didn't say a word—not in front of the driver. *Where did someone start with all this?* Anything that formed in her mind seemed too inadequate.

Strangely, a wealth of information passed in that simple look. She tried to hide her accusation, but it was out there for him to see. Followed swiftly by exasperation and then love. His was an apology tinged with fear, a little defiance and then awe. He held her eyes in wonder all the way home without a single word being spoken. Maybe that's what love was.

The car pulled up and Seb held her hand to help her get out and they walked together to the house. Inside, there was no sign of Lynn and she remembered she was staying at Colin's. She was glad they were alone. Grabbing a pint glass of water and a cold flannel for a compress, just in case, she led Seb to her room.

Together, they shed their clothes without a single thought of shyness and slid into the cool sheets in a kind of shock. It robbed them completely of the ability to act normally. She guessed it was natural when something as weird as this was shared and could no longer be ignored or brushed aside.

Facing each other, Seb moved in closer until their lower bodies were touching. He smoothed the hair away from her face. She wanted to shout at him how stupid he'd been, but it died before it came to her lips.

Eventually, Seb broke the silence. "You went through all this alone for weeks?"

She nodded and rubbed her thumb under his sore-looking eyes. "You both thought I was going mad as it was."

He smiled weakly, closed the gap and put his mouth softly over hers. He took his time kissing her lips several times.

"Have you any idea what you've done, Seb?" she said, eventually.

He rolled on top of her, taking his weight on his elbows. "I knew it after your first session with him."

She looked into his eyes, startled. That was even before her. She couldn't believe it, but she quickly realized he was being deadly serious.

"He started to turn up at the places I was at: bars, gigs, just walking down the street. He's not the sort of guy you miss. I didn't make the connection first of all."

Rachel's heart was beating so hard she thought he would feel it through her chest. "I had no idea," came out more like a whimper.

He swallowed hard. "In the end, it had to be that way,

Rach ... I was confused, ashamed." He shook his head like it was hard to think about.

She didn't understand and frowned.

He was searching her face like he'd find the words he was searching for.

"What is it, Seb? ... You can tell me anything."

He nodded and swallowed with difficulty. "There's something you don't know. Something I have to tell you, but I'm not sure I can."

Fear was creeping through her veins and constricting her throat. "Please, Seb, just say it."

He closed his eyes and pushed off her in one fluid move. He sat up and ran his fingers through his hair. She sat next to him, holding his moving arm gently before he pulled his hair from the roots. "Whatever it is, you can trust me, OK?"

He turned his head and looked intensely into her eyes as if deciding whether he could. He looked devastated and hopeless.

"Seb!" she said, shaking him gently.

"I kissed him—I mean, we kissed ... something happened between us. I dunno. I mean, I'm not even gay, Rach." He got out of bed and began to walk around the room, shaking his head. "But I did it. I kissed him." Then he stopped and hung his head, defeated. "And I liked it." He looked straight into her eyes. "Since then, I've tried to hide it, but I've been all over the place."

Rachel stared at him, open-mouthed, stunned. She'd put everything down to him being hot and cold with her and now it all made sense. "When?"

He shook his head and shrugged at a loss. "I dunno. Early on. Not long after your first session." He was looking at her imploringly.

She tried to think back over the time they'd got close. "What ... before we kissed?"

He frowned briefly as if he couldn't see how it mattered. "Er … yeah … I think it was."

She tried to decide whether it really mattered when, but that threw up a whole load of other questions. *Was Grigori after Seb all along? Or covering all his bases.* "Did you kiss me to prove to yourself you were straight?" Her mind was in freefall.

He laughed and went to her immediately. Sitting down next to her, he took both her hands in his. "Please don't think it had anything to do with the way I feel about you. I was trying not to mess you around, keeping away rather than coming on to you."

Rachel thought about it and it sounded true. All the staying out and being distant did fit with what he was saying.

He smiled sadly at her. "You of all people should know I'm straight. I think some tendency would have shown itself before now."

She searched his face, looking so earnestly back at her. She had no idea he'd been dealing with this as well. They'd both been living in their own private turmoil, with Grigori pulling the strings.

Then a strange feeling of it all starting to make more sense than either of them realized crept over her. The fight orchestrated after the gig. Grigori saving the day, then healing him.

Seb watched her closely, not able to follow her internal monologue.

"He gave you the option to go to Abaddon in my place after the fight?"

Seb nodded, not getting the significance. "Yeah."

"So, when I thought you were upset because of me …"

His eyelids lowered and he nodded. "I wasn't sure if you were pulling back because you knew something about him and me—Fuck! I didn't even know what it was."

Rachel sagged in defeat. "Until the night of the fight." Grigori had been several moves ahead from the moment they'd met. Nicola had been right about everything.

Seb took her silence for anger and held his forehead in his hand. Rachel gently took hold of his wrist and spoke softly. "It's not your fault, you know." She had been angry initially. She thought Grigori wanted Seb because he liked men, but that was far too simple. Grigori only saw interesting leverage. He was telling the truth about labels. He was a cunning strategist, just like Nicola said.

Poor Seb was still waiting for her anger and inevitable rejection that he felt he deserved. *Hadn't she kissed him, too, and two other angels?* "Don't feel bad, Seb. Angels have some sort of drugging pheromone in their saliva."

Seb was looking deeply into her eyes for signs she was just trying to make him feel better. "Sorry to damage your ego, but he was just controlling you." The corners of his mouth began to twitch until he was grinning and he pulled her to him in a tight hug. They held it for a few moments until she pulled away to look up at him again. The look he gave her then was so full of adoration, she wished she could bottle it and keep it forever. "Listen, can't we start a new slate from today? Now we both know everything?"

He nodded and his face relaxed in her hands to a beautiful smile of relief. He went to speak, but she put a forefinger to his lips. In the end, he kissed her finger gently. "Tonight, we're two prisoners on death row. Neither of us knows when our time is up." She wished she could smooth out the furrow in his brow that came when she said that.

Instead, he bent slightly, lifting her off the floor and kissing her fiercely at the same time. It was a whirlwind that landed them on the bed. It consumed and disoriented her. They rolled over and over while she straddled and moved over him. Seb stopped her, reached over with effort for his jeans and pulled out a small packet. She was grateful one of them had good sense. In less than a minute, they both gasped with a gentle hitch of breath as they joined and moved together. Moaning what they wanted in whispers, as they became everything they needed in each other. For the first time, both were secure in the knowledge that they knew what the other was feeling.

When at last the overwhelming release overtook them, Seb's fingers held her tightly at each hip, grinding her to him until she fell onto his chest, welcomed by the warm drum of his heart. They lay breathless in exhausted bewilderment. Rachel knew instinctively they were both thinking the same thing: How they could hope to keep this closeness with Death's scythe coming between them at any time.

They slept deeply after that. Until Rachel woke, draped over Seb, raging like a furnace. He had the fever that always ravaged a person after one of Grigori's tattoos. At least she knew what it was now. She gathered cooling wet flannels and draped them over his burning skin until he eventually slept peacefully. His fever broke sometime the next morning, meaning she could relax with him at last. The two of them slept late.

Rachel knew how weak Seb would feel, so she left him sleeping and went into the bathroom to call Nicola.

She picked up immediately. "Rachel?"

"Yeah, it's me." She caught her up on the previous night's events.

"Oh, my God, so he has both of you as collateral for the other. It's unbelievably clever."

"I know." Rachel had to hand it to him; he'd played a blinder. "But I've told him I don't accept the sacrifice Seb made and I'm going to fight him."

"OK."

Rachel wished Nicola's response had been said defiantly, but it wasn't. It didn't bolster her up or motivate her to stand strong at all. "Nicola, I need you to be a guide in all this. You've got to help us. Can you come here? I'm going to try to read the last chapter."

"Of course, … I'll come Monday, when Seb's had time to recover. I'm not going to kid you, though, Rachel. This is a dangerous gamble that you may or may not both come out of. Xenon's played a genius hand and may have everything sown up."

Rachel closed her eyes and nodded, even though Nicola couldn't see her down the phone.

"He obviously wants you very much," Nicola said more softly.

She wasn't sure about that, but he had ruthlessly and single-mindedly played her. Now it was time to stack the cards in her favor.

"You will still have to meet him tonight to get your owner's mark. I'm sorry, Rachel, but he will just come and get you. His blood tells him where you are."

Nicola was right. She couldn't miss it; besides, she needed to know all the plays of the game in order to fight it.

SEB SLEPT most of the day. When he woke a couple of times, Rachel explained what was happening to him and he seemed to understand. However, he hated that she still intended to go to the tattoo shop and was going alone. "Please rest, Seb, I've done it loads of times. Grigori is a shit, but I don't think he'll hurt the merchandise."

Seb relaxed back into the pillows and smiled wryly. They both knew she was right.

As promised, her car was back outside her house. She set

off for the shop at 8.45 to arrive at nine. Despite having done the journey so many times, her hands still shook and her heart palpitated. It was a mixture of adrenaline and her growing addiction to Grigori, which she despised. There was no radio on or roof down tonight. It had all been a valuable lesson. *What was all this shit—these things, if you don't have the people you love?* She guessed Grigori had even tried to teach her that, too, in a weird fucked-up kind of way. He was certainly an enigma. Little wonder he managed to pull them both in. He was so confusing, he actually made you think he cared.

"Come in and take a seat," Grigori said the moment she got there from his usual spot, lit in the darkness. Except tonight they weren't alone. She felt it immediately.

The heat dropped around her at least a couple of degrees and her mouth went dry. She could see an outline of a tall man sucking the darkness from the shadows. She couldn't see his face and was terrified of walking further into the room. "Who's there?" She turned her face anxiously to Grigori, who turned and smiled a little regretfully.

The man finally stepped out of the shadows, just like he did in everyone's nightmares. He was dressed entirely in black. His roll-neck went right up to his chin and his black slacks hung perfectly tailored to cover his expensive shiny shoes. His baldness reminded her of the angel on the Angel's Ink logo. This must be him, the one all this was about.

His eyes were completely black and his cheeks dark and hollow. He smiled slightly and nodded as if he followed her thought process. It made her shudder.

She blinked and he was standing right in front of her. The shock almost made her pee herself. He put out a bony ring-covered hand for her to take. If an angel could choose the physical body that they could take, then this one was chosen deliberately to instill fear. She swallowed hard. "Is this ..." She couldn't finish her sentence. Instead, she looked over at Grigori, who nodded. He looked like a ghoul or an angel of death.

CHAPTER 30

Rachel instinctively wanted to shrink away from him, but she felt paralyzed. There was no running away. This was the thing that would own her after tonight. "But I don't want the contract. I can refuse, can't I … free will?" she whimpered.

The thing in front of her smiled, showing large yellow teeth shaped like gravestones. His sallow skin stretched over his cheekbones.

"Abaddon is an ancient, even for me," Grigori explained. "He's lived long and seen everything—every kind of badness … and purity."

A sick feeling began to crawl through her veins as the thing's eyes lowered. At first, she thought it was from modesty, but his eyes began a slow, appraising graze of her body. Her insides bubbled and turned to liquid, making her want to throw up. She turned her head to Grigori in fear. Bile was reaching her mouth. "Him?" She wanted to run to him to protect her, but that made no sense.

"Don't worry," he said softly. "It's usual for him to be here for the fourth session."

For some strange, unfathomable reason, Grigori's eyes grounded her at that moment because she was sure she would have bolted. She swallowed and looked back at Abaddon, whose eyes hadn't left her. "What are his terms?" She tried to sound strong and keep the wobble out of her voice.

The thing smiled slightly, and Grigori nodded appreciatively. "She is a strong one," it said. Its voice hit her ears like ringing glass and ran through her mind like winter rain, leaving icicles around her heart. "I refer the boy back to you, Xenon." Its eyes left her and went sideways to Grigori for the first time.

He nodded once in understanding.

"Mephistopheles has made a bid for this one, but I've decided it is a wrong fit. I will keep her myself. She interests me."

Rachel swallowed hard and she tried to breathe to slow down her heart. "What are your terms? I haven't agreed to anything yet."

It laughed, a shrill, ringing sound. "Are you aware of who I am?"

She felt as good as dead anyway. "I know who you are: Abaddon, the Angel of Death."

He nodded slowly, once. "Then you know I can take you now if I so wish."

Her knees were shaking violently, and she prayed he couldn't see it. "But you won't because of the scales."

He looked across at Grigori and raised an eyebrow.

Grigori grinned like some proud parent.

"You wish to know what I can offer you if you choose to come with me and what I can take anyway?" He looked back at her with his eyebrows raised in a question. It was a threat masked in mild amusement.

Then she threw at him something that had been going around in her head for a while—something that had stayed with her from Bible study many years ago. "Or I could simply end my own life here and now." Her hand was in her bag, rummaging for the sharp nail file attached to her keys. She didn't know what the hell she'd do with it, but it would help her make her point. "God hates a person to take their own life when it's not theirs to take and so do you, don't you?"

Abaddon narrowed his eyes and Grigori looked amazed at the direction she was taking.

"Scripture says no resurrection for those ones, that means to you too, doesn't it? We'd go straight to the end game." It was a huge gamble with a being who was unbelievably clever, but she knew her scriptures.

There was a split second where a glimmer of surprise flashed across its features. However, he smiled wickedly and turned to Grigori. "Put in a clause that in the event of the first party's death, the boy reverts straight to me."

Panic and frustration threatened to tip her over the edge, but she got a hold of herself quickly. "We've made a pact. We'll do it together." She knew she sounded too wild and desperate to be taken seriously. "And don't think about imprisoning us or brainwashing us or anything, because it's meant to be freely given … scales, remember?" she threw in at the end, thankful for the moment of genius bringing the argument back in her favor.

Abaddon's eyes glittered and he smiled despite what she'd just said. He nodded once. "I understand why you kept this one close, Xenon." His eyes bore into hers. "How I will enjoy dealing with you." He let his words sink in for the longest moment, which made her swallow. "Very well, terms." He turned his head to Grigori, who took the pencil from behind his ear and held it ready to write on a small notepad. "The boy reverts to you." He looked back at her and smiled. "For the duration of his life—untouched—unblemished, providing the subject: Rachel Fairweather, does not dispute or sabotage the said contract."

Rachel's heart and mind were racing, searching for any loophole. He was cunning and the wording was vague. Try as she might, it seemed watertight. She shouldn't be surprised. They were always going to use Seb as leverage. It had been the point all along.

"He will want for nothing." Grigori's tone was the softest she'd ever heard it, almost sympathetic.

Abaddon's creepy black eyes remained on hers. "And you will no longer be under the jurisdiction of any Grigori. From this day, you will have my personal protection."

When she looked across at Grigori to see what that meant, she could see that even he was surprised.

"I will groom you as my protégé. I haven't taken an assistant in centuries," he said, almost wistfully. "Knowledge and purity of spirit should not go unnoticed and unrewarded. They are essential attributes for the serious work you will undertake."

What he was suggesting was truly terrifying. Every word was embroiling her more and more, so she could never escape, but she had to keep a clear head to hear him out and get all the facts before she went back to Nicola. "Are you getting all this down?" she flung at Grigori, not missing the small smile that played on his lips. *How fucking dare he find this funny.* "Does that mean I'm going straight to Hell?" she had to ask. *Weren't everlasting souls what all this was about?*

Abaddon smiled his weird, creepy-looking smile. It looked translucent, stretched over his cheekbones. "There is no such place."

She scoffed. "So, are you trying to tell me there's no Devil? Where does he live then?" She remembered vaguely something Nicola said of a place she'd never heard of.

His smile widened as he turned to Grigori. "Education is needed, Fallen."

Grigori nodded and wrote it down like an item on a grocery list.

When he looked back, there was no amusement in his features. His demeanor had totally changed. "Enough now. The terms have been set. You will dwell out your natural life-span on the Earth to learn your new profession, during which I will summon you at will to the place imparted to you by The Fallen, Xenon of Kryta."

His words were terrifying and bewildering in their finality. She truly had no idea if she could get out of this—even with Nicola's help. They were foolish to even think they stood a chance against these beings. "What will my new profession be?" Her breath stopped for the axe to fall.

"You will aid me in my work of weighing the scales of the people of the Earth."

She stood unmoving, letting his words sink in. It wasn't what she was expecting. She wasn't sure exactly what that was. "What are you saying? I have to help you get souls for the Devil, or something?" Her abhorrence dripped from her voice. "Trick people and pull them in like me?"

"Rachel!" Grigori gently reprimanded. His eyes were guarded, giving nothing away. "Have a care."

"Yes," Abaddon said, drawing out the S as if his patience was wearing thin. However, he wasn't answering her; he was speaking to Grigori. "Education in the last two sessions." He continued to study her and narrowed his eyes. "Did your scripture study teach you nothing, child? 'Wide and spacious is the road leading off to destruction, but long and winding is the road that leads to life … and few find it'. Understand that, and you will understand your purpose in life … and in death."

She gasped. Not just because she knew the verse well and

was astonished that someone as evil as him—a co-worker of Satan himself, should be quoting it back at her, but he was alluding to it being linked to her fate.

"The scales balance for everyone, whether they are aware or not."

"The way they live their life sorts them," she said, desperate to hold on to what she'd always believed: that good people are rewarded with everlasting life. It was unbearable that he was trying to rationalize an abhorrent occupation of tricking and damning the people he came into contact with.

He smiled then, but it never really reached his eyes. "Mortals choose. The Grigori, The Fallen and the demons themselves sort them, with me as the final judge of which path they take." He began to turn.

Rachel was astounded at what she'd just learned. Even she knew that she'd just been privy to insider information that no living human could know.

"I myself see to it," he said as he stepped back into the shadows and disappeared completely.

She was left staring at the space where he'd last been. Finally, she swallowed, began breathing normally again, and looked over at Grigori. He hadn't said a word. He was smoothing his hair back with his hands and putting on his cap just like an ordinary day at the tattoo shop. "Sit!" he said.

Although she was still in shock, her feet began to move, and she approached him. Strangely, it felt like familiar ground and, after what she'd just witnessed, oddly comforting. She unconsciously climbed into the chair and turned her head to the distinct sound of his chuckle.

She couldn't actually believe that he found something funny, or even laughed at all; it was so rare. "I can't believe you threatened the Angel of Death with suicide." Then he let loose and laughed loudly, shaking his head.

It was so unusual that she couldn't help smiling too.

"How did you know this?" he said, smiling, conspicuously close to her on his stool. Her nerve endings began to light up as they always did when she got near him.

She shrugged, now grinning. "Bible study 101, der-brain," she said, pointing at her own temple. She didn't know how she could be joking about all this. It was probably the hysteria a person got before they faced execution or went into madness.

He laughed again and nodded. "The jeans need to come off," he said, wiping the grin straight off her face. The atmosphere immediately plummeted to sub-zero, danger territory.

Rachel unbuttoned her jeans, slipped them down, and dropped them on the opposite side of Grigori. She tried to find his eyes to gauge his mood, but was unable. He pumped the lever on the chair and sat back on the stool. "Lie on your side. The next tattoo needs to be on your left hip, travelling downwards to balance the others."

She did as she was told, so her left hip was in the air facing him, but he made her yelp by kicking something and spinning the chair, so she had her back to him. Her eyes darted while she waited. There was no point in arguing with him; they were way beyond that.

"Pull them over your hip."

She quickly pulled her panties higher, so nothing interfered with the curve of her body, leaving it resting in the dip of her waist. The only comfortable place for her head was to lean up on an elbow to rest it on her hand.

"Good!"

She peered over her shoulder while he took the familiar marker pen from behind his ear. He began to sketch quickly over the skin of her side, a design roughly the size of a beer mat with a perfectly circular line around it. There were several squiggly line symbols at the compass points of north, south, east and west. It seemed very basic and almost child-like compared to the others he'd done.

His eyes flashed to hers as if he knew what she was thinking. "This one isn't for beauty but for the message it contains."

"What language is it in?" There was nothing about it she recognized.

"The earliest—predating Sumerian. It outlines the contract you just made. Below ..." And he pointed to what looked like a cross with a circle on top with a second bar across it like cow horns, then changed her mind to wings, "is Abaddon's symbol."

Then above the circle, it looked like a thin vertical triangle with the point facing downwards, a bar across the top and two smaller triangles at either end. It looked like a crude picture of scales with a circle above it like the sun. "That's me?"

"That's the symbol for apprentice or assistant."

Then she got it. It was the contract written in ancient pictographic script, with her at the top, touching the circle, and the details of the deal in the middle. Abaddon was below it, overseeing it all.

When Grigori had finished drawing, he pulled out the familiar doweling from his drawer and held it out to her across her body.

She couldn't help swallowing. "Painful, eh?"

His look was almost apologetic.

"Is it? Tell me."

He looked thoughtful for a moment, which worried her. "It isn't so much the placing this time but the ink itself. It has something added for permanence."

She had no idea what that meant.

Grigori's eyes were direct. "It must burn."

Hers went wide in horror as panic began to set in. For a brief second, she thought of running.

"I'll be with you. The design won't take long, an hour, hour and a half, max."

She could no longer look at him; her disappointment in him was too much. "Don't you get fed up being someone's lackey?" It was out before she had time to check herself.

He pulled her back roughly by the shoulder, so he was staring down at her. Strangely, she wasn't even scared. He seemed to sense it and recoiled slightly. She blinked slowly with contempt.

"No matter who you are in the universe, there is always someone higher, good or bad. The Grigori have Abaddon, he has Lucifer, even he …"

"Waits for the axe to fall," she finished for him. She could no longer bear to look at him, letting her feelings of doom and hopelessness wash over her. "Just get on with it," she said in little more than a whisper.

The machine whirred, and when it touched her skin, nothing happened—well, nothing out of the ordinary. It stung, but there was no horrific burn. She kept quiet, hoping for some reason she'd escaped it.

Grigori was bent over her hip in concentration. She could see him out of the corner of her eye. Her sense of security was shattered when he said, "I will tell you when to bite down." His eyes flicked to the doweling lying on the chair in front of her.

Oh shit. Her mind raced and she tried not to tense. "I need to talk," she said, torn between not wanting to be friendly but needing to take her mind off the waiting. It was torture itself.

He adjusted his position to get a better angle. "So, talk."

"So, what did he mean when he said there is no Hell? Does the Devil even exist?"

Grigori continued to work. "He does."

"Where does he live then?" She flinched as Grigori touched her hipbone. Then she twisted her upper body to look at him.

He sat up and loosened his shoulder muscles by moving them in circles. He always drew attention to his physique. She wondered if it was deliberate because it always made her lose her train of thought.

"Lucifer, Abaddon, Mephistopheles, all are simply Fallen Angels, but they fell at the very beginning."

"And Satan? Lucifer," she corrected. "He was the first?"

He nodded with a sigh and looked off into the middle distance. "There are many realms or dimensions. Tartarus is one and Gehenna another."

"That's where he lives?" She understood then. It was the place where the old kings of Judah sacrificed children by fire. It was symbolic and humans had somehow morphed it into a fiery hell.

Grigori nodded. "We call it Wode, which means the place of hopelessness and despair." He seemed to go to that dark place in his mind as if he'd been there. "The dimensions are close, existing side by side. Sometimes they even rub together, meaning they can be crossed." He moved in with the machine in his hand again and continued to work.

While the familiar sting was tolerable, she thought of the room at the top of the stairs and the way Abaddon appeared and went the same way.

"Abaddon is very old and can cross dimensions at will."

"Even Heaven?" she asked cautiously. Without him even saying, she could tell he never wanted to touch on the subject of God and the other angels that still dwelt with him. Suddenly, she realized what a truly privileged position she was in. To be able to find the answers to questions that scholars had asked themselves for centuries.

However, her heart plummeted when the reason she was allowed came to her: there was no going back. Like an insane serial killer telling his victim how clever he'd been and revealing his whole plan. Because he knows his victim will be silenced by death very soon. That was her right now.

CHAPTER 31

Grigori shook his head. "The heavenly realm was closed off to us long ago." A sadness crossed his whole body like a dark shadow. That would have been the last time he had contact with the Angel he loved.

"And the others—the good ones … they can come and go?" She could have kicked herself for her choice of words.

He checked her expression to make sure she wasn't joking, frowned and was silent after that.

Feeling a little guilty, she changed the subject. "So, I'll have nothing to do with you once all this has concluded?"

He let out a single blast of air through his teeth. "You would prefer it?" he said, his eyes flashing to hers.

"No, I'd prefer none of this to have happened at all and be simply getting on with my life, actually."

He tipped his head. "And so you will, except you will receive instruction from Abaddon. You'll accompany him and be protected by the whole of the spirit realm because of this," he said, nodding towards the tattoo he was working on. "But you will see me regularly as your agent here," he gave her a small rueful smile.

It still didn't make much sense. "And Seb … what will you do with him?"

He continued to work, but his smile grew, making her increasingly uneasy. She was starting to think he had more carnal designs on her boyfriend. However, he schooled his features. "You have relegated him to collateral. He will go on to do great things. He will rise to do whatever he wants to the highest degree, but he will always be indebted to me for it, and for that I will stay in his life."

He paused and took in her worried expression. "I will be in the shadows, taking any and all that I choose. That will be his price on the scales."

Rachel's heart sank. "People he cares about, you mean," she said, heart sick. She thought she'd saved Seb and she wanted him to have a successful life and career, but his sacrifice hadn't been entirely forgotten. She may have saved him from a fate with Abaddon, but the price of all the good stuff happening to him was a heavy debt to Grigori. It was heartbreaking and hopeless.

Without even looking up, he said, "Remember the road leading off to destruction, Rachel?"

She hated that he threw that up at her then. "You're not actually trying to tell me you are performing a public service?" she said, not even trying to keep the mockery out of her voice.

"People are neither all bad nor all good, Rachel. I am saying exactly that. Soon, it will be your job to pass sentence on which road they take. I will identify them, but you will carry the scales."

Her heart dropped into the pit of her stomach. She wanted to scream no at him, but even she couldn't help thinking it through and being fascinated by the notion of it. That it should be part of some huge scheme of things.

Her eyes went to the small symbol that depicted her—the

bar across the neck like a yoke with a triangle at each end. Now she could see they were the scales. Her heart dropped even further. This was way bigger and more complicated than she thought. All her life, she thought people did bad things and went to Hell, and good people went to Heaven. This was so much more than that. "Where do they go then, the bad people?" She thought her nan's dying had knocked her faith, but this rocked her to the core.

"The grave, ultimately. The ones we weigh either resist or are put to work in return for their good fortune. Some are called by Lucifer and he toys with them for a while, usually in order to gain others. The good ones live their lives, die and lie in the dirt waiting in the hope of a resurrection."

"How did they resist?" She'd not wanted any of this. How did she end up here, in the chair with everyone she loved in danger? That couldn't be right.

His look was almost apologetic when he said. "You took a small step into the dark and you came. Your own footsteps brought you here."

She looked at him, frozen in shock. He removed his eyes from her and resumed working. Surely it couldn't have been so easy as simply ignoring Rose's message of doom and not going to Angel's Ink in the first place. "I don't believe you. I've seen my nan. She's in Heaven."

He bobbed his head as if that was entirely possible. "Some are weighed and called to Heaven at the point of death. 'In the twinkling of an eye,' he said, quoting scripture again.

She scowled at him.

"It could also be demons playing tricks on you. What better way of perpetuating the lie of everlasting life for all than producing a dead relative. Most people simply cease to exist, Rachel. They become a memory on the wind, in the hope of being remembered by Him on the last day."

"The resurrection," she spoke softly to herself. The

knowledge literally blew her mind. "I know I saw her. She warned me about you."

He didn't argue. "Then cherish the memory, because they will be few."

It was said through tight lips and she knew he was thinking of his own loved one. The horror of it all wrapped around and constricted her throat so she couldn't breathe. Their polar positions made seeing him impossible and so it would be in her case too. "What happens in the last two sessions?" she asked in a cracked voice.

"Instruction and small symbols, mainly. No more great works of art," he said dryly. "The last being your own seal." He looked directly at her then. *How did he do that?* That look that pulled her in from the very first day. Deep, intense and infinitely sexual. She recognized it now. Something had shifted. She wasn't as naive as she used to be. He was referring to her own signature on the unbreakable contract and the final full stop to everything, but his eyes said so much more.

He sat back. "It is finished."

A wave of relief flooded over her. "That's it? It was nowhere near as bad as he made out.

"Not quite." And he pointed to the doweling.

She frowned and picked it up.

"Now you will need it."

She put it in her mouth, totally bewildered. Then all she could do was watch in horror as he gave her no time to think. He produced a gas lighter from nowhere and put it against the skin of her new tattoo. His large hand came up as a barrier to shield her eyes. She dodged her head on instinct to look through his fingers and watched as the ink ignited like a fuse. The pain followed a second later.

Grigori was now on his feet, holding her down by the shoulders while she screamed through her teeth, gripping onto the doweling. It seared the symbols of the tattoo like a line of gunpowder, covering every single stroke he'd made. Her eyes were now tightly shut in her agony, but she felt its progress over every part of it. The five or so seconds felt like ten minutes. It was excruciating. By the time the burning stopped, she lay exhausted and covered in sweat.

Her eyes fluttered open. She spat the doweling out and it clanked onto the floor. Before she could utter a word, Grigori swooped down and covered her mouth with his. He kissed her long and deeply, swirling his tongue with hers. The extreme pain dulled and was replaced by warmth and excitement, running through her veins like molten metal. By the end of the kiss, he had completely dwarfed her pain.

She was left looking at him, amazed, when he pulled apart from her. Those eyes looked through her in his direct way that turned her insides to liquid.

"An angel's kiss has hidden properties," he said, and moved away.

She was left stunned by him as always. The moment had gone, and she wasn't sure it had ever happened in the way she thought. He had basically just said he'd given her the angel version of an anesthetic.

Rachel must have passed out shortly after because the next thing she knew, she was at home in her own bed. Seb slept soundly next to her with soft, warm breaths on her shoulder. Sleep dragged her down again.

THE FIRST THING that Rachel felt when she woke was her hip. It felt like a chunk of her skin had been ripped off. Seb stirred next to her as if he was aware, even in his subconscious. Sunlight poured into the room where no one had closed the curtains the night before.

She sat up cautiously, wincing. The slightest movement

killed. She was dressed exactly as she had been the previous night—minus the pants. Grigori must have brought her straight home in what she'd worn in his chair.

There was some kind of surgical dressing over it, rather than the usual protective gauze.

"Hey," Seb said, sleepily blinking and turning onto his back. "How was it?"

She smiled and frowned as the memories of the whole thing started to ping into her mind.

"You were out a full day and a half, I was getting really worried."

Her eyes widened. She couldn't believe she'd been out that long. No wonder she was starving. "How are you?" she said, remembering he wasn't in great shape when she'd left him either.

He turned onto his side and pulled her hand to cover the bulge in the front of his boxers. "Better," he said, his smile as sexy as ever. "And don't dodge my question."

She grinned and kissed him. "It went OK ... I think," she said, frowning. Then she remembered what day it was, if she'd been out that long. There was no time for indulging in Seb's body, however tempting. "Get up," she said, already pushing off the bed. "We need to meet up with Nicola."

He groaned behind her. "You know I'm not a morning person."

She giggled. "It's not morning anymore, Seb. Get up!"

He sighed and she felt him get up behind her and kiss the crook of her neck. She found a light shift dress to cover her that wouldn't rub the wound. "Come on, I'll explain every-thing there."

He followed her, a little shakily. She had to remember he would feel very weak still after the first exposure to the ink. She pulled him with her across the hall into the bathroom and turned on the shower.

He had to hold onto the sink to step out of his boxers. She pulled the dress over her head and stepped into the shower. He followed. "What did you get this time?" he asked, pointing to the dressing that she was already trying to pull down slowly. The surgical tape wasn't too bad, but the dressing was agony as it had stuck to the wound.

She gasped with the pain and remembered the all-consuming kiss Grigori had given her after the burning. The same heat flooded her body at the memory and the stinging subsided.

"Why is that over it?"

"Hang on, I'll show you." With a final wince, she managed to get the whole thing off. Grigori hadn't said she had to keep anything on it. She stared down at it.

"Fucking, hell, Rach. What is that?"

She knew exactly why his anger was building. It looked like a red angry brand like the ones cowboys gave cattle.

Seb dropped down to his knees to study it more closely. She could tell his mind was scattered, thinking a number of things. "Why'd they … who the fuck did you get?"

Rachel let out a ragged breath as the enormity of it all came crashing in. "The Angel of Death," she whispered.

Seb looked up, straight into her eyes, but remained on his knees. She didn't think she'd ever forget that angelic, heart-breakingly concerned look. The irony wasn't lost on her. Water was cascading down from her and splashing onto his face and hair, making him spit the water out a couple of times. How beautifully innocent he was and how tragic that their roles had reversed so much.

The moment was heavy with no other noise other than the crashing water of the shower and his expression softened when he realized she didn't want to talk about it right then. Instead, he closed the gap between his mouth and her abdomen, and without breaking eye contact, began a trail of kisses downward, gently sucking her skin and swirling his tongue as he went.

She threaded her fingers through his hair. He was gentle and so reverent. "I'm done being careful, Seb. Take it all the way."

It was gratifying to see his pupils dilate and register what she meant. She was forced to grab the rail as he dipped his head and mercilessly tortured her. His fingers separated her folds and ventured in and out, first one and then two. He pulled the leg from her good side over his shoulder and lapped the small bundle of nerves, nipping and circling until she literally came apart in his hands.

He stood slowly and turned her, covering the hand that held the rail with his own and kissing her shoulder, while he gradually fed himself into her from behind. It felt like he pulled her apart. She gasped and he groaned, taking the skin of her shoulder between his teeth. She was so full she almost came undone. He paused and she breathed. Then he began a tortuously slow rhythm. She loved that he was so passionate yet gentle. Her hip had been relegated to a dull ache.

"Sorry, I don't think I could lift you today," he whispered.

She half gasped, half laughed, and put out her hand to pull him in behind her tighter. It was new and strange, and he filled her completely. This way, he could move with her and hold her in place with his other sinful hand straight between her legs.

She wondered if he got it at all that their days together were numbered. Maybe on some level, he did. If that was so, it only served to drive them hotter, higher and totally over the edge. His thrusts built in strength and she welcomed it. This was the perfect distraction that they both needed. It was visceral and real, cutting through all the other bullshit in their lives at the moment.

His mouth captured her loud sigh over her shoulder.

Maybe he was thinking Lynn could hear, or maybe he just wanted everything. Whatever it was, it pushed them on. The sensation crawled up her spine and spread its burn through every vein and neural pathway. He was forced to support them with one hand on the tiles to stop them collapsing when he followed. Pulling out of her, she felt the hot jets against her back. *Shit,* it had been so all-consuming that she hadn't given safe sex a thought. She was losing her mind.

She braced her hands on the wall on either side of her to ease her cheek that had been pushed into it. Seb held her waist while his own breaths slowed, until he pulled her back against him, cupping her breasts.

He bit her shoulder playfully, just above her iris tattoo, and ran his thumbs over her nipples. They were hard and exposed and he made her feel wild and sensual. She couldn't help pushing her backside against him and he crushed her tighter. His arms dropped to circle her waist and she rested hers over them. He was completely encircling her. She turned inside his arms to face him.

How did he manage to look so dopily sexy? His hair was all over the place and his bloodshot eyes half closed.

"Thank you," she said, holding each side of his face. "I think I needed that."

He laughed and pulled her to him, linking his arms behind her back. "You're so sexy, you know that?"

It seemed a strange thing to think, but she was beginning to. Then she could only think of how cruel the timing of all this was. She picked up the shower gel and the sponge and made a lather in her hands. "Come on, we have to meet Nicola soon, and we don't have much time. I need to catch you up with everything that's happened."

CHAPTER 32

They went back to her room and dressed in silence after that; Seb in his customary black, and she in some loose yoga pants and a white t-shirt. Both felt the weight of what lay ahead.

As promised, her car was left at the front of the house and they held hands over the central console while she drove them into town.

Life was so cruel. Part of her wanted to cry at how unfair all this was. Seb seemed to know and squeezed her hand. It was a relief that she no longer had to hide any of it.

She pulled into the car park of the cafe where she'd met Nicola the last time. They went inside and found her already sitting at a table, waiting. Seb went to the counter and bought coffee and croissants and they settled in their chairs opposite Nicola, just like any other weary shoppers taking a break. Except they weren't. The three of them were as damned as any person could be.

They all sensed it. Rachel wondered if it was conspicuous. She eventually broke the awkward moment by introducing Seb and quickly explained his part in everything. Skimming over the fact that their new sexual status played a huge part, and the kiss he'd shared with Grigori to save his embarrassment.

Nicola nodded along to everything while she sipped her coffee and listened closely.

Rachel finally got onto the events of Saturday, right down to the tattoo being burned into her skin.

"Do you mind if I see it?" Nicola said.

Rachel angled herself away from onlookers and pulled the side of the yoga pants down. Nicola pretended to pick something up off the floor to peek at it under the table. Seb kept watch.

"Was your fourth session like that?" Rachel asked.

Nicola came back up and, shuffling to get comfortable again, she shook her head. "No." She frowned and sighed deeply. "I don't know much about this stage with others. It's where I normally lose them, but no one I know has reported anything like that."

Rachel didn't know what to say. This was the one person she expected to have all the answers.

"I can only think it's because of who it is."

She looked at her so sadly then that Rachel knew there was no coming back from this. However, she was grateful she didn't voice it for Seb's sake. All she said was, "I can't lie, Rachel. It doesn't look good." Her eyes that bore into hers said way more than words: It was burned on because it was permanent—more so even than ink that contained the blood of an Angel.

Seb wasn't stupid. "Ink is permanent," he said moodily, straight at Nicola.

"That can't be covered over … ever," Nicola said, pointing at Rachel's lower body. "Burning reaches the soul." Then she averted her eyes.

Rachel saw the moment that Seb fell in with what she

meant, and her heart went out to him. "We need to look at the book, Nicola."

"Did you bring your copy?" Nicola said.

Rachel patted the large bag at her feet. "Did you bring yours?"

Nicola nodded. She looked around her. "But not here."

"We can go to the library if you want?" She remembered Mabel had a few days booked off, so they'd be left alone without too many questions about why she hadn't been at work.

They all agreed, finished their coffees and made the short drive across town to the library.

THE LIBRARY WAS modern and light. It had WiFi and a cafe if they needed it and some comfy sofas in the quiet corner. Mabel's fill-in librarian was so engrossed with customers that she wasn't aware of them. They whisked through, straight to the corner where they managed to bag some armchairs around a low table.

Nicola took off her leather backpack and pulled out two copies of the familiar black book and passed one to Seb. "Yours!" she said.

Seb looked at her, puzzled, but took it anyway. "Why do we need our own copies?"

"Your way of resisting might be different from Rachel's. And you'll need to refer to it a lot."

He nodded as if it made sense, but Rachel's cheeks prickled red at the look she shot at her. They both knew that he would probably be the only one coming out of this. "To resist, we all need to read the last chapter."

"I think you should read up on all the other chapters too, Seb," Rachel said softly, smiling at him.

He looked at her a moment too long, then cracked the

spine and began to thumb through. She had to rein in her emotions, otherwise he'd see right through the bullshit and guess this was a one-way ticket for her.

She pulled out hers, which was already pretty dog-eared. She'd marked specific sections with sticky notes. "Show me yours," she said, leaning across to Nicola.

Nicola quickly flicked to the back of her own book. Rachel saw only blank page after blank page. She passed it to Seb to see if he saw the same. "Can you read it?"

He took the book from her hands and turned the pages far too easily for something to be written there. "Nothing," he said, shaking his head.

Rachel looked again and shook her head, not fully understanding what it meant.

Nicola took back the book, looking troubled. "It's what I was afraid of."

"What?" Rachel and Seb both said together.

"I think the last chapter is different to everyone … which means … "

"Only one person can read it," Rachel finished for her.

"Wait! You wrote the original last chapter, right?" Seb said, looking at them both as if the answer was simple.

Nicola nodded. Yes, but I checked my computer files this morning and it never stays. It always disappears."

"Can't you remember the gist of it?" Seb said.

Nicola shrugged and shook her head. "That's just it, I can't. There's a huge hole in my memory there."

"But you've saved loads of people, haven't you?" Seb was beginning to sound desperate. "Can't we contact them?"

Nicola looked sad, as if she felt terrible about saying it. "That's not how it works, Seb, I'm afraid. They have no memory of anything. If they escape, their memory of it is taken and they disappear. I never hear from them again. And if their soul is owned, then they won't dare say anything.

Think about it, even if they did, they won't know theirs is any different to anyone else's and we won't be able to read it to know by how much."

"They've got it completely sewn up," Rachel said, shaking her head.

"Except you," Rachel said.

Seb became alert and nodded too. "Yeah, why only you?"

The light seemed to drain out of Nicola's eyes as she spoke, like the inevitability of everything simply drained her. Rachel couldn't imagine the weight she carried. "You could argue that it's my fate to remember. I have to. To be of any use to anyone, they allowed me to keep it." Her eyes went to Rachel's and the words "you will too" went unsaid. But they came through loud and clear.

Rachel looked at Seb nervously, but he was clearly pondering what Nicola had just said. It worried her that Nicola was already treating her as a lost cause, *but wasn't she doing the same?* The thought of spending even a day with Abaddon made her shudder. She had to get a grip. The whole point of today was to find some sort of loophole or way around it that didn't implicate Seb.

Her voice of reason constantly picked at her, taunting and jibing, that beings that had lived longer than the Earth itself would have made any contract watertight by now, but she couldn't allow her mind to go down that burrow. That only led to despair and madness. "Turn to the last chapter," she said, coughing as her voice broke.

While he shuffled the pages, she stared out of the large bank of windows. The sky was dark, and rain was now lashing them.

"Blank," he said. "Blank, blank, blank. He turned every page until he got to the back of the book.

Rachel sighed as if their day couldn't get any worse. She

put her hand over the pages to stop him from turning them frantically. "Stop!"

His breathing was labored, as if he was only just keeping his temper. Rachel was shocked; she'd never seen him so upset.

"You've got to want to fight it, Seb, I mean really want to," she said, softly, like she was talking him down off a ledge. Then she slowly removed her hand.

He swallowed and looked intently at the pages again. "I am … I don't know. There's nothing." He slammed the book closed and pushed it to the floor.

Rachel reached out a hand and held his wrist before he went to get up. "Maybe he can't control it now, maybe it's all on me." She reached down and retrieved the book from the floor. She opened it and went straight to the back, to the heading that said, *How to beat the tests.* A thought struck her. "Seb didn't have the tests." *Could it be as simple as that?* He was owned at his first tattoo.

She looked down. The paper seemed to move and swirl. It was blurry at first. "Something's coming."

She felt Seb come closer as his knee brushed hers. "What does it say?"

"OK, I can see it. I'll read it all."

FOR MOST, the final chapter assumes you have gone through the five sessions prior to it and are ready and willing for the last. This is your signature on the deal, if you like. However, that's not always the case. For some, there are no tests. They have offered themselves or been given by a loved one to stand in their place.

This is called the sacrifice service or pledge. It is an offering by proxy that has equal weight on the scales. It is binding if accepted, but doesn't automatically free the original subject. It only frees them of certain aspects of the deal. They become collateral for each other. The Grigori will own both of them, holding their contracts for the duration of their lives. Their sacrifice service (we will call 'Proxy' from now on) can refuse, right up to the point of being marked by the Grigori.

RACHEL LOOKED up into Seb's eyes then. She couldn't speak.

FROM THAT POINT ONWARD, their fate lies solely in the hands of the original subject. They alone can decide whether to relieve them of their service. If they decide on that course, they can go on with their lives without any knowledge of the transaction. However, there is a catch: they will always be owned by the Grigori who marked them. We can only assume their fate is the same as that of all the others marked for destruction.

RACHEL BLINKED BACK tears when she looked at Seb again. She'd brought him into this, and she hated herself for it. It was made so much worse because he didn't. His eyes looked misty but determined. He knew damn well he was marked, and it was too late for him. They all did. She just had to find a way to get him away from Grigori.

"It's your turn," Nicola said, snapping her out of her thoughts.

With a deep breath, she put Seb's book down onto the coffee table and opened hers in her lap. She went straight to the back of the book where she'd placed a bookmark.

Again, it took her a few moments to focus. The first sentence was the same, except this time it listed the six sessions and their relevance to the subject.

- *Session 1: The pivotal point in your life.*
- *Session 2: The journey that brought you to this point.*
- *Session 3: The mark of the Grigori.*
- *Session 4: The contract construct (The deal).*
- *Session 5: The submission.*
- *Session 6: The mark of the subject—final signature.*

FOR MOST WHO *read this chapter, you have reached sessions four and five and are about to sign on the dotted line. Some would have managed to use their willpower to resist the temptations offered prior to this point—Rather like Jesus, who was offered all the kingdoms of the world when he was alone with the Devil in the wilderness. For some lucky subjects, that would have been all that was needed—a simple emphatic 'no'.*

Unfortunately, for some of you, it hasn't been that simple. You have come to the notice of the highest-ranking of The Fallen, or even the demons themselves. You have the qualities they need to do something for them. They want to enlist you in service.

You will probably be scholarly, well-read, maybe well-versed in scripture, pure of spirit, or have no conscience at all. It is unclear whether all or which is required. Suffice it to say that, if you are chosen, your only hope is to cut the best possible deal for your loved ones, because if you are past session four, you're too deeply in.

RACHEL STARED at the page that went to nothing after that. At first, she thought her tears had affected her vision, but when she wiped them on the back of her hand, it was as though the rest of the words had been rubbed out. It didn't even explain five or six. A sob escaped her and her hand went to her mouth. "It's gone … there isn't anymore."

Seb's face was thunderous. "That's it … she just gives in?"

He said it too loudly and got loads of dirty looks from browsing customers. Rachel was worried he'd punch something. She'd never seen him so angry.

Nicola moved further to the edge of her seat and motioned for them to come closer and do the same. "Look, I know it sounds bad, but the book has given you a major clue."

Rachel and Seb both pulled confused faces at each other and looked back at her again.

"There are still deals to be made."

Rachel frowned, not so sure.

Seb looked like he couldn't take in much more.

"We just need to think about it carefully. It needs to be clever and achievable, as I think it will be a one-time thing, and it needs to be pitched before session six. Otherwise …"

She didn't need to finish. Rachel got her drift perfectly. The deal will stick for the rest of their lives. She didn't miss the look Nicola gave her. Whatever they did now, the major part of it would be for Seb. For the time being, they would let him assume they were working to free them both. She and Nicola both knew that was a lost cause. The main objective was to save Seb's eternal soul, and in order to free him, they had to come up with something creative and fast. Then, he must never know.

CHAPTER 33

*E*ach of them got to work after that—Nicola and Rachel with their laptops on their knees and Seb on one of the library desktops.

Rachel looked over at Seb a couple of times. How sexy he looked with his serious, concentrating face on. She had to smile as she saw it so rarely. He was one of life's breaths of fresh air. Little got him down. He was the joy and brightness that lightened every room he was in. Whatever happened, she would save him at any cost.

She decided to concentrate on the deal—what Grigori's strengths and weaknesses were and hers too. His strengths were daunting, given the length of the list. Physical and mental strength, fighting ability, intellect, wit, cunning, the list was endless. When she started to dwell on his washboard abs and beauty—in a lethal, life-threatening kind of way, she decided that was no help whatsoever. Except it brought her to his own stunning array of tattoos and his lost love. The teardrop was the key. Layke was Grigori's only weakness. How she wished she could speak to him.

An hour and a half passed quickly when Nicola called a

break. They all went and sat in the library's coffee shop. "So, what do we all have so far?" Nicola said, putting a coffee down for each of them, stowing the tray and settling into her seat. "I concentrated on the scales aspect and whether the transaction was legal and of equal weight when bringing Seb into it."

Rachel nodded. It was a good start.

"The main point of the scales is justice," she explained. Even though they're Fallen, the concept of all things being equal comes from God himself. A good point to argue could be that while you came off your path of righteousness and looked for them willingly, Seb was an innocent, making it not like for like."

Seb frowned and grinned his lopsided grin. "Or not so innocent."

Rachel chuckled. The idea of Seb being labeled as innocent in any sphere was preposterous. It did make a kind of sense though. She had slept with him and then saved his life, pulling him into it, but then she remembered. "Yeah, but he freely offered himself for Grigori's mark. Wouldn't that negate that?"

Nicola bobbed her head and sighed. "Perhaps. It's a tough call."

"I looked up the Jewish calendar—I guessed these guys worked off the same background of religious stuff?" Seb said.

Rachel's eyes widened. It was a great idea.

"Yom Kippur is coming up on the fourteenth of September—the tenth day of Tishrei." He looked over at both of the women as if they should know this stuff.

Rachel's mouth was open.

"The atonement of sins," he said, looking from one to the other. "Where the fate of a person is sealed."

Rachel looked at Nicola, who was looking equally as gobsmacked.

"What?" Seb said, half laughing. "I'm Jewish, so what!"

"I think you could be onto something," Rachel said, and reached for his hand under the table. "So, what do you normally have to do on atonement day?"

Seb shrugged. "Usual stuff, you know. Fasting, prayer, abstaining from physical pleasures," he said, not able to keep the grin off his face.

"Your last session falls on the fourteenth of September," Nicola said, cutting right through Seb's playfulness. "It might not be a coincidence. What did you get?" she said, switching her attention directly to Rachel.

"I looked for Grigori's weaknesses and came up with only one."

They both looked surprised that he had any at all. She explained what little she knew of Layke. There wasn't much because he barely spoke of him. Just that he was the artist of his many tattoos, that his teardrop was for him and that they were meant to Fall together, but he didn't stay. However, something in her made her hold back the details of the depth of Grigori's love for the Angel. Despite what he'd done —was still doing—she wasn't comfortable betraying him that way.

Seb and Nicola agreed that it could be a major chink in his armor, but neither could offer any idea how it could be of use to them.

Rachel did, but for that, she needed to go back to church. As much as she hated the idea, she needed to call Cynthia. With what Seb had hit on as well, there had to be some significance to all this.

She searched her contacts immediately, grateful she hadn't just discarded her number. Guess that was the good little librarian in her. Neatly tucking it away in the "never know when you might need it" section.

She picked up after the third ring. "Cynthia?" The other

two were watching her make the call, silently drinking their coffees.

"Yes,"

"Hi, Cynthia, it's Rachel."

"Oh, Rachel, I'm so relieved to hear from you. How—"

Rachel cut across her. It wasn't a social call. "I need a favor, Cynthia."

"Erm, well … of course, if I can."

"I need to speak to Pastor Andrew. Can you get him to meet me at the church later? It's kind of urgent."

"I will, of course, my dear. I'm thrilled you have decided to come back to us."

Rachel tried to keep the impatience out of her voice. The woman would keep her on the phone forever, so she ended it quickly, saying she was at work. The lie, even after everything that was happening, made her cheeks go pink. "It's set then. Hopefully, he'll agree to see me tonight."

"I'll go with you," Seb said.

She gave his hand a squeeze. "No, Seb, I need to see them alone." Then she turned to Nicola. "You go home, and I'll ring you later."

They all agreed. At least it was a start. Any action was better than nothing.

Rachel dropped Nicola off at the station. "Call me," she said with a comforting squeeze of her shoulder. It was starting to feel like she was going off to war and wouldn't be coming back.

She and Seb went home to wait it out. Bible group ended at 8.30. She guessed that was when the pastor would see her.

Their mood was somber. Lynn flitted in and out, thankfully, not asking too many questions. They'd agreed not to bring her into it any more than she was already for her own safety. It was handy; she assumed their preoccupation was down to them being so into each other and left them to it.

There was something in the air though, that made her suspect that Seb had caught on to the clock ticking on their relationship. Whether Seb really understood how final it had to be, she wasn't sure. That afternoon, they made love as if it were one of their last times, and it was heartbreaking and beautiful.

They'd got so close in such a short time. The physical lust-filled part had happened like a flash fire, so the risk was high that it couldn't last. Wasn't the saying "the light that burns twice as bright burns half as long"? She had to remain tough. Leaving him was the right thing to do.

Cynthia texted early evening, exactly as expected. Rachel was to meet the pastor at the church at 8.30 at the close of Bible Study group. The time came for her to go and Seb drew her to him, kissing the top of her head. "I'll be at Jack's if you need me."

She nodded and breathed in his wonderful Seb scent through his t-shirt on his chest. She hated that he watched her go with such sadness and worry in his eyes. They were still on her all the way down the path and into her car. This couldn't continue. She was tearing him apart.

Cynthia greeted her as soon as she arrived. She waited patiently outside while they were all filing out of the door from their study group. She shook hands and kissed cheeks as she'd done on many occasions before with her nan. She felt a weird detachment now. She was here for a purpose and nothing more.

After literally pulling her inside to where the pastor was piling chairs from their bible group, Cynthia finally left her with a squeeze of encouragement and a cloud of violet scent.

"Good evening, Rachel," Pastor Andrew said in his soft Jamaican accent. She'd forgotten how warm the sound was. He smiled and continued putting the chairs away from the discussion circle.

Rachel helped him, but kept her eyes on him the whole time in case he said something more. He was a handsome black guy with grey peppering over his temples. He was sixty-something years of age, but you wouldn't know it from the line-free dark skin.

When they were done, he came and stood right in front of her and gave her his warmest smile. "Welcome home, Rachel. What brings you here on such a dark and windy night?" His eye held an infectious twinkle that instantly made her relax.

She wondered if he thought this meant she was back for good, but somehow, she didn't think so. "It's just a flying visit, Pastor Andrew. I've come for advice, really."

The pastor nodded once and led her by the elbow to the rows of chairs at the front of the church. "Well, you've come to the right place," he said, and indicated for her to sit with him in the front row. He waited patiently for her to speak with his hands resting in his lap. She was sure he would have waited for her all night until she was ready. How lovely and simple her life would have been if her nan hadn't died. She'd have remained comfortable and cocooned in these walls. However, apart from her loss, she would never have swapped living with her friends, and to an extent, even meeting Grigori, who had brought her into this horrible mess. "I want to know how to contact a particular angel?" she blurted.

The pastor looked genuinely surprised and then confused.

"I'm not talking about a dead person, a séance, or anything like that, I mean a proper angel like Gabriel or someone like that."

His eyes widened and he took a minute to think about her question, then frowned again. "Whatever do you need that for, child? You know you can't pray to one directly; you can only pray to the Father through Jesus. They'd never respond directly."

Rachel knew what he was saying was true and looked down at her hands. "It's not for me, it's for a friend." She wasn't sure exactly what to tell him that wasn't going to be construed as evil, however she put it. Saying it was for someone who'd lost someone they cared for deeply wasn't going to sound any better without some sort of explanation. That was something she wasn't prepared to give. She'd only put the pastor in danger then. Maybe she already had. She went to get up.

"Wait, Rachel!" he said, taking hold of her hand gently. "I'm not sure what's going on, or what trouble you are in, but I suspect it has something to do with your grandmother." He was looking intently into her eyes. "Such a sad and terrible loss. She is always in our hearts and our prayers."

She returned his direct gaze, waiting to see where he was going with this.

"You could ask Jesus to intercede for you. If your request is genuine and good, I'm sure he would listen."

She wasn't sure what she expected. She guessed something a little more concrete than that. "OK, I will," she said, standing more slowly this time.

The pastor stood too and picked up both her hands. He looked directly into her eyes and she wondered what he saw there. Whether he saw that she'd changed, or the small, timid girl who held onto her nan's skirt as a child? He'd made no comment about her hair or clothes. A tear escaped her eye. He really was a good man. "Thank you, Pastor Andrew." She realized this would probably be the last time she ever saw him. Soon, she wouldn't be worthy. She smiled and pulled away, her shoes clip-clopping on the hard floor as she made her way back to the entrance.

"You're always welcome," he called out, making her pause

and turn her head. "Whenever you're passing by," he said, with a kindly smile that seemed so knowing. "Remember, even in our darkest hour, someone is always watching and there is hope, Rachel."

He didn't know how eerily true those words were. "Even if you've strayed from the path, pastor?" Tears welled and she fought them back.

"Especially in those times."

She turned and left the warm glow and comfort of the building for the cold and the dark outside. She began to run and didn't stop until she got to her car. The unshed tears fell all through the drive home.

The streets were still busy. Cars, people, everyone carrying on with their lives, oblivious to what was going on around them. She sobbed for her nan and the life she had that she could never get back, and her first love that she knew was on borrowed time. To keep him would damn him alongside her. No, she would have to free him, whatever it took, and accept that he would know nothing of their relationship together.

There was something in what the pastor had said about loss and carrying a piece of the person with us always. Despite what Grigori had said about the dead, she was sure her nan had tried to warn her a couple of times. That meant she was watching, or at least someone was. How much more capable would a powerful angel like Layke be? Surely he would watch over Grigori. It gave her a little comfort.

She wondered what he looked like. Perhaps all the good angels were golden like the one she'd dreamed of that night in her room. That's how she imagined them: beautiful, glowing creatures with white wings tipped in gold. It made up her mind. She hadn't prayed for a very long time. Tonight, she'd pray like never before.

CHAPTER 34

It was ironic that the thing Rachel craved most in the world was normality. To be an ordinary person, even if it was just for a short while. It was with that thought that she went back to work the next day. The wait until the weekend was going to be agonizing enough.

Nicola contacted her while on her break. "Any news?"

Rachel relayed what the pastor had said and the bones of her plan. "The only chance we've got is to strike a deal just for Seb."

Nicola agreed that it was their best shot. They both understood it would be a one-way ticket for her. "Seb must never know, though," Rachel begged. "Otherwise he won't go along with it." When she pointed out the sacrifices Nicola made in her own life, she could do nothing but agree.

And so, Rachel settled into a rhythm of life, albeit somewhat stiffly at times. Lynn spent a lot of her time with Colin, and when she was home, seemed amused, assuming that her's and Seb's weirdness was the honeymoon period of young love. How little she knew.

Rachel woke early on Saturday morning with a feeling of

impending doom in her heart. Seb slept with his arms tightly around her as if something would take her in the night. His head was on her stomach with his messy hair spread over her up to her breasts. Despite the ease of everything physical between them now, a subtle wedge was sliding between them and she felt helpless to do anything about it. By keeping him in the dark, communication between them was breaking down. It was starting to feel like sex was all they had left to stay close.

She ran her fingers through the loose mop of black hair. Tonight, she would leave him for Grigori for the submission session. No lover would be OK with that. It was in the title. The chasm was doomed to widen; it was inevitable. She'd checked the last chapter a hundred times and it always said the same thing. Her only hope was to barter a deal for Seb and offer herself unreservedly. She'd have to deal with Seb's hurt as and when she came to it. They'd all looked for loopholes all week and there were none. Saving Seb was the only good outcome from a shitty situation.

IT WAS TIME TO GO. Seb held her tightly at the door and kissed her soundly. It was as though he knew at some level what she was about to do but wasn't sure enough to voice it. He wasn't stupid; he knew the enormity of the session. He kissed the top of her head when she really had to go.

"I'll be back as soon as I can," Rachel said, looking up into his eyes. These last few days seemed to have sucked all the happy-go-lucky joy out of him and she hated that she was the cause.

"You sure I can't go with you?" He rubbed the pads of his thumbs over her cheeks.

She shook her head slightly. "I don't know what it'll be,

but I know I need to be alone." The thought of putting Seb near things like Abaddon turned her blood to ice.

He nodded reluctantly and kissed her for the last time. "Message me as soon as you're out of there."

She went to turn to walk away and he didn't let go of her hand until the very last moment. It broke her heart and so she didn't look at him again. She jogged to her car, got in and pulled away, knowing that he watched her until she was out of sight.

Everything was exactly the same as usual when she got to Angel's Ink. It was 9 p.m., the streets were almost empty and the corridor was in semi-darkness.

The door to the shop at the back was on the latch. After closing it, she quickly scanned the room for any more surprises and found Grigori at his usual place, at his station, preparing for the session. "No more weirdoes for me to meet tonight, then." Her words were acid, but, even as she said them, she was taking in his battered low-slung jeans just barely resting on his hips and baggy white t-shirt that should have done nothing, but accentuated his oozing masculinity.

He turned and grinned. "No, we get out of here tonight."

Her heart stopped. "Where are we going?" There was a certain amount of security in the shop. He could be taking her anywhere. She might never come back. The thought of never seeing Seb again sent her into a blind panic.

A small frown played on Grigori's forehead. "We have almost finished our journey, Rachel. It is time to see the world you will live in through new eyes. I thought we could let our hair down if we are to spend eternity together." His gaze was intense and made her literally gulp. Her mind went from Seb waiting patiently for her to get home and then stalled at eternity. "That wasn't the deal. My natural life, Abaddon said."

Grigori frowned, leaned back against his counter and

folded his arms like he always did. "Don't be ridiculous, Rachel. Abaddon wouldn't spend his time training you to give you up in the blink of an eye. A human lifespan is nothing to the millennia he has already lived."

Suddenly, there didn't seem to be enough air in the room. Rachel gasped for breath and felt the blood drain out of her cheeks. Within a second, Grigori's arms came around her. "Breathe slowly," he whispered next to her ear. "In, one two, out, one two ... that's it," he said when she began to copy him.

When she finally calmed down, she became aware of his presence all around her. The smell, the feel of him, his height and warmth, everything felt so familiar. She realized then that she'd done this many times. Whether they were dreams or not, they had felt real enough. She craned her neck to look up at him.

Without her even realizing, he had taken it; he gently released her and handed her her own phone. "Text home. It will be a long session tonight." She preferred to think that he was being thoughtful so that Seb and Lynn didn't worry, but she strongly suspected it was more to do with the risk of Seb coming there to find her.

Her hands were still shaking from her near faint, but she nodded and did as he asked. There was no way she wanted Seb turning up. Her mind raced from where he might be taking her to whether it was usual to be taking her anywhere at all. "But I thought ... what about the tattoo?"

He put his head to the side to gauge her expression. It seemed childlike for such a big, scary guy. How easy it would be to be drawn in by those strong lines and unusual eyes that looked almost orange in the light. "You will have your tattoos by morning."

Before she could speak, he took her by the hand and led her to the door. They followed the corridor to the staircase and began climbing. Her heart was thumping more with every step for fear of where he was taking her. She didn't want to go back to the forest to the other scary angels. "You said tattoos. How many will I have?" she asked, staring at his broad back while he pulled her with him upwards, past the door and towards the roof. Wondering what on earth could be up there, she went back to the thought of where more tattoos could possibly go. She didn't want to be completely covered.

"There will be three for the submission. They represent your hands for your service and your mind for your free will."

It didn't feel like free will just then.

They reached the roof and Grigori opened the metal door with a clang. It was a clear night and stars were all around them. Grigori turned and cupped the side of her face with his large hand. "Stop worrying, Rachel. You passed the worst of it last week. Tonight is about learning to put your trust in me." His stunning eyes were looking down into hers intently, with a hint of vulnerability which she instantly dismissed as preposterous. "Do you trust me, Rachel?" He laced his hand with hers.

She pulled it free and glared up at him. "Isn't all that beside the point? I belong to Abaddon, don't I?"

He frowned a little. "As his protégé, yes, but you will spend most of your working life with me." He smiled wryly. "That is, unless you want to live with him in Wode?" He laughed and picked up her hand again. It dwarfed hers. The laughter died on his features as if he was thinking the same thing. "For most people, life is shit and you die, Rachel. You have an opportunity to remain mortal but live indefinitely. I have only seen it a handful of times."

She was watching every small movement in his face as he spoke. He was right and she could almost think he cared. However, she could not allow herself the luxury of that. She didn't trust him or any of this new world she was falling into. Bartering for Seb seemed such an impossibility now. Perhaps that had been Grigori's plan all along. He'd completely outmaneuvered her. The thought of outliving everyone she loved ripped open her heart and terrified her. What hope was there but to go along with it all for now. "What if I simply refuse? … What if I can't trust you enough to submit?"

He seemed to sigh and shift his weight onto the other leg. Then he rubbed his thumb under her eye to a tear she hadn't even noticed falling. "I don't think we need worry about that."

His arrogance made her recoil, but on further inspection, she could tell it was just confidence born of thousands of years of experience. It still blew her mind and she swallowed hard. Everything was so direct and sexual with him. Nothing failed to hit her in the gut. He probably just meant Seb would take her place, so he won either way, but his hooded eyes suggested so much more.

"Come!" he said. "Tonight, your senses will be unveiled, and you will see the world through the eyes of angels. He led her to the corner of the roof and, with the loud snap like a sail, his wings came open and covered the entire width of the building. In the time it took her to take in a breath, he had her pulled to him and her feet left the ground to rhythmical beats. She quickly grabbed onto his neck. Terrified, she clung with her eyes tightly closed. "Turn," he said. "I've got you."

Grigori turned her easily in his arms so she could see where she was going. Her nails dug into his forearms as she gripped him so tightly. However, as the sight before her came into focus, she allowed herself to relax just a little to take in the wonder that was before her eyes.

Everywhere as far as the eye could see, amongst the light pollution in the sky and streetlights, were the majestic wings of angels flying, taking off and landing. They were walking along streets, landing onto rooftops and soaring like darts through the sky. Many had the black wings of The Fallen, like Grigori, beautiful nonetheless, but nothing compared to the splendor of the ones completely in white. They were like doves, appearing less often than the black. Rarer still were the ones with wings tipped in silver and gold. They seemed to carry their own light source, glowing against the night sky. They were the most beautiful creatures she'd ever seen. "Angels," she whispered in wonder.

Grigori heard her. "Free to come and go from the dimension of the heavens."

She turned her head to see his stubbled jawline. "And you can't?"

"No. All the Fallen are banished to earth. If it wasn't for the work we do for Abaddon, the Grigori would never get out of Tartarus."

She looked at all the black wings. They were everywhere, outnumbering the white easily, five to one. So, all of those black ones aren't like you?"

"No, there are a few thousand that followed us into Tartarus. Most are merely followers of Lucifer. They roam the earth meddling in Earth's affairs, keeping themselves occupied until the last day."

She didn't want to dwell anymore on that. Instead, she found herself relaxing into their flight. He seemed pleased and she felt sure his fingers caressed her a couple of times. She became filled with wonder at the gift he was showing her. All this was under human beings' noses every single day and only she was privileged to see it. "Are they there during the day?"

"Yes—except the Grigori."

She nodded in understanding.

"Don't get any ideas, Rachel. We might be imprisoned, but we can still get around in spirit form in those hours."

He was smiling when she turned her head to look at him. "Do you think I should have some wings written into my contract?"

He laughed, a deep baritone sound that vibrated right the way through her. "You will be trouble enough without wings."

The way he spoke then, with endearment, made her look at him for a long moment. She almost missed that they were beginning to land on a flat roof of an old building in a more industrial part of the city. Which one, she had no idea. Her feet touched the ground gently and his wings closed and disappeared quickly. "Where do they go?" she said, already wondering how that worked with clothes.

The white angels had nothing on their top halves and went around like Greek gods. A shimmering gold material appeared to cover them below the waist to the knee.

"It is an illusion. Our wings are there all the time. Clothes are created just how we want to present ourselves on our fleshly bodies. In reality, without it, we would appear like dimmer versions of the heavenly ones you see."

She looked at him intently, trying to imagine him like a dark version of Michelangelo's *David*, and she couldn't. She just couldn't visualize him as a dimmer version of anything. He emitted power. He would have been some powerful angel.

Two other Fallen landed near them. They quickly averted their eyes and bowed slightly. "Grigori," they both said, and continued walking to a shed-like building she guessed was to the stairs downward. It was then she realized that Grigori was someone to be feared even among The Fallen.

His eyes lowered as if he'd followed her train of thought. "Come!" he said, and began to walk in the same direction. He opened the door for her, and they travelled down a dark staircase to the sound of muffled beats getting louder and louder. It sounded like a nightclub.

She followed him ever downward until the light began to get brighter and the music louder and more discernible. At the bottom, the place was like nowhere she'd ever seen. At first, she thought it must be some kind of goth club, but on closer inspection, she was shocked to see it was more like a fetish club she'd only ever heard about on TV and in books.

Once inside, the music was loud but not unbearable. It felt more like an old mansion than an industrial block. It had nooks, low ceilings and places to get lost if you wanted. Dark wood lined the walls and the floors, and the dividing curtains and seating were in dark red and black velvet. Everyone wore a lot of makeup and dressed up—even the men. The Fallen were easy to spot. They were big and muscular, dressed casually, and wearing no makeup. They mingled with the crowd as if casually searching for someone. It made her shudder; they were looking for easy prey. The other thing that became glaringly obvious was that there was not a single white angel in the building.

Onlookers began to clear a path as they walked through. None of them met Grigori's eyes, but bowed their heads. They had no such qualms about her and eyed her up and down with interest. It made her hold onto Grigori's arm for protection. He continued at a purposeful stride and accepted the adoration and respect from the crowd as his due.

They came to a stop at the long wooden bar. "Vodka—bottle," he said to the barman who came straight to him despite the three-deep bar. While he got their drinks, she looked around and noticed, on closer inspection, that the room was done out with wood paneling like a Tudor house. The whole place felt like it had been plucked from five hundred years ago, apart from the music and the bar that held all the neon lighting and refrigeration of the twenty-first century.

The barman appeared with a bottle of the best Beluga vodka and two small frozen glasses. He poured and pushed them towards them. She allowed herself to absorb the place filled with loud, painted people and electronic dance music, while the oily, strong liquid burned down her throat. People were smoking freely; many with substances she was sure were not legal.

Grigori passed her a full glass. "*Za nashu drzjbu!*" he said, throwing it back in one. Then he immediately poured another while she watched him.

"What did you say?" she said, taking a small sip of her own.

He frowned. "Drink!" he said, waving her on with a hand.

She did as she was told and then grimaced. It did warm her insides though.

He watched her, mildly amused. "I spent many years in Russia. It is northern hemisphere and the harshness of it suited my character. It was a simple toast to our friendship." He poured her another and enticed her to drink it quickly.

"What is this place? Is everyone … you know?"

He grinned, filling her glass every time she emptied it. "It is a place for us to relax. There are three in this city."

She looked around and he seemed to read her mind. "They are mostly human here. Kind of like you."

"Owned, you mean," she said dryly. The drink was making her say every thought that entered her head, completely unfiltered. She looked around at the garish costumes and decided, "No one's like me."

He bobbed his head. "No, they are not. What I meant was, they are under contract with someone and their eyes are unveiled … like you." He looked intently at her then and she was sure his eyes looked the strangest she'd ever seen them.

The flecks of amber almost danced like flames against the black. *Shit! She had to lay off the drink.*

"They are not like you, Rachel, because these are the easy sheep that flock to The Fallen. The Grigori are a little more discerning. Their subjects have to have worth."

She chuffed a blast of mirthless laughter. *Worth. That's a joke.* The drink was making her see very clearly. Since meeting him, she was forgetting all that her nan had taught her, her church and its teaching she'd lived her whole life by, even her job meant nothing. Her friends barely knew her and now Seb. Here she was running the night with another man while he stayed home worrying about her. It didn't feel much like she was a person of worth right then. "To get out of Tartarus," she added. The looks she was getting from those around her, she was nothing more than a high-ranking prisoner let out from house arrest.

The way he looked at her with interest, it was hard to tell if he couldn't make her out or understood her too well.

"Why aren't the white ones in here?" she said, looking around her.

He looked at her a moment too long before speaking, his mind always churning and calculating. "They are on official business. They have no dealings with us, particularly here. They merely occupy the same space as us for the short time required." He took another hard shot to mask his bitterness, but she didn't miss the tic in his jaw.

"Have you ever seen him … you know … since?"

He leaned on the bar and his hands gripped it so she could see his knuckles go white. He looked down at his boots between his arms, only just containing his emotions. "No," he said, so quietly she almost didn't hear him. Then he turned his head sideways and his look was so desolate he took her breath away. "Fallen and Angels don't mix."

She pushed on, knowing she was on dangerous territory,

but he was talking, and time was very definitely running out. "But you could, though … if you wanted to. Isn't there a single place even?"

He slammed his hands down on the bar, rattling the glasses and making her jump, but she didn't stop. "Where is it then?"

He looked up at the ceiling and back at her, exasperated. "Is this how it will be for eternity?"

She was pushing him to the brink and she knew it. The drink, her situation, she didn't know what the hell was driving her, but despite his eyes glowing like they'd flame any moment, she glared back at him, not letting him off the hook. "Education is needed, comrade," she said, doing a poor impression of Abaddon's nasal British accent.

His mouth twitched and she thought he would actually crack a smile, particularly as she was grinning now.

"Fuck!" he said, pushing off the bar with both hands. "There is one angel: Hadraniel. He petitions for The Fallen if they ask for it."

"How do they petition?" A plan was forming in her mind, and she had to try not to look too excited.

He narrowed his eyes, seeing through her immediately. "He has no sympathy with humans, Rachel. That isn't his calling."

She swallowed. "OK, I get it." She did get it. This could be her only way in, and she would take it.

CHAPTER 35

"Answer me, then?" Rachel said.

Grigori let out a long breath and rolled his eyes. "I am beginning to think you have been sent as a penance for me, Rachel." He looked at her wearily. "It is usually the highest point of every town. It can be a rooftop or a hill. Contact with Hadraniel can be made there."

"Have you ever tried to do it?" she asked, instantly sorry for him. Imagining a heartbroken young Fallen, trying to be heard to speak to his lost love.

"No!" he said, and the shutters were down. "Come!" He grabbed a new bottle of vodka the barman had brought over, along with the two glasses, and motioned for her to follow him through the club.

Her mind was slow now, but she tried to think clearly about what she'd learned that night. People's faces were smiling and blurry. They all seemed taller than her and watched her wide-eyed with curiosity. Words like "Grigori whore" and "dead girl walking" caught her ears on occasion and she turned to glare at them. They were soon swept away in the hordes of people smelling of liquor and pungent perfume. The whole place dulled her senses with overload. It totally reminded her of a Marilyn Manson video she'd once seen on MTV.

They came to a corner of sofas, where people were chatting and drinking. They took one look at Grigori's huge frame and all stood, bowed their heads and left. Grigori flopped down into one and Rachel sat down more gingerly next to him. Looking around, she could see that it was as though they had a twelve-foot bubble around them. Literally no one invaded that space. "Why are they so scared of you?" She turned to him as he leaned forward to pour them each another drink.

His eyes looked at her wearily then, and he passed her a glass. "Because they know who I am."

He was trying to be intimidating, but she kind of felt done with it by then. She didn't miss a beat when she replied, "But I know you and I'm not scared of you."

He let out a long, exasperated breath and she could tell he was trying not to smile. "Maybe, because you are foolish, Rachel." He was looking sideways at her through narrowed eyes.

She couldn't help but wonder if it was weird that while the eyes of onlookers were burning into her and whispered behind hands, all she could think of was how incredibly hot he was right then, like literally smoking.

His expression changed to one of curiosity as he nudged her to drink. "Forget them." He turned in his seat, bending his knee so he could face her squarely and leaned back into the sofa. "You have something to hash out with me." Then he motioned for her to continue with his hand. "You have some kind of pitch?"

She frowned in slightly drunken confusion. He was going from scary to sexy to annoying. *What the hell?* She didn't know what to say. She thought this part would go on while he tattooed her. "Hey, you got me drunk on purpose." She wasn't sure how he knew she was going to barter with him. *Maybe all his victims do.*

It was a sobering thought that she was just one in a long line. She had to stop thinking she was in any way special to this guy.

"Don't worry. You'll have your tattoos by morning," he said with a smirk.

Now he was annoying the hell out of her. He was so arrogant. "Why would I submit to you, Grigori? What does it even mean?"

He reached for the bottle and she was shaking her head before he could top up her glass. He ignored her and filled it anyway. "Because you've come this far, and you can't go back. Because if you were honest, you wouldn't even want to."

He was moving forward, so his mouth was close to hers. Then he pulled her closer so he could speak close to her ear. His breaths were warm on her cheek. "Because you like the person you are becoming, and I am the source of it all. I am the flame you are drawn to, little moth."

She turned her head in anger and his lips were right there. Like, literally right there, millimeters away. The familiar shakes started going through her at his close proximity. His blood was calling to her; she wasn't stupid enough to assume it was anything else.

He laughed and moved back into his seat. "Just say what you need to say, Rachel. You have already said you aren't afraid of me."

She studied his amused face. He left her body reeling as he always did. He was toying with her, but she could tell he was genuinely interested in what she would say. She topped up his glass this time and passed it to him. His smile widened as he took it from her. He was so good at making her feel like she was the first to do stuff like that. He was definitely a master at hooking a girl in.

He drained the glass with his eyes on hers the whole time, waiting for her to speak.

"Look, I know it's too late for me, but surely it's not for Seb? I never consciously offered him. You took it upon yourself to take him." His face didn't change while Rachel spoke, making her want to kick him. "I don't want him stepping in or involved in any of this at all, Grigori."

He rubbed the stubble on his jaw, which she knew he chose rather than grew, for his materialized body. Then he frowned and shifted in his seat as if he was really considering her words. "He bears my mark, Rachel. That is irreversible."

"Can't you just void it and send him back to the world? Please, Grigori." She wondered if there was any real empathy behind the burnt-orange lion's eyes. Then she didn't know why she said it, but the words came tumbling out. "And you only want him because he's good-looking."

Grigori almost spat out his drink; his laughter came upon him so quickly and loudly. Everyone was looking at them open-mouthed and asking, 'Who was the girl that made the Grigori laugh like that?' When he composed himself, his eyes held amusement and warmth, as if he found her truly entertaining. "You think I would keep someone as a plaything?" he said, raising one eyebrow.

"I think you can do anything you want to do." Then she looked down at her fingers in her lap. "He told me you kissed him." Her feelings were confused on this point and she hadn't fully worked them out. She honestly couldn't tell if she was upset that Grigori actually fancied someone and not her. The ridiculous thought itself made her angry. She should be concentrating on the danger Seb was in. "It completely messed with his head, Grigori."

When she finally rested her eyes on his again, he had stopped laughing, but he was smiling at her. In fact, his face was the most relaxed she'd ever seen it. "I admit I manipulated a situation, but in answer to your question, no, I don't want to have sex with your boyfriend." He sipped his drink, waiting for her response.

The moment was laden. She was more relieved than she cared to admit and wondered what he was saying behind those eyes. Had it all been to truly trap her because he wanted her on some level? Or was she simply reading too much into this, like always? "Then set him free ... for me," she added.

He was still studying her, but his brain was whirring in the background. It always did.

"The reaper doesn't want him, he said so," she added, wanting him to say something, anything. He never gave a damn thing away.

Grigori sighed and leaned into the chair a little more. "He would have to revert back to me at death."

"No, you throw him back in the pond ... but watch him and don't let anyone else have him," she added as an afterthought, knowing how crafty his mind was.

Laughter bubbled under the surface; she could see it, but he tamped it down. "I'm not a guardian angel, Rachel." He regarded her for a full minute, considering what she'd said. "He couldn't keep his memories."

"Done!" Rachel said, not believing she'd actually won a small victory.

"You understand that means you can never be in his life?" He was watching her closely to see how she received the terms. "For me to watch him, he must still be contracted to me." Before she could protest, he held up a silencing hand. "Because of this, seeing you or having anything at all to do with you could spark a memory, and the moment that happens, he will be back in the game. Do you understand that, Rachel?"

She took a ragged breath and nodded. Her mind was reeling, trying to make sense of the terms and whether she'd gained any ground. She thought she did, but with her foggy brain, she couldn't be sure he wasn't just tying her up in more knots.

"He will always bear my mark, Rachel. No matter how much you might want me to, it can't be undone."

"Can't you change it to something else? Please, Grigori, he doesn't deserve any of this. He deserves every success in life. He deserves his life back." She hadn't intended to cry, but the tears came anyway.

Grigori watched her with an impassive face. Of course, he couldn't feel sympathy for a silly crying girl; he'd lived far too long for that. "I could cover it in any kind of ink to make the picture different, but in the end, the blood in the original tattoo marks him and flows through his body." He nodded when she got a tissue from her bag and blew her nose. "I will, however, consider your terms in return for complete submission."

Rachel stared at him then. *Wasn't that what they were here for anyway, the submission thing?* "What if I could give something to you—something no one has ever given you before?"

His head went to the side and he scrutinized her with genuine fascination.

"Five minutes with the one person you love more than life itself." There it was, her wild plan, out there before she had time to think or have any real idea of how she could deliver.

The smile dropped from his face immediately and the temperature around him dropped ten degrees. She gulped, literally thinking he'd kill her on the spot. She yelped as he pulled her up with him so quickly and put his mouth next to her ear. "You get that, Rachel, and we will all be free, because hell will freeze over." Then he tugged her roughly by the arm, pulling her along, through the parting crowds and up the stairs to the roof.

Truly terrified, her heart was palpitating, and her breaths were shallow hitches all the way. Everything was going so well, and she'd had to go and open her big mouth. She should have worked on getting it before actually saying something like that to him. She was just hung up on the deal she felt had to be struck tonight.

When they reached the edge of the roof, he grabbed her to him and took off again. With no softness in his hold and his anger rolling off him in waves, he didn't utter a word. All she could do was try to calm herself by taking in the many Fallen landing on rooftops, the rivers and the fields. In the end, she had no way of knowing if they were even in the same country.

Eventually, they landed on a large penthouse balcony attached to a shiny glass apartment building, surely built for the very rich. The thing that struck her the most was that it had no safety rail, meaning it was a purpose-built platform for people with wings.

They landed on it easily. This time, the looks they got were more curious and less like the looks of fear they'd received in the club. It became apparent that this crowd was much higher up on The Fallen social scale.

The music was a fairly low-level rhythmic dirge to a beat. Someone welcomed them to New York, blowing her next question. The cool air of the journey had only sobered her temporarily. Now she felt drunk. She guessed you would after more than a bottle of vodka.

The people wore stunning Venetian-style masks and chatted in huddles. Some reclined on cushions, wrapped in each other, in deep conversations. It made her feel she was intruding just walking past. She gasped and averted her eyes at a semi-naked threesome, tangled together on a fireside rug. A small crowd of onlookers had gathered around them. It was shocking and compelling at the same time. She'd never seen anything like it.

She took a sly glance up at Grigori. He walked through without taking notice of what was fast appearing to be some sort of high-class orgy. She guessed someone as jaded as him had seen it all before. She, however, hadn't, and it made her very uncomfortable. She needed to get out of there. It was starting to feel like he was punishing her for saying the wrong thing.

The apartment was huge and appeared to occupy the whole top floor of the building. Whoever lived there was super-rich. They eventually came to a huge living room with white leather sofas sunk into a circle of highly polished black marble floor. The walls were white, displaying what appeared to be expensive works of art. Installations and modern sculptures filled up areas of space. Nothing was functional. All was for aesthetics. The owner collected beautiful things and liked to show them off.

As they got closer, she could see that the people on the sofas were fawning over one man—correction, Fallen. The one with hair and eyes of a raven. The one that reminded her of the darkest hour of the night—Raephe.

He leaned back into the sofa while a young man and woman sat on either side of him and placed a hand on the chest of his open shirt. He smiled and his face was beautiful. It was fine and chiseled with a cruelty so apparent that she couldn't find him attractive. This was The Fallen who had ensnared Nicola. She couldn't help but wonder what he was like when they interacted alone. "Ah, the lovers on submission night," he sighed. He looked sloe-eyed and as drunk as they were. It must be late, possibly almost morning.

He kissed the woman who was supermodel beautiful. It made her think of poor Nicola, tied to this faithless being forever, while she clearly loved him. *Would that be her fate? It made her shudder.*

Raephe whispered something to his guests and they cleared the sofas. She followed Grigori down the small stairs and they sat opposite him.

Raephe clicked his fingers and another bottle of ice-cold Beluga was brought for them and the familiar shot glasses. She longed for something to mix it with. "How goes the pet project, Xenon?" he asked, flashing his crow eyes at her and smiling widely.

Her blood began to rise. The man-whore, angel, or whatever he was, incensed her so much. Maybe it was the alcohol or that she was strangely lucid for the amount she'd drunk, but she couldn't control the anger she was feeling.

"Well."

How she loved Grigori's monosyllabic answers then and she couldn't help smirking at Raephe.

He laughed loudly. "Oooh, Xenon. I like this one. If looks could kill, she would slice me open." Then he narrowed his eyes at Grigori, a little puzzled. "And yet you …"

He didn't finish what he was saying, and she didn't have time to overthink as Grigori glanced sideways at her. She guessed she must have been scowling. *To hell with it.* "Where's Nicola tonight?" she threw at Raephe, making his eyes widen. "Shouldn't you be looking after your charge with the dangerous job she does … for you, I might add?" At that moment, she felt desperately sorry for Nicola, tied to this disgusting creature.

Raephe's eyebrows rose and he bobbed his head at Grigori, but his laughter had subsided into cautious amusement. "Your Iris has teeth, Xenon … I like!" A girl bent down behind him and rested her hands on his shoulders, but he shook them off. It was the only giveaway to his annoyance.

However, the use of her nan's flower in reference to her quickly put her in her place. These weren't people, but powerful beings that could snuff her out in an instant—almost as powerful as the devil himself. "I'm not the iris, that was my grandmother," she said, trying to keep the emotion out of her voice. She hadn't noticed, but she had moved closer to the protection of Grigori.

Raephe put his head to the side and looked up to the ceiling dramatically. "Is it, though?" He was tapping his fingers on his chin.

"Raephe!" Grigori said in warning. Her eyes shot to him as it was the first interesting thing he'd said since they'd got there.

She looked back to Raephe for the answer.

"He hasn't told you, has he?" he said, his smile widening. "Bad Grigori! Shameful withholding of information."

Her eyes went to Grigori's fists, clenching against his legs. "What hasn't he told me?" Her hand went straight to Grigori's legs the instant she felt him stiffen to jump up. "No, I have a right to know. It's submission night, isn't it? All cards on the table."

Raephe's eyes glittered and his smile was wicked. "Oh, I like this one, Xen." He grinned and studied her, as if he was looking for more information from her appearance alone.

In the blink of an eye, he was in her face, centimeters from her mouth. She felt Grigori react at the same time, but something was holding him in place. Raephe spoke so she could feel his hot breath on her lips. "The Iris represents The Pontip."

Grigori was struggling next to her. She vaguely felt beings behind them, but she couldn't tear her eyes from Raephe's. "That is, Layke of Pontip."

He allowed her mind to catch up with him. *What Layke—Grigori's Layke?*

"When you walked innocently into the shop and it was evident the tattoo you would have, your fate was sealed then." He looked ruefully at Grigori. "The six sessions were always academic." He put his head to the side and looked genuinely apologetic when he said, "You see, your fate and his have always been intertwined and you never stood a chance."

"Wh—what?" she stuttered.

He ran a long talon down her cheek, leaving it stinging. "And my feisty little mannerless human, you will be a vassal just like my faithful Nicola."

She tried to move, but whatever held Grigori held her too. She tried to turn only to look into the eyes of the hateful female angel, Oleander. Raephe pulled her chin back to face him. "You will, of course, have your work with Abaddon and your principles to justify the fact that all you live for is to quench your thirst for your Grigori's blood. The blood that runs in your veins, his heavenly touch and the bed that compares to no one else's. This is the truth he will not tell you, that you must know on submission night. From this night onward, you will be his slave. I know it, he knows it, and every other person in this room knows it." With those last words, he pushed away, and whatever held them let them go.

Grigori shot to his feet and pushed off the people around him with such force that they shot to the walls, knocking people in their way like skittles. He reached down with his hand, which Rachel instinctively took, and pointed at Raephe with the other. "I won't warn you again. The Iris has no greater meaning than a marker."

Raephe straightened his clothes and smirked. "Are you sure she's not his?"

With that, Grigori flew at him. Girls screamed and scrambled away as Grigori's fist connected with Raephe's jaw, and they began to roll and grapple at lightning-fast speed. They smashed against walls, making huge holes and crashed through priceless statues and glass tables.

Eventually, Oleander and the one she recognized as Bohdan got between them and they stood glaring at each other amongst the rubble they'd made of the apartment.

Suddenly, just as Rachel thought the pandemonium had died down, the lights flickered and dimmed to an eerie blue. The temperature dropped several degrees, making the hackles on the back of her neck stand up. Breaths hitched and heads turned to the figure standing at the edge of the room by the balcony. Dressed entirely in black was *Abaddon*. He seemed even darker and more menacing than she remembered. He sucked all the light and life out of the room. His wings snapped shut behind him and they disappeared, leaving him to walk freely, which he did with a cat-like grace. He stood without robes in just his plain black sweater and perfectly tailored pants. He didn't need the dramatic look to exude evil. "Games are over. It is time." And he turned his icy smile to Rachel. His words totally threw her and all she could do was stutter. "Wh—?" and look to Grigori for help.

"You have the boy and now she comes with me."

An invisible force pulled both her arms out in front of her roughly, turning over her wrists so they were upwards. "She has no submission in her. She refuses you, Xenon, and so she comes to me."

CHAPTER 36

Rachel didn't understand what was going on and was grateful for Grigori's hand reaching for her arm. She looked up into his pain-filled, bleary eyes. He'd barely recovered from his blind rage. Looking at him, she then realized that she had submitted. She would always choose him rather than Abaddon.

Grigori seemed to read it in her and looked back to Abaddon. "She does submit. She has merely been bartering for her sacrifice. I have given her till the last hour because of it."

Abaddon's mouth twitched into a malicious smile. She wasn't sure if he was angry or pleased with the outcome. "See to it. She comes to me after the signature."

She looked back at Grigori to see his nod of agreement. The signature was the last session. She only had one week left of her old life.

In the moment it took her to have that thought, Abaddon was gone. "We go back," Grigori said. However, they didn't leave by way of the balcony this time. He led her through the crowd to a circular doorway that looked like a bank vault.

As they went through the thick metal arch, she felt the familiar disorientation and blurred vision. It was a portal to Tartarus. This must be Raephe's way into their weird dimension.

"It's quicker this way."

She felt woozy, like she'd been spun around. She smelled the leaves and the earth of the forest until they came to a tunnel of darkness. She was terrified, as she had no memory of this. It was amazingly fast, because the next thing she knew, they were coming out of the door at the top of the Angel's Ink staircase. Now she understood why Grigori had forbidden her to go there; the door to mortal danger was literally on their doorstep and she'd knocked on it several times.

The corridor felt hot after the forest. It was a relief to finally walk into the tattoo parlor. She headed for Grigori's chair and climbed straight in. Grigori was already choosing ink from his many bottles. "I don't get it. What was tonight all about? How was it anything to do with submission?" She watched Grigori's profile closely.

He stopped what he was doing, looked up at the ceiling and sighed deeply. It was the first time she'd seen him appear to be under any signs of stress. He closed his eyes as if mustering strength and moved closer to the side of her chair. He picked up her right arm and turned it, so the delicate skin was upwards. "The submission is in three parts. Three marks very similar in appearance are placed on the inside of each wrist and at the back of the neck, just below the hairline. The language is early Sumerian. One represents the heart," and he picked up her left wrist. "The right—the soul, and the neck—the mind. Each must be given to me freely."

She was listening to him so keenly that she hadn't realized that her teeth were clenched, and her nails dug into the palms of her hand. "Not Abaddon?" she said and relaxed them.

Grigori reached for his baseball cap and smoothed his hair back while he put it on. "No … your contract is with me. I make the promise to pay Abaddon. Everything … must be submitted to me."

His eyes lowered and heat surged through her body. Everything always implied something deeply sexual with him, but he'd never laid a hand on her. Even now, when her body literally sang to him to be touched, all he did was guide her slowly in the chair to turn around to expose the back of her neck. She quickly took the band from her wrist and tied up her hair. Her heart was hammering with panic. "I know what I must do, but I don't think I'm ready to fully submit heart and soul." Tears were already wetting the back of the chair. How could any of this be classed as freely given?

Grigori took a step towards his old stereo system and the first bars of a rock anthem built in the air. "Then we will start with the mind. I can live with that."

The sketch was done in red with a steady hand in seconds. It felt like nothing more than a hieroglyph.

She had difficulty swallowing and her eyes darted in fear as he picked up his machine. Out of all the weeks she'd sat in this chair—sometimes for many hours, she'd never felt so damned.

The familiar whirr sounded and came closer. "It contains your blood?"

"The highest concentration. It is a sign for all to see, High or Fallen."

"High?"

"It's what we call the ones above."

Rachel noticed that he could barely mention Angels, and she was sure it had more to do with Layke than any hatred of them in general. "Will it make me ill?"

"I doubt it. You're too far in now."

Her heart sank even lower at the finality of those words. His hand was already working, and she felt the familiar sting. Of course, he had been distracting her with conversation. As he worked at what felt like very thick black lines, her heart sank so low it was an ache in the pit of her stomach.

It took no time at all—probably fifteen minutes, tops. He gave her a hand mirror and held one behind her so she could see it. It was nothing really—a collection of triangles just below her skull, no bigger than a fifty pence piece. It appeared to be a horizontal bar with two tiny downward-pointing triangles at each end, then an X between them. It looked like a weightlifting bar above the X, which undoubtedly represented Xenon, but then she guessed they must be the scales everyone kept going on about. There was also a tiny line through the apex of the X.

Grigori taped the usual protective gauze over it and she quickly pulled up the neck of her shirt. She turned slowly and leaned back as he changed the chair with a pump of his foot to a regular upright position.

Tears were streaming down her face; she just couldn't stop them. She'd never felt such a hopeless sense of self-loathing. She was already craving the next touch of the tattoo gun, yearning for the ink like a thirsty person needing water. Her hands were visibly shaking, and her forehead perspired. She had to do something, anything.

He stood directly in front of her and turned up both of her wrists, then he pulled his stool closer and sat so her knees were between his. It felt like he was all around her, capturing, owning her. "What if I'm not ready yet for heart and soul?" She willed him to look her in the eye.

She was rewarded with a gaze that shocked her with its intensity. He looked locked in a battle of his own. "Doesn't the submission have to be real?"

Without answering her, he took off his cap, ran his fingers through his hair and replaced it. Then he took up her left wrist, meaning heart came next, and marked out a pattern with his red marker pen. They just looked like more triangles in a different order.

Strangely, all she could think of right then was how many times he'd done this. How many women with heaving chests had been craving his touch like this? It was that thought that sickened her, but she couldn't help thinking it, nonetheless. "Will I be one of many?"

His eyes flashed to hers as if he was surprised for a moment, but he didn't answer. Instead, he said, "These are your choices, Rachel: You go to Abaddon, now, in this moment, alone and at his mercy, or you submit to me, spend the week with your precious friends and go in a week's time with my eternal protection." His look was hard with no sentiment at all. He was hammering home a point, each word like nails in a coffin. Definite, final and no room for softness at all. She didn't know why that still surprised her. The injustice of it reared up in her. "What if I simply said no and went home?"

He put his head at an angle and a small breath of laughter escaped him. "Then you will find no one there, for they will be in this chair."

A sob escaped her. 'Even Lynn?"

Grigori shrugged. "Maybe not straight away, but it won't take long for the boy to implicate her. And she already has a little of my blood as a kind of holding clause."

The daisy. Her illness. How could she have been so stupid to miss that? "I hate you." Her words were ice spat through gritted teeth, and in that precise moment, she meant them.

He simply leaned closer, pressing her wrists into the arms of the chair with his weight. His mouth was mere inches from hers. Even then, her pulse raced at the thought he might kiss her again, and she despised herself.

His eyelids lowered as if he knew exactly the effect he was having on her. He moved closer to her ear and she held her breath. "Hate is good. Nurture it, Rachel. It will keep you sane." Then he moved back into his seat again. "When will you learn that your life as you know it has gone? Your journey is nearing its destination and you can't ignore it or pretend it's not coming."

She closed her eyes and wished he'd just get on with it. All she could think of was how close she'd come to his mouth and the feeling of his warm breath next to her cheek. How it would feel to have those lips on her. However, every time she thought they were building a genuine connection, he did something deliberately to smash it in front of her eyes.

She remembered Nicola's words: how they used their sexual prowess mercilessly around humans to trap them and get what they want. "I know what you're doing," she whispered.

He'd barely sketched anything this time and was already bringing the machine close to her left wrist. "And what is that?"

She felt the cold rub of alcohol before the sting of the needle. "You use seduction to get what you want."

His head was low over her wrist and the pain level was high because of the nerves that travelled through to her hand. As she tensed to ride it out, she could still see the twitch of the corners of his mouth. "You don't deny it?" she said, straining with the pain.

Grigori sat up to relieve his back for a moment and grinned, then he leaned back in and went over the same thick line he'd been making. "I have no interest in you in that way. If that had been the case, I'd have been between your legs on your first visit."

Her mouth dropped open at his crudeness. It was ridiculous, but it felt like a cold slap across her face. She should feel glad, but instead she felt hurt and insulted. "Because you prefer boys and the reason why you took Seb," she said, to grab just a little of her pride back.

His grin widened and he flashed his eyes at her and continued to work. He seemed genuinely amused this time. His mood swings made her dizzy.

He sat up and appeared to think about her question. Then he bobbed his head. "I do like Seb. I can see what you see in him." He appeared to ignore the look of horror that appeared on her face and folded his body over her wrist again. "I have already told you I don't accept labels. I don't choose a particular gender." His eyes flashed angrily at her again. "The point of The Fallen is that they take all whom they choose."

It made her swallow. Just when she ventured closer to him, he slapped her right back into place with who he was. It reminded her of Layke, who chose not to, and she was sure he was thinking of that too.

It also occurred to her that she was some kind of precious cargo. He'd done a lot of inferred intimidation and scared the shit out of her with his sheer presence, but he'd never actually touched her. It made her a little braver. "Sounds like you're in denial. There are support groups for people too scared to come out." Despite her bravery, she held her breath.

He merely raised a brow in warning and shook his head and continued. Maybe she'd hit on the truth. She pushed him again. "Doesn't the submission have to be real … you know, physical?"

"You always try to box me in human terms. I am not human." When he looked at her then, something inside her sighed in contentment. The amber flecks of his eyes mixed in a crucible of red. What she wouldn't give to know what he truly felt.

He said no more on the subject. The left wrist was done. It looked exactly the same as the one on her neck, except this one had another triangle blacked out on the left side of the X. It was a basic picture depicting the scales and the heart, all held by the X. It was perfect in its simplicity.

He scooted a little to his left to turn his attention to her right wrist—her soul. "And what do you intend to do with it?" she said, finding it difficult to swallow now they were on the last one.

He frowned, pulling out the pen from behind his ear.

"With my soul," she prompted.

He put his head on the side as if the answer should be obvious. "Guard it with my life."

He left her staring at him in shock while he bent and marked out the last symbol. His hands were steady as he drew what looked like a sideways eight or infinity symbol inside a circle. Then he placed four dots outside the circle to make the infinity symbol turn into an X, depending on how you looked at it. It was a clever perspective thing.

With a wipe of alcohol, he was soon bent over her, scratching her skin with his needle. Despite his harshness, she had an overwhelming urge to touch him. He was so close she wanted to just feel his hair and connect with him in any way she could. He reminded her of a damaged boy who'd grown up making the best of a shitty life, making a warped sense of the world around him with his broken version of love or lack of it.

"What would you do if I did manage to get Layke to see you?"

His grip on her hand tightened so she squirmed, and he looked up at her through his eyebrows in warning.

She winced. "Stop glaring at me like that. If we're going to be together forever, then you have to stop throwing your weight around every time I say something you don't like."

A flash of emotion glimmered in his eyes for a second before he managed to pull it in and get a hold on it. Then his look became sardonic." I have been on this earth for thousands of years as an angel and many more still since I fell, and never once in all that time have I ever caught a glimpse of Layke." He let out a chuff of mirthless laughter and continued to work on her wrist.

Rachel tried to absorb just how long that was. It simply blew her mind the length of time to be alive, let alone being in Grigori's kind of misery. To be heartbroken for that long, no wonder he was cynical. "Why do the others call him The Iris?"

He let go of the trigger and his gun stopped whirring.

She held her breath, terrified she'd gone too far. What Raephe said needed answers. She'd never had the chance to question it until then. "Am I here for more than my scintillating conversation?" Her weak idea of a joke fell flat.

A muscle ticced in his jaw, he pressed the trigger on his gun, and it came back to life. He blinked slowly and bent down over her wrist and worked until it was done.

The marks were all so small that the session couldn't have lasted more than an hour. It was done and now there was nothing at all that could reverse it. She expected to feel different, but she didn't. She simply felt empty. She just sat and watched while he stood, took off his baseball cap and threw it onto the bench. He looked exhausted. "Grigori!" she said, not able to let it go. "I'm not stupid. I heard the things the other Fallen have said."

He slammed down both hands on his bench, making the bottles scatter and roll in all directions. Her eyes stayed on the broad shoulders hunched over the desk where his head hung low. He was gathering himself together and reining in that formidable temper. After a moment, he turned his head sideways to look at her in the chair, and for the first time, her trembling was from fear.

"That first time you came, I knew your loss and the name of that person, Iris. It was the same as my loss." His look was pained and piercing right through her. "I knew things like that just didn't happen by accident in the universe."

He held her in rapt attention of fear and curiosity and she daren't look away. He slowly straightened and turned to face her squarely; every muscle coiled and tense. Then, as if he realized it himself, he relaxed back against the bench in his usual position, as if the fight ebbed out of him. "I knew you'd been sent by him or for him. Your purity of spirit and body, your enquiring mind, all sang of him and called to me. Outwardly, those things were desirable enough alone, but in reality, I knew you could have only one owner."

She flinched at being owned by anyone, but right then, it was an accurate description and one she wasn't arguing about in his present mood. His mind was miles away.

"I needed to get my blood in your veins and your body marked as quickly as possible by any means necessary."

She coughed to clear her throat. "So, you admit it wasn't done entirely with my free will?"

Before she could praise her own initiative for seizing control of the conversation, he pointed a finger and laughed. "Nice try. I don't admit this. Once you got a taste, in your heart, you knew what you were doing." He looked up at the ceiling and she wondered what he saw when he did that. It was always done as if he would find some answer there. "As I began the first piece," he said, his eyes falling on her again. "It became a benediction. It soothed both our souls as much as it called to him, like an unspoken prayer." His eyes appeared to glow with his fervent look, and with his frown, he looked more vulnerable than she'd ever seen him. "You became so tangled up and a part of him that I didn't see you took on a life of your own." His eyes were in the distance again.

"I wasn't ever going to get away, was I?" she said, quietly and resigned.

He took a deep breath and shook his head. "I don't believe you were ever meant to. I still can't make up my mind whether you were sent for him or by him."

Part of her wanted to rail at him and call him out for his blatant disregard of her as an individual, but there was something so unstable about him tonight. It was a side, she was sure, that few had seen. "And Seb?"

He dismissed it with a hand. "That story you know. You had to come to me and Seb had to be the leverage you so graciously gave me."

She looked at her hands in her lap. He was right, she did know, but it didn't make it any easier to hear her stupidity out loud. "You still haven't answered my question, Grigori. You got what you wanted. Will you throw Seb back with no strings attached?"

He ran his fingers through his hair as she was beginning to notice he did in times of stress and sat back down on his stool. He picked up the tube of ointment and her wrist and gently rubbed it into the angry, raised mark. She watched every movement made with the utmost care. When his eyes found hers again, the amber and fire in them seemed alive. She knew exactly what Nicola had meant. In that moment, he could have anything he wanted, and she would be glad to give it.

She stiffened when he reached out a hand and gently tucked a piece of hair behind her ear. Her heart raced while he held his hand there.

"Go home, Rachel." He said it so softly and so gently that she found herself leaning into his hand. He had the power to make everything go away. "Go and enjoy your life for one last week."

The unusual tenderness in him sent a tear tracking down her cheek and he caught it with his thumb. "What about Seb?" she said absently, watching enthralled as he brought his thumb to his mouth and tasted her tears.

His eyes never left hers the whole time. "If you are willing to let go of everything and submit wholeheartedly to me, then I will think about your request."

It wasn't a definitive answer, but it was the best she was going to get. He was already demolishing her good sense. She needed to get out of there before he spread her legs right then and she let him like the brazen hussy he'd made her.

She slid off the chair and, in doing so, was forced to stand between his knees. He didn't move and looked up at her speculatively at what she would do next. He was level with her chest and so touchable. Her knees were trembling so much she swore he must feel them, and her stomach swirled.

If he took hold of her now, she would surely be lost. However, his eyes looked weary and ancient. Like he'd seen this a million times before. It sobered her and made her take a hard swallow. "I'll go," she said with a broken, barely audible voice.

He bowed his head slightly and rolled back to give her space. She stooped to pick up her discarded bag.

"Bring what you need when you come next week because you won't be going home."

She should have been firing questions at him then, like where and how she would live, but all she did was stare at him in some weird, highly charged showdown. He was still inquisitive, waiting for anything she would do or say. It gave her a curious sense of power to think he was either a great actor or genuinely didn't know everything she'd do.

The moment went on for so long, she became aware of it

and embarrassment followed. She turned and walked towards the door.

"In answer to your earlier question, you will not be one of many, Rachel. For there are none who peer through the frozen bars of my heart."

In the time it took for her to turn, he had disappeared.

CHAPTER 37

It was 6.45 a.m. when Rachel tiptoed into the house. She'd said goodbye to the scandalously good-looking driver she was quickly becoming accustomed to and put Grigori's disappearance down to the fast-approaching sunrise.

She always forgot he was a condemned prisoner, only allowed out on good behavior. That being said, she was sure he went around unseen. It made her slightly uncomfortable to think he could be here with her now. She'd have to have a conversation with him about that.

She felt beyond exhausted as she climbed the stairs. It was hard to believe everything that had happened in one night. Every single emotion had been wrung out of her and she still had no idea what she'd tell Seb when he asked her.

He was a soft bundle wrapped in her quilt when she got to her room. She shed her clothes, watching the slight movement and listening to the soft sounds of his breaths. She eased herself in under the quilt, careful not to wake him.

Instinctively, he drew her into his body and wrapped

himself around her. His heat, the alcohol and the weight of the night she'd just had sent her to sleep in minutes.

She came to sometime later to the hushed tones of Seb's voice, trying to talk into his phone without her hearing. She cracked an eyelid enough to see him sitting on the edge of the bed with his back to her.

The bedside clock said 11.30. Her eyes stung, and despite really wanting to eavesdrop, there was no way she could wake herself up long enough to listen to more than a few words. "Yeah … she was out all night. OK, but she's still asleep. I'm sure she'll ring you as soon as she gets up. *Nicola* was her last thought before she drifted off.

Another two hours passed before she woke up to the smell of toast. She stirred with a groan and her eyelids fluttered open and squinted in the bright light.

Seb held out a mug. "Come on, eat and drink something," he said with a frown of concern. He sat down next to her on the bed.

She smiled and tried to sit up awkwardly against the headboard, holding her head, remembering the inevitable hangover. It wasn't as bad as it should be, probably because of the time she'd spent in Grigori's chair.

She watched Seb's face closely, grateful he didn't appear to be angry with her for staying out. She thought of all the times he'd done it before. The clock said 13.40. "Sorry, I came home so late." She took a loud bite of the toast and washed it down immediately with a huge gulp of tea. She couldn't remember the last time she ate. About lunchtime yesterday, she supposed. A thousand years ago.

"How was it?" he said, pointing at her wrist.

Rachel blew over the top of her tea. "Both wrists and the back of my neck."

"What are they?"

She could detect the hardness already growing in his voice as he sensed her avoidance. "Symbols, that's all." She took a bite of her toast to fill her mouth as much as possible so she couldn't talk.

"Then what took you so long? I didn't come to bed myself until five and you weren't back, so don't try to lie to me."

She looked directly into his eyes. He was already withdrawing—assuming she'd spent the night with Grigori. She almost laughed. In a man's mind, she guessed that was the logical interpretation of submission. If only he knew it was so much more. *Still*. Maybe it's better that he thought that. "Not much … he just took me to some places … you know, in his world." She dropped her eyes so she couldn't see the turmoil behind his. He was joining dots to imagine a place that was probably so far from the truth. He now looked angry and hurt. It was understandable, but annoyed her too. Because his ego was such that it wasn't because she'd given in and sold her soul, but that he believed she'd spent the night with another man. Right then, even if she told him the full story of her night, she wasn't sure he'd believe her, and she wasn't sure she wanted him to. She found herself hardening in front of him. A clean break on Saturday was best. They had so little time together. By Sunday, he wouldn't even remember her name. She wanted to shout at him that he could rest assured that if she'd had sex with Grigori, then they'd be over anyway, such was the power and the magnetism of the most dangerous of all The Fallen.

For now, she just played along with his hurt and the notion that it was all part of a master plan to win this thing for both of them. Then, after Saturday, they would go back to being an ordinary couple, working, dating and having sex together.

Even that felt odd and gave her pause. Like there was a time limit on it. Even if she did win and come home, how long would it take for a leggy blond to turn Seb's head at one of his gigs and sweep him onto her broomstick? All she'd be left with was the "it just happened" conversation. "It didn't mean anything," and "it's kind of an occupational hazard for a musician". Then, "it was great while it lasted" followed swiftly by, "we always knew I wasn't forever material".

That made her the saddest of all, because she did know that, but she cared about him a great deal, and he didn't deserve to be damned because of her stupidity. She reached out a hand and touched Seb's face, making her wobble in her conclusions over the last few minutes. Nevertheless, she had to push through with her plan. "I have to act how he is expecting me to."

Seb stared at her blank face. He was deciding whether he believed her or not. She wanted to say she hadn't slept with Grigori yet, but what would that do? She'd imagined it a hundred times anyway. Wasn't thought a precursor to deed? He'd been lured in enough to kiss Grigori himself.

He sagged in front of her. "I'm sorry. You've been through hell and I'm giving you a hard time. It drives me insane here waiting for you to come back."

She climbed into his lap and put her nose into his neck. He smelled deliciously of pure Seb. Although his arms hung slack around her. "Please don't withdraw from me, Seb. Not when I need you the most."

Her words seemed to do the trick. He tightened his arms around her and drew back to look into her face. "I'm sorry. I'm a selfish bastard." He kissed her gently, brushing his soft lips against hers. He crushed her to him, his hardness growing beneath her through the soft fabric of his shorts.

They seemed to realize what a flimsy barrier it was at exactly the same time. He shifted his weight and she lifted hers and they were gone. They both groaned when they were skin to skin, her wetness moving across him as her hips began to move instinctively over him.

This time, when he took her mouth, it was with a fierceness she'd never seen in him before. It was strong, with an urgency that felt like a claiming. It lit something in her, and she responded gladly. She shifted from her knees to her feet, and his hand went between them, placing himself at the perfect point, and she slid down onto him with ease. They both gasped loudly, without a care for who might hear them. His hands kneaded the flesh of her backside and she held the sides of his face while she kissed him deeply. She moved on him slowly, pushing him more deeply within her to prove the night was his. Despite what he believed, while she moved on him, she was the driving force and he took what she had to give him as his due.

It drove them hotter and higher in this moving embrace. In that moment, she knew that leggy blondes may come and go, but this moment would be forever etched somewhere in Seb's psyche as a time that could never be equaled.

Their chests pushed together, and nipples grazed against skin. He bit and sucked, drawing them into his mouth while she threaded her hands through his hair and pulled hard. She scratched his back and pulled him into her more tightly, grinding into him as she began the glorious feeling of floating.

It was that exact moment she thought of Grigori. The worst possible time and paradoxically the best. It drove her hurtling over the edge. There was something so absolutely carnal about him. As her eyes went up into her head, she was assured there was absolutely nothing spiritual about this. It was pure lust-governed pleasure, shared by consenting adults, and yet she took it completely for herself.

Seb felt her tighten around him and whispered, "Yeah … come with me." He bit onto the soft part of her shoulder and groaned through his teeth. Despite the confusion of her thoughts, she gripped him and felt him pulsate deeply inside her, and all she could do was let herself go. In freefall, she was already registering the lack of barrier or contraception at all.

Seb drew her with him and flopped back onto the bed. His boxers were still bunched around his knees. She lay collapsed onto his chest, which was working up and down, while he caught his breath too. *Shit!* was all she could think of over and over and rolled off him.

He turned his head to look at her and chuckled. "You destroyed me," he said, bleary-eyed.

She grinned. She had come a long way from shy librarian, she guessed. "Go and switch the shower on. I'll be in in a minute, I just want to call Nicola first."

He nodded and rolled straight off the bed. She waited until she heard the bathroom door click before she texted Grigori. Their lack of self-control had thrown up an angle she hadn't thought of before. *Is pregnancy a deal breaker?* She was sure it must have come up before, but she had to at least ask. With no idea how he would take it and her mind in freefall, she hit send.

Next, she dialed Nicola. She picked up on the second ring. "Hey, you OK?"

"Yeah, it's done."

"Seb was worried. He phoned me three times last night."

Rachel smiled a little, but it was a regretful smile. Whatever he felt about her was pointless now. "Grigori took me all over before the tattooing. We even crossed continents, I think. He showed me the world … well, his world. You know … with unveiled eyes." She wondered if everything was exactly the same for Nicola. Somehow, she couldn't imagine the dark one, Raephe, doing anything but preening his crow feathers.

Nicola had gone quiet until she said, eventually, "Yeah, I remember that. It seems so long ago."

"I saw Raephe in New York." She didn't want to hide anything from her and wondered how much she knew about her Fallen.

She heard a deep sigh. "I don't want to know anything about him, Rachel." It was said abruptly, with a hint of anger and hurt.

It confirmed her suspicions. "You sound like you care a great deal for your Grigori, Nicola."

There was silence again.

She felt a little bad about pressing her in areas that were none of her business, but it was very relevant to her own situation and how she behaved going forward.

"I can't help it, Rachel. You'll understand soon enough."

She guessed, on some level, she believed her. There was something so dark calling her about Grigori that, if she gave in to it, she was sure there would be no coming back from it. Perhaps that's what Nicola meant. She hoped she didn't come out as hopeless and resigned as Nicola sounded now.

"So, I guess it's all steam ahead now for your jump of worlds next Saturday?" She sounded too upbeat for the subject matter, but she appreciated the change in subject.

Rachel looked over at the door and still heard Seb singing in the shower. "Yes, but listen, Nicola. I heard there's a place in each town—on the highest ground, where The Fallen can make their appeals for the angels to carry above. Is that true?" *Oh, God,* she hoped that it was.

"Yes, I've heard of it. But it's not for humans, Rachel."

"I know. It's not for me. I want to send a request to Layke."

"Are you mad?" Nicola shrieked. She was sure she'd never heard her so rattled before. "That's insane. Your own Grigori or definitely one of the others will kill you for that. Layke is Grigori's one weakness and that weakens them all."

"That's right, but don't you see? That's what makes it so perfect and have worth … The scales," she reminded her. "But I can't do it without you. I need you to ask Raephe to help us. He must care about you. Wouldn't he do this small thing for you? We'd be including one of them and not going behind their back."

"He's not going to help you break your contract, Rachel." Her voice sounded dead and flat, as if the mention of Raephe had lost her all sympathy.

Rachel tried to lower her voice to appeal to her more calmly and reasonably. "I'm not trying to hurt Raephe or any of the Grigori—far from it. I'm simply attempting to free Grigori of his past. He's so broken, Nicola. And, in doing that, I'm hoping he'll agree to free Seb. I promise you, I fully intend to honor my contract, but I won't condemn Seb with me." Just the thought sent the blood in her veins to ice. They'd both lose their lives to be locked into some toxic threesome with Grigori.

She gave Nicola a long minute to think, until she eventually said, "OK, I'll try. But I can't promise you how he'll take it. Raephe is extremely unpredictable—particularly where Xenon is concerned."

Rachel let out a breath. "Thank you … And, Nicola?"

"Yes?"

"I'm glad we'll have each other." It was truly the only heartwarming thing in this whole messy situation. Nicola was a good person and she was lonely, and they could guide each other through.

The line went quiet. "Me too," she said softly.

Rachel let out a ragged breath. "Well, OK then. Can you let me know as soon as you've spoken to him?" It all sounded so wild and hopeless, but she had to try something. She was all out of options.

"I will," Nicola said and ended the call.

RACHEL SPENT the whole of Sunday in bed with Seb.

"Ew, you're like a pair of bloody rabbits!" Lynn shouted from the hallway. But then they heard her shriek and then stomping feet as she was chased by Colin. So, 'pot' and 'black' came to mind.

It made them both laugh and threatened to put Seb off his game; however, Seb's appetite was voracious, as if he knew their time was running out as much as she did.

He leaned over her, propping himself up on an elbow. Sweat still beaded on his brow as he searched her eyes and smoothed the hair off her face. It was a moment of taking each other in.

Despite Seb's past of being a lovable rogue, he was honest and good. She could get lost in those gorgeous eyes. She knew there were real feelings behind them. It was something you couldn't fake or hide in moments like this.

It made her wonder if maybe they could have gone the distance if she'd never met Grigori. Or perhaps Seb wouldn't have noticed her unless she did. She would prob- ably never know for sure. "I want you to know, Seb, if anything happens on Saturday, that these past weeks have been the best of my life, and I wouldn't have changed a thing. I'm glad it was you." She wasn't even solely talking about losing her virginity, but any experience with boys at all. He was the first man she'd ever learned to trust since the father who'd run out on her. Maybe that was why it had taken her so long. "Why do you think you have so many girls, Seb?"

He tilted his head and half-smiled at the strange question.

"Do you think it was because you lost your mum?" she said.

He let out a blast of air and shrugged as if it never occurred to him before. "Maybe ... I just think I'm a people person. I feel easy around them." His smile was already widening with her train of thought. But then he frowned, got serious again and ran a finger along the furrows on her forehead. "That was in the past, Rach. It kind of sounds like you're saying goodbye."

Her blood pumped at being seen through so easily. She really was a rubbish liar. "I just want you to be happy, just in case something happens, you know?" It was the best she could come up with that he would remotely believe.

He smiled instantly and planted the softest of kisses on her nose and then her mouth. "You're real girlfriend material," he whispered and grinned against her lips.

"But are you boyfriend material?" she threw straight back, making them both laugh. In all the time she'd known Seb, she didn't think she'd ever seen him with the same girl more than a few times.

"I mean it. You can remind me of this conversation after Saturday," he said, understanding her completely.

A tear escaped the corner of her eye. She couldn't help it. He was trying to give her hope and she loved him for that. "I will," she said, with a hiccup.

LYNN WORKED that evening and they ordered pizza in. While they were eating cross-legged on her bed, she announced she was going into work the next day.

Seb looked at her curiously, obviously biting his lip. She knew there didn't seem much point and he was thinking the same thing.

"If we come out of this, I guess I'll still need a job, Seb."

However, as soon as she said the words, she felt awful. She knew damn well she was saying goodbye to her old life. She would never see anyone again, but she couldn't just abandon Mabel without so much as a goodbye.

IT WAS rainy and grey the next day. Weirdly, she still hadn't heard from Grigori after her impulsive pregnancy text. She didn't know how to take that. It had been a false alarm anyway, but his radio silence was out of character.

To take her mind off it, she drove to work playing all Seb's favorite songs: The Clash, The Ramones, Sound Garden. She was determined to fit as much of him in as possible in one week.

The traffic was slow, holding her up at the lights right outside Shebangs. She wondered whether the terms of her contract would allow her to go back there. She hoped so. Even people like Gavin, who were fairly new in her life, had suddenly become precious to her. She understood why she couldn't keep in contact with Seb and Lynn, but surely a haircut now and then was harmless?

Her emotions were a huge knot in her throat by the time she got to work. She was a little early and Mabel had only just opened up. "Ah, there you are. All better now?"

She almost gave herself away when she looked vacantly back at Mabel. Then she remembered all the time she'd taken lately had been because she was sick. "Yeah, sorry to leave you in the lurch like that, Mabel. It was such a nasty bug." She found it hard to lie to her face and went straight out to their little kitchen to put the kettle on.

Mabel's voice was warm when she called after her, "Aw, poor love. Glad you're better."

Rachel made the tea and handed her a cup with slightly

trembling hands. "Actually, I have to tell you something, Mabel, and I'm not sure how to say it exactly,"

Mabel picked up her hand and gave it a squeeze. Her eyebrows were pinched in concern. "What is it, love. You can tell me."

"I have to leave. This will be my last week."

The disappointment made Mabel sag. "Oh no, love. I thought you liked it here?"

Rachel felt awful and squeezed her hand. "Oh, I do. It's been the best job ever, it's just my great aunt is sick, and after Nan …" She was the worst person ever to barefaced lie to a person as kind and loving as Mabel. "I need to take care of her," she said with a weak, pathetic smile.

Mabel was already shaking her head. "Of course you must. It's last-minute, but I can arrange cover for you. Take as long as you need unpaid … but don't leave."

Her excuse had backed her into a corner and all she could do was nod. "OK. That's so kind of you, but I've no idea how long it'll take—whether she'll rally or …" She burst into tears at that point.

Mabel, of course, thought she was upset about her fictitious aunt, but she was really crying for the loss of someone as lovely as Mabel, her job and the choice she was having to make.

Mabel immediately pulled her into her ample bosom. She was warm and soft, smelling of flowers. She stroked her hair and let her cry. "There, don't worry, my love. You just do what you have to do. Your job will be here when you get back. Don't you worry about that." Her kindness reopened the gates of tears.

Eventually, when it was obvious that she had an audience of early library goers, Rachel extricated herself from Mabel's arms. "Sorry," she said, giving her nose a good blow.

Mabel squeezed her shoulder and served the first

customer. Rachel watched her work for a few moments while she composed herself. There was so much about her that reminded her of her nan. She was mumsy and caring, and when she had to be direct with anyone, it was always coated in kindness. She took herself off to the loo and cleaned herself up and redid her hair.

She paused and studied the person she'd become in the mirror. She wasn't the person she was before. She was strong. It was hard, but she was laying the trail for her disappearance to protect the ones she loved.

CHAPTER 38

Seb was at band practice when she got home, and Lynn had already left for work. It was actually really nice to be alone in the house. The walls held so many lovely memories for her. She could revel in them for a few hours as part of her goodbye. Doing simple things, like taking a long soak, made her feel normal and gave her a break from the looming shadow of doom. Life had felt far from it for the last six weeks. *Had it really only been weeks?* It felt so long since she'd walked into Rose Beauregard's tent.

Rose! She had been the one who had known everything from the very beginning. She'd warned her about the Grigori long before she'd even met Nicola. The hairs on her arms stood up despite the warm water. She wasted no more time and got out of the bath and hurriedly wrapped a towel around her.

She padded across the hall to her room and opened up her laptop. She quickly dried herself as it came to life, and she searched for 'Psychic Fairs' in her area on Google. Within seconds, she found what she was looking for. A community center in the next-door town this Thursday. She prayed it was the same one. They were a collective known as the Romany Rovers and had a webpage. She clicked on it and it showed the places and dates for the rest of the year. It was due to be back at Lynn's sister's kids' school in November. It had to be the same one. The "about" page listed the stalls and there she was: Rose Beauregard – teller of fortunes.

She threw on some old sweats and stepped into some bunny slippers. She needed to calm down. There was nothing that could be done before Thursday.

She went down to the kitchen, figuring she should really try to eat, and stopped at a bottle of Lynn's wine cooling in the fridge. She grabbed it, vowing to replace it the next day. She poured a huge glass that Lynn would be proud of and toasted the air to her friend. It tasted good and helped with her raw nerves.

Bunging two slices of bread of dubious freshness into the toaster, she sat at the table and sipped her wine. It felt like a lifetime ago that she first set foot into Angel's Ink.

But did she regret it?

Yes, her life was in turmoil, but would she prefer to never have met him, to remain the old Rachel, hiding her light with no confidence at all? She doubted Seb would have really noticed her for more than a novelty. No, in her heart of hearts, she would probably have done the same thing again. Apart from putting Seb and Lynn in danger. That she would erase. But the rest—the excitement—she thrived on and she kind of liked the person she'd become.

Grigori was right about that. Before, she wasn't living. She'd learned to step out into the open now and become the person she was meant to be, and that was down to him.

Seb reeked of alcohol when he came home. He stumbled into her bed and pulled her onto his chest. "Will you work tomorrow?"

She nodded without looking up at him.

"Isn't there loads you would rather do this week?" It was said awkwardly, as if he'd missed off the words, 'just in case'. Then she understood. He was supposed to have no idea that she was resigned to her fate and believe they were still fighting this thing as a couple. However, by the way he was beginning to act, she had a horrible suspicion that he was starting to think she was giving in on purpose. Maybe she was leaving him to be with Grigori out of choice. "I just want things to be like they always were," she said, honestly, looking up at him with a hard swallow, searching his face to see if she'd guessed right.

The room was dark, but there was enough light to see the stark lines of his profile staring up at the ceiling. Seeing him this low made her want to cut out her own heart. She'd been so wrapped up in her own life and saying goodbye to it that she hadn't given much thought to what was going on in his mind. He was still unaware of the full terms of the contract. He didn't know what would happen to him either—whether or not he'd still be here after Saturday.

Rachel leaned up on an elbow to look at him and played with one of the tags on his many necklaces. "Seb ... there's something I've been meaning to tell you."

He took his eyes from the ceiling to look at her. "What?" Despite his alcohol level, she felt his body tense, waiting for the blow.

She reached across and switched the lamp on to see him more clearly. "It's just me all this is going to happen to." She watched her words sink in and confusion spread across his face.

"You know that, do you?" His eyes were bloodshot and angry-looking, confirming her suspicions that he'd been drinking a lot.

"I do. It's just me. I promise you." She carefully omitted

the fine print that said she couldn't be in his life. She just wanted to make him feel better and not hate her too much.

However, confusion turned to anger very quickly, and he tried to sit up to look at her more squarely. "What, the guy's just going to let me off? … Convenient." Then he squinted. "And what did you have to give him?" His smile held only spite.

Instead of arguing with him, she cut him off by covering his mouth with hers. He kissed her for a few seconds before he pushed her away. "You're so wrong, Seb." She tried to keep the wobble from her voice, but failed.

He continued to stare at her, still unsure of what she was saying. His look darkened. "What bullshit is this, Rach? It's him, isn't it?"

She shook her head as it all began to spiral down.

"It's always been him. I should have guessed. What a mug."

"I'm telling you the truth, Seb. Please believe me. I got us into this. I rejected your sacrifice, so you're off the hook." Pain was leeching into her face and she couldn't hide it. "When I go there on Saturday, it will be to sign for me alone. That's it, Seb. That's the truth."

A range of emotions washed over his face in a matter of moments. Then a scary kind of drained acceptance. "So, it's done, and you never thought to discuss it with me." It was said flatly and not a question.

She deflated sadly and watched the light slowly and irrevocably go out of his eyes. "Yeah, it's done. There's nothing you can do. Please, Seb. Let's just enjoy the week. I want to carry on as normal as possible."

His blankness turned into a bewildered frown while he processed it as best he could. Then he pulled her to him, almost crushing her. "Fuck, Rach, what have you done? I would have done it for you," he whispered into her lips.

"I know you would." And she did, without any doubt.

WEDNESDAY EVENING WAS Lynn's night off. Seb had a big drinking session planned with his friends and she didn't want to deter him from it. Despite her coming clean, he wasn't handling it well. The light seemed to have gone out of their relationship.

She took a ragged breath, shook the maudlin thoughts away and concentrated on the perfect excuse for girl time. "Do you fancy a girls' night in, like old times?"

Lynn agreed straight away, clapping. She wasted no time and phoned Colin to tell him what they were doing, then ordered Chinese food and two bottles of white wine.

They settled in their PJs, wearing face masks, and painted their toenails. They talked and laughed like they'd done many times before, all the while Dirty Dancing then Pretty Woman went on in the background.

"Hey, do you remember that time I got you to drink that glass of Advocaat from my mum's drinks cabinet and you were sick?"

Rachel pulled a face at the memory. "It was disgusting."

"You didn't have to drink it," Lynn said, laughing.

"I did, you dared me and called me a square, who'd even bore the pants off Jesus. I remember the words you used distinctly." Rachel was already laughing before she finished speaking

Lynn was doubled over, trying to breathe. "I did, didn't I?"

Her laughter was infectious and soon Rachel was joining her. "You were right!" And they both laughed harder till their stomachs ached and tears filled their eyes. It was the medicine she needed.

They finally managed to pull themselves together. "We

needed this," Lynn said, more seriously. "I thought I'd lost you for a while," she said, looking directly in her eyes.

Rachel stared back for a long moment. It broke her heart. "Wouldn't happen," she said, tears welling up in her eyes. Whatever happened on Saturday, she'd find a way to stay near her oldest friend.

Without speaking, Lynn topped up both their glasses. "Let's make a promise right now, that whatever happens, wherever we end up, we will always be best friends."

The lump was so big in her throat that all Rachel could do was nod vigorously. They clinked glasses and Lynn knocked hers back in around three gulps. Then she pulled her into a tight hug to hide her own emotion. Rachel clung on, her mind torn and reeling. She wanted to be honest, but it would only hurt her and ruin the last few days they had. "Who else would I get boy advice from, right?"

It broke the tension and Lynn laughed. "Yeah, you are kind of hopeless."

They both laughed then.

Lynn refilled her glass and grew more serious. She was studying her closely.

"What?" Rachel said.

"Aren't you getting in a bit too deep with Seb, a bit too quickly?"

She was right. In Lynn's eyes, they'd gone from nought to sixty in about six seconds—well, six weeks to be exact. She had no idea they were cramming everything in because it would be over by the weekend.

"Because you know he's a dog, right?"

Her prime choice of words and the look on her face made Rachel laugh. It was so Lynn, but she was coming from a good place. Six weeks ago, she would have been a lamb to the slaughter with Seb. She had no way of knowing she'd live a hundred years in that time. All she could do was nod. "Yeah, I know." And maybe she should be hurt or upset knowing all that about Seb, but in the short time they'd been together, he'd been different with her. She'd learned to trust, but so had he. She really felt that he'd only ever allowed her in, emotionally. And for that, she felt terrible, but sentiment had no place in what she had to do to save his life and possibly Lynn's too. It put things in perspective. She had far bigger fish to fry in one dangerous, brooding, sexy, fallen angel. The person she'd be bound to for the whole of eternity, who would undoubtedly chew her up and spit her out.

Seb would revert to his line of groupies. It would be all he'd have after Saturday with no recollection of her, so she couldn't begrudge him that. "Don't worry, Lynn, I'm under no illusions." She gave her a weary smile. "Don't get me wrong, I care about him and I'm glad he was my first, but I don't think he's my future." It broke her heart to deliberately lead Lynn to the unfair, not the full, story conclusion. It was so disloyal to Seb, but there was nothing that could be done.

Lynn stared at her for a long moment as if she sensed the sadness in her. "The girl went and grew up," she said softly. Then she instantly brightened and clinked her glass with hers again. "To Mr Right Now, and not Mr Right!"

The laughter that followed felt hollow with guilt. "To Mr Right Now," she echoed. The familiar lump came back up in her throat while she took in every line and contour of her best friend's face.

THURSDAY COULDN'T COME QUICKLY ENOUGH. Seb didn't come home at all the previous night. Even though she guessed he wouldn't, it still hurt that he couldn't find it in himself to spend precious time with her. He was already protecting himself from the loss to come by distancing himself emotionally and physically.

However, to dwell took time—a luxury she didn't have. Instead, she got up early and went to work in good time to please Mabel.

The morning passed quickly.

Mabel let her take an early lunch break of 12 to 1 o'clock and she called Nicola.

"Rachel?" she said, after one ring.

"Yeah, it's me. Have you spoken to him?"

"Tonight. He's acting weird. He's difficult to pin down—more than usual."

"This weekend is the very end of the moon cycle Seb spoke of. If ever there was a chance to speak to the mediator, then it has to be now."

"I know. Tonight, I promise."

Rachel could hear the fear in her voice. She hadn't met Raephe much, but he seemed a lot more volatile than Grigori. "There's something else … I'm going to find Rose Beauregard. She must know something about getting an audience."

"She could be anywhere, Rachel."

"Actually, I think she's at a community center in a town quite near me tonight. They work a county circuit. I'm going to go. It's on between 4.30 and 6."

There was a wary silence for a moment. "Well, let's wish ourselves luck, then," Nicola said, sounding like they were going off for execution.

Rachel felt a pang of guilt. Maybe Nicola was risking a lot more than she realized. "Yeah, good luck."

IN ORDER TO get to the psychic fair in good time to make sure she got a slot with Rose, she had to get off work early. She grabbed her coat, bag and said goodbye to Mabel at around 4.30.

She swore at the traffic that conspired to hold her up at every set of lights. The stress was making her temple throb. At last, she pulled into the community center carpark at a little after five. She was lucky, as someone was already leaving and she could fill their parking space.

She slammed the car door and ran inside. She paid her two-pound entry fee and hurried to the lady in charge of the list of slots for the various services. She realized Rose Beauregard was popular and breathed with relief when she managed to get one of the remaining slots at 5.45. She had about half an hour to wait.

She messaged Seb in case he worried about where she was. A small paranoid part of her wondered if he still cared. It was warming when he messaged right back: *Will you be OK? Do U want me to come with you?*

She answered, *No, I'm OK. Traffic bad. Will be fine.*

He ended with a heart emoji. He could be so sweet at times. She guessed that was why girls swooned at his feet.

Next, she messaged Nicola to let her know she'd got there and was just waiting for her turn.

She messaged back: *Raephe's agreed to see me at 7. I haven't seen him for a while, but I can't help feeling something's up. Be careful, Rachel. I'm terrified.*

Their interaction seemed strange to her, like he was granting her an audience. It was so different from her and Grigori, who was more like a stern teacher. She also suspected that Nicola had strong feelings for Raephe and her fear had a lot to do with that. She felt the pull from Grigori and shuddered to think what that must be like with Raephe in control. *Good luck. Ring me straight after. I'll be home by then.*

She was left staring at her phone. It still bugged her that

Grigori hadn't been in touch after her last text. *Oh, what the hell,* and she tapped his number. "Rachel?" he said after a couple of rings.

"Oh, so you are alive then?"

He ignored her sarcasm. "Where are you? Is everything OK?"

"You mean after being scared half to death, I could be pregnant. I'm at the doctors now, though little you care."

He sighed as if she tried his patience. "You are not pregnant, Rachel. I know this."

"How could you know when you haven't even bothered …" She stopped in her tracks and said more softly. "Yeah, how do you know?"

"Subjects cannot fall pregnant, Rachel. It would not weigh equal on the scales. My blood prevents it." The information flabbergasted her. It was kind of an essential piece of information in the interest of freedom of choice, they kept harping on about. "Thanks, a bloody lot, Grigori!" She was furious with him. Everything was getting harder and harder, and the further things went, the more she realized she was in the dark.

"What is the matter, Rachel?" His voice was lulling and soft. Drawing the anger out of her to leave her exhausted with everything. "You are angry about something which has not happened. What is really troubling you?"

She sagged. He was right. It was a lot of things, but she guessed the main thing was Seb. After everything she was going through, she couldn't help being desperately disappointed in him. She knew he was using his safety defense mechanism to protect his feelings, but it still hurt on top of everything else. "What is it with men? I mean, I get so sick of all the double standards." Her mind was racing, thinking of Seb and even Raephe taking advantage of Nicola's love all the time. "They sleep around and yet they want a girl to be just for them. Sex means nothing. They go here, they go there, they get it anywhere they want." Her voice was getting louder and people started to turn their heads to look at her.

Grigori chuckled.

"What's funny? You're just going to say I'm being naive now, aren't you? Well bollocks to that!"

He laughed more loudly. "Well maybe a little." He was infuriating, but his good mood drained her anger till, in the end, she even heard the whine in her own voice and laughed begrudgingly. "OK then, comrade, what's your take on the human male and sex?"

He sighed. "I can only tell you my observations as a watcher of people. It doesn't apply to me."

As usual, he threw up a whole load of questions, but she didn't want him to clam up now. "Go on then, give me your pearls of wisdom."

"You want to know why they sleep around or why they choose one woman?"

"Yes." It was exactly what she wanted to know. "Both!" Her thoughts were all over the place on the subject.

"Mmm," he said, sounding like he was giving it great thought. "You think women guard sex as a sacred thing and men think it's something to throw away, but it's simply not true; it is the other way around."

She went to argue, but he cut her off. "Women sleep with men quickly and impulsively in order to pull them to them. Even if they do not love the man, but hope it will come after. The mistake they make is to think that sex will hold a man. It does not."

"You see, I am right, sex means nothing to a man!" Rachel said, feeling totally vindicated.

"No, on the contrary, in order for a man to choose one woman, he has to believe he is winning in some way. He must be the first or the best. She must have social standing, the most beautiful or coveted by his friends. When a woman sleeps with a man just to gain his attention, she devalues herself in that currency system. So, in effect, that one act of sex means more to the man than it does to a woman. Because from that he learns if he is special or not. Of course, he will repeat this with woman after woman, enjoying the journey."

She wanted to argue, but it was so amazingly insightful. He was, of course, the absolute expert on human nature. She was feeling hurt and angry because she didn't know exactly how she fitted into that philosophy with Seb. All she knew was how it felt, and she instinctively felt Seb pulling away. "And you're not like that?"

"No, I'm not."

Suddenly, despite being on the phone, she felt her temperature rising. "What are you like then?" She coughed as her voice disappeared completely.

"There are no hearts and flowers with me, Rachel."

Their hypothetical conversation suddenly felt very personal. "So, I'm right then. Sex is purely physical to you." She said it as a statement and not a question. She wasn't sure how they'd found themselves in this territory of conversation and she could already sense his annoyance. "Love and sex are completely unconnected ... with me." He left the final words hanging, so she had no doubt they were directed to her.

She wanted to throw the question of Layke at him, but she definitely didn't have the courage. By then, he seemed to have calmed down. "Not all men move on because they search for something better, Rachel. For some, it is self-preservation. They simply cannot expose themselves in that way."

She knew then that he was speaking about Seb and had known what she was feeling all along. A lump came up in her throat and she could no longer speak. He had that uncanny knack of getting straight to the point of what was bothering her. He had managed to deflect the heat from him, but he had spoken kindly, and she knew he was right. "I have to go," she said, and ended the call before he could say anything further. It was time to see Rose.

CHAPTER 39

*A*t last, 5.45 came and she hovered outside the tent for the last appointment to leave. A young woman came out, full of giggles, to join her friend. Her heart went back to the time she'd done almost the same thing with Lynn. How little she knew that her life would change immeasurably from that moment.

She walked warily into the darkness of the tent. It was empty like last time.

"Hello again, Rachel Fairweather," came from right behind her. She jumped around holding her chest. *How did she do that?* Her breath caught when she had the startling thought that maybe Rose operated outside of this world, just like all the other weird beings she'd met over the past weeks. It made her question whether she was even standing in the Earth dimension at all at that moment. "Hello, Rose," she said, regaining her composure.

Rose gestured for her to sit on the familiar low cushion next to the small table with the crystal ball covered in a cloth. "What brings you back to Rose? How goes it with your Grigori?" she said, taking her seat opposite her with guarded but curious eyes.

Rachel frowned. Perhaps no one had ever come back to her after she'd sold them out. She sensed she was more than a little wary. "A lot has happened since the last time I saw you."

Rose nodded as if it was unsurprising and didn't enquire how.

"So, you know?"

She bobbed her head. "Whispers between the spirits."

"Then you know I am for the Reaper?"

Rose bowed her head slightly and a lot more cautiously than the last time. She was afraid. It gave her a curious sense of power in her reversal of roles. "After Saturday, I am to work alongside him with my Grigori as my benefactor."

Rose couldn't look her in the eye, but she was listening closely, swallowing a little too often. The woman was now scared of her. *Good!* It was how she wanted her. How many people had she damned over the years? She would make her pay.

The way she couldn't meet her eyes meant she understood. Then, before she knew what she was doing, Rose was prostrate on the floor in front of her. Her forehead was on the mat and she was groveling.

The old Rachel would have pulled her up and brushed her down immediately, but not the new. The woman deserved this, and she would see to it that she got it. "I need something from you."

"Anything," she said, still not looking at her.

"This weekend is the last moon for atonement, and I wish to arrange something in offering for my Grigori."

Rose remained silent, waiting, but she could see her eyes moving rapidly.

"Sit up!"

She obliged sheepishly and sat cross-legged.

"You know of the mediator angel?"

She frowned. "He holds audience for The Fallen who wish to petition the heavens. It is on the hill of Gadsby Park. But there is no place for humans," she said, raising her eyes at last.

"You hold a special place in the spirit world, don't you?" She was flying totally in the dark here.

The woman nodded. She hoped not from flattery but from genuine standing in all this stuff. "What do you want me to do?" She met her eyes boldly this time.

"Listen to me carefully. You may want to write this down," she said, with a wave of her hand.

She rummaged in the pocket of the apron she was wearing and found a small pencil and a notepad.

"I don't care how you manage it, but it's important that a petition gets made to Layke the Pontip—got that? Layke the Pontip. To grant the wish of his humble servant, Rachel Fairweather, apprentice to the Reaper, Keeper of the Scales." Then she outlined the details of her plan and what she wanted to happen. "Make sure he hears the name, Xenon of Kryta, OK?" She repeated the name so many times that Rose had to say, "OK, got it!"

"Make sure he knows I make the entreaty on his behalf and not for me, so technically it isn't for a Human."

Rose nodded while she scribbled frantically. As she watched Rose scrawl, she genuinely wanted it for Grigori. Despite her own imprisonment and her need to free Seb, she wanted Grigori to be free of some of the guilt and bitterness he carried. She really did.

Rose caught up and dotted the last word with a heavy full stop.

"How will this get there?" she asked. Rose was as human as she was.

"I will give it to one of my Fallen contacts to carry it for you."

"And you have faith in him? Because, rest assured, I will know."

Rose bowed her head. "I will do this thing for you in the hope of the relationship we will build in the future." Her eyes raised to hers speculatively.

Rachel tried to hide her abhorrence of the woman. It wouldn't hurt to have a contact in her, albeit a slimy one. She never knew when she would need it. "Then we understand each other. Do this thing for me, and I will see to it that all concerned will know the part you played."

It seemed to satisfy Rose, and she touched her forehead and bowed low again. Rachel used the opportunity to stand and leave.

"Don't you want me to consult the crystal before you go?"

She looked over her shoulder at the woman waiting expectantly for her answer. "Can it predict the decision of an angel?"

Rose shook her head. "Such things are out of this realm."

Then, deciding that everything rested on that, she walked out into the light, saying, "Make sure my message gets delivered."

RACHEL WAS AMAZED at her own gumption. She guessed needs grew balls when a desired outcome required it.

She said nothing to Seb when she got home. She didn't get a chance. He was off out again and she'd be lying if she said it didn't hurt. Part of her wanted to scream at him, what did he expect? Everything she was doing was to save him and the least he could do was be supportive and grateful. However, when she really thought about it, he would still be losing her to Grigori, and that was at the bottom of all this.

Whatever she told him, Seb knew it was a goodbye of sorts. He was a man at the end of the day. With pride and an ego like all of them.

Seven passed. Then eight, nine, and ten. At eleven, the phone call from Nicola finally came. She was grateful Seb wasn't there then to hear her anguish. "What happened?" she said without even a hello.

"Sorry it took me so long. We … I had to … Raephe can be demanding when he sees me."

Rachel could imagine and didn't need it spelled out. Maybe what it was like was a conversation for the future when they were closer friends. "So, tell me what he said?"

"I waited till he became relaxed in my company, then I broached the subject. I put it to him like you had a dilemma."

"What did you say, exactly?"

"I kind of said the truth; that Xenon had these demons because of Layke. That you wanted him to have closure if you were to join him for eternity. You know, that it was a barrier between you."

Rachel was shocked and appalled at her take on it, first of all. It was completely wrong. She was not contemplating a relationship with him. *Was she? Was she living in some sort of denial that others could see?*

No, that wasn't it. "That's not entirely true, Nicola," she said, exasperated with her. "Through this process, I came to understand how deep his loss was. It was similar in a lot of ways to my nan and me. I just thought if I could give him some sort of solace, then …"

"He'd free Seb. Yes, Rachel. I know what you told me, but this is me, remember? I deal with a Grigori too. I know how they make you feel. They know and understand you like no human man ever could. Please don't try to kid me or yourself in all this, because that would be a lie and do you no good."

Rachel physically blanched at Nicola's strong words.

She'd never been so harsh with her before. She wanted to call her out on it and shout she was wrong and being a complete bitch, but she stopped herself. Instead, she took a breath and simply said, "So what did he say ... in the end?"

After a beat of surprise, Nicola said, "He asked me where you were, and I told him you'd gone back to the fortune-teller. He agreed to personally see to it that your message reaches the mediator. I think it suited him to remain in the background so as not to anger the other Grigori."

Rachel breathed a sigh of relief. It was clever. When it came to it, Rose could take the blame. "Thank you," she said, thinking that maybe Raephe wasn't as bad as he came across. However, one thing did bug her about him. He seemed more of a competitor than a friend to her Grigori. "Did he say why he was prepared to help?"

"Kind of. He said that Xenon was a lone wolf and a loose cannon set to go off at any moment because of his loss. He'd been that way for centuries. He thought you might be the stability that he needed—that they all needed."

She felt oddly comforted by that. "So that's good, right? If the others want that too ..."

"Not exactly. There is rivalry between them. They band together, but they are all for themselves. They are co-dependent, shall we say. Oleander lusts after Xenon herself and he has always rejected her, so she will hate you. Be extremely wary of her, Rachel."

She listened carefully, grateful for Nicola's insight. She would never forget that she risked herself tonight. Raephe was an unpredictable animal who could have turned on her any minute. "Seriously, thank you, Nicola. I owe you," and she totally meant it.

"Don't thank me yet."

She ended the call feeling that at least she had one good friend left out of all this, after Lynn and Seb had gone.

. . .

IT WAS LATE when she finally got into bed. Secretly, she hoped Seb would relent and come home; they didn't have much time left, but he didn't.

She reminded herself that it was selfish to expect him to invest feelings into something that was doomed. However, even she had to admit she was making excuses for him now. He was probably deliberately too drunk to drive or think as deeply on their relationship as that. He simply wasn't allowing it.

The thing was, there was no point in even calling him out on it. In two days, he wouldn't even know she existed. In the end, after much soul searching, she fell asleep alone.

THE NEXT DAY, she pushed on regardless. She went to work and tearfully said goodbye to all her regular, well-loved customers and, in the end, Mabel, who openly cried on her shoulder. She patted her back and cried along with her. They all thought she was just leaving for pastures new and not the scary life she could scarcely come to terms with. She was living in a kind of shock.

"I will pop and see you from time to time," Rachel told Mabel, not entirely sure if she'd be able to. They had only said she couldn't go home.

After much kissing and waving, she got into her shiny sports car that had now come to represent all that was wrong with the world and made the short drive home. She took the scenic route, going through the center of town. Past all the familiar places that she, Lynn and Seb had frequented a thousand times.

Queuing at the lights directly next to Wethy's pub, she

reminisced on all the boozy "happy hours" she'd passed with her friends.

Her heart stopped. Seb pushed open the large cinema-like doors with an arm draped around the shoulder of a blonde she vaguely recognized. He was unsteady on his feet and could barely open his eyes. He looked drunk and like he'd not slept for days.

Guess she had her closure there. He didn't see her, *thank god,* but she did war with herself not to wind her window down and give him some verbal abuse. Instead, she watched them walk in the direction of home.

The lights went green, and as she cruised past them, she wondered if he would recognize her car. He showed no sign. The moment passed and so did the image of the two of them in her rear-view mirror. They were gone, just like her old life.

She guessed in Seb's mind it was over, and this was his way of dealing with it in his inimitable style. Well, she didn't have to wait around and watch. She made up her mind. As soon as she cleared the town center, she was home in minutes. She rushed into the house, ran upstairs and threw down her case from the top of her wardrobe. Then she threw in as much stuff as it would take. Lastly, she picked up her phone and dialed Lynn, who picked up, but with a very noisy background. "Hey! What's up?" she said.

"Guess who I just saw?"

Without giving her time to impart her gossip, Lynn answered for her. "Seb with that skinny girl from last year."

She couldn't help smiling. It was such a Lynn-type answer.

"You wait till he sobers up."

Now laughing, Rachel cut across her; "Lynn … Lynn!" She had to repeat herself to get her to listen. "Don't worry about it. I love you, right?"

Lynn laughed in relief. "Love ya, babes."

Rachel ended the call before she got too emotional. She wanted to remember her just like that, the Lynn she knew and loved. Then she wrote one final text before she turned off her phone for good. She knew exactly what she had to write so he would understand. *Coming now, a day early, of my own free will.* She knew exactly what it meant and how it would be taken: the total submission he had been waiting for.

CHAPTER 40

The door to the shop buzzed open like it had done many times before, except this time it felt like it had been expecting her. It made her shudder. She hurried through to the back.

"Up here," Grigori's voice said from the darkness at the top of the stairs. It was enough to make her halt her steps. "Come up!"

Not sure what she expected, but she guessed it was for him to be in the shop, even though the appointment wasn't till tomorrow. She climbed the tiled steps slowly. Each step reminded her she'd jumped into the deepest sea without a lifejacket and there was no going back. She was throwing her lot in a whole day early with a powerful being who frightened the life out of her and yet made her feel more alive than anything else. And here she was, not able to make a louder statement of full submission.

The door was ajar when she reached the landing. She couldn't help looking around her because that had never happened before. Soft music came from behind it. He was waiting.

Cautiously, she walked through the weird, disorienting hallway. The perspective felt wrong and always made her feel sick. It felt like a strange place to take her for the night. Perhaps they weren't staying. Her weird dreams had taught her that she would soon come out into the clearing in the woods; the whole thing reminded her of Narnia.

No sooner had she had the thought than the hallway seemed to dissolve, and she reached it. The familiar speckled light through the trees that cast an otherworldly light and the smell of earth and leaves that quickly hit her nose. The whole place bombarded her senses and never failed to amaze her. Birds chirped, trees rustled and snakes slithered. It all sounded a little too loud, as if the volume on life had been turned up.

She touched the side of her head, feeling like she was getting a migraine. Seeing a fallen log, she stumbled over to it and sat down. As she pinched her nose, four feet appeared directly in front of her. Her head shot up. *Bohdan and Oleander. Shit!*

She looked around for Grigori, but he was nowhere around. Raephe was lounging against a tree a little way off.

The two Fallen eyed her suspiciously, making her feel instantly uncomfortable and nervous. "I'm here to meet with Xenon," she said, hoping that was enough to make them stand down.

Oleander smiled an unfriendly smile. "We won't keep you long."

The woman literally made fear creep up her spine. It suddenly occurred to her that Grigori might not know she was here at all.

Bohdan smirked, wolf eyes fixed on her hungrily.

"A little birdie tells me you have been meddling in things that don't concern you."

Rachel found herself pulled to her feet with just a curl of

Oleander's finger. She looked anxiously across the clearing to Raephe, whose face remained guarded. Was he staying out of the whole thing, or had he been their "little birdie"? It was hard to tell. "I don't know what you mean," she said, facing Oleander again.

Bohdan pulled her chin around to face him and held her with his icy eyes. He was right up in her face. "I am the Watcher of the South and I see you, tamperer. You are the lurer, the destabilizer … Yes, I see you." He grinned, showing perfectly white teeth, and then licked his lips like he would eat her whole.

Her eyes widened with fear.

"Do you seek to turn our brother from the task he has sworn to for eons?"

She was shaking her head manically, terrified of what they planned to do to her.

"We need surety," Oleander said, dragging the attention back to her. She scratched the skin beneath Rachel's chin and drew blood.

"I don't know what you mean," she rambled. "All I've been doing is finding ways to free my boyfriend. That's all I want," she answered, truthfully.

"Liar!" Oleander shrieked, swiping her across the face.

"Enough!" Raephe said, breaking his silence at last and coming over.

Rachel rubbed the side of her smarting face. Adrenalin kicked in, bringing with it the calm of shock. They'd brought her there to kill her.

"Fools! Marking her like this. Have you taken leave of your senses? You will incur Xenon's wrath. You see how much she has become a part of him. I say, give her what she wants. Control her and we control him."

When Rachel looked into his infinitely dark eyes, she could see he was playing. He was acting a part, but it was clear that he was playing his own tune and he enjoyed the fact that she knew it as well as he did. He was crafty in the extreme.

The other two just looked at each other. She wasn't entirely sure they weren't telepathic.

Raephe continued to watch her. His dark, aquiline features homed in on her the whole time. "Why then do you seek Layke?" he said, holding up an arm to immediately stop the others butting in.

She could see now that even if he had helped her, he needed to know this for himself. She had no idea what to say. All she could do was stutter, "I ... I..." Hoping to God he had delivered on his promise to Nicola.

He rested his head at an angle to indicate he was still waiting for his answer.

"I thought if I could give Xenon the opportunity to speak with Layke and he could get some kind of peace, he would free my friend."

Raephe closed the gap and drew her to him by the throat. She could feel his hot breath on her lips, so close she swore he thought about kissing her. "Do you have any idea what will happen if Layke convinces Xenon to repent? Even if he kills him, the Watchers' agreement will be broken and we will be permanently imprisoned in Tartarus, never to walk the Earth again. You want this?" Raephe said, snarling in her face.

"No ... no, I swear."

"You would see us annihilated on the last day?"

All she could do was try to shake her head in his painful grip while tears began to spill. "It wasn't like that. I need him," she said, honestly. That would be catastrophic for her too. Leaving her completely unguarded with the Reaper.

His demeanor softened as if he was pleased and he released his hold. "So, you hoped to bargain," he said softly, nodding slowly with understanding. His beady eyes then roamed her face, assessing her.

"She lies," Bohdan whispered in his ear. "I say we take her for ourselves and to hell with the consequences."

Raephe laughed. "And risk Xenon's anger?"

"Better that and keep him, miserable though he may be."

Raephe bobbed his head. "He does have a point."

The more Raephe spoke, the more she got to understand he was a game player.

"Xenon, bitter and devoid of emotion, is an effective machine for us. Abaddon and even the Devil himself recognize this," he said, raising his eyebrows at her. "Your position will always be precarious as they will watch your influence on him closely."

She recognized the warning he was giving her. She understood perfectly. It was to everyone's benefit to keep Xenon doing what he did best, focused, single-tracked and ruthless. Her helping him risked all that.

"So, you see our dilemma," he stated, walking a little apart from her. "So, I ask myself, what can we do?" he said theatrically on a sigh and tapping his cheek. The others were watching him closely.

Bohdan smirked. "I say just kill her!"

Raephe rolled his eyes. "But those tiresome scales," he said with a rakish smile.

Rachel looked between them all anxiously. "But I'm already tied to Abaddon, aren't I?"

Raephe laughed loudly and pointed a finger at her. "That you are," he laughed. "See, I told you," he said to the others. "This one's clever."

Oleander sneered at that. "I can think of a hundred ways to make it not so."

Raephe's face became serious. "I am beginning to think she won't hurt Xenon at all. I suspect she cares a great deal for him already." He tilted his head to study her more closely. "And when she finally succumbs to him, he will own her completely. I say let her go to him, but we'll take some insurance for ourselves."

Rachel swallowed hard; her mouth was completely dry. This was something she wasn't going to talk her way out of.

The other two closed in shoulder to shoulder with Raephe, intrigued, all eyes on her. An invisible force held her arms to her side and she was moved towards the flat table of the plinth. "Wait!" she called over her shoulder. "Was my message delivered?"

Oleander ignored the question and said to Raephe, "What will you do?" moving her along with his mind. "Putting a clause in the contract."

"Shouldn't she be willing?" Bohdan said, excited, despite his words.

"Blood is blood," Raephe said ominously. "Little can be argued by that."

Rachel writhed and struggled against the force holding her as her feet left the ground and she was laid out on the table.

Raephe lowered his mouth to her ear. "All of this would be redundant if not," he said so only she could hear.

She had no time to process the words when her wrists were turned outwards. "Just a small addendum to your contract," Raephe said.

A sharp sting made her jump. Then another and another. Then, a warmth of skin covered it after, and she watched in horror as each of the three Fallen licked their wrists. "It is sealed," Raephe said. "Blood with blood for the four winds. If aught should fail, dominion shall fall to the remaining Watchers." He was saying it in a hushed tone like an incantation. Then he ended with, "This blood signifies the subject bound to all."

The other two followed with, "So be it."

Rachel could barely breathe, and her eyes were wide with terror. *Where* was *Grigori when she needed him?*

"Behind you," came from the other side of the plinth.

The light seemed to drain from the place as if a cloud had come over. A great blackness engulfed them all. The temperature dropped dramatically, and snow began to fall.

He's here, she breathed.

Grigori stood on the other side of her, but he wasn't alone. Abaddon stood with him. She glanced anxiously at the three on the other side of her, and for the first time, she saw uncertainty on Raephe's face.

However, it wasn't Grigori who spoke first, it was Abaddon. "You dare tamper with a subject already promised to me?"

Grigori's eyes were on her, already checking her over for damage, warming everywhere they touched. She was so pleased to see him. *Boy, did she have Stockholm Syndrome.* Her invisible bonds were instantly released, and she managed to sit up. She slid off the plinth and immediately went to Grigori's side. "They did this." She held up the wrist they'd marked. It was then she realized it was the wrist that represented her soul.

Grigori took the shortest glance, covered it with his hand, then looked at the others thunderously. The pain instantly eased at his touch.

She followed Grigori's line of vision. Oleander had regained her composure and looked as beautiful as ever and posed and preened in front of him. Bohdan looked wary and ready to fight and Raephe just smirked.

"Abaddon, is it not illegal to take a subject already submitted and bound?"

Rachel looked up at Grigori sharply. *Was he bluffing?* They still hadn't slept together. He glanced down at her quickly, his face still showing the anger bubbling beneath the surface. "Submission comes at the thought, not the act itself."

She was left absorbing that while Abaddon replied, "Indeed it is."

Grigori's hand on her wrist tightened. "I defer judgment to you as the wronged party."

When she saw the corners of Abaddon's mouth twitch, she wanted to scream not to do that. She didn't trust any of them.

Raephe looked completely composed when he addressed Abaddon directly. "We merely recognize the special favor shown this subject and sought to bind her to the four winds for your safety and security sire," he said, slightly bowing his head. "Merely business. It is an uncertain world we live in, is it not?"

No, no, she wanted to scream, but Grigori squeezed her wrist to keep her quiet. She looked up at him and felt worried for the first time. He was watching the situation intensely, like he didn't know himself how it would go.

Instead of addressing them, Abaddon turned and faced her and motioned for her to put out the injured arm to him. After looking in Grigori's eyes and getting a slight nod, she did as he asked.

He narrowed his eyes and looked at Grigori. "It seems your brethren trust you not." Then he looked back at the others. "Know this. Each of you is allowed your freedoms solely because of me. If any one of you so tamper with my charge, Watchers or not, you will be weighed and sentenced." Then he turned to Grigori. "And that includes her guardian. The addendum stands as surety of that."

She looked up at Grigori just in time to see the shock. Oleander laughed. Bohdan clapped and Raephe smirked but looked straight at her. He'd played a master stroke. He'd won in every way tonight and she felt suddenly nervous of the way he looked at her.

Grigori simmered. "Outrageous," he said, ominously low.

Abaddon was already turning and walking away. "Insurance, Xenon. If she lives up to expectations, then naught is lost on any side." He paused and looked over his shoulder with his grimace-like grin. "It will be in your interests to keep her that way." He was already beginning to disappear. "Until tomorrow night," he said, his words floating on the wind.

Without facing the others, Grigori snatched her to him, and the next thing she knew, they were walking into the studio. Grigori's reaction was scaring her more than anything. Suddenly, everything in this new world was uncertain and terrifying. She hoped she was strong enough to survive it and Grigori stable enough to protect her.

HE WENT STRAIGHT to his workstation and leaned back against his bench as he always did with his arms folded. His eyes rested on hers, hard and unyielding. He was pissed.

Rachel stared at him a full minute with wide, wild eyes, her chest rising and falling as if she'd just run for her life. "They tricked me," was all she could say.

They both stood rooted to the spot, taking each other in. He seemed to calm down eventually, his gaze remaining steady, intense and fixed on her. "I can't offer you love, Rachel, only obsession."

It was brutal and openly honest, and she kind of respected him for that. From anyone else, it would sound conceited, but from him, it was the hopeless truth, and she understood. She swallowed hard and slowly approached him, taking it as permission granted at last. She came to a stop close enough to have to crane her neck up to look at him.

"The contract remains unchanged?" she said, fully intending to still free Seb. After the debacle of a few minutes ago, it was good to get clarification.

He shook his head. His eyes changed from hard to speculative.

It was strangely liberating. She wanted this new start. There was something between them; there always had been. It may not be love, but it was there nonetheless, and he felt it just as surely as she did.

He put out a large hand to the side of her face and cupped her cheek. Then he caught the stray strands of blue hair and pushed them back. The softest gesture she'd ever seen him make. "You are sure?"

Her heart was beating wildly, and the honest answer was no, but she recognized there was no going back. She could barely breathe as he ran a thumb along her cheekbone. She swore he emitted pure electricity. The mind boggled at what the whole him would feel like. She nodded. "Yes."

Blackness swept her up with velvet wings.

CHAPTER 41

The feeling of him holding her through the cold of the night felt different. As his huge wings beat a slow rhythm against the sky, his arms held her in a proprietary way for the first time. She wondered if he felt the change in their status as keenly as she did.

She had no clue where they were going, but she felt the steady drop in temperature and guessed they were heading northwards, towards his own lands. Snow soon covered everywhere below them, and her breaths were visible in front of her face. She was grateful when Grigori's feet touched down on the platform of a penthouse at the very top of a tall modern building. They were high above a bustling city. A castle of chrome and glass, and not of stone, which she kind of expected of him.

Large plate-glass windows parted as he walked in his fluid gait towards them. Welcome warmth immediately hit her when she followed. Everything in the huge space was black. The highly polished marble floors, smooth walls, leather sofas—even the subtle mood lighting—were all black. There was a large wall-mounted TV and a kitchen area with an island and breakfast stools in the far corner and a smoked-glass wall she guessed hid the bedroom. No woman lived here. This was his place.

It made her think of her life after Saturday for the first time and panic raced through her. "Where will I live?" she said, turning to him. He'd walked past her to the kitchen, where he grabbed a bottle of vodka from the freezer and poured it into two small glasses.

"Anywhere you like—except with anyone from your past life," he said with a bob of his head, then he knocked back his drink. It hit her how utterly alone she would be, and her future felt bleak.

When he walked, she was reminded of the predator he was. Every movement was easy, fluid and mesmerizing to watch. "This is my private space," he said, coming to a stop right in front of her and passing her a drink. His eyes seemed to draw from the blackness of the room, and she had to swallow.

"Can I stay for a few days?" she said, her voice suddenly gone to a husky rasp.

His eyes bore into hers while he touched her face again. He was analyzing whether he could stand her there. Then he took the untouched drink from her hand, knocked it back and nodded. "You can stay as long as you wish, but I suspect it won't be for long. Abaddon will put demands on your time and I'm not easy to live with." His hand wrapped around the back of her neck while his thumb stroked her jaw. The smile he gave her was filled with his own pain and uncertainty. This was going to be difficult for him too. She was now precious cargo he would have to guard at all costs, judging by the farce they'd just gone through in Tartarus. She also guessed it would cramp his style, having a subject in his home when he had his work to do, corrupting others.

The corners of his mouth twitched at that.

It made her draw back. "Oh my god, you can read minds!"

His smile widened. "Not always. But your thoughts are loud, Rachel." He laughed, that rare and beautiful sound, and then got serious. "And God will no longer help you." He raised a brow. "You have fallen now, like me."

It sobered her instantly. In all the upheaval and worry, she hadn't ever thought about it like that.

"And in answer to your unsaid question, very few have been here. I seldom let anyone this close." As he said the words, he took a step closer, until the heat of his body seeped through her clothes. She found herself wondering about the obsession he spoke of earlier. *Whose?* And whether that was the reason she couldn't stay with him. "What will it be like with you?" she whispered, dragging her eyes up from the ribs of muscle she could clearly see through his clothes, up to his eyes.

His answer was to glide a finger down the side of her face. "You are very astute." He bent his head and brushed his lips against hers, instantly pulling a sigh from them. Her body ignited as if he'd flipped a switch. It was so fierce it took away her breath, giving her her answer. "I don't stand a chance, do I?"

He shook his head slightly, then licked across them. Her heart-rate quadrupled. "You never did."

A ragged breath escaped her. Resigned and already coiled in excitement, she guessed she'd always known it right from the lust-filled look he'd given her that first night in the full-length mirror. Her body had called to him even then. Perhaps she'd always known this time would come.

He began a trail of gentle kisses along her jaw to her ear, then down the column of her neck to the soft part of her shoulder. Each one was lighting a trail to her groin, which was already pooling wet between her legs. She had to speak while she could still string a coherent sentence together.

Despite knowing he'd lived for millennia and sounding ridiculously childish, she had to tell him how she felt. "I can't stand the idea of being one of many, Grigori. I don't think I'm strong enough for that."

He didn't answer. Her feet left the floor and he carried her past the smoked-glass screen that hid the biggest bed she'd ever seen behind it.

He placed her down gently and climbed onto it next to her. His hands continued where his lips had been, smoothing back her hair and caressing her neck. The buttons of her shirt were nimbly loosened. Despite finally admitting to herself that she had fantasized about him from the beginning, she honestly never expected to end up here in reality.

"Sex is a simple animal transaction of the body, Rachel, and nothing to be scared of."

She frowned as her shirt fell apart to reveal her bra and his finger travelled across the delicate skin above it. *Surely the human mind made it more important than that?* "And yet it was enough for you and a third of the angels to leave Heaven," she said, looking at him with more defiance than she felt.

His hand stopped and his look darkened, making her quickly regret what she'd said. For a long moment, neither of them moved until he looped a finger into the waistband of her jeans and yanked her to him. She was brought flush against him in a single tug.

He brought his lips down next to hers. "You are right," he said against her lips, driving her temperature up and making her want to nip at him. "Some need a sense of belonging—a touch to make the soul soar."

His breath tingled on her skin while he spoke, and she felt herself already yielding to him. She instinctively knew she'd be a hopeless wreck after this. He sensed everything and his tongue entered her mouth and began to tangle with hers. She gently sucked it and let it go. "You have nothing to fear," he said, between kisses. "I will take great care of my earthly iris."

The potency of his kiss was already spreading through her veins and taking her over. Soon she would be lost.

"Please say the words, Rachel. I must hear them clearly," he whispered, nipping along her jaw. "That you offer yourself to me, body and soul, to do with as I will." He ended the sentence by kissing her with the full force of a whirlwind that almost left her unable to speak.

"I do," she panted. All she saw or wanted now was him. "I give myself," she breathed and panted again. His hips were undulating with hers. "Body and soul, of my free will."

As she lost herself in another all-consuming kiss, she wondered how someone being kissed by a being this powerfully sexy could ever speak and their statement be construed as admissible in any court of law.

Once she'd said the words, he surprised her and drew apart from her, lying on his side. It gave her time to breathe. His eyes were still bleary and a little bloodshot.

"What?" she gasped. "What's the matter?"

This close, his eyes reminded her of deep space with small flecks of amber novas. It was as if they were both in shock at what just happened. "It is enough … we need go no further."

She gasped, not believing what he was saying to her. "Was it something I did?" She was panicking, she knew. Her body was still heated for him, and he was turning her down at the last moment. "What changed?"

He reached out a hand to her lips to stop her speaking and ran a soft finger along them. "Nothing has changed. All is the same. You have submitted and I have accepted as in the terms of the contract."

"But …" She felt foolish and rejected, as if he'd led her on in the cruelest way. "You don't see me in that way," she said flatly, dying in the worst depths of humiliation.

He shook his head and drew her closer to him, even though she tried to remain where she was. "We have a very long time together, Rachel. I don't want to reduce you to a quivering mess on day one," he said, a small smile playing on his lips.

Her frown subsided while she absorbed and understood what he was saying to her. It thawed her humiliation slightly. "You're so arrogant."

He bobbed his head and shrugged slightly. "But truthful."

"How do you know that I won't reduce you to a quivering mess?" she said, starting to smile.

He threw his head back and laughed, rolling on top of her easily. She found herself holding her breath again, not knowing what he would do. He nodded and searched her eyes. "Maybe one day we will find out."

Then, before she could come back with anything at all, he pushed off her and got up off the bed. "You will live here," he said, already walking off.

She sat up and was left reeling, wondering what the hell just happened.

She took a shower and mulled it over. She supposed, in a weird kind of way, him not taking advantage was a good thing. It showed a level of respect.

She dressed simply in some yoga pants and a loose-fitting top, dragged a brush through her wet hair and went and looked out at the snow-covered city below. The view was stunning through the wall of smoked glass that spanned the apartment. It was still dark, but it glittered with different colors from the tall buildings and streets, like a fairyland.

Grigori came up behind her and put his arms around her waist. At first, she stiffened, then relaxed into him. It was such an easy boyfriend-like gesture that it took her by surprise. He kissed the top of her head and she looked out in shock for a few moments. This new whatever-it-was was going to take some getting used to.

They stood for quite a few moments. "I had no idea what led me here to you a day early," she whispered in all honesty.

It took him a while to answer. "In truth, I don't know why I brought you here," he said above her head. "Since the beginning, I have been trying to piece together the meaning of it and it always comes to the same thing."

She waited, barely breathing, continuing to stare out at the winter city. "What's that?" she said, eventually.

"That you were sent to me for him."

Part of her was always let down by the way everything always came back to Layke. She guessed she was envious of that kind of love. How beautiful to be a part of something like that. Surprisingly, she harbored no jealousy over it. *He was an angel, for god's sake.* She could never hope to have such a claim on him. It was then that she got a small glimpse of how Nicola must live from day to day, living for the small morsels of affection that Raephe threw her way. *Obsession.*

He walked away to the kitchen area to grab himself a drink. Her breath caught when she saw him in nothing but jeans. It was the first time she'd ever seen him relaxed in this way.

The heavenly scene in black and grey was revealed on the smooth skin of his back. It was a masterpiece worthy of Michelangelo himself. It depicted two embracing angels in full flight, rising up to the shining gates of heaven. The artwork was stunning; however, it was the expressions captured on the angels' faces that drew her in. It was one of pure wonder, ecstasy and contentment; so delicate and drawn with something in the hand that more resembled a brick than a pen. If Layke truly did that, then he was a master artist.

He closed the fridge and grinned at her when he caught her watching him. He walked back and passed her a bottle of juice. "Well," she said at last. "If you have no room for another and I'll be ruined for other men, then I would say we're a perfect pairing."

He glanced at her sideways and assessed her in his calculating way. Then he picked up one of her hands, dwarfed by his, and nodded once. His eyes dropped immediately to her lips, giving away what he would do with them.

Her heart sped up and she smiled tentatively while his eyes roamed her face. She still wasn't quite sure how she walked out on her old life this morning and ended up here with an angel of the most sinful kind, hoping he'd do the most wicked things to her. She really had sold her soul.

It was almost daylight when her eyes left his to look back out of the smoked-glass window. "Where are we?" she asked, absently.

"Norway," he said, pulling her against him again.

She reveled in the feel of his warm skin and wonderful smell. Her heart was skipping, still not understanding their new dynamic. Even without getting physical, he commanded her responses.

Then she could see the sun on the horizon. The land of the Northern Lights—long nights and shorter days—and his home and its location made sense. The black walls and decor of the apartment all prolonged the night as long as possible. It was daytime and he was still corporeal.

With miraculous timing, she felt his arms disappear around her. "I'll be back soon," he said, like an echo on the breeze.

CHAPTER 42

*R*achel waited restlessly in Grigori's apartment on her own. She watched TV, made coffee and wandered around opening cupboards just to see what a fallen angel would keep in them. She was disappointed to find nothing at all. She was beginning to understand that for these beings, physical things were like props. They really had very little use for them. They just manufactured them out of thin air as they needed them. It was a troubling thought when she thought about Grigori's achingly hot body.

With no idea what the time was or the time difference to the UK, she tapped Nicola's number.

"Hey!" she answered right away.

"I'm at his apartment in Norway," she said, unprompted. Sounding just as surprised as she felt.

"Wow, he took you there? That's huge, Rachel."

"Don't get too excited, his heart is still Layke's. Have you spoken to Raephe recently?" She wasn't sure how much to tell her about what went on in Tartarus. She decided it could wait.

"Yes, but he's guarded about the whole thing."

She remembered the distrust and the fear they all had of Grigori being reunited with Layke and her heart began to sink. "You don't think he helped us?"

"No, I believe him. The message was delivered, he assured me that. There are just rumors spreading through the underworld. Oleander and Bohdan must be getting wind of it."

"Underworld?" She thought there was no such thing.

Nicola laughed a little. "Down here on Earth is what they call the underworld. The angels are above, and the Fallen are under."

She got it. "So, what now?"

"We just wait. You go and do your final signature as planned. It's the Eve of Atonement, so I guess if miracles do happen, tonight is the night."

They wished each other luck and ended the call. Guilt pricked her conscience at not telling her about Raephe's addendum to her contract, but she hadn't wanted to complicate things this late in the game and she'd explain everything when it was over.

Night came early and Grigori returned. He brought with him new clothes and a faux fur coat. The jeans hugged her perfectly and the gossamer-thin sweater accentuated her curves. They were her perfect size. "Thank you," she said, eying him curiously.

"I have lived a long time," was all he said in answer to her unsaid question.

After she'd changed, he led her out onto the large balcony that gave her vertigo and swept her up and away into the freezing night air. It felt good to be held in his arms. She did wonder why they'd flown, but he quickly explained, "I won't risk you in Tartarus tonight."

She wondered if he meant the night of sealing her tattoo contract or the night of atonement, if all Fallen were aware of it.

Miraculously, they arrived at the shop a little before nine, she guessed, for probably the last time. Possibly never coming back, even to her hometown. Fear gripped her for a second. They hadn't discussed specifics yet. There was a strange feeling of anticipation between them, as if neither really knew what to expect after tonight.

She climbed into Grigori's chair as she'd done so many times and watched him take the many bottles of ink from his old-looking wooden box. *The special ink.* It made her wonder where he made it and when he extracted his blood to mix with it.

The mood was awkward between them. "Do I call you Xenon from now on?" she said with a grin to lighten the mood.

He looked sideways at her like he knew she was taking the piss. "That, or master," he said, raising a brow.

Her eyes went wide. "Bugger off!" she laughed. *Stockholm!* she thought, shaking her head.

It was his turn to laugh.

She couldn't help looking at him and thinking there was never a more screwed-up situation.

He turned to her with a scary-looking syringe in his hand. Her eyes went from it to his, warily. "That's better than some of the names I could call you right now."

He smiled sympathetically and looked genuinely sorry. "I just need a little of your blood this time." He picked up her wrist and ran a finger up to the crook of her arm to find a good vein. His touch was gentle and as electrifying as always. These angels were lethal. It was definitely wise to ban them from fraternizing with the female population. When he looked intensely into her eyes, she nodded her permission and he very expertly pierced her arm and took one vial of blood. Even that quickened her pulse. She guessed she'd had his blood mixed into her tattoos; it made sense that her signature should contain hers.

After he was done, he checked her eyes and put a wad of cotton wool on the small wound and asked her to press down. She watched, fascinated, as he began to pour half the blood into a small ink bottle, giving it a shake, and the other into a tiny cut-glass bottle, which he sealed with a stopper. "What's that one for?"

He wrapped it up in a black velvet square and put it back in his box. Then he turned around and pulled his stool closer with his foot. "I keep it. The first and most valuable part of your education: the soul is in your blood. It *is* your signature. Science is only just catching up with what we have known since the dawn of creation. When it is spilled, whether in violence or to an owner, it cries out to the whole spirit world. All now know who holds your soul."

It was astounding and yet made a weird kind of sense. Scientists can decipher everything that makes us into who we are from our DNA. Rachel found it heartbreaking how every time a living thing dies, the spirit realm knows of it. What a weight to carry. It threw new light on the scales.

He sat on his stool and rolled closer, scraping back his hair and putting on his baseball cap. Then he nimbly clipped the different parts of his gun together, placing the ink bottle containing her blood on the top. "Whoever possesses that, possesses you," he said, nodding towards his wooden box with the small bottle inside.

Things were becoming very scary and very real. Rolling around with him in the sheets was one thing, but that was just a diversion from this, the point of it all. "And Abaddon? You give it to him?" The thought of him owning her made her stomach turn.

Grigori shook his head. "He wants to buy it."

Her heart sped up at the idea that he wanted to keep it

himself. "I decided to just sell him a license to use you … like publishing rights," the corners of his mouth twitched into a mischievous smile. "To be reviewed on a year-by-year basis." He couldn't hold in his laughter then.

She scowled, wanting to hit him. None of this was a laughing matter. However, suddenly it was. It was hysterically funny and it bubbled up inside her like steam needing release. In the end, she had to shake her head and the madness away. "Shit, Grigori. I'm not livestock." He was unbelievably clever. It was a way of softening the threat of Raephe's addendum, if her actual owner was in fact one of them and not Abaddon after all.

He moved in closer with his gun and touched the side of her face with his free hand. He was the man of last night again, looking at her intensely with those eyes and those lips she could kiss despite what he was doing to her. "You need to take off your top and your bra," he said softly.

She swallowed and did as she was told. Part of her thought how heartless he was being, then she remembered that much of this was now for her protection. They were just too far along to go back.

He was already in business mode, examining his mark already there on her chest.

"What will you do this time?"

"There will be two marks. I will make a small iris, probably here." He pointed to the end of his X mark. "And you get to make a small X on me to complete the contract."

She grinned. Finally, payback. However, there was no humor in his look, as if he was already sorry. It made no sense. Then a chill began to creep through her veins. She couldn't be the only one who had completed the tests with him. She continued to wait in shock while he leaned over and switched on his stereo, cranking up the haunting rock music.

Nothing out of the ordinary followed, if you discounted the sex god, fallen angel marking up your body with an expression of steely determination. In the end, it was a perfect small flower that she had to admit softened the monstrosity of his mark. "That's it!" he said at last, pushing away from her on his stool. His eyes flashed to hers as he took off his cap and pulled his t-shirt up over his head.

Even now, she mentally drooled over his physique. She hated the idea of marking him up with an awful, unskilled tattoo done in her own hand.

"Don't be afraid. All you have to do is make a small X and it's done." He gave her simple instructions on how to operate the tattoo machine. She had no idea how he could create such works of art with something so cumbersome.

He put his back to her. Though when he turned to look over his shoulder, he didn't meet her eyes. "Look at the piece on my back." It was the way he said it that began to alarm her. She ran her eyes over the beautiful flying cherubs in all their majestic glory, clouds, sun rays and everything, then her eyes finally dropped to what appeared to be the sea boiling up below it. Every single part of the churning waves was made up of tiny Xs. It reminded her of a needlepoint tapestry.

"Many have faded. There are many layers," he said softly, but still hammering home his point. He was Fallen and this was what he did. The very thought she'd had earlier that day came immediately to mind. *I don't just want to be one of many.* It halted everything. How foolish to ever think she could be special to a being like him. His whole existence had been to take souls for thousands of years. Here were their marks made with their own blood and their own hands. It was as gruesome as it was heartbreaking.

"Don't overthink it," he said, understanding immediately where her mind was going.

"So many," she whispered, her words catching in her throat. How would she even pick a place to put her own insignificant cross? "Have you kept them all?" The thought suddenly occurred to her that if he held their contracts, then he held their souls. They could all still be alive somewhere, longing for him as pathetically obsessed as she was. *I can only offer obsession.* It was clear now.

He finally looked at her over his shoulder. He seemed sad, as if he knew how she felt. "You don't need to be in the sea, Rachel. You can be a bird in the sky, flying off into the distance."

She moved closer and ran a hand over the skin that had caused pain to thousands, deciding where to put her own misery. She wanted to see if there were any other stray Xs that had received a similar concession. "There are no others there," he said, reading her perfectly as usual.

Her hands shook as she switched on the machine, as he'd shown her. It vibrated, making the shaking worse. She must be losing her mind to still be going along with it. She moved achingly slowly towards the soft skin of his back.

"You *are* special," he said when she was almost there.

She decided on a tiny cross just beneath one of the sun's rays. It seemed fitting to be a small bird flying directly into its heat for certain destruction.

He took a breath and his head went back as the machine made contact with his skin. It was as if he enjoyed it.

She bit her lip with concentration, and she made the tiny X. In the end, it was so small that an outsider would barely know it was there.

Grigori reached behind him and held her free hand. "Total submission is a great gift," he said quietly. He turned slowly and took the machine from her hands like it was a loaded gun and laid it back in its cradle. It was only then that she realized they were both facing each other, topless. He moved his stool closer, pulling her legs over his so she was almost in his lap.

Nothing shocked her anymore. She found herself smoothing tendrils of his hair away from his face to reveal the tiny tattoos in his hairline. "Maybe I should have put my mark here, so you are reminded of me every day."

His smile lit up his face and then became serious again. "They are angel kills."

It made her freeze. It was one of those occasions he threw her straight back into reality. He always had to remind her of who he was. Then, to confuse her all over again, he pulled her into his lap so she could feel him grow beneath the fabric of their jeans. He was already nuzzling into her neck and making her hot. "Don't try to humanize me because you will always be left disappointed," he said, leaving a trail of kisses along her collarbone.

Then he turned his head suddenly to the side, making her jump. "Who's there?" he said, putting her away from him and standing up.

She looked in the same direction, but all she could see was the black gloom of the corner of the shop.

"Put on your clothes," he said without turning around.

She scrambled down, quickly picked up her sweater and put it back on. Her hackles were rising with fear. "Is it Abaddon?" She wasn't ready to go yet. It was too early.

He shook his head, still facing the darkness. "It is not the appointed hour."

She came and stood directly behind him for protection. That was the one sure thing about him; he would protect her at all costs, and she was grateful for it.

"Someone is coming," he said, scaring the life out of her.

She tried to peer around him to see into the darkness. Three forms stepped from it together. She recognized them immediately: *Raephe, Bohdan and Oleander.*

"What do you want? You can see we're busy sealing the contract," Grigori said, pulling her more tightly behind him.

She could feel him taut and coiled, like a panther ready to fight.

"It is already done, Brother," Raephe's eyes twinkled with enjoyment as they fell on her. "We merely came to offer our congratulations to you both and wish you a long partnership." He tipped his head slightly at her and smiled.

Grigori didn't relax a single muscle at his outward show of friendship. Despite bowing his head in return, he seemed to ready his stance.

"And to deliver a friendly word of warning," Bohdan said.

Grigori waited, as if all this was just a prelude to a fight.

"On this night of Atonement, your subject, that you guard so closely, sought to petition for your sins behind your back."

Grigori said nothing but shifted his weight while he thought about it. Rachel didn't know whether to step back or further into the shelter of his body. Bohdan was twisting everything and making it sound terrible. Her mouth had gone dry and her heart was racing. She peered around Grigori's arm and looked straight into Raephe's eyes, alive with mischief. This was his doing and he was enjoying it.

"This one isn't like the others, Xenon. She will destroy us. She went to the mediator," Oleander said, pointing at her.

"You expect me to believe that an angel would ever listen to petitions from a human?" he said, low and ominously, taking a threatening step forward.

Rachel began to slowly move away from Grigori. When he blew, she didn't want to be anywhere near him. However, Raephe spoke up, looking directly at her and pointing. "She asked me."

"You!" Grigori said, flatly.

Grigori was slowly turning to look at her, shock and horror clearly etched on his face.

"Of course, I didn't do it myself," Raephe was saying. But it receded into the background as all Rachel was aware of was the disappointment in Grigori's face. Suddenly, the fact that he thought she'd betrayed him became more important than what he would do to her at that point.

Raephe was still talking, on and on. She wanted to scream at him to shut up. "She's clever, this one. On the surface, she would have you believe she seeks to save her friend when, in reality, she seeks to drive a wedge between us to save herself."

She was shaking her head, all the while studying the emotion on Grigori's face. It was all the more devastating because it was seldom seen.

"Your earthly iris sought to buy her freedom this night from her counterpart above."

This was all wrong and her heart ached that Grigori appeared to be buying it. How stupid she'd been. "No ... listen to me, Grigori. It's me, Rachel. You would know instantly if I was up to something. I can't lie to save my life, remember?"

His eyes narrowed.

"It wasn't for me, it was for Seb, but mostly for you."

His look turned so venomous that her knees literally shook. She never knew that was actually a thing, but it was. She was quaking in her boots. "I told you, remember?" she said more quietly, so only he could hear her. "I asked you what you would give me if I got him for you, and you said it wouldn't matter because Hell would freeze over. Remember that, Grigori?" She was beginning to cry. A brief flicker of indecision came and went, and his anger returned.

"We are here to see the scales adhered to, Xenon," Oleander said from behind him.

She couldn't look away from Grigori's face. She daren't.

"She's using the night of Atonement against you,"

Oleander purred, enjoying herself far too much for someone who genuinely cared about him.

"Of course, it would seem a selfless act worthy of The Pontip himself," Raephe said, as the final poke to Grigori's anger. The reference to Layke was all it took. She saw despair whiplash into anger and crouched down as low as she could. Grigori turned and there was a blinding flash of light.

CHAPTER 43

A huge man stood between Grigori and the others, surrounded in a golden glow. She knew instantly who it was. He smiled at her. "My namesake," he said. His voice sounded smooth and relaxing like fresh rain and he was utterly beautiful. His smile transformed his chiseled, flawless face. His hair was the lightest blond in soft waves around it. His muscles rippled and corded on his bare chest as his stunning white, gold-tipped wings gently folded behind him. Despite his strength, he radiated warmth and kindness.

"Layke," she whispered.

"We share a common flower," he said, able to calm her with his mere presence. He simply commanded the room. Then he slowly turned his gaze on Grigori, who stood dazed and motionless in front of him.

His shirtless golden skin glowed with swirls of red and ochre markings. His legs were covered in a thin shimmering material that wrapped around them to his knees.

He turned his head briefly to the other three and nodded once to Raephe. "Thank you for alerting me. You may go. My business here will be concluded in a matter of minutes." His voice was clear, refined, and melodic. His authority undeniable, as the others looked at each other cautiously, stepped back and disappeared.

It was confusing as hell, as it seemed that Raephe had delivered the message after all. She wondered what it all meant. She looked at Grigori again. His eyes had never left Layke. The fight had drained out of him and he stood lifeless and in shock. She became suddenly conscious of the private moment it now was, so she stepped back to the edge of the room, a little away from them. She didn't feel safe enough to leave completely. Instead, she stayed on the sidelines and watched the sweetest reunion she'd ever seen.

She could see what Grigori loved about him. Goodness simply radiated from his pores along with a golden glow. Even his hair shone gold. His wings glittered majestically behind him. What a contrast Grigori was next to him, now flopped down onto his stool like a broken man. With his head hung low, he looked so dark in comparison. His skin was tanned and heavily inked in black, his body no less beautiful, but lethally so. It was then she noticed that there were four others standing sentry around the room.

"Are you not able to look at me?" Layke said, his gaze enigmatic and intense.

Grigori raised his head slowly to look at him, blinking as if the light was too bright. "You are an archangel," he said, as if it was news to him.

"Recently appointed," Layke said, his eyes raking over Grigori as if taking in every part of him.

The love between them was undeniable and obvious, even from where Rachel was standing.

Silence hung in the air like a great chasm. "Your subject has great loyalty to you already." Layke's gaze flicked to her and made her stand up straighter. "Take care of my namesake."

Grigori nodded. "She brought you here?"

"At great risk to herself." Layke reached out to touch Grigori's hand, but he retracted it as if he'd been burned. Then he relented and allowed Layke to pull him to his feet. At his touch, Grigori's huge black wings appeared behind him. "Black becomes you," Layke said, drawing him closer into an embrace.

He bowed his head and began to talk softly into Grigori's ear. She couldn't hear what was being said, but Grigori nodded occasionally. His head rested in the crook of Layke's neck. When his huge shoulders began to shake, Layke's wings came around him to shelter his emotion.

Rachel watched with tears rolling down her own cheeks while their exchange went on for some minutes and said far more about love than sex ever could. She could only look on in wonder. Never in her whole life had she seen anything more heartrending nor more beautiful than seeing an angel comforting his fallen brother.

Eventually, Layke put him away from him by the shoulders. He looked across at her, still standing next to Grigori's workstation in the corner. "Come here," he said.

Rachel approached cautiously, not because she was afraid of him but because he commanded so much respect. When she stopped a couple of feet away, she didn't know whether to bow, curtsy, or what. Instead, she simply kept her eyes on his beautiful face.

"Xenon has vowed to take care of you on my behalf. From this day, you, Rachel, the innocent lamb, will be known as Eireen: the rainbow that brings the soul peace.

Just for a moment, she thought she may have secured her own freedom, but his face was regretful when he sadly looked from her to Grigori as if he was speaking to them both. "You have chosen your path. Your destiny is with Abaddon, but Xenon will protect you with his life. It is his atonement." Then he smiled beautifully. "It is a good night for it, is it not?"

"And Seb, will he be released from his obligation?" Not sure if she'd spoken out of turn.

Layke nodded slowly. "Xenon will protect him as he protects you, as his mark is upon him, but at the weighing of the scales, neither you nor Xenon will be called to mind for the whole of his natural life. He will not be recalled unless he puts his soul in peril again, then Xenon must claim him, for to him he does belong."

"So, his life is his own?" she said, almost not containing her excitement. It had worked, everything had worked.

Layke nodded. "When I leave here this night, with the end of the final test, he will have no memory of you, nor will anyone else connected with that household."

A lump came up in her throat. She already knew the consequences of what she'd achieved tonight, but that didn't make the loss hurt any less. She nodded. The scales were equal. "Thank you." She looked across at Grigori, who was looking bemused between them both. "We both lost someone who meant the most."

The angel tilted his head to the side. "And yet you asked nothing for yourself." He smiled. "It was the very thing that brought your petition to my ears." He searched her face again. "Ask me what you will."

She swallowed hard, racking her brains for the single best question that would satisfy her the most. She got the impression this was a one-time thing. "Is she happy?" she said, before she could overthink it.

He smiled beautifully then, that light-giving warmth that filled her heart. "She rests peacefully in sleep until the last day, secure in the Lord's memory."

As she suspected, her mind was then filled with follow-up questions, but she decided it was enough. It made sense that she wasn't floating around on a cloud somewhere but was waiting for that resurrection promised to all those on that narrow path. A tear escaped her eye. It was all she could ask for.

With a single nod and a gaze that rested a moment longer on Grigori, Layke stepped back. The four others had appeared directly behind him, signaling it was time to go. They were a majestic sight. She wondered if she'd ever see him again.

He smiled beautifully. "Live well and decide wisely." Then he was gone, and the room was a cold and empty place without him.

Rachel wondered what he meant by that and remained rooted to the spot, stunned. There was so much in this new world she still didn't understand. Grigori hung his head. She immediately went to him, put her arms around his waist and her head against his chest. His head came down into her neck, and she held the big, bad Watcher as long-forgotten emotion wracked his body. Her mind scattered at what she'd managed to achieve that night. It was nothing short of a miracle. It would even seem that Raephe had actually helped her, despite his actions. There was no doubt the other Watchers were still a threat. However, Seb was free, but she was not. Her future was tied to this creature she held together in her arms. She guessed coming face to face with a painful ten-thousand-year past would do that to someone, however powerful they were. The night had been a success, but seeing him like this, she had to wonder whether she'd done the right thing.

When he relaxed at last and pulled his head up from her shoulder, he studied her face with red, swollen eyes. "In all my thousands of years on this earth, I have never met one such as you, Rachel—Eireen," he corrected with a smile. "You were named by an archangel himself."

His smile was infectious, and she grinned back at him. "It is pretty badass, isn't it?"

He widened his eyes playfully. "Do you realize how much you are worth now?"

Her face dropped and she scowled and punched him in the shoulder, but he was playing and wouldn't allow her anger. He crushed her to him and kissed the top of her head.

She was already looking into the shadows, drawn to the great blackness there. The lone black figure stood and pushed back his hood. *Abaddon.* She swallowed hard. He'd come for his charge to begin her education.

They pulled apart and she looked up into Grigori's eyes. Something was different between them now. She could tell he didn't want her to go. She was scared, but she was encouraged by his single nod.

She turned and took a step towards Abaddon, but he held up his hand. "The time is not now." He was talking directly to Grigori. "You have one more thing to do before she comes to me once and for all, and remember, I will be watching closely."

Grigori's look was stern when he bowed his head. "We have somewhere to go." Rachel looked confused between them. Something was wrong. This wasn't what she expected. "Come!" Grigori said, steering her by the elbow.

Abaddon stepped back into the shadows and disappeared. "I look forward to your return."

Rachel was still looking up to gauge Grigori's expression while he pulled her with him to the roof. There was no time for conversation as he stepped straight off the edge with her into the night.

"You sure they can't see us?" Rachel said, standing shoulder to shoulder with Grigori.

"No one in this world can."

It still baffled her that she could stand on the opposite side of the road to her old house, with Grigori, wings and all, and not be seen.

It was very late and there were hardly any cars. Most of the houses were in darkness, but there were lights on in the place where she'd lived up until a couple of days ago.

It seemed more than a few hours since Layke had come to her last signature session. Abaddon delaying his collection of her still didn't make any sense. She still couldn't fully believe it, but wouldn't allow herself to hope she had somehow escaped him. Besides, she understood what a privileged position she was in. Standing there, watching her old house unseen, she went over in her mind all the many things she'd already learned.

The spirit realm that held Tartarus and the space she stood in now ran directly parallel to the earthly one. If only people knew it was a hair's breadth from their faces the whole time. Yet they were oblivious to it. Wode was another place altogether, where the Devil and his close circle of Fallen resided, and Heaven another still. All were separate universes operating side by side and only certain people could travel between them.

Grigori was observing her closely, as if he enjoyed watching her marvel at it all. She smiled up at him. "I don't really feel damned, you know," she said, still gripped, watching the lights come on and off in her old house. Lynn was still awake in there, just a few feet away.

She looked up at him at the sound of his smirk. "It's not such a bad place with your Fallen, then?" His sense of humor made her heart flutter. There had been a subtle change in him since Layke's visit. He seemed calmer, more at peace now. Perhaps he had the closure he needed. She hoped he did.

Just then, a noisy old van entered the road, pounding the air with muffled beats of indie rock. *Seb.* Smoke billowed out of the exhaust as he parked it in the small driveway behind Lynn's little car.

Jules got out of the passenger side, followed by two girls. She recognized the one from Friday. Seb got out of the driver's seat.

She felt Grigori's eyes assessing her. A pain jabbed her heart at how quickly Seb had moved on. But it only lasted a moment. She had no right to feel she owned him. Especially now he never knew she existed.

The girls giggled and one stumbled on her heels. They were drunk. Seb caught her and pinched her butt, which earned him a shriek of laughter and a playful slap.

For just a moment, she longed for her old life, but then she looked up at Grigori, still watching her closely, probably for the same reason. It was just hard to wrap her head around the fact that Lynn and Seb didn't know her anymore.

All their fun times together and the things they shared were lost to them.

"*You* still have them," he said, following her thoughts perfectly.

She nodded. In her own heart, perhaps. However, she paused. There was something strange in his expression.

"Hadn't you better go in and kick somebody out?"

She frowned, not following him at all. "What? I thought I wasn't allowed anywhere near them?"

"Hell froze over. You're free!" He wore a look somewhere between amusement and amazement—one she'd definitely never seen.

She looked from him to the house and back again, confused and at a loss for words.

"It was my promise to Layke. He wanted to offer you one final opportunity—against my better judgement, I might add," he said, with a bob of his head. "Don't worry, I'll always be close. I've a feeling I'll be needed."

The implications of what he was saying began to hit her in waves. Suddenly, Abaddon deferring her education made sense. She looked up at him, shocked.

He nodded. "Layke smoothed things over with Abaddon, but, needless to say, if you mess up, Rachel, then it's all back on … I stipulated that part," he said with a small, roguish smile that broke her heart.

Joy at what he was saying bubbled up in her, then deflated immediately. "But you … you'll be all alone."

His smile widened with real affection then. "The scales were not equal for us, Rachel," he said seriously, with what seemed real regret.

Still not believing what he was saying, she looked back at the house containing Seb, floundering, in a mess. Dealing with his problems the only way he knew how. "It won't last," she said, more to herself.

"Nothing in this world is permanent, Rachel. Both you and Seb must learn to take a chance on life." She looked at him in wonder at his wisdom and the great gift he was giving her.

"Their memories are intact … for now," Grigori said, with a frown. "He will at least remember you."

Then it hit her, and her eyes brimmed with tears. "But I won't remember you, will I?"

He shook his head sadly.

It ripped out her heart and felt like she lost either way. She knew then what Layke's last comment meant. This was her *real* last test. Layke knew it, Abaddon knew it and Grigori knew it. She could go into that house and have everything back in her old life and take a chance on a wonderful first love with Seb and all the troubles and anguish that would bring. However, if she did that, she would forget everything that had happened over the last six weeks.

Or there was the alternative; she could go willingly right now with her dark angel, forever having him satisfy her darkest desire. Her eyes would be opened to every wonder in the universe and she could live many lifetimes.

"Only obsession," Grigori reminded her, knowing exactly where her mind had gone. There would be no love with him. He only had room for one person, and he had wings tipped in gold. Her heart broke at the thought of him alone in his apartment in Norway, visiting parties like Raephe's orgy in New York, remembering being devastated in the arms of his archangel. "I don't want to forget you," she said, wiping away her tears. She guessed she really had grown to love him over their time together.

"I will not forget you, though, Rachel. Nor will the rest of the spirit world. You are Eireen, beloved of an archangel and tamer of The Watcher of the North. I will not be permitted to ever live it down," he said with a wry smile.

She stepped into him and he stooped so she could kiss him on the mouth. The heady taste and sensation she craved hit her instantly. She took a deep inhale of his scent at his neck and pushed her fingers up through his soft hair. She took one last, lingering look at him, mapping features that would be lost to her, then she turned and walked away.

"My blood still flows through your veins, Rachel, and yours in mine."

She slowed her steps a little and continued on towards her house. Her heart leaped at the idea of that.

"Stay away from fortune-tellers," he said with laughter in his voice.

She reached the doorstep and put the key she still had in the lock. It was no use, she had to take one last look over her shoulder, just in time to see his huge wings expand and then disappear into particles on the wind with his laughter. "I'll be Watching."

CHAPTER 45

*O*ne week later

Seb and Rachel spent Sunday morning lazing around in bed, eating last night's cold pizza so they didn't have to get up. She'd come home last week and actually caught Seb and Jules entertaining a pair of skanks in their own living room, with the excuse of being drunk and high after a gig. He'd been a contrite lover trying to make it up to her ever since. She loved having the upper hand.

In fact, he'd moved permanently into her room now, even though Lynn thought she'd forgiven him too easily. She enjoyed milking it for all it was worth.

She lazily dragged her fingers over the new tattoo he wore on his shoulder. He maintained it was a declaration of his undying love for her. The skeleton being him waiting for her to get ready for them to get out any time soon.

It made her laugh, but she recognized it as a lovely gesture though, just for saying the hot, naked girl was her. She had to admit it had a lot of similarities; blue highlights and everything, but she wasn't completely convinced. She was so glad she only had the small flower on her chest.

Seb planted a kiss right over it. "I still don't get what the X means?"

She tried to remember what the young guy at Nicks had said about it exactly. "He said it was some kind of ancient rune for protection, or something. Like my nan is watching over me like a guardian angel. I kind of liked the idea."

He bobbed his head as if it satisfied him.

Just then, there was a knock at her bedroom door. "Come in," she called out.

Lynn put her head around the door. "I'm off to work, Colin said he has something important to ask me." Her eyes were wide with excitement, conveying what every girl thought it might be. "Oh, and I almost forgot. My sister called. That Psychic fair is coming back in a few weeks. You coming?"

***

In the mood for another Dark Valentine? Download and read Star Child right away.

458

WHAT'S NEXT?

Have you tried the Sirens Series yet? Download from any platform absolutely free: Soul Breather

And to receive your two free 21st Century Sirens Novellas, and be the first to know anything relating to T's books, leave your details here: https://mailchi.mp/d18c89c14f50/tstedmannovellas
And please don't forget to leave a review. I really appreciate the feedback.
Much love
T

COMING SOON

Embedded, Book 2 in the TinBoiz Series by T Stedman, to
be released in the spring of 2026

You can also find T Stedman at:
www.stedman.com
Facebook
TikTok
X

Dark Valentines Collection

The Watchers
Diablo
Star Child

21st Century Sirens Series

Soul Breather
Blood Sister
Shield Maiden
Tiger Lily
Night Goddess
Darkly Begotten

The Novellas

Protector
Lost Moon

The YA Books

TinBoiz

Entanglement

Young Atlanteans

Two Tribes
Cross Heirs

Night Shades

The Blackwood Curse
Demon in the Attic

Non-Fiction

My Migraine Story

www.ingramcontent.com/pod-product-compliance
Lightning Source LLC
Chambersburg PA
CBHW031927110726

47902CB00001B/67